Once an
Heiress

Elizabeth Boyce

Author of *Once a Duchess* and *Once an Innocent*

CRIMSON
ROMANCE
F+W Media, Inc.

Crimson Romance
an imprint of F+W Media, Inc.
10151 Carver Road, Suite 200
Blue Ash, Ohio 45242
www.crimsonromance.com

ISBN 10: 1-4405-7347-6
ISBN 13: 978-1-4405-7347-7
eISBN 10: 1-4405-6194-X
eISBN 13: 978-1-4405-6194-8

Printed in the United States of America.

10 9 8 7 6 5 4 3 2 1

This book is available at quantity discounts for bulk purchases.
For information, please call 1-800-289-0963.

Dedication

For Sarah, who loves it when my girls get hardcore domestic
and
For Aunt Minnie, who forgot.

Acknowledgments

Many thanks to superwoman Jennifer Lawler, and the whole team at Crimson Romance. Tara Gelsomino, thank you for swooping in and being awesome. Thanks, too, to J.C. Kosloff.

To my sister Crimsonistas, thanks for the laughs and support. You ladies are the very best.

If one can thank entities rather than people, then I must thank PBS and Wikipedia for a great many reasons. I'm going to keep donating, and you should, too.

As ever, Michelle and Sarah, I couldn't have done it without you.

Kids, thank you all for reaching school age, so Mama has time to work.

Berkeley, no one keeps my notes warm like you do.

Finally, thanks to my wonderful husband for reading this behind my back—and liking it.

Chapter One

Lily Bachman squared her shoulders, lifted her chin, and drew a deep breath. Behind the study door was another dragon to slay—or perhaps this one would be more like a pesky dog to shoo off. Whatever the case, one thing was certain; in that room, she'd find a man after her money. He was the fourth this Season, and it was only the end of March.

She smoothed the front of her muslin dress with a quick gesture, and then opened the door.

The Leech, as she dubbed all of them, halted whatever nonsense he was blathering on about and turned at the sound of the door opening, his jaw hanging slack, paused in the action of speaking. Her father sat on the sofa, situated at a right angle to the chair inhabited by the would-be suitor.

"Darling." Mr. Bachman rose. "You're just in time. This is Mr. Faircloth."

Lily pressed her cheek to his. "Good morning, Father."

Mr. Bachman and Lily were close in height. He was of a bit more than average height for a man, while Lily was practically a giantess amongst the dainty aristocratic ladies. She stuck out like a sore thumb at parties, towering over every other female in the room—just another reason she detested such functions.

The man, Mr. Faircloth, also stood. He was shorter than Lily and lacked a chin. The smooth slope marking the transition from jaw to neck was unsettling to look upon. He wore mutton-chop sideburns, presumably an attempt to emphasize his jawline. They failed miserably in that regard, serving rather to point out the vacant place between them where a facial feature should have been.

"My..." Mr. Faircloth wrung his hands together and cleared his throat. "My dear Miss Bachman," he started again. "How lovely you look this morning."

Lily inclined her head coolly. She settled onto the sofa and folded her hands in her lap. Mr. Bachman sat beside her and gestured Mr. Faircloth to his chair.

Mr. Faircloth cast an apprehensive look between Lily and her father. "I'd thought, sir, that you and I would speak first. Then, if all was agreeable, I would speak to Miss…" He lowered his eyes and cleared his throat again.

Good, Lily thought viciously. He was already thrown off balance. She knew from experience that when dealing with fortune hunters and younger sons, one had to establish and maintain the upper hand.

"When it comes to my daughter's future," Mr. Bachman said in a rich baritone, "there is no such thing as a private interview. Miss Bachman is a grown woman; she's entitled to have a say in her own future. Would you not agree?"

Mr. Faircloth squirmed beneath the intense gazes of father and daughter. "Well, it's not how these things are usually handled, sir, but I suppose there's no real harm in bucking convention just this—"

"Mr. Faircloth," Lily interrupted.

The man swallowed. "Yes?"

"I don't recognize you at all." She raised her brows and narrowed her eyes, as though examining a distasteful insect. "Have we met?"

"I, well, that is…yes, we've met." Mr. Faircloth's head bobbed up and down. "We were introduced at the Shervingtons' ball last week. I asked you to dance."

As he spoke, Lily stood and crossed the room to her father's desk. She retrieved a sheaf of paper and a pen, and then returned to her seat. She allowed the silence to stretch while she jotted down notes: name, physical description, and first impression. *Younger son*, she decided, *a novice to fortune hunting*. She glanced up with the pen poised above the paper. "And did I accept your invitation?"

Mr. Faircloth gave a nervous smile. "Ah, no, actually. You were already spoken for the next set and every one thereafter." He pointed weakly toward her notes. "What are you writing there?"

She leveled her most withering gaze on him. "Are you or are you not applying for my hand in matrimony?"

His jaw worked without sound, and then his face flushed a deep pink. "I, yes. That is why I've come, I suppose you could say."

"You suppose?" Lily scoffed. "You're not sure?"

"Yes." Mr. Faircloth drew himself up, rallying. "Yes, I'm sure. That's why I've come."

So there is a bit of spine in this one, after all, Lily thought. "That being the case," she replied, giving no quarter in her attack, "it is reasonable for me to keep a record of these proceedings, is it not? You are not the first gentleman to present himself."

Mr. Faircloth sank back into himself. "I see."

"Tell me, what prompted your call today?" Lily tilted her head at an inquisitive angle, as though she were actually interested in the man's answer.

Mr. Faircloth cast a desperate look at Mr. Bachman.

"That's a fair question," her father said. Lily loved many things about her father, but the one she appreciated more than anything was the way he treated her like a competent adult. Most females were bartered off to the man who made the highest offer, either through wealth or connections. When he spoke up for her, supporting her line of questioning, Lily wanted to throw her arms around his neck and hug him. Later, she would. Right now, they had to eject the newest swain from their home.

Mr. Faircloth grew more and more agitated with every passing second. He fidgeted in his seat and finally blurted, "I love you!"

Lily drew back, surprised by the tactic her opponent employed. She waved a dismissive hand. "Don't be ridiculous."

"It's true," Mr. Faircloth insisted. "From the moment I saw you, I thought you were the most beautiful woman at the ball. Your gown was the most flattering blue—"

"I wore red," Lily corrected.

Mr. Faircloth blinked. "Oh." He rested his elbows on his knees, and his head drooped between his shoulders.

He was crumbling. Time to finish him off.

"Let's talk about why you've really come, shall we?" Lily's tone was pleasant, like a governess explaining something to a young child with limited comprehension. "You're here because of my dowry, just like the other men who have suddenly found themselves stricken with love for me."

"A gentleman does not discuss such matters with a lady," Mr. Faircloth informed his toes.

"A *gentleman*," Lily said archly, "does not concoct fantastical tales of undying affection in the hopes of duping an unwitting female into marriage. Tell me, sir, which son are you?"

"I have two older brothers," he said in a defeated tone.

Lily duly made note of this fact on her paper. "And sisters?"

"Two."

"Ah." Lily raised a finger. "Already an heir and a spare, and two dowries besides. That doesn't leave much for you, does it?" She tutted and allowed a sympathetic smile.

Mr. Faircloth shook his head once and resumed his glum inspection of his footwear.

"I understand your predicament," Lily said. "And how attractive the idea of marrying money must be to a man in your situation." She tilted her head and took on a thoughtful expression. "Have you considered a different approach?"

The gentleman raised his face, his features guarded. "What do you mean?"

She furrowed her brows together. "What I mean is this: Have you considered, perhaps, a profession?"

Mr. Faircloth's mouth hung agape. He looked from Lily to Mr. Bachman, who sat back, passively observing the interview.

"It must rankle," Lily pressed, "to see your eldest brother's future secured by accident of birth and to see your sisters provided for by virtue of their sex. But do consider, my dear Mr. Faircloth, that younger sons the Empire 'round have bought commissions and taken orders, studied law or medicine, accepted government appointments. The time has come," she said, pinning him beneath her fierce gaze, "for you to accept the fact that yours is not to be a life of dissipated leisure. Instead of hoping for a fortune to fall into your lap, your days would be better spent pursuing a profession."

Mr. Faircloth wiped his palms down his thighs. "Miss Bachman, you've quite convinced me."

She blinked. "Have I?"

"Yes," he said. "I am well and truly convinced that marriage to you would be a nightmare from which I should never awake until I die. Sir," he turned his attention to Mr. Bachman, "I see now why you offer such a large dowry for your daughter." He stood. "It would take an astronomical sum to make the proposition of marriage to such a controlling, unpleasant female the slightest bit appealing."

Lily's mouth fell open. "Why, you—"

Her father laid a restraining hand on her arm. Lily exhaled loudly and pinched her lips together.

"Thank you for your time, Mr. Bachman." Mr. Faircloth inclined his head. "Miss Bachman." He hurried from the parlor. A moment later, the front door closed behind him.

"Well!" Lily exclaimed. "Of all the sniveling, puffed up—"

"You wore blue," Mr. Bachman cut in.

"I beg your pardon?"

"The Shervingtons' ball. You wore blue, just as Mr. Faircloth said." He stood and crossed to his desk, where he poured himself a brandy from a decanter.

"Did I?" Lily murmured. "I could have sworn I wore red." She tapped a finger against her lips.

"No, darling," Mr. Bachman said with a sigh, "you wore blue. I'm quite certain, because your mother fretted that the color washed you out and no gentleman would notice you."

"Ah, well," Lily said. She rose and briskly rubbed her palms together. "It doesn't signify. One more Leech gone."

Mr. Bachman's chest heaved and heavy, graying brows furrowed over his dark eyes. "My dear, you cannot continue in this fashion. You know I'll not force you to marry against your will. But marry you must, and it *is* my desire that your marriage elevate this family's status."

Lily straightened a pile of papers on the desk as he spoke; her hands paused at this last remark. Indignation mingled with hurt slammed into her like a physical blow. She idly slid a paper back and forth across the polished desk and kept her eyes studiously upon it as she recovered, hiding the force of her emotions behind a casual demeanor. However, she could not fully suppress the bitterness in her voice when she spoke. "Fortunate, then, that Charles died. A mere ensign and son of a country squire would not have provided the upward mobility you crave."

Mr. Bachman's glass boomed against the desk. "Young lady, guard your tongue!" Her eyes snapped to his mottled face. His own dark eyes flashed rage, and his nostrils flared. "Had poor Charles returned from Spain, I would have proudly and happily given you in wedlock. Indeed, it was my fondest wish to unite our family with the Handfords."

A humorless laugh burst from Lily's lips. Turning, she twitched her skirts in a sharp gesture. "A fact you made sure to educate me upon from the earliest. I spent the whole of my life with the name of my groom and date of my wedding drilled into my head."

It was an unfair accusation, she knew, even as it flew from her mouth. Yes, she had been betrothed to Charles Handford since time out of mind, but for most of her life, it was simply a fact she'd memorized, along with the color of the sky and the sum of two and two.

There'd been plenty of visits with their neighbors, the Handfords, but Charles was ten years her senior and rarely present. Her earliest memories of him were his visits home from Eton and Oxford, and later, leaves from his lancer regiment.

Their betrothal only became more relevant as her twentieth birthday neared, bringing the planned summer wedding that was to follow on its heels—an event postponed when Charles's regiment could not spare him, and which was never to be after he died that autumn.

The silence stretched while her father regained his composure. Gradually, the angry red drained from his face. "Now, Lily," he said in a more moderate tone, "I'll not be portrayed as some chattel dealer, looking to hoist you off without a care for your feelings. Since last year was your first Season—and you just out of mourning—I did not push the issue. I still wish you to make your own match. The only stipulation I have placed is that the gentleman be titled—either in his own right or set to inherit. Surely, that is not too onerous? There are scores of eligible gentlemen to choose from."

"I don't wish to marry an *aristocrat*." She dripped disdain all over the word. "They're a lot of lazy social parasites with a collective sense of entitlement, just like that last one—"

Mr. Bachman's brows shot up his forehead. "Lily!"

She ducked her head. "I'm sorry," she muttered, abashed. "My mouth does run ahead of me—"

"And it's going to run you right into spinsterhood, if you don't mind yourself."

Heat crept up Lily's neck and over her cheeks.

"Now, dear," Mr. Bachman continued, "poor Mr. Faircloth certainly *was* here because of your dowry. It's big on purpose, and no doubt about it. But he also knew what color gown you wore to a ball last week. Do you know the last time I noticed a woman's gown?"

Lily shrugged.

"Thirty years or more," Mr. Bachman proclaimed, "if, in fact, I ever noticed to begin with." He lifted her chin with a finger. Lily raised her eyes to meet her father's softened expression. "You are an exceedingly pretty girl—"

"Oh, Papa…"

"You *are*. The way society works, however, renders it almost out of the question for the right kind of man to come calling, even if he thinks your dress *is* the most becoming shade of blue. Your dowry clears a few of those obstacles." He took her hand and patted it. "Now, let us be done quarreling and speak of pleasanter things."

Lily nodded hastily.

She happened to disagree with her father on the issue of her dowry. To Lily's mind, the "right kind of man" would want to be with her, fortune or no. She thought of her dearest friend, Isabelle, Duchess of Monthwaite. Even though she and her husband, Marshall, went through a horrible divorce—reducing Isabelle to the lowest possible social status—they still found their way back together. Marshall didn't allow Isabelle's reduced circumstances to keep them apart once they came to terms with their past.

For the thousandth time, Lily wished Isabelle were here. But she and His Grace were in South America on a botanical expedition-cum-honeymoon. They'd be home in a couple of months, but oh, how time dragged when Lily so needed her friend's advice. Fortunately, Isabelle's sister-in-law, Lady Naomi Lockwood, would soon be in town. She'd written to Lily that her mother, Caro, would be sitting out the Season to remain in the country—a singularly odd choice, Lily thought, considering the dowager duchess' responsibility to see Naomi wed. Instead of her mother, Naomi would be chaperoned by her spinster aunt, Lady Janine.

Lily would be glad to see their friendly faces. She didn't get on well with *tonnish* young women, and there was always the suspicion that men were only interested in her money. Lily often found herself lonely in the middle of a glittering crush.

"Are you attending?" Mr. Bachman said.

Lily blinked. "I'm sorry, Papa, what was that?"

"I asked," he repeated patiently, "if you've decided on a project."

Lily's mood brightened. *This* was something she would enjoy discussing. "I have."

"Excellent!" Mr. Bachman sat in the large armchair behind his desk, the throne from which he ruled his ever-expanding empire of industry. He moved the chair opposite the desk around to his side. "Have a seat, dear."

Despite the tempest that had just flared between them, Lily felt a rush of affection for her dear father. Since she was a girl, he'd shared his desk with her. When she was young, he'd held her on his lap while he spoke to her about things she didn't understand then—coal veins and shipping ventures; members of Parliament and government contracts.

At the time, it all blurred together into Papa's *work*, but as she grew, she began to make sense of it all.

She understood now that all her life he'd treated her as the son he never had, the heir apparent to the name and fortune he'd made for himself. Never had he indicated any doubt in her capability or intelligence on account of her sex. He took pride in his daughter's education and emphasized mathematics and politics, in addition to feminine accomplishments such as drawing and dancing.

Just before they'd come to town this Season, Mr. Bachman presented Lily with a unique opportunity. He desired her to develop a sizable charity project. He would fund her endeavor, but Lily had to do the work to bring her plans to fruition. She jumped on the proposal, glad for an occupation beside the *ton's* vapid entertainments.

Mr. Bachman rummaged through a drawer and withdrew a sheet of paper covered with Lily's neat writing.

"So, here is the list of ideas you began with. What have you settled upon?"

Lily pointed to an item halfway down the page. "The school for disadvantaged young women," she said. "I should like to keep it small for now. Girls would receive a sound education, plus some accomplishments that would enable them to take positions as governesses, ladies' maids, companions, things of that nature."

Mr. Bachman cupped his chin in his hand and listened with a thoughtful expression while Lily enumerated her ideas for the school. When she finished, he slapped his fingers on the desk. "Marvelous, my dear."

Lily swelled with pride at her father's approval.

He took a fresh sheet of paper and jotted a note. "I'm putting my solicitor at your disposal. The two of you can select an appropriate property for purchase. Meanwhile, you also need to secure a headmistress, who can, in turn, hire the staff. You'll need tutors, a cook, maids…"

As the plan came together, Lily's confidence in the project soared. There was nothing she could not accomplish once she knew how to approach a problem.

She kissed her father's cheek at the conclusion of their meeting.

"Just think, m'dear," he said on their parting.

"What's that?"

"When you marry one of those lazy aristocrats, he'll have scads of free time to help with your work." He winked and patted her arm.

Lily scowled at his back. He seemed to think a man in need of her dowry would also, in turn, look kindly upon her efforts to care for those less fortunate than themselves. She snorted. Such a man did not exist.

Chapter Two

Thump. Thump. Thump.

In the hazy place between sleep and waking, it was the sound of the fat man plodding upstairs, unwittingly leaving his mistress in the company of his rival.

It was the sound Ethan's pulse made when Ghita appeared in the parlor doorway like a succubus rising from the mist, her slender hips swaying provocatively within the silken confines of her gown. One golden strand fell from her updo, curling against her collarbone like a finger crooked in invitation. In the light of a single candle, huge doe eyes blinked up at him.

Dainty fingers grazed the shoulders of his blue superfine coat before slipping around his neck. "Eeethan," she crooned. "You have to leave. He'll find us." Her operatic training and years on the stage gentled her Italian accent. Even as she murmured against his neck, her voice was a song. A seduction.

Ethan brushed the top of one small, high breast. "Let him," he said, nipping his way across her jaw. "Maybe he'll learn by example how to properly satisfy a woman." He dipped into the neckline of her dress and fondled a taut nipple between his first and middle fingers, rolling the bud back and forth. Ghita whimpered and pressed her hips against him.

In reply, Ethan grasped her pert bottom with his free hand and rocked against her mound. Pressure built at the base of his spine. His erection twitched, eager to bury itself in hot, wet flesh.

"Ooh, you must hurry and find a wife, Eeethan. One who is dripping with money like my Quillan. She'll be so happy to own you, she won't care what you do. Then we can be together."

Thump. Thump. Thump.

The sound roused him enough to bring awareness to his very real, very hard condition. He burrowed his head into the crook of his arm and touched himself. Images from last night flashed behind his eyelids.

Ghita. His desire. His temptation. His friend's mistress.

He saw her as she was earlier in the evening, across the card table, draping herself over Quillan's shoulder to give Ethan a view of the tight slit between her breasts. She nibbled her corpulent protector's ear, all the while treating Ethan to a heated look, telling him without words: *This could be you.*

His own hand became the remembrance of hers, stroking through his trousers while Quillan awaited her upstairs. Despite the lust blazing between them, Ethan had not taken her to bed. Ghita was, after all, a professional. A very *expensive* professional.

Thump. Thump. Thump.

His memory jumped; his hand fell away. This time, the heavy noise became the sound of Ficken's winning cards hitting the table with ominous finality. The poseur, with his over-pomaded hair and ill-fitting clothes, turned beady eyes on Ethan. "That's hate thousan' ye owe me this month, moi lor'."

The butcher-turned-professional-gambler's mangled King's English made Ethan's guts roil. He kept his eyes trained forward, refusing to acknowledge the jumped-up East Ender. No matter how much money the man took from the pockets of the aristocracy, he would never be a true gentleman.

Ethan signed the promissory note and passed it to Ficken.

Ghita's lips made a sympathetic moue. Ethan tried to forget the gaming debts and thought instead about sliding into that pretty mouth. He threw back the remainder of his drink and set the glass down with a resounding—

Thump. Thump. Thump.

Gradually, the heavy sound teased his eyelids open. The swirling pattern in the plaster ceiling of his study started to come into focus. It only spun a little.

He pressed the heels of his hands to his eyes and groaned. His cock ached with need and his head hurt like the very devil—so badly he could *hear* the blood thudding in his temples.

No, that didn't make sense. He hoisted himself up, swinging his long legs over the side of the leather sofa on which he'd fallen asleep after stumbling home in the early morning hours. Except for the sickening new debt and the all-too-brief encounter with Ghita, the details of last night's disastrous basset game were shrouded in an alcoholic blur.

What *was* clear as the morning sun streaming through the window was the blasted thumping coming from the stair, as though a heavy object was being dragged down. Whatever it was, it hit the landing, and after a moment, he heard the sound of the object dragging across the wood floor of the entrance hall. Mrs. Oliver, the housekeeper, would have someone's head if a careless maid had scratched the wax finish.

Slowly, Ethan stood. Last night's coat, bunched around his right arm, was only half-removed. "Pretty bad, old boy," he muttered.

He peeled the garment off and tossed it in a rumpled ball back onto the sofa. He stretched, arching his back and reaching his arms overhead, his fingers brushing the ceiling. Around his throat, his cravat still trussed him up like a roast duck. He nimbly worked the knot. A sigh of relief escaped him as he scratched the liberated skin.

The noise outside the study increased. More feet tromped up and down the stairs, inconsiderate of the fact that the master of the house had only been abed—or asofa, as the case may be—for a few hours.

Maybe Mrs. Oliver had a bee in her formidable bonnet to undertake some heavy cleaning. He sighed and collapsed into the chair at his desk then adjusted his trousers to ease the strain of his ebbing morning arousal. No sense leaving the sanctuary of his study; he'd only be underfoot, or find himself with a dust cloth in hand.

A pile of unopened correspondence stood in the middle of the desk. Ethan glared accusingly at the pile, squirming against the cold knot it aroused in his belly by the mere fact of its existence.

He grumbled and snatched a letter from the top of the pile. He cracked the seal.

Thorburn,

he read.

> *It has now been five months since I loaned you the sum of one thousand two hundred pounds. You promised prompt repayment, and I trusted you to make good on your word. It grieves me that this has not been the case. I must now insist in the strongest terms—*

Ethan tossed that one aside. He opened another.

My lord—

> *I still hold your promissory note for seven hundred pounds, dated 17 January. I hear I am not the only one with your worthless notes. Is this why you no longer show your face at Brooks's?*

It joined the first note.

Letter after letter demanded compensation for debts Ethan couldn't begin to pay. It seemed he owed personal loans and gaming debts to half the *ton*, not to mention his bills from numerous tradesmen and mortgage payments to the bank.

He dropped his head into his hands. How had it gotten so bad? Not for the first time, Ethan considered giving up gaming. The cards and dice had been against him since…He gazed out the window, thinking.

The last good win he'd had was this very house. He won the deed in a game of cribbage about a year ago. Since then, he'd been trapped in a downward spiral of loss after staggering loss.

He let out a frustrated growl. How could he give up gaming? He had no money with which to pay his debts, so he had to make money. To make money, he had to gamble, but doing so inevitably ended with him further in debt.

After last night's loss to Edmund Ficken—Ficken! The very name offended him with its coarseness—Quillan had teased Ethan. *"For Christmas, Eth, why don't you ask your father if he'll do you the courtesy of dying?"*

If only the old bastard *would* die, Ethan's life would improve in so many ways. He'd inherit the fortune needed to clear his debts. He'd finally be free of his sire's condescending disapproval. No more would he have to see the regret in his father's eyes that it was Ethan who would be the next Earl of Kneath, instead of Walter, the firstborn into whom their father had poured all his hopes and dreams, only to have them killed along with the man on the dueling field three years ago.

The wretched man was immortal as Satan himself. He'd clung to life through illness after illness just to spite his son, Ethan was sure. He delighted in making his wastrel offspring beg for every penny. Refusing to dance to the old man's tune any more, Ethan had cut off all communication with the earl. He hadn't spoken to his father in almost two years.

Ethan shook his head. He was being morose. Breakfast, he thought. Something in his belly to sop up last night's gin. He tugged the bell pull.

A few minutes later, the butler, Jackson, entered the study. The tall man carried a new stack of correspondence. Ethan bit back a curse. More dunning letters. Would he never be free of them?

"Breakfast, please, Jackson," Ethan said. "Tell Cook nothing too heavy. Just some toast and ham—"

"No, sir," Jackson cut in.

Ethan's brows drew together. "I beg your pardon?"

"I said, no, my lord." Jackson extended his arm. He dropped the papers into the middle of the desk, where they landed on top of the other letters with a soft thud.

Ethan stared at them. "What's this?" he asked, suspicious.

"These, my lord, are letters of resignation for the entire staff." The butler's thin lips turned up in a smug, satisfied smile.

Ethan gaped. He shot to his feet. "The entire—why?"

"You've not paid wages to a single one of us in two months' time, and before that it was months of half wages. *You* might be able to live on credit, my lord, but the rest of us cannot. We have families to feed, parents and siblings depending on us—"

Ethan flung a hand into the air. "Spare me the melodrama." He huffed through his nostrils. "So the entire staff is revolting? Who put them up to this?"

Jackson shook his head.

"Well, I don't accept your resignations!" Ethan yelled, jabbing a finger toward the butler.

He strode across the study and yanked the door wide.

What he'd taken for the sounds of heavy cleaning, he discovered, were, in fact, the sounds of an exodus in progress. He employed a dozen servants—most of whom had come with the house—and every last one of them stood in the front hall, their voices mingled in angry tones.

When Ethan appeared, a hush fell over the group. He felt the weight of twelve irate glares. He held his hands out and spoke in a raised voice.

"Everyone," he said, "I know you're distraught. But if you'll just bear with me for another week or two, I'll have your wages—"

"Where's it going to come from?" a footman called. "We all know you haven't a farthing to your name."

"Just like the *Quality*," a maid jeered, "trampling all over honest working folk without shame. Do y'even have a heart, my lord, to treat us so? After all our faithful service?"

"Here, here," cried another servant. The rumble of voices rose up again.

"Now, now," Ethan said, trying to calm them.

"To hell with you!"

Ethan didn't see who said it. But once it was out, a chorus joined in. Ethan stood stock still while his servants rained curses upon him.

Then one of the men picked up a valise. The others followed his lead and hoisted their own belongings. In a silent line, they filed past Ethan toward the servants' door at the back of the house.

His housekeeper averted her eyes as she passed. "Mrs. Oliver," he said, reaching for her arm.

She wrenched free of his grip and shot him a look of hurt and anger then continued on with the others.

Disbelief began to give way to annoyance. What was he going to do with no servants in the house? "Don't think I'll give any of you references!"

There was a knock on the door, which intensified to an insistent pounding.

Ethan looked to Jackson expectantly. "The door?" he prompted.

"Answer your own bloody door," Jackson returned. "The mechanism which opens it is called a knob. It should not be beyond even your comprehension." With a final withering sneer, he stalked after the other servants.

Ethan glared at the disloyal retainer's retreating back and made a sound in his throat. He wrenched the door open.

A short man wearing a neat brown suit doffed his hat. At his heels loomed four great brutes, each dressed in rough trousers and shirts. A hackney coach waited at the curb. Behind it was a team of four draft horses hitched to a large wagon, followed by another team and wagon.

The small man squinted up at him. "Ethan Helling, Viscount Thorburn?"

Ethan frowned at the men and their train of vehicles. "Yes?"

"Mr. Steven Laramie, bailiff of the court. I've been charged with carrying out the magistrate's orders." He rendered a brief bow, handed him a piece of paper, then shoved past him into the house. The large men followed. Ethan sidestepped to avoid being crushed.

Mr. Laramie gazed at the walls and floor with avid interest, like a visitor to a museum. He glanced up the stairs and then strolled down the hall, opening doors and touching objects.

Ethan skimmed over the paper the bailiff gave him. He recognized the names of numerous tradesmen to whom he owed money. A cold rock dropped in his middle.

"Here's the dining room," Mr. Laramie called. "Begin here."

The laborers lumbered down the hall to where Mr. Laramie pointed.

Ethan followed, watching in horror as the men grasped either end of a valuable sideboard and carried it into the corridor. "What are you doing?"

"I understand there is no entailed property on the premises," Mr. Laramie said. "Is that correct?"

Ethan stared at him, all agog. "No, nothing here is part of the tail. Why? What is happening?"

"By order of the magistrate," the bailiff said with the tone of an official pronouncement, "your property will be auctioned and the proceeds split amongst the listed complainants. Some of them," he added in a scolding voice, "have waited two years and more for payment."

Ethan's mouth snapped shut. The hulking workmen returned to the dining room again and started disassembling the long table dominating the center of the room.

"But these are my things," Ethan protested.

Mr. Laramie gave him a tight smile. "Not anymore."

He looked from the vacant hall back to his quickly emptying dining room. Then he took himself to the staircase. He plopped down on the bottom step and watched dispassionately as Mr. Laramie and his lackeys carried out nearly everything of value in his home.

Just as well, came the bleak thought. With no servants to keep the place up, he didn't need all these things standing around collecting dust, anyway.

*

It was amazing how quickly one's life could be dismantled, Ethan mused. In the space of a couple hours, he'd lost his entire household staff and most of his belongings. As he walked through the house, the sound of his footsteps bounced off naked walls.

Mr. Laramie had left the study untouched. Ethan sat down and idly flipped through his pile of correspondence, soothed by the familiar action. If he kept his eyes on the desk, it was easy to forget the rest of his house was an empty shell.

In a way, it was good all this had happened, he decided. Being a bachelor, he never should have had so many servants. A single

manservant and one or two maids would have sufficed. Ethan had
only kept Jackson, Mrs. Oliver, and the others out of a sense of
obligation. It wasn't their fault their previous employer had lost the
house in a game of chance—they'd become his responsibility with
a turn of a card. Neither would he ever have considered selling off
his furnishings, but now that he had no choice in the matter, some
of his debt would be retired; the thought offered a sense of relief.

He fished through his papers, searching for the bills from the
tradesmen named on the bailiff's orders. A few pieces of post fell to
the floor. When he bent to retrieve them, Ethan spotted familiar
stationary amongst the litter. He cracked the seal and unfolded
the paper, releasing the faint odor of roses.

My dearest Thorburn,

*Too much time has passed since I saw you last. Please come to
me. Do not forget your own—*

Vanessa

Ethan traced the V with his index finger. He wondered when
she'd sent the note; the date at the top of the page was worthless.

Briefly, he considered calling on Ghita—but no. A visit to
Nessa would be just the thing. There, he could concentrate on her
and forget his own troubles.

He found the limp, wrinkled cravat in the blanket and tied a
hasty knot. He plucked his wadded coat from the sofa, shook it
out, and wrestled into it.

With something approaching a spring in his step, Ethan left
the hollow shell of his house behind him.

*

Vanessa lived in a graciously appointed town house. The neighborhood was perfectly respectable, populated by successful tradesmen and professionals. From the clean, stuccoed exterior to the urns full of flowers flanking the stairs, nothing about the unremarkable house drew attention to the fact that inside dwelt a kept woman.

The butler, Higgins, exhaled in relief when he saw Ethan. "Thank goodness you've come, my lord," he said in a harried tone. A sheen of sweat was evident on his upper lip. "Madam is…"

Ethan handed the servant his hat. "Bad today?" He glanced toward the stairwell.

As if in answer to his question, a blood-curdling shriek split the air, followed by a stream of incoherent language. The sound was briefly louder when an upstairs door opened, then muffled when the door closed again. Footsteps pounded down the stairs, and a woman wearing a gray dress and white apron burst into the hallway. Her thin face was pale and tear-streaked, her white cap perched at a precarious angle on her head.

She shot a fiery look at Ethan. "That's it, I'm done. No more."

"Wait." Ethan grabbed her arm. "Please don't go. You know she can't help herself," he said. "Please, whatever it takes. You're the best nurse she's had. She needs you."

The woman's chin trembled. Tears slid down her face. "I can't take any more, my lord. She's been screaming all morning, accusing me of thievery. She threw a picture at me. Look!"

The nurse turned her head and pointed to just below her right temple, in front of her ear. A purple lump was raised there, with a ferocious red line in the center.

Ethan winced and sucked his breath through his teeth. "Did you send for the doctor? Shall I?"

She shook her head. "It's not too bad. But that could have been my eye."

"I understand," Ethan said in a mollifying tone. "Take the afternoon off—"

The nurse laughed bitterly. "The afternoon? Attend, milord. I said I'm done. You'll have to find a new nurse to take her abuse, because it won't be me."

Ethan followed her to the door. "Please reconsider," he called as she descended the front stairs. "Take a few days…"

The woman didn't look back.

Ethan pinched the bridge of his nose and squeezed his eyes shut. It was too early to have to deal with so many catastrophes. He opened his eyes and met Higgins' fretful gaze. "Send a note to her solicitor, Mr. Logan. Have him put out an advertisement for a new nurse."

"Yes, my lord."

"I'll see her now," Ethan said. "Let me know if this one comes back." He tipped his chin to the door. "Even if she demands a higher wage, it would be better to keep her than to have to find a new one."

With Higgins' assurance that he understood the orders, Ethan climbed the stairs and walked down the hall to her bedchamber.

At the door, a knot formed in his chest. Ethan braced himself, uncertain what he'd find on the other side. His fingers trembled as he twisted the knob.

The aroma of roses—her scent—greeted him at once. Thick carpet dampened his footsteps as he slowly made his way across the room. The French influence was obvious in the furnishings of the elegant style favored by Marie Antoinette and her court.

Soft blues and greens reminded one this was a feminine lair, but invitingly so. It was the kind of room a man could lose himself in when he needed nothing more than the soft ministrations of his lover.

Through the sheer white curtains surrounding the bed, Ethan saw Vanessa's slight figure reclined against a pile of pillows. She'd fallen silent, perhaps asleep.

Evidence of the morning's outburst was scattered about. A vase of white roses on the bedside table had toppled; a water stain darkened the carpet beneath it. The picture that had struck the nurse lay facedown beside a tufted ottoman. Though only about four inches wide and six inches tall, the oval gilt frame was hefty. If Vanessa's aim had been a little better, she could have done the nurse serious harm. Ethan turned it over—

And stared into his own face.

Not *his* face, but one remarkably similar. The man in the miniature wore his hair long, while Ethan's was clipped short. The artist had captured the bronze hue the men's hair shared. The gentleman in the painting had the same strong, straight nose and slate blue eyes. The largest difference in features was the jawline. Ethan's was a touch narrower than the square face in the painting.

"Thorburn? Is that you?" asked a tired voice.

Ethan straightened. He set the miniature upright on a table. "Yes, Nessa, it's me."

The woman wept softly. "I asked for you and asked for you. Where have you been?"

His body responded to her distress with a pain in his heart. He couldn't bear her tears. "I'm sorry, darling." Ethan crossed the distance to the bed. "I came as soon as I could."

He drew the curtain aside, revealing the bed's occupant.

Vanessa's long white hair lay like silvery rays of moonlight against blue pillowcases. Her skin was deeply lined and thin as vellum, showing the veins in her face and hands. Her eyes, though, were as bright and vivid as they had ever been, a rare violet that had inspired poetry and beguiled royalty on both sides of the Channel.

Now those eyes, brimming with tears and childlike fear, turned upon him.

Ethan lowered himself onto the edge of the bed. "I heard you argued with your nurse."

Vanessa thrust out her lower lip. "She hides my things, just to be mean. Today, she took my brush and wouldn't give it back."

Ethan glanced at the vanity. As he knew it would be, the silver brush lay alongside the comb and hand mirror, right where they always were. "I think I see it," he said in a patient tone. "Would you like me to get it for you?"

"No!" Vanessa's hand shot out and caught his. "Don't leave me, Thorburn," she whispered. "You've been spending so much time with that wife of yours, and hardly any with me. Are you...are you tired of me?" Though her voice was reedy with age, her eyes pinned him with a ferocious intensity.

His heart lurched. "No, my love," he said, reciting the script that would calm her, words from a time long past. "I could never tire of you."

Vanessa tugged his hand. "Then come to bed."

Ethan sighed and stretched out beside her, on top of the coverlet. He propped up on some pillows and reached for her.

Vanessa nuzzled into Ethan's chest and made a contented sound. The frail woman felt insubstantial in his embrace. He rested his cheek on her forehead and kissed her brow, just to assure himself she was really there. "What shall we do this evening, Nessa?"

"I'd like to go to a ball," she answered on a happy sigh. "You buy me so very many pretty things. All the ladies will be jealous. Their husbands don't do half for them what you do for me and it infuriates them. They can look down their noses at me all they like, but I see their envy. They wish they had things like mine. They wish they had a love like ours…"

Her voice trailed off into a mutter, and then she was quiet. She inhaled and exhaled slowly. Her weight increased against him as she sank into sleep.

When he judged it safe to do so, he reached for the bell pull beside the bed.

A maid opened the door and crossed the room, her eyes wary upon Vanessa.

"Could I have something to eat, please?" Ethan asked in a whisper. "Something I can manage with one hand."

The maid glanced at her sleeping mistress and offered Ethan a sympathetic smile. "Of course, my lord. And may I say," she hesitated before continuing, "God bless you, sir. The care you give madam…" She shook her head. "Well," she concluded, "we're just fortunate you don't have bigger things on your mind."

She curtsied and tiptoed from the room. Ethan stared after her, stupefied. *Didn't have bigger things on his mind?*

For the first time since he'd arrived, he remembered that when he went home, it would be to a house stripped to the bones, and creditors banging down the door.

Ghita's insistence that he marry once again floated through his mind. The Italian woman had even mentioned a name, to which Ethan had paid no attention. Brock-something, maybe? Marriage was repugnant to him, thanks to the twice-damned Earl of Kneath. Ethan didn't want a bride, but gaming had driven him to ruin.

If only he possessed a useful skill, he could seek respectable employment. Perhaps a diplomatic post or a royal appointment?

But no. He could never abandon Vanessa. She was his responsibility—the only one he'd never fouled up. If he left

London, she'd be alone, vulnerable to malefactors who would take advantage of her condition. Long ago, he'd vowed never to let that happen. He didn't dare lower his guard.

Which left him, in regards to his debts, with little in the way of options. Did he risk losing more money to Ficken and his ilk and digging himself deeper into debt, or did he enter into a detestable marriage of convenience? Both were intolerable.

Ethan glanced down at the frail old woman sleeping in his arms. He had wanted to come here to escape his problems.

Even in that, he'd failed.

Chapter Three

Lily disembarked from the carriage and joined her father's solicitor on the walk. In the last two weeks, they had viewed numerous properties under consideration as possible homes for the school.

She looked up and down the row of stately homes. "Isn't Bird Street a little much for what we have in mind?"

It would be the matter of only a few minutes to walk to Brook Street, turn the corner, and find oneself in Grosvenor Square, where scions of the wealthiest, most influential families lived in imposing grandeur.

Lily's friends, the Duke and Duchess of Monthwaite, would reside on the Square when they returned to England from their South American expedition.

"Ordinarily, I'd agree," said Mr. Wickenworth, the solicitor. He was a short man, round in the middle, balding on top, and almost always smiling. Lily had no idea the law could prove to be such a jolly profession, but Mr. Wickenworth seemed to find handling Mr. Bachman's affairs the epitome of good living.

He removed his spectacles and wiped them with a handkerchief. Then he dabbed the bit of forehead showing beneath the brim of his hat before returning the spectacles to his face. He wrinkled his nose and blinked. "However," he said, "the owner is eager to sell and might be persuaded to accept an offer more in line with our budget."

She looked up the walk, where a fashionably dressed lady and gentleman strolled arm in arm, along with a small terrier on a lead. A fine phaeton rolled past, drawn by a matched pair.

She looked at Mr. Wickenworth. "Even if we can convince the owner to sell to us at a reasonable price, I'm concerned the neighborhood might not be appropriate for the school."

The solicitor patted his belly. A gold ring circling his pinky finger winked in the sun. "That is something to consider," he agreed. He gestured to the front stairs. "Still, we're here. Let's have a look."

Lily ascended, careful to hold her skirt and dusty blue military-style pelisse free of the water collected on the steps. A general air of neglect hung about the property. Spots of rust blemished the wrought-iron rail, and the brass knocker was tarnished.

She wrinkled her nose. "How long has this house stood vacant?"

"It isn't." Mr. Wickenworth reached past her to knock. "I'm told the owner lives here."

Lily raised a brow. She very much doubted anyone possessed of the fortune required to reside in this neighborhood would permit his house to go without such basic maintenance as sweeping the front steps or polishing the brass hardware.

Several minutes elapsed with no response from inside the house.

"There, you see," she muttered. "This has been a wasted trip."

Mr. Wickenworth's features drew together, putting Lily in mind of a punched ball of dough. "I made an appointment through the solicitor handling the sale," he insisted. He reached for the knocker again and rapped a full ten times.

After another minute passed in silence, Lily said, "Maybe they left the door open for us."

She reached for the knob, but jerked back at the sound of a loud clatter, followed by a muffled voice. A moment later, footsteps pounded down stairs and the door opened.

The eyes of the man standing there hit Lily with a stunning force. They were deep blue—the color of the restless sea after a storm, and their scrutinizing regard took in her face and then boldly roved down her length and back up again.

Heat prickled the back of her neck. She couldn't breathe. She couldn't remember *how* to breathe.

The man's hair was cut very short. It was reddish brown, and the top was tousled and stood up about two inches in short twists that would curl, given another inch. She realized with horror that her hand had begun to reach toward that hair and snatched it back.

He wore a black suit, rather than livery. *He must be the butler*, she decided. The coat seemed reasonably well tailored, but it was hard to tell for certain because it was rumpled to within an inch of its life, as though it had been slept in. She frowned and shook her head at the ludicrous thought.

"Yes?" the butler said in a bland tone, seeming not to have noticed her wayward extremity. "What do you want?" His eyes flicked to Wickenworth, giving Lily opportunity to further study his face. His brows were long and heavy, but not oppressively so. Rather, they complemented the firm, straight line of his nose. Dark stubble shaded his strong jaw. She clutched her reticule tighter to keep from reaching for him again.

"I'm Wickenworth," the solicitor announced, "representing Mr. Bachman." He gestured to Lily. "This is Miss Bachman."

The butler's heavy-lidded gaze fell on her again. Lily's stomach flipped.

"We've an appointment to tour the property," Wickenworth continued.

The man stared blankly at the solicitor for a moment, then he shook his head as though clearing it. "Oh. Yes. Come in."

As Lily passed the handsome young butler, every nerve in her body stood on end.

The door banged into the frame behind them. She startled.

"Sorry," the butler muttered.

For a moment, the three of them stood in the dim entrance hall. The walls were bare. In one spot, a nail protruded from the plaster with a bit of hanging wire dangling from it. A layer of dust lay on the parquet floor. Next to the front door stood a ladderback chair. A gentleman's hat hung on the top of one of the back posts, while a great coat had been draped across the seat.

Something tugged at her attention. She turned to see the butler watching her with frank interest. Their gazes locked. Lily unconsciously bit her lower lip and tucked a strand of hair behind her ear. The man followed each minute movement with his fathomless eyes, a mocking smile twitching the corners of his lips. She swallowed, willing her nerves to calm.

"May we look around?" she asked with more confidence than she felt.

He nodded slightly, his gaze holding fast to hers.

Lily turned away and closed her eyes; her heartbeat pounded in her ears. What on earth was wrong with her? She'd seen handsome men before—she'd even kissed one or two. This was only a man, and a servant besides. She scolded herself for acting like a ninny.

She walked up the stairs, glad that Mr. Wickenworth had placed himself between her and the butler. From the landing, she crossed to a door and opened it. The room appeared to be a parlor. Carefully, she made her way through the gloom to the windows. When she pulled the drapes open, sunlight streamed through the glass and illuminated a cloud of dust stirred up by her movements. It was as though no one had touched the room in weeks.

The parlor was bare, except for a decorative plate in a stand atop the mantel. The carpet was marked by the footprints of chairs that were no longer there.

She wrinkled her nose as she dragged her finger across the windowsill. It looked for all the world as if the most recent occupant had long since moved away. Mr. Wickenworth must have been mistaken. Surely.

"Does someone *actually* live here?" she asked, turning toward the door.

The butler stood just inside the room, casually leaning with his shoulder propping up the wall. His eyes narrowed at her question. "Yes," he said in a jeering tone, "someone *actually* lives here."

"That was uncalled for," Lily muttered.

Handsome as he might have been, the man had no sense of his station. She stalked past the rude servant to a door across the hall. She reached for the knob.

"Wait!" He grabbed her upper arm, bringing her to a halt.

Lily's startled gaze flew to his face. He was a few inches taller than she. Being quite tall for a female, this was a little out of the ordinary. Lily stood equal in stature to—or even taller than—most men of her acquaintance. The butler radiated an intensity of presence; his maleness oozed from every inch. His warm, spicy scent softened her other senses. Awareness flared between them, and Lily once again felt herself drawn in. She started to sway, shifting her weight closer.

"Yes?" she said breathlessly, her lips parted in a pout.

His eyes were riveted to her mouth. Then his brows puckered slightly, as though it took some effort to remember what he'd wanted to say. "I'd rather you didn't go in there," he said at last. "That's my—"

"Nonsense!" Mr. Wickenworth cut in brusquely. "How can we appraise the place if we don't see the entire property?"

Lily looked from the solicitor to the man. She looked down at his hand still on her arm. Annoyance flared through her as she realized that a perfect stranger—and a servant, at that—had manhandled her.

She pulled her arm out of his grip and drew a breath, fighting to regain mastery of her suddenly traitorous body. "Mr. Wickenworth is quite right," she said. "We've come to view the property, and view it we shall."

The butler's lips drew into a thin line as though he wanted to argue.

Lily's eyes narrowed in a challenge.

She saw the instant the man's shoulders relaxed a fraction. Lily felt her equilibrium returning. His handsome face had briefly thrown her off balance, but she was once again in control of herself and the situation. She turned on her heel and marched into the room.

Several steps in, she stuttered to a halt; she felt herself enveloped by...him. The entire room smelled like the gorgeous stranger. A twinge of uncertainty gave her a moment's pause before she continued to the window on the nearest wall. She opened the curtains, once again kicking up dust.

This was a study. A desk at the far end of the room was buried under messy piles of papers. She thought of her father's massive desk, exactingly neat. No one could function in chaos such as this.

She wondered who lived in a largely vacant house, with only a presumptuous and incapable butler for a servant. Something had happened here, she reasoned. No matter what the butler said, it was patently obvious that the bulk of the house's interior was not lived in.

A roaring sneeze startled her. Mr. Wickenworth held his handkerchief to his face.

"God bless you," Lily said.

"Excuse me," the solicitor said. He took several steps into the study, the butler following close behind.

Mr. Wickenworth sneezed again. He blew his nose. "I'm sorry," he said. "The dust is aggravating my nose. I'll just step outside for a mo—" He interrupted himself with another sneeze.

"For heaven's sake, go." Lily shooed him out with a wave of her hand.

The front door closed behind him. A heavy, uneasy silence followed as Lily realized she was alone with the butler and his too-penetrating gaze.

She clasped her hands behind her back and took a turn around the study. There was a leather sofa in the middle of the room. From behind, she saw that the wooden floor in front of it was darker than the surrounding boards, showing that a rug had covered the area at one time.

When she reached the other side, she found a rumpled blanket lying across the cushions. A heavy glass bottle was on its side on the floor beside the sofa.

She remembered the bang she'd heard when they knocked on the door and eyed the bottle warily. She had the overwhelming feeling of having stumbled into a primitive masculine den. There was nothing refined about it—a jumble of papers and a place to bed down with a bottle of whiskey. It was the barest degree of civilized living she had ever encountered in fashionable Mayfair. This was all better suited to an overcrowded tenement house.

Once again, she felt the handsome stranger watching her. She met his eyes, and heat shot straight to her lower belly. Her heart thudded against her ribs.

"This is squalid," she stated, striving again to regain a sense of balance. How could he jumble her thoughts with a look?

"You have a great many opinions, don't you?" he rejoined. "Why do you want it, *Miss* Bachman, daughter of *Mister* Bachman?" He gave a derisive intonation to their prefixes. "This isn't a neighborhood for upstarts."

He started toward her in slow, deliberate steps. A hungry glint in his eye made Lily decidedly uncomfortable. He looked at her as though he were a wolf, and she the little lamb separated from the flock.

She retreated backward a step. He took up entirely too much space; he sucked the air from the room. "A sch—school," she stammered. "I'm opening a charity school."

The predatory posture relaxed. He rubbed a long finger across his chin. "A charity school?" he murmured. "It would be nice to see something good come of the place."

A realization slapped Lily across the face. "You're not the butler!" she exclaimed.

The man's eyes widened in genuine surprise. Then he threw his head back and let out a laugh, clear and loud. The sound sent a shiver of delight through Lily. She couldn't help but chuckle along with him.

"The butler?" he said. "You thought I was the *butler?*" He laughed again.

A flush of embarrassment heated Lily's face. It was one thing to laugh at her mistake the first time. Now he was just mocking her!

"What was I supposed to think?" she snapped. "You answered the door in *that*," she said, waving her hand up and down to indicate his dark attire. Now that she looked at it again, she saw that it was a gentleman's eveningwear, not a butler's uniform. "The men I know aren't still wearing the previous night's apparel at eleven o'clock in the morning."

The humor left his face and the penetrating look returned. "You don't know many interesting men, then, do you?" The easy, aristocratic drawl in his voice was unmistakable, now that she expected it. How could she ever have taken him for a servant?

She swallowed. "I know a great many interesting men." She raised her brows pointedly.

He stalked forward again.

Lily's pulse thrummed in her ears. She felt the edge of the sofa against the back of her legs an instant before she lost her footing and sprawled onto the cushions. She hadn't even realized she'd stepped back.

His mouth spread into a lazy smile and his eyes took on a heavy-lidded appearance.

"You sleep here," Lily said, grasping for something, anything to keep him at bay.

"Usually," he answered. "But there's a rather large bed upstairs that hasn't seen any use in a while." His teeth flashed in a wolfish grin.

Lily froze at his insinuation. Then she was angry. How dare he? *No one* spoke to her that way. Lily Bachman was not some lightskirt who'd come tripping into his dilapidated abode to subject herself to his torment.

She pressed her hands into the sofa and shoved back upright. The blanket slid off the smooth cushions and pooled behind her ankles.

"Sir," she began. She cast a contemptuous glance around the study. "If you truly live like this, then you have my pity, but I'll not be purchasing your hovel. This run-down sty would offend even a bushman accustomed to dwelling in a mud hut."

The man's mouth fell open in astonishment.

Lily's lips curled in an icy smile. "There will be no need to tour the rest of the property," she said. "I'll show myself out."

As she passed the man, she shivered. He stared at her in wrathful silence.

She felt a twinge of guilt for putting down his home without knowledge of his circumstances, but he'd made her feel completely out of her element and so helpless under his hot, penetrating eyes.

On the front step, she drew a deep breath and felt the tension slowly drain from her body.

Mr. Wickenworth stood beside the carriage. "Completed the tour already?"

She shook her head. "I could tell it didn't suit."

From inside the house, she heard a bellowing roar, followed by the sound of shattering glass; she immediately recalled the bottle beside the sofa.

Lily fled down the stairs and nearly dove into the coach. "Take me home at once, please."

She eyed the house warily as the coach rolled forward, glad she'd gotten out when she had. Between the way the stranger inside had ignited her blood and her temper, she was fully aware that she had almost completely lost control of herself. She never wanted to feel that way again.

Chapter Four

Ethan finished dealing out thirteen cards to each of the other three players at the table. The last card, his thirteenth, he turned face-up—the three of clubs. A quick check of his hand confirmed that he had four high-ranking cards of the trump suit. He could win this hand. If his partner had even just a few good cards to complement his trumps, it would be a done deal. The old, familiar excitement coursed through his veins.

He cast a longing look at the next table, where an intense game of *vingt-et-un* was underway. Bishop Holyland looked up and caught Ethan's gaze. He nodded in greeting, then returned his attention to his cards.

He would've given anything to join that game, but he simply didn't have the money—or the credit with the other gentlemen—for the staggering sums those players were throwing around. When Ethan had approached the table an hour ago, half the men had refused to acknowledge him. Bishop had pointed out the ladies needed a fourth for whist.

It was a lowering moment, but Ethan refused to give anyone the satisfaction of laughing at him. A dowager's money spent the same as any other, after all. He'd thanked Bishop for the suggestion with an easy smile and sauntered to the dowagers' table as though nothing in the world could give him greater pleasure.

He flashed the women his roguish grin. "Care to make it interesting, ladies?"

"Thorburn, there you are!" Quillan's booming voice drew the attention of everyone in the card room. He sidled up behind Ethan and clapped him on the shoulder.

"Ladies," he said. "I hope you'll forgive me if I steal Lord Thorburn away—we've some deadly dull politics to discuss."

"Thorburn doesn't sit in Parliament." The guileless eyes of one of the dowagers blinked at Ethan.

"Truer words have never been spoken, madam." Quillan nodded to the woman. "Nevertheless, there's a proposed public road improvement near his family seat, and I'd like his input on the lay of the land."

Smooth, Ethan thought appreciatively. If he didn't know Quillan any better, he almost would have thought his friend gave a rat's arse about some road project.

He issued a dramatic sigh and rose. "My apologies, ladies. Duty calls."

Ethan allowed Quillan to guide him away from the card room. They paused in the hallway just outside the door.

"You looked in need of rescuing," Quillan said cheerfully.

Ethan snorted. "I could've won that set. Did you have any idea Lady Bryer refers to clubs as puppy toes?"

"No," Quillan blinked owlishly. "I generally don't lower myself to gambling with dowagers."

Ethan's lips pursed. He saw how it was. He was the easy target of his friend's jibe.

Not long ago, Quillan had been the one who needed this friendship more than Ethan did. Ethan was the one the ladies had flocked to. He was the one with a well-cultivated reputation for fast living and a lust for life. Years ago, when they'd met at Oxford—and then as two young men new to town—Quillan was chubby, awkward, and easy to overlook in a crowd. The only thing that recommended him at all was his title, and that only mattered to husband-hunting misses.

Ethan introduced him to the more interesting set and helped him overcome his debilitating shyness. With Ethan's guidance, Quillan found his stride.

And now the nature of their relationship had changed. Quillan was the one welcome in every ballroom and parlor. He was the one who had secured a contract with the most sought-after courtesan in London. It was he who did Ethan favors now—usually in the form of loaning him money. At present, Ethan owed him upwards of ten thousand pounds.

The tone of their friendship had shifted. Ethan needed Quillan, and Quillan knew it. And sometimes, such as now, he reminded Ethan of the fact.

Well, before much longer, Ethan would give Quillan a small taste of comeuppance when he took his mistress right out from under his nose.

They strolled into the ballroom where several hundred bodies were packed in close proximity to one another, a teeming mass of elegant attire and false-bright smiles.

"How is Lady Umberton?" Ethan asked casually.

Quillan gave him a sharp look.

The only, *the only*, subject remaining that Ethan could possibly hold over Quillan was his marriage. Ethan warned his friend the fair object of his infatuation might only be after his title.

But Quillan refused to listen, believing instead the sweet nothings his intended whispered in his ear. They'd married her first Season out, a few months after Quillan met her.

And he'd regretted it every day since, for the past five years.

Immediately after the wedding, all of Lady Umberton's sweet pretenses fell to the wayside. His countess took to spending Quillan's money and brandishing her title over inferior acquaintances like a duck to water.

Ethan stood by his friend's side, resisting the urge to ever once breathe a word of the *I told you so* that had hung in the air between them all these years.

But if Quillan was going to persist in rubbing Ethan's debts into his face…

Quillan made a disgusted sound in his throat. "She's big as a house and a misery to be around, if you must know," Quillan said. "I hope she delivers soon, and pray God it's a boy. If I never have to touch that harpy again, it'll be too soon."

Ethan tactfully nodded and gave his friend a neutral sounding, "Hmm."

He took a glass of champagne from a passing footman. Despite the lines of twirling dancers in the middle of the ballroom, a flurry of activity on the other side of the room grabbed Ethan's attention.

A woman in a scarlet gown stood out like a rose against black velvet, surrounded as she was by a coterie of gentlemen in dark eveningwear. Her hand rested on the arm of her escort, though the distance between them suggested she bowed to politeness, not preference. From here, Ethan detected the haughty lift of her chin, the way she ate up the floor with confident strides, rather than mincing, ladylike steps, forcing her entourage to trip over themselves and each other to remain beside her while avoiding collisions with the other guests.

"That's her," he breathed. Admiration mingled with distaste. While she was certainly a rare beauty and no shrinking violet like so many society misses, he couldn't forget the numerous set downs she had heaped upon his head just minutes after they'd laid eyes on one another.

"What was that?" Quillan turned to look in the direction Ethan was staring.

"That girl," Ethan amended. Quillan knew he'd lost his possessions, but he didn't know Ethan was forced to offer his house for sale. There was no way for Ethan to describe how this infuriatingly rude vixen had toured his home and insulted every inch of it without further abasing himself in Quillan's estimation.

His friend chuckled. "There are a hundred girls here, Eth. To which do you refer?"

Ethan nodded to indicate the direction. "The one in red with a round table's worth of gallants swarming around."

Quillan scanned the crowed until he spotted the tableau. "Miss Bachman, you mean?"

"Yes," he murmured, "Miss Bachman."

As they watched, Miss Bachman dropped her escort's arm. Another man materialized at her side, proffering a cup of punch. She waved a hand, turning down the offering. A rival stepped in front of her with a flute of champagne. This she also refused.

She was tall for a woman, taller even than most of the men nipping at her heels. He hadn't noticed her height when she'd been in his house. She was shorter than he, which was all that registered—but so was every other woman he'd ever met. Now that he saw her in comparison to others, he gained an appreciation for her stature.

A woman that tall, he suddenly thought, *must have miles of leg under her skirts.* His mouth went dry as he contemplated this revelation. "Do you know anything about her?"

Quillan turned a quizzical expression upon him. "You mean you *don't* know anything about her?"

Ethan frowned and shook his head. "Should I?"

Quillan barked a laugh. "Old man, Miss Bachman is the dark horse catch of the Season. She's got the regular brood of would-be wives in a tizzy. All those pathetic chaps over there aren't yapping around a woman of no consequence whatsoever because of her pretty face."

"Then why are they?" he asked, lifting his champagne to his lips.

"Ethan," Quillan said with laughter in his voice, "Miss Bachman has a dowry of a hundred thousand pounds. Have you been under a rock all year?"

Ethan choked on his drink. The effervescent liquid shot up the back of his throat and burned his nose. "A hundred thou—" he croaked.

"Astonishing, isn't it?" Quillan said. "This is her second Season out, but word of her fortune just leaked this spring. There hasn't been a dowry like that on the Marriage Mart in years."

"But who *is* she?" Ethan asked. "And how can this only be her second Season? She's no young miss." Indeed, he thought, recalling his provoking encounter with Miss Bachman, her rapier wit bespoke a woman of some experience. If she was a green girl, then Ethan was the King of Siam.

The vision in red turned her back, giving him ample opportunity to examine her figure. Chestnut hair looped and twisted in an intricate updo, leaving the column of her long, creamy neck bared for his consideration. He followed the line of her neck down. It swept his gaze over a graceful but well-defined shoulder. No timid bits on that one, no. A narrow waist flared out to generously curved hips. His body tightened as the first hints of arousal thudded through his veins.

In his study, she'd both infuriated and intoxicated him. He'd written it off as the effect of drinking too late and rising too early, but with a similar feeling again stealing over him; perhaps it hadn't been the alcohol, at all. If she could transfix him so from a distance of twenty paces, he must well and truly be attracted to the infuriating female.

As he watched, she made an annoyed, regal gesture with a gloved hand, sending some poor sap on his way.

"If by 'Who is she?' you mean to inquire about her connections," Quillan said, seemingly unaffected by the siren across the room, "then I can tell you that the family is of no account whatsoever. Her father is richer than Croesus—coal, I hear—and has some government contracts. He's won a seat in Commons. It's new money. Quite crass."

Ethan's gaze wandered from Miss Bachman to the unassuming older couple standing nearby—her parents? The woman was talking to some other older ladies, and the gentleman had the blank look on his face of a man who would much rather be elsewhere. The pair didn't look extraordinary in the least. They would have blended right into the local assembly rooms in any small town.

"So now," he concluded, following the trail of Quillan's story, "Miss Bachman's marriage—to a nobleman, of course—will cement the family's status. They will have, as they say, *arrived.*"

"Just so," Quillan agreed. "She was previously affianced to an Army man, but the Peninsular did him in before they wed. Last year was her first Season out of mourning, and her first in town."

Ah. That explained the discrepancy in her age-to-Season ratio. "Any son?" Ethan asked.

"No." Quillan tapped a manicured nail against his glass. "Miss B is the only child. Of course, Mr. Bachman *is* actively engaged in industry. The stench of trade is all over his money, in any event. But when there's just so very *much* of it and still more coming in all the time…" He waggled his brow. "One begins to acquire an appreciation for the aroma."

"No title," Ethan mused out loud as his disbelieving gaze crossed the room again to settle on Miss Bachman, now seated and hemmed in by seven men vying for her notice. "New money. No tail tying the fortune to a male heir." A tingle shot up his spine. "He's leaving it all to her, isn't he?" he said, turning astonished eyes on his friend.

Quillan nodded. "She's not just an heiress, she's *the* heir. That's the rumor, anyway—not only the dowry, but the inheritance to come when Mr. B passes to his eternal reward."

Ethan swallowed, his throat suddenly dry. "And how much would that be?"

"Nobody knows. But if *her* dowry is a hundred thousand, how much more must *he* have?" Quillan lifted his glass and tilted his head. "Makes me wish I wasn't already shackled, I tell you."

Ethan's mind reeled. With a dowry of a hundred thousand for his daughter, Mr. Bachman himself could easily be worth a half-million, or a full million, or more. Ethan could pay off his debts. He could afford Ghita. Hell, he could afford *ten* Ghitas.

Something soft and feminine jostled against him.

"Oh, excuse me, my lord."

He glanced down to see a petite blonde pressed against his side.

"Lady Elaine," he said, inclining his head.

She batted her eyelashes at him in what he supposed was meant to be a flirtatious fashion but fell miserably short. "This has turned into quite the crush. One can scarcely breathe," she simpered. "I couldn't help but hear you talking," Lady Elaine said. Her small eyes disappeared behind the apples of her cheeks as she flashed him an ingratiating smile.

Ethan and Quillan exchanged a nonplussed look.

"Were you discussing Lily Bachman?" the woman pressed.

Her name is Lily. He filed that information away in his mind. "It would do no good to deny it, as you've already owned to eavesdropping."

The young woman drew herself up, oblivious to his rebuke, and crossed her arms beneath an unimpressive bosom. "I can't stand her," she said with a sneer. "No one can."

"That's quite a claim." Ethan tipped his glass toward the portion of the room where Lily Bachman held court. "It would appear a great many people tolerate her perfectly well."

Lady Elaine's nostrils flared like a bull preparing to charge. "They're only after her obscene money. No one likes her. Look at her," the woman said. Envy etched its ugly imprint across her features. "Tall as a giraffe. She stomps about like a man and holds herself apart, like she's too good to talk to anyone—*her!* A complete nobody, lording around over *actual* lords and ladies. And when she does open her mouth, she doesn't have a nice word to say to a soul."

Ethan was tempted to point out the hypocrisy of her diatribe, but held his tongue.

"Just look!" Lady Elaine gestured with a hand.

He looked.

Some oaf dabbed with a handkerchief at what appeared to be a punch stain on the thigh of her skirt.

Color flooded Lily's cheeks. She swatted the swain's hand. Ethan understood that she didn't want the man touching her leg. The place he kept swiping at *was* awfully close to Eden.

The man kept insisting, kept touching.

A frustrated knot formed in Ethan's chest. Why didn't anyone stop the fool pawing her? He made a disgusted sound.

"Exactly," Lady Elaine said. "See how she berates the poor fellow?"

Ethan's brows furrowed as he suddenly felt a protective urge. He started forward, intent to pull the man off Miss Bachman, when she took matters into her own very capable hands.

She jumped to her feet and rounded on the offending gentleman. Ethan couldn't hear her voice over the music and rumble of the crowd, but he saw well enough the sharp gestures of her hands, the way her teeth were bared as she spoke. He saw, too, how the man seemed to crumble under her verbal evisceration.

Finally, the man hurried away, swiping at his cheek.

"By Jove," Quillan said, all astonishment. "She made him cry!"

"Horrible," Lady Elaine sneered.

Ethan let her declaration hang in the air, unanswered, as the inexplicable anxiety he'd felt for Miss Bachman drained away. He didn't know that he'd call Miss Bachman *horrible*, as Lady Elaine insisted, but having already been on the wrong end of her sharp tongue, he wasn't ready to jump to her defense, either.

A moment later, he noticed the space at his side had been vacated. Lady Elaine had evidently gone elsewhere to spread her vitriol. He breathed a little easier.

"So," Quillan said.

Ethan looked at him. "Yes?"

"What do you think?"

"Of what?" Ethan asked.

"Miss Bachman," Quillan said.

He shrugged. "What is there to think?" She had turned her back on the punch-spiller. Ethan had a nice view of her profile, which was dominated by a spectacular pair of—

"Ethan," Quillan said.

"What?"

His eyes still roved Miss Bachman's assets. She'd been modestly buttoned up in a pelisse when he'd met her before. *Hiding those lush breasts should be a hanging offense*, he decided.

"The gleam in your eye, Ethan, reminds me of the last time you had a decent hand. When was that? Remind me; it's been a while."

Miss Bachman's money offered freedom from a bleak future. It was comfort, security.

As he watched her skewer another hopeful, he felt something

akin to the same blissful state he remembered from sailing with his grandfather. Exhilaration and peace all at once.

Well, maybe not peace, he considered. Not with Miss Bachman part and parcel with her hundred thousand.

Of course, he mused with a thoughtful tilt of the head, he didn't really *like* peace all that much, did he? A little fire to keep things exciting might be just the thing.

Besides, marriage didn't mean an end to his life. Plenty of people, Quillan included, lived virtually separate lives from their spouses. Marriage was just a contract, names scribbled on a license. It didn't really *mean* anything as he knew from his own parents' wildly unsuccessful union. His own life could go on just as he wished.

Maybe Ethan *could* offer Miss Bachman a mutually beneficial arrangement. He had the title she wanted, and she had the money he needed.

He smiled. "Quillan, my friend, I've decided it's time I marry."

"And I won't insult you by asking the identity of the lucky lady. Only one has the charms," he said while rubbing his thumb and first two fingers together, "to catch your eye. When do you start your pursuit?"

Ethan looked across the room where the future Lady Thorburn was conversing with one of her hangers-on with a bored expression on her face.

Ethan's smile deepened. He handed Quillan his glass. "Right now."

Chapter Five

Lily cast a longing look at one of the two chandeliers hanging above the ballroom. It glittered like a thousand shards of ice the morning after a winter storm.

She wondered if it would support the weight of a noose from which she could hang herself. It didn't even matter if the chandelier couldn't support her for long. Once the noose snapped her neck and ended her misery, the chandelier could crash to the floor and send a few of these milksops to hell, too.

Gradually, she became aware of anticipated silence surrounding her.

She blinked and lowered her gaze to the man standing in front of her, a pockmarked fellow whose name she hadn't even attempted to remember. "I'm sorry, I wasn't attending," she admitted. What did it matter if she offended him? All to the good, if he left her alone. "What did you say?"

"Not at all," he said with an ingratiating smile. "I merely commented upon the quality of the entertainment." He nodded toward the musicians' nook behind a screen at the end of the great chamber. "Rarely have I heard such precision in a ballroom."

Lily sighed wearily. Really? She had to comment upon the *precision* of the ball's musicians?

She cast an unhappy glance around the room, where other groups of people her age were laughing together, having a grand time dancing and talking.

Meanwhile, she was isolated like an oddity at a county fair, held apart from everyone else and only approached by the most intrepid—or desperate—men.

The women all hated her, Lily knew. They didn't appreciate interlopers in their midst and resented competition for *their* men.

An angry thought directed toward her father crossed her mind. He was dead wrong if he thought her dowry was going to land her a decent husband. No honorable man would come after her money to begin with. If he'd made her dowry more modest in size, she might stand a better chance. As it was, she had the outrageous hundred thousand pounds hanging around her neck, an embarrassingly large albatross that marked her for a ruthless social climber when she was really anything but.

She was once again aware of the lapse in conversation.

Oh, right. The musicians. The *precise* musicians.

Five gentlemen stood around her in a circle, each making a good show of caring what she had to say about the musicians.

Might as well have a little fun, she decided. She smiled slyly. "I suppose they're fine. So," she said, changing the subject, "that war…"

That war was always a heated topic of conversation. The news out of France came fast and furious this spring. The Allies had taken Paris, and Bonaparte was bound for exile. Everyone had something to say on the matter.

"It's about time they got Boney," said one man. "Wellington made some blunders in Spain. He should have had this wrapped up last year."

Spoken like a man who's never worn a uniform, Lily thought crossly.

"My mother can't wait to get back to Paris and buy a decent bonnet," drawled another.

She rolled her eyes and bit her tongue. Thousands of men, including her betrothed, had died freeing the Continent of a maniacal emperor, and people were concerned with *bonnets*?

The pockmarked man spoke up. "I just wish they'd put *him* up in front of the firing squad and be done with it."

"So eager for blood?" Lily curled her lip. "Hasn't enough been spilled?"

"W-well," the man stammered. "That is…I don't mean to imply…"

"Exile is an appropriate punishment," Lily said. "Bonaparte is an emperor, after all. Or would you have us start taking the heads of kings? *Vive la révolution*, gentlemen?"

Her group of suitors fell into shocked silence. There was nothing quite like raising the specter of *the Terror* to get the titled class quaking in their boots, she thought with satisfaction. At least they'd ceased their namby-pamby efforts at conversing with her.

A warm hand pressed into the small of her back. "Careful," a velvety, low voice rumbled in her ear. "You begin to sound like the sympathetic rabble. Makes the aristocracy *very* nervous."

She turned to face the speaker. The arm attached to the hand slipped around her waist.

"Good evening, Miss Bachman," said…the butler. Who wasn't a butler. Who was, perhaps, the handsomest man she had ever seen, and had his arm around her waist, and was looking into her eyes with a silky heat that she felt in her belly—

The world went off kilter. She was faintly aware that she was standing in a ballroom in the arms of a man whose name she did not even know. "Good evening, my lord," she murmured.

He flashed a devastating smile and that, too, contributed to the simmering heat in her lower regions.

"Come, let's dance." He tilted his head toward the middle of the room, where couples formed up for the waltz.

The light skipped across his russet hair, picking up hints of auburn in the brown. It was as tousled and refusing to be tamed as it had been the day she first saw him.

"Thorburn," piped up one of her suitors. "Miss Bachman has already promised me the set."

Lily lowered her eyes, unaccountably disappointed. "It's true, my lord, I have." She slipped out of his arm.

She dragged air into her lungs, clearing her mind, even as a residue of heat remained where he'd touched her. Who was he, anyway, to come 'round and lay claim to her? They hadn't even been introduced! He was a boorish lout, even if he was devilishly good-looking. Handsome men were the worst sort, anyway—they knew they were in short supply, and were always insufferably full of themselves.

Lily started to turn toward her promised dance partner. Thorburn's hand clamped around hers.

"You've got all night to dance with these toads," he said into her ear as he tucked her hand into his arm. "Couple with me now."

There was something suggestive about his words, but when she turned her widened eyes on him, his face was all innocence.

Couple with me.

Lily's chest tightened.

As the music began, his arm slipped around her waist again. His hand fit into the curve of her back, warm and firm.

She laid a hand on the shoulder of his evening jacket, black as a raven's feathers. The snowy linen of his cravat was neatly folded into an intricate knot. How could she ever have mistaken his attire for a butler's uniform?

"Are you going to open a door for me?" she teased.

His slate blue eyes flashed sudden annoyance. "Are you going to insult me if I do?"

The nerve. Lily didn't have to put up with this. She pushed against his chest and attempted to pry her hand out of his. His grip tightened and he put a little more force into twirling her around the floor.

"Tell me, Miss Bachman," he said in an even tone, as though he hadn't noticed her effort at escape, "do you typically compete with your dance partners, or do I alone have the distinction of doing battle with your slippers?"

Lily glanced down where her feet were, in fact, making a muck of the pattern, refusing to fall into step with his. She blushed.

"Allow me to remind you," he said, arching a brow, "*I am* leading this dance."

Any number of retorts pranced across her tongue, but the firm set to his jaw made her think better of issuing one. She didn't care to get into an argument in front of the *ton*, or draw attention to the fact that she was dancing with a gentleman to whom she had not, in fact, been introduced.

She met his challenging gaze, then silently acquiesced to his lead. It was just a dance, not a battle. There was really no reason to make it one. Lily adjusted her steps to cooperate with his.

An appreciative smile touched the corners of his mouth. He drew her closer.

As she relaxed and enjoyed the music—the musicians actually were quite good—she became aware of how harmoniously their bodies moved together. She felt the muscles of his shoulder tighten and release beneath her fingers. His hand on her back exerted a light but constant pressure, somehow taking some of her own weight off her feet.

Or maybe she was just floating at being in the arms of a handsome man who had yet to say a word about her money, or an insipid remark to win her regard. *That* was something to recommend him, even if his manners left much to be desired.

His eyes roamed her face, then traveled down to her décolletage.

Lily felt her breasts tighten in response to his scrutiny. She inhaled sharply.

"Are you warm?" he asked, a knowing glint in his eyes.

How could eyes such a cool blue hold so much heat, she wondered.

"A little," she admitted.

As a turn in the waltz brought them near the French doors opening onto the balcony, he pulled her out of the pattern of dancers and drew her out into the night.

The fresh air cooled Lily's addled senses. "Just a moment, Lord Thorburn, was it?" She laid a hand on his bicep and immediately wished she hadn't. His arm was solid. How could living flesh be so firm? She found herself wondering what his bare arms looked like, what it would feel like to touch them.

"Are you quite all right?" His voice held a teasing note.

He *knew* what he was doing to her, the insufferable man—he was probably doing it on purpose. She lifted her chin and met his hot gaze with a cool one of her own. "I did not consent to accompany you anywhere," she said imperiously. *There.*

His lips quirked in amusement. "Have I abducted you against your will?"

"Well…no," she faltered.

He tucked her hand into the crook of his arm and strolled toward the stairs. "I'd be happy to return you to your group of admirers, if you'd prefer their company."

The thought of going back to that lot was nauseating. She made a sound that expressed her feelings. Thorburn chuckled, a throaty, wicked laugh. It crawled over her skin and sent a shiver up and down her spine.

She made no further protests as they descended into the garden. They strolled past other couples and exchanged greetings with acquaintances. It was all very respectable.

Why, then, Lily wondered, did she feel that stepping into the night with this man was an act of rebellion?

Why did her heart pound so as he led her farther away from the house?

And why was he moving around the hedge and pulling her into a shadowed alcove?

Alarms sounded in her mind. "My lord—" she started.

He gripped her waist and swung her around so her back was to the tall hedge.

She couldn't see the house at all now. Only the faintest wisps of music and laughter filtered to their secluded hiding place. His features melted into the darkness, rendering his face a study of shadow-on-shadow. There was only his overwhelming nearness and the warmth of his hands on her waist.

Her heart hammered madly. She had to get out of here. This wasn't a good idea. In fact, her overwrought mind pointed out, this was a very *bad* idea. She'd have been better off discussing the various precise attributes of the musicians with her swarm of fortune hunters, rather than allow herself to get carried away by Lord Thorburn's many charms.

Her throat was dry. She swallowed. That didn't help—her mouth was dry, too. "My lord—"

Then his mouth was on hers, extinguishing her voice like a snuffer on a flame.

The contact shocked her. Her eyes went wide.

His lips were soft, yet exerted firm, insistent pressure. Strong arms snaked around her back and drew her against his hard length. *No!* her mind protested. *He didn't ask. I didn't say he could...*

She placed her left hand on his shoulder and pushed herself away. At the same instant, she brought her right hand swinging up.

His hand clamped around her wrist like a vise before she made contact with his face.

"That's rather uncalled for, isn't it?" he asked, his voice full of mirth.

He was *laughing* at her—again! Never had she known someone who laughed at her as much as he did. It was lowering in the extreme. "I didn't give you permission to do *that*," she said.

His hand slid from her wrist to cover hers. His thumb traced small circles on her palm. Tiny convulsions of pleasure shot up her arm and her eyes fluttered closed in spite of herself. "I'm leading this dance, remember?"

Lily's arm went limp under his touch. "We're not dancing anymore." Her voice was small and weak in her own ears.

"Of course we are." He guided her hand to his neck. Of their own volition, her fingers burrowed into the short hair at his nape.

His hand still covered hers, keeping her firmly anchored. His other hand rose to her face and grazed her cheek with the back of a finger.

She jerked a little, turning her face toward his touch. The part of her mind that had sounded the alarm bells now notified her she was being drawn in by a practiced seducer. But the warning voice scarcely made an impression against the pleasurable sensations rolling through her.

His finger traced its way to her mouth. Lily pursed her trembling lips to meet his.

He gasped and let out a soft chuckle. "That's it," he said in a low voice.

Thorburn's gloved fingertip was warm. He pressed against her bottom lip, parting her slightly.

Blood rushed in a whoosh through Lily's ears. A steady thrumming of heat built in her lower belly. She felt heavy between her thighs.

He lowered his head again, replacing his finger with his lips. This time, Lily was poised to receive him. She tilted her head back into his hand.

There was nothing timid or asking about his kiss. He very simply took—without preamble, without consideration of her virginal sensibilities. His mouth slanted over hers, soft at first, but increasingly more demanding. His hands roved the curves of her back, molding her yielding body against his hard form. Everywhere he touched left a trail of fire on her skin. Lily was burning alive and all she could do was whimper. Her experience with any kind of kissing was limited and nonexistent when it came to the erotic provocation of Thorburn's mouth.

His tongue flicked at the corner of her mouth. Tentatively, she parted her lips. He groaned his approval. She felt the soft warmth of his tongue probing against hers. It was delightfully wicked, and Lily *never* did anything wicked. She opened further and drew him into her mouth, exulting in the passionate *newness* of it all.

She felt herself leaning against him, as though her legs could no longer support her—didn't *want* to support her. She wanted him to hold her, wanted to be as near as she could. She clung all the tighter, clumsily trying to convey her need—

He lifted his head.

Lily made a tiny sound of protest. *Come back!*

He drew a shuddering breath and exhaled. His breath was a warm caress against her cheek. Then he removed himself from her embrace.

Thorburn squeezed her shoulders. Lily swayed forward and nearly stumbled when he stepped back. He was still hidden from her sight by the darkness. "Miss Bachman," he said in his wry, detached voice. "Thank you for the dance." He kissed her hand then melted into the dark garden path.

He was gone.

Lily stood in the bushes, alone and dazed. Her skin still burned from his touch. Her knees still wobbled. But he was gone, and she was alone.

A stone bench crouched in a pool of torchlight a short distance toward the house. She dropped onto it. Dimly, she was aware of what had transpired. She'd allowed Lord Thorburn to kiss her, and she had kissed him back, allowing herself to be swept into lust. Slick moisture dampened her upper thighs.

She'd gone out of her mind and lost control of herself with one measly kiss. Hot shame stabbed through her. What would her mother say if she found out what Lily had done—what would her *father* say?

Lily drew several deep breaths, forcing herself to calm. The throbbing in her lower portions began to abate. She tried to order it away entirely, but her body refused to obey. So, she'd kissed a man, she reasoned. What of it? Men and women kissed each other all the time. There wasn't anything special about *kissing*.

Only there was.

She touched her lips. Thorburn had touched her mouth just so…Lily jerked her hand down. It didn't do to dwell on such things.

She made her way back to the house. As she approached the ballroom, the music seemed garish, the lights too bright. It was all overwhelming. The ball had taken on the not-quite-real quality one feels upon being woken out of a dream.

Lily stepped back into that illuminated cave teeming with bodies. She squinted against the light.

"Miss Bachman!" One of her suitors bounded to her side. "There you are. Are you all right?"

Lily stared at him. Was she all right?

Was she?

"Yes," she finally murmured. "Quite all right, thank you."

"Are you sure?" he asked. "Would you care for some punch?"

She nodded. "That would be lovely. Thank you."

The man looked at her with a hint of disbelief on his face. Then he grinned and nodded. When he returned with her punch, Lily allowed him to escort her to a seat, where several of her most devoted suitors soon flocked.

Their conversation washed over her unnoticed. She docilely answered a few direct questions. Her mind was too distracted to summon her usual disdain for all the men who wanted her fortune.

She looked around the ballroom for the one man who suddenly mattered very much, the one who had turned her ordered world topsy-turvy with a waltz and a kiss.

He was nowhere to be found.

Chapter Six

Lily poked half-heartedly at a bit of egg. She lifted her fork to her mouth and went through the motions of chewing and swallowing, only to discover the egg was still on her plate.

"Such a crush last night," Mrs. Bachman said. "Lady Northington-Jones must be thrilled, but I fear the air was not good for my lungs. So much going and coming, the air never settled."

"I found it stifling," Lily said. "Fresh air is better, anyway, Mama."

Mrs. Bachman pulled her shawl tighter around her shoulders. "I disagree. After all, you don't leave the windows of a sick room flung open, do you? Of course not. Warm, still air is more recuperative."

Lily took a sip of tea and replaced her cup in its saucer. Around the rim, fanciful peacocks in the Oriental style flew against a wide blue band. The service altogether clashed with the breakfast room's traditional décor, but Mrs. Bachman insisted the set was the crack of fashion. Lily hadn't the heart to tell her mother that *chinoiserie* was already *passé*.

"What is that you're wearing?" Mrs. Bachman asked, her cheeks drooped in a frown.

Lily glanced down at her dress. "What, this? It's new. This is the first I've worn it."

Her mother lifted a lorgnette and squinted. "Is it muslin?"

"Chintz." Lily broke a morsel off her bread.

"I don't recognize the fabric," Mrs. Bachman said.

Lily dipped the bread in her tea and popped it into her mouth. "You were present when I selected it."

"Was I?" Mrs. Bachman dropped the lorgnette. It fell against her ample chest, dangling from a chain around her neck. "I must say I don't recall. I certainly don't think I'd have approved the color. The blue of those flowers does nothing for you. And there it is again in that ribbon 'round your..." She gestured below her own bosom. She clucked her tongue. "Not a thing for you, my dear."

Lily closed her eyes and counted to twenty, so as to not lose her temper at her mother this early in the day.

She'd only gotten as far as twelve when there was a rap at the front door.

Lily startled. Her eyes rested on the breakfast room door. Quite a few callers had come in the week since she'd danced with Lord Thorburn, but not him. She'd convinced herself he would come, outing himself for a Leech like all the rest.

But he hadn't.

Lily didn't know whether she was relieved or disappointed that he never came. If he had, she'd have been happy to see him but sorry he was only interested in her money. But since he hadn't, she was deprived of laying her eyes on his handsome face again, even if she was still put out at him for kissing her. And then leaving her. She wasn't sure which offense put her out more.

Gah, she was a mess. She drummed her fingers on the table.

"No, no, that is most inelegant," Mrs. Bachman scolded. "Very mannish. And with your unfortunate height, you simply cannot utilize such gestures. The Duchess of Monthwaite could," she said with a nod. "Such a petite, pretty thing. It would be quite modern of her and soon become all the rage. But it just looks odd on you, Lily. I don't suggest you continue."

Lily groaned and pushed back from the table. "I'm sure you're right, Mama." She dropped a daughterly kiss to Mrs. Bachman's cheek. "I shall strive to curtail my hoydenish ways."

She went to the entrance hall to see who had called.

The butler, Wallace, was arranging several bouquets on a platter. He glanced up at her approach. "I was just bringing these to your room, miss."

Lily looked over the assortment of colorful flowers. "Who sent these?"

Wallace handed her a collection of calling cards. "Several gentlemen have stopped by this morning. I took the liberty of noting which gift is matched to each card."

"Thank you," she murmured. With trembling fingers, Lily flipped through the cards. "Mr. Faircloth?" she muttered. "Still?" She tossed it onto the sideboard and looked at the next. No, no, and no. None of them were from Lord Thorburn.

She scowled. "Box them up, Wallace," she directed. "Send them to the Navy hospital."

With a heavy sigh, Lily took herself to the library, the one room in the house where she could be reasonably certain of privacy. Mrs. Bachman had not read anything more intellectually strenuous than the scandal sheets for as long as Lily could remember. The cozy room offered a sanctuary in which to work on her school.

She unpacked her papers from a decorative box on a large mahogany table tucked into the corner of the book-lined walls. So far, she and Mr. Wickenworth had viewed five properties, including Lord Thorburn's. None of them were quite what Lily envisioned for the school, but the time was coming to make a selection.

She laid out her notes and then withdrew a fresh sheet of paper. On it, she listed each property down the left side of the page, then proceeded to jot down a few words for each, describing the strong and weak points of the houses. Beside the address of Lord Thorburn's Bird Street house, she wrote, *Advantages: Taller than I;*

Handsome; Kisses quite well. Disadvantages: Arrogant (insufferably so); High-handed; I ought not be in the position of knowing he kisses quite well.

She scowled at the paper and drew heavy black marks through that line of text. "The house doesn't suit," she muttered. "Neither does the man. And that's an end to it."

Forcing Lord Thorburn's mocking smile from her mind, she set aside the property list, determined instead to review the letters they'd received in answer to the advertisement for a headmistress. There were several who seemed suitably qualified—on paper, at least. This was another decision that needed to be made soon, as she wanted to leave the hiring of tutors and staff to a competent headmistress.

Several hours passed with Lily engrossed in her work, scarcely noticing the passing of time. The sound of her mother's voice wafting down the hall alerted Lily to an impending interruption.

"There you are!" Mrs. Bachman declared from the doorway. "I see you've not dressed for company though it's now gone noon. You know it's our day to receive visitors, and only look who's here!" She stepped inside the library and waved to an unseen guest in the hall, gesturing them forward.

Lily's heart skipped. Had Lord Thorburn finally come?

Her disappointment at two female figures appearing lasted only an instant when she saw who it was.

"Naomi!" Lily cried, springing to her feet.

Lady Naomi Lockwood, the youngest sibling of the Duke of Monthwaite, squealed when she caught sight of Lily. She wore a lilac muslin dress with a lightweight shawl draped over her arms. Her reddish-gold hair was done up in a simple twist.

She embraced Lily and stepped back, her hands resting on Lily's arms. "You look lovely, my dear. Please give me the direction of your modiste—that chintz is divine."

Lily's lips twitched and she shot an amused glance in her mother's direction.

"Miss Bachman!" said the other newcomer. "I trust you are engaged in an improving activity."

"Yes, Lady Janine," Lily said, wrapping her arms around Naomi's aunt.

"Pray, do not make me correct your address yet again, m'dear," the woman said.

Lily laughed. "Yes, Aunt Janine," she replied.

Lady Janine had never married, and so took particular interest in the doings of her niece and nephews. She had taken both Lily and Isabelle under her wing last Season, and insisted they also address her as "Aunt." The older lady was a hopeless bluestocking, forever absorbed in some course of study, and shamelessly encouraged the young ladies to follow suit.

"Shall we adjourn to the sitting room?" Mrs. Bachman was already moving toward the door.

"Oh, no," Aunt Janine replied in a faraway voice. "This will do very well." She walked the length of the massive bookshelves, running her fingers over the spines of the numerous volumes.

"Bosh," Mrs. Bachman, argued, "not a bit of it. No one wants to hang about these dusty old books. This room always puts me in mind of a tomb. Let's repair to the sitting room. So much pleasanter."

Aunt Janine's jaw dropped open in horror.

"Mama," Lily said firmly, forestalling any further offense toward Aunt Janine. "This will do."

Mrs. Bachman looked from her daughter to Aunt Janine and back again. Then she sniffed. "Very well." She took a seat near the fireplace and gestured for the others to join her.

"How is Her Grace?" Mrs. Bachman inquired of Naomi. "I was surprised to hear she would not be to town this spring; I trust she's not unwell?"

"Her Grace fares well at Helmsdale," Naomi answered in an ambiguous tone that sparked Lily's curiosity. "Aunt Janine is staying with Lord Grant and me here in town."

Tea arrived. Naomi helped her serve the older ladies, then they strolled around the room together. When they'd reached the opposite side of the library, Naomi asked, "Have I missed anything?"

Lily shook her head. "Just the usual preening and posturing."

"Hmm," Naomi said. She threw a sidelong smile at Lily. "We only just arrived yesterday, but I've already heard one interesting tidbit."

"Oh?"

Naomi inclined her head toward Lily. "I heard," she whispered, "that *someone* has had to ask all her suitors to form an orderly queue at the door."

Lily snorted. "I believe what you've heard has been exaggerated."

"But no betrothal?" Naomi asked. "After so many offers already?"

"No." Lily shook her head. "I'm really not interested in marrying just yet. Besides," she said, inclining her head toward the table where her papers were still laid out, "I have work to occupy me."

She hoped to steer the conversation away from her gaggle of hopefuls, but Naomi refused to be redirected.

"Has no one captured your notice?"

A picture of Lord Thorburn's provokingly handsome face sprang to mind.

"There is someone!" Naomi giggled. "You're blushing. Now you *must* tell all."

"There's nothing to tell," Lily insisted. "The only man who has captured my notice has done so because he's insufferable and rude and—"

"Handsome?" Naomi supplied.

"That, too," Lily admitted, "but it doesn't matter when his character is so—"

"Who is it?" Naomi asked.

Lily pressed her lips together.

"Out with it!"

"Lord Thorburn," Lily whispered.

Naomi's eyes flew wide. "Thorburn!" she yelped.

"What was that?" Mrs. Bachman looked over at the two girls.

"Who mentioned Thorburn?" Aunt Janine asked.

Lily winced.

Naomi had the good grace to look abashed. "Sorry."

"Lily waltzed with Lord Thorburn," Mrs. Bachman volunteered. "She ought not have done so, because they hadn't even been introduced. But you can't tell young people anything anymore."

"He's thoroughly disreputable," Naomi said. "You must be careful, Lily."

Aunt Janine snorted. "If debt renders one disreputable, then half the *ton* are notorious."

Lily frowned. "Is he badly in debt?"

"Oh, yes," Aunt Janine answered. "His proclivity for gaming is no secret, though with his past, it's no wonder he's picked up a vice or two." She turned back around in her seat and sipped her tea.

Don't be interested, Lily told herself. Thorburn's history wasn't any of her affair, didn't signify in the least. Besides, if he was in debt as Aunt Janine said, then he must certainly fall into her category of Leech.

Lily stared at the back of Aunt Janine's head. Then, like a moth inexorably drawn to a flame, her feet carried her to the sitting area. She lowered herself onto the sofa.

"What of his past?" she heard herself say. *No!* shouted a warning voice in her mind.

But, she argued with herself, if she learned about him, perhaps she could relegate him to the proper compartment in her mind and forget that foolish kiss. As it was, he was an enigma she'd built up to mythic proportions.

The scholarly lady set down her teacup; her face took on a faraway look. "The poor boy didn't have a chance of reaching manhood unscathed," Aunt Janine said. "His father, the third Earl of Kneath, is known to be a cruel man. Lady Kneath was a lovely girl in her time, but after their wedding, she was seen more than once with bruises on her face and arms."

Lily made a disgusted sound.

"How awful!" Naomi said. Lily hadn't noticed her friend had joined her on the sofa, but she seemed as engrossed in Aunt Janine's tale as Lily.

"It was," Aunt Janine agreed. "His wife tried to leave him once. Kneath caught up with her, carried her home again, and beat her worse than ever." She paused to take a sip of her tea. "She lost that babe."

Naomi's cup clattered to her saucer. Mrs. Bachman let out a cry and pressed a hand to her cheek.

"She was *with child*?" Bile rose in Lily's throat.

"Oh, yes," Aunt Janine said with a sad nod. "And almost died herself. She had a son soon after, and another—the current Thorburn—about four years later. After the children were born, she embarked on a career of cuckolding her husband at every opportunity, although from what I hear, she has been settled with her Greek lover these several years now."

"In Greece?" Naomi asked.

Aunt Janine nodded. "Lady Kneath has not set foot in England in ten years or more. It's truly one of the most spectacularly failed marriages I've ever beheld."

Lily shuddered. She couldn't imagine the abject terror Lord Thorburn's mother must have felt on a daily basis, knowing that at any moment, her husband might turn on her. And what of the children?

"You said there were two boys," Lily said, "an older one. What happened to him?"

"Duel," Aunt Janine replied. "Killed by his lover's husband."

Naomi wrinkled her nose. "Not much respect for the institution of marriage in that family."

"Not much respect for it anywhere," Aunt Janine rejoined.

A gloomy silence fell over the group. Lily thought about the Duke and Duchess of Monthwaite, who had been divorced but were now married to one another again. The duke was Naomi's brother and Lady Janine's nephew. She wondered if that was where the others' minds had gone, as well.

"Mr. Bachman and I have been happily married twenty-eight years this June," Mrs. Bachman declared. "Not every couple strays from the vows." She looked at Aunt Janine. "I'll remind you there are two unmarried ladies present, and thank you not to scare them into spinsterdom."

Aunt Janine subjected her to an icy smile. "And I'll remind you there are *three* unmarried ladies present. I am a spinster, Mrs. Bachman, yet have managed to enjoy a fulfilling life. I wonder if you can say the same."

Mrs. Bachman's mouth fell open. "Why, Lady Janine, I'm not sure I appreciate the implication—"

"Bravo!" Aunt Janine exclaimed. "I am astonished a word with as many syllables as 'implication' has found its way to your vocabulary. I commend you, madam."

Naomi pressed a hand to her eyes and shook her head.

"Aunt Janine," Lily said in a raised voice. "Mama!"

The two older ladies ceased their squabbling. Mrs. Bachman's cheeks flushed with embarrassment, while Aunt Janine looked as though she was enjoying every moment of the exchange.

"You were telling me about Viscount Thorburn's family," Lily reminded her.

"Oh yes." Aunt Janine cleared her throat. "Kneath—Thorburn, then—didn't pay much attention to the present Thorburn, as he was the younger son. It's probably for the best, when it comes right down to it. I know I'm not the only one who worried about those boys after their mother had been so ill-treated. The eldest Helling son, Lord Walter, seemed to be turning into a replica of his father. Honestly, it's just as well that duel did him in. The younger one, Lord Ethan, was left to run wild. His grandfather is the only one who took any interest in him, the poor thing, but he died some fifteen years ago. When Lord Walter died, their father went into mourning and still hasn't come out of it, even though it's been three years. He stays at the family heap and won't acknowledge Thorburn any more now than during his childhood."

A surge of pity for the young Ethan Helling and his miserable childhood shot through Lily. She squirmed in her seat. She didn't need to feel pity for him. He was a grown man now, and whatever he'd made of his life—debts and all—was his own doing.

She cleared her throat. "At least that settles one thing," she said. "If he's badly in debt and not receiving funds from his father, then he's almost certainly a fortune hunter."

Aunt Janine tilted her head to the side. "A fortune hunter he may be, m'dear—but he doesn't seem to be hunting yours. That must be a relief."

Lily forced a smile. Somehow, said her despairing heart, it wasn't any relief at all.

Chapter Seven

Lily set the letter of reference down in her lap and rubbed her eyes. She'd thought the park would be a pleasant setting to settle on her choice of headmistress before her meeting with Mr. Wickenworth this afternoon. Instead, the sunlight glaring off the white papers gave her the beginnings of a headache.

At the other end of the bench, her lady's maid, Moira, sat with her ankles crossed and her hands clasped across her belly. Her chin rested against her chest, which rose and fell steadily while she dozed. The warm air *was* rather soporific. Lily's jaw cracked. She covered her mouth with a hand, arched her back in a stretch, and yawned.

"Miss Bachman! This is an unexpected pleasure."

Lily startled. She opened her eyes to see Lord Thorburn standing there, his left hand covering the brass head of a black lacquered walking stick. In his right hand, he held what appeared to be a letter. He quickly folded it. As it passed over his waistcoat on the way to his inner coat pocket, Lily caught a glimpse of a florid V at the top of the stationery.

Her stomach flipped at his sudden appearance. It was his fault she couldn't concentrate on work at home. She still hadn't decided whether or not he was a rotten bounder like the rest of the Leeches, but she had given up on him coming to call after her fortune. But now here he was, unexpectedly showing up at her park bench. Had he followed her? Was he full of mercenary intentions, after all? She eyed him suspiciously, trying to divine some meaning from his gray morning coat and blue waistcoat, as though they were scrying stones.

"I have interrupted you," Thorburn said. "Forgive the intrusion." He touched his gloved hand to the brim of his hat. He was going to walk away, and Lily hadn't said a single word to him!

"No, please," she blurted. "I've cobwebs in my skull this morning."

Thorburn paused. A small smile touched his lips.

Lily swallowed, her innards fluttering. "What are you doing?" She realized as the words escaped her lips that it was an impertinent question. It wasn't her business in the least what Lord Thorburn was doing this morning. Heat flooded her cheeks. *Why haven't you come to call?* That was the question she really wanted to ask, but it would be exponentially more outrageous to voice that than the question she'd already posed.

Thorburn didn't seem to mind. "I'm on my way to visit a friend," he answered, "though I'm in no hurry. It's such a fine morning, I thought I'd enjoy a walk before I called."

Lily furrowed her brow and nodded. She looked down at her hands in her lap, unaccountably stung that he was going to call upon someone other than her. He'd not so much as popped in for tea, even though he'd dragged her into the hedge and kissed her.

From the corner of her eye, she caught the motion of him swaying, on the verge of departure. He hadn't followed her or anything of the sort, she realized. He'd happened upon her by chance and stopped to be polite, and she was making a muck of it.

"Would you care to sit down?"

A shadow crossed his face at her invitation, reminiscent of the hungry wolf she'd glimpsed in his study. Then he blinked, once again the image of polite civility.

"Thank you," he said.

Lily picked up the folio of letters and moved toward the middle of the bench, closer to her abigail. Thorburn sat on her right. Her heart pounded in her chest. She was too aware of him; his solid masculine presence radiated confidence and authority. As much as Lily liked to command situations, it was often work to do so when men were involved. They always came around to her perspective eventually, but it sometimes took her entire arsenal of biting words and feminine charms—usually only one of those, sometimes both.

But Lord Thorburn…now, here was a man who had dispatched her whole group of admirers at the ball that night by strolling over and claiming her with barely a word of protest raised by the others. And then he'd claimed her further with that kiss.

That kiss. That stupid kiss that wouldn't get out of her mind and had made a wreck of her this whole week past. Well, he was here now, she thought, drawing herself up. Time to grab the bull by the horns and find out once and for all what kind of man he was—

"Miss Bachman," Thorburn said. "I feel it incumbent upon me to apologize."

Her eyes flew to his face. His expression was unreadable, his eyes shuttered. "Apologize?" she asked. "Whatever for?"

"I want to assure you," he said, "it is not my habit to accost young ladies in gardens."

Her lips pinched together. He was apologizing for kissing her before she had the chance to express her extreme displeasure on the same point! Why did the man have to continually knock her off balance?

"Oh?" Lily said archly, still hoping to score a hit. "Where do you usually accost young ladies? If you'd be so good as to give me the address, I shall be sure to avoid it in the future."

For an instant, his eyes widened. Then he chuckled. "*Touché.*"

Lily's fingers clutched together. Butterflies buffeted her stomach, but now was not the time to retreat. He might not wish to argue with her, but she still had to know. "Why did you do it?"

Thorburn crossed his legs and gazed over the park.

Lily followed his gaze and swept her own eyes over the scene. It was still too early for the afternoon social parade. Children played with governesses. Dogs walked on leads in the care of footmen. It was the time for all the entities who dwelt in the houses of the high but who were not welcome at their balls and suppers. Just like Lily. No wonder she preferred to come here before noon.

"I suppose I got carried away," Thorburn said. "You have quite an impressive…stature."

Lily did not miss the way his gaze flicked to her chest. Heat prickled up her neck. "You kissed me because of my height?"

Ethan shrugged. "It was novel. I've never kissed so tall a lady before."

Lily glanced at Moira. The maid was still asleep, oblivious to her mistress's inappropriate conversation. She shouldn't be talking to Lord Thorburn about their kiss, but he made it so very easy to do things she oughtn't.

"How did you find it?" she asked. The heat creeping up her cheeks belied her bravado. She only hoped he didn't see the flush.

His lips turned up the barest bit at the corners. "I have often gotten a crick in my neck from bending over so far. Thanks to your considerate height, I did not experience that problem. It was quite pleasant."

"Pleasant?" she cried, unable to keep the dismay from her tone. *Pleasant?* That one erotic embrace had thrown Lily's life into turmoil all week long. She'd been unable to concentrate on work. Every time she went out, she hoped to catch a glimpse of him. Her normally logical mind had become possessed by an indecisive madwoman; she hoped he'd come calling just so she could see him and dreaded the day he knocked on the door and outed himself as a Leech.

And now, she was thinking about that blasted kiss yet again with Thorburn right beside her, his thigh mere inches from her own. Her body reacted in a way she was coming to associate with his presence. Her breasts tightened; her woman's flesh felt swollen. She was becoming aroused right here in the middle of the park in broad daylight. How did he do that? It would be nothing to shift a little closer, to make him see that kissing her was more than pleasant.

Unless he was being generous as it was, and hadn't actually enjoyed their kiss at all. The thought stabbed through her gut. He *had* left rather quickly, abandoning her in the hedge like an unwanted heel of bread.

Thorburn gestured to the portfolio in her lap. "Have you been sketching?"

Lily shook her head, clearing her mind. He was sensible to change the subject. With her emotions reeling from one extreme to the other, she was liable to make a fool of herself if they continued down that path of conversation.

She opened the leather binder. "They're letters of reference. I have to select a headmistress for my charity school by three o'clock when I meet with Mr. Wickenworth." She exhaled a sigh of despair. "How do I choose? They all seem qualified. My father has hired dozens of employees over the years. I don't know how he does it!"

"I daresay it comes easier with practice," Thorburn said. "I could help you, if you'd like. I have experience with headmasters."

Lily brightened. "You do?"

His eyes twinkled with mischief. "I became well acquainted with the disciplinary methods of any number of headmasters during my ignoble adolescent tour of the nation's institutions of learning. If you'd care to hear a discourse on the relative merits of the paddle versus the strap, I'm your man." He made a bow from his seat with a flourish of his hand.

How could he make light of being beaten and tossed out of schools? Then she recalled Aunt Janine's story about the unwanted second son, who suffered God only knew what torments at his father's hand, and her heart constricted. School must have been a welcome respite, even if he earned the unhappy attentions of a few headmasters.

Thorburn reached for the stack of letters. "May I?"

"Please."

He scooped several into his hands and leafed through them with his long, slender fingers. He paused at the list she'd written out, detailing the good and bad points of each applicant.

Lily sat quietly while he read, becoming more agitated as time passed. Something about him holding her papers and reading her private thoughts struck her as intimate, even though the subject matter was utterly mundane. Her insights into each applicant were laid bare, and he might find her judgment wanting.

Thorburn looked at her, his expression thoughtful. "You make a good point here." He pointed to an item on the list. "Mrs. Burns' years as a *duenna* do not give her the experience needed to run an entire school. She only ever had one charge at a time and might not be prepared for a dozen, plus administrative concerns."

Lily beamed at his compliment of her observation. She riffled through the papers and extracted another letter. "What do you think of this one?" she asked. "For qualifications, I think Miss Cuthbert is ideal—but there seems to have been some tawdry business in her past. It *was* twenty years ago, however. Would you let that stand in the way, or should I give her a chance?"

Thorburn took the paper from her and glanced over it. His lips parted as though to speak, but then he caught her gaze. His mouth closed again.

She detected something almost pained in his eyes.

He handed the letter back to her. "I'm sure you'll make the right decision," he said. All the playful banter had fled from him, leaving behind a detached, bored aristocrat.

He stood and took hold of a watch fob, then pulled a silver watch from his pocket. "It's time for me to be on my way. I'm expected."

"Of course." Lily scrambled to shove all the papers back into the binder. She rose from the bench. "Good morning, then. And thank you," she added.

Thorburn bowed. "Good morning, Miss Bachman." He touched the brim of his hat with the brass head of his walking stick. Then he turned and strode across the green expanse of park toward the streets of Mayfair.

Lily admired the view of his retreating figure. The walking stick touched the grass lightly—a decorative piece only. His form was one of perfect health, moving with a masculine grace that suggested regular physical activity—boxing, perhaps, or riding.

Or wenching, she thought. She lowered her eyes. He *was* known as an inveterate rake; gambling, drinking, and womanizing to excess. No doubt he got plenty of exercise in the beds of his many lovers.

On the one hand, Lily was relieved to have determined that Lord Thorburn was not after her fortune. On the other, she couldn't stanch the disappointment she felt that he wasn't after *her*, either.

*

Vanessa's butler led Ethan to her rooms. She sat before a crackling fire, a large book open in her lap.

She glanced up at his entrance. "Thorburn!" She stood to greet him; the forgotten book slid from her lap onto the carpet. "Oh!"

"Allow me." Ethan scooped up the volume. He flattened the creased pages, plates of French landscapes.

Vanessa's eyes filled with tears and her chin trembled. "That was silly of me. I'm sorry."

Ethan tossed the book onto the chair. "Not a bit of it, Nessa."

He wrapped his arms around the elderly woman's thin shoulders. She stepped into his embrace and rested her cheek on his waistcoat.

Ethan stroked her back, his fingers slipping across the peach satin of her dressing gown. It was refreshing to see her out of bed and neatly dressed—her hair was even styled in a simple twist. Today must be better than normal. She might even know him as himself. Still, he didn't want to risk upsetting her fragile mind. "How are you feeling?"

Vanessa pulled back in his arms. "I'm fine, of course. Why shouldn't I be?"

Ethan shook his head. "No reason. I'm just making sure."

She touched his cheek with stiff fingers. "So solicitous," she said. "Always thinking about me, never taking care of yourself."

Ethan was still unsure.

She pulled out of his arms and picked up the garden book, which she carried to a little table. Vanessa carelessly deposited it before picking up the miniature portrait, the one she'd thrown at her nurse. She cradled it in her hands, touching the face and whispering endearments. Then she looked sharply at Ethan.

"You cut your hair." Her eyes narrowed in suspicion.

Ethan took a step forward. "My hair always looks like this, Nessa."

Vanessa clutched the portrait to her chest and backed away from him. "No." She shook her head. "You look—" Her brows drew together as she examined his face. Finally, she brightened. "You look just like young Ethan!"

"I *am* Ethan," he snapped, slapping a hand against his chest. He muttered a curse. Patience escaped him today. He wasn't in the right frame of mind to deal with Vanessa's mental infirmity.

"You are?" Her voice was small and confused. "But I haven't seen Ethan in…oh, Ethan!" she cried piteously. "I'm so sorry." Her head dropped, and her shoulders shook with silent tears.

He sighed. Her solicitor hadn't hired a new nurse yet, and Vanessa's poor servants were run ragged caring for their ill mistress. If Ethan didn't take care of her, one of the footmen might drop her off at the gates of Bedlam. It had already come close to that once before. Ethan could never allow such a fate to befall Vanessa, not after the years of unfailing kindness she had shown him.

With gentle firmness, he pried the portrait from her hands, then led her back to the sitting area. "Shall I call for tea?"

She sniffed and nodded.

After he'd summoned a maid and requested the refreshments, he plopped down into a chair and glowered at the glowing coals on the grate.

"We must speak." Vanessa plucked at her skirt. "This isn't easy for me, but it must be said."

Ethan's brows drew together in a frown. "What is it, Nessa? You know you can speak with me about anything."

"It's time for you to marry," she said in a rush. Then she clamped her hand over her mouth and turned her face away.

Damnation. She'd slipped into the past again.

"Don't argue with me," she said vehemently. "I know you must do your duty, and I'll not stand in your way." She laughed humorlessly. "You'll think it strange, perhaps, but I want you to find a good woman, someone you won't mind spending time with when you aren't with me. She'll be the mother of your children—you *should* get on well with her."

Even though she wasn't really talking to him, her words made Ethan think about Lily. The way she'd looked at him in the park when she'd asked his advice on the headmistress applicants had shaken him to the core. He'd seen that look in the eyes of females before…that misplaced look of trust.

He should be glad she was so easily drawn in—this was exactly what he wanted, for God's sake! He could practically taste her money, it was so close. And yet, he didn't want her trust. He would only let her down when she found out what he really was. In the past, it had always been easy enough to skip out when women started looking at him like he could be counted on, but blast it, he *liked* how he felt when Lily looked at him with both lust and admiration, as though she was as equally interested in his thoughts as she was in the considerable attraction between them.

"I think I've met someone," he said miserably. With his elbow on the arm of the chair, he dropped his forehead into his hand, covering his eyes.

Suddenly she was beside him, stroking the back of his neck. "It's all right, darling," she murmured. "I want you to be happy. Well," she amended, "not *too* happy."

A maid came with the tea. After she served and departed, Vanessa returned to the topic. "You were telling me about your future bride."

"I don't really want to—"

"Thorburn!" A wounded expression creased her brow. "You have never withheld anything, my love. Do not hold back from me now."

Ethan's lips twisted. As pointless as it would be to burden

Vanessa with his thoughts, he *did* want to talk about Lily Bachman. He was in a turmoil, especially since his most recent encounter with her this morning.

He cleared his throat. "Well, her name is—"

Vanessa raised a hand. "Wait." Her voice was thin and reedy. "I'm so tired all of a sudden. Help me to bed."

He sighed. "Of course, dear." He set his tea aside and assisted the elderly woman to her massive bed. It was nonsensical for him to have wanted to share with Vanessa, anyway. It wouldn't mean anything to her and might instead resurrect old pain.

As he tucked the blanket around her, she caught his hand in a claw-like grip. "Please stay, Ethan," she said. "I would like to hear about your lady after I rest."

He inhaled a sharp breath. That made twice today she'd recognized him. Hope leaped in his chest. Perhaps she was recovering, even though the doctors all said there was no coming back from dementia such as hers.

Whatever the case, today was a good day; he had to cherish it while it lasted. "I'll stay," he promised, giving her fingers a squeeze.

Her lips wavered in a sleepy smile; she looked like a small child in the middle of her vast bed. "Good," she murmured. Then she muttered a few incoherent words and was lost to sleep. Her hand slipped from his fingers to the coverlet.

Over the next several hours, he looked over Vanessa's affairs. He wrote to her solicitor, inquiring after the search for a nurse. Then he reviewed the accounts with the housekeeper. He cringed at the number of servants in Vanessa's employ. Her solicitor had control of her finances, while Ethan saw to Nessa herself. Therefore, he didn't know how much she had in savings, but it couldn't have been much. If her funds were depleted, what would become of her?

Ethan would gladly provide for her himself, if he weren't

already destitute. He bit back a curse at the stupid gambling habit that had gotten him into this mess.

He jabbed at the long list of expenditures. "You must find ways to economize. Are you trying to drive Mrs. Myles into the poorhouse?"

The woman's mouth dropped open. "Of course not!" She drew herself up. "I'm proud of the way I run this house, given madam's considerable problems—"

"Just don't make them worse," Ethan said, moderating his tone. "Perhaps we should consider closing off part of the house and letting a maid or two go."

The housekeeper's mouth drew into a pinched line. She dropped a curtsy and excused herself.

Ethan realized she'd made no commitment about economizing. He couldn't afford to be as foolish with Vanessa's money as he was with his own. She depended on him to make sure she had a comfortable home to live in, even if she didn't realize it.

When he returned to her rooms, Vanessa was already out of bed and eating a light meal at the dainty table in the corner. A maid hovered nearby, watching every journey of the spoon from the bowl of soup to Vanessa's lips.

Her violet eyes brightened when she caught sight of him. "You stayed."

He exhaled a breath he hadn't known he'd been holding, relieved that she seemed still in her right mind.

After she ate, he escorted her to the sitting room, which had a lovely aspect of the street below. For a moment, they stood in silence, watching the flow of carriages and pedestrians.

"I don't think I've been in this room in quite some time," she said.

Ethan glanced down and met her pained gaze. "No, darling, you haven't been."

"I'm trapped, aren't I?" She touched a hand to her temple. "Trapped in here. I'm scared, Ethan, of how it's all going away. Sometimes—even now—I don't know people I should know." Her eyes slid over his shoulder. "The butler," she whispered. "I think he's been here a long time, but I can't remember his name." Her eyes glistened with unshed tears.

Ethan pressed a handkerchief into her hand. "Today is a good day," he said calmly. "We'll spend it together, all right? Would you like to go for a ride?"

For an instant, she seemed pleased at the idea. Then her face fell and she shook her head. "I'm frightened to go out of doors. What if I get lost?"

"I'll be with you," he reminded her. "You wouldn't be lost."

"No, what if I get *lost*?" She covered her forehead with her hand, and Ethan understood. She licked her lips and plucked at the hem of his handkerchief. "What if I never come back?"

"Shhh. Come now." Ethan drew her away from the window and led her to a chair. When she was settled, he sat down in the chair's mate on the other side of a little side table.

"You were going to tell me about your wife," Vanessa said, changing the subject.

Ethan smiled, delighted she remembered their conversation from before her rest. "She isn't my wife—not yet, anyway. Maybe never. Who knows?"

Vanessa waved a hand. "Bosh. The ladies adore you, Thorburn. You have your pick of the *ton*."

He crossed his foot onto the opposite knee and breathed a laugh. "I don't know about that." Vanessa knew nothing of his current financial woes or how he was barely tolerated in the same ballrooms he'd once had the run of.

"Tell me," she pressed. "We might not have another chance to talk."

Saddened by her humbling words, he nodded. "Her name is Lily Bachman," he began, "and it would be wrong of me to marry her."

Vanessa tilted her head. "What an odd thing to say. What does she look like?"

Her image sprang to his mind: lush curves and full lips; hair he wanted to bury his hands in while he devoured her with kisses; long legs he imagined wrapping around him in bed . . .

He let out a strangled sound. "She looks like Aphrodite, as drawn by a bawdy adolescent." He glanced around the room. "Isn't there any brandy in the house?"

"She sounds lovely," Vanessa said. "And you're such a handsome young man. You'd make a fine-looking pair. Tell me about her."

Out of luck in his desire for alcohol, Ethan dropped his head against the back of the chair and gazed at the frescoed ceiling, where centaurs and pans gamboled across a fanciful landscape. "She's maddening. She says the most outrageous things." His lips twitched as he recalled how she'd made that buffoon cry after he'd spilled punch in her lap. "But she's marvelous, too, with a more generous, noble heart than any born aristocrat."

Vanessa listened while he spoke of Lily, and the misgivings he felt about marrying her. He divulged the sordid story about Ghita, even. Vanessa stopped him to ask questions every now and then, or to offer a comment. But mostly, she just listened. It was such a relief to finally be able to talk about the whole horrible mess with someone.

He was unaware of how much time had passed until he noticed the light outside growing purple.

He glanced at Vanessa. She was staring into the air, as though transfixed by something unseen. "Oh, God." He crouched beside her chair and touched her hand. "Nessa?"

Her startled eyes flew to his face, blank but for the fear he saw in their depths. She snatched her hand back. "Don't touch me! How dare you, sir?"

A cold rock fell into his middle. "Come, Nessa, let's go back to your room now." He placed a hand on her back to help her up.

She sprang from the chair with the spry energy of a woman a third her age. "No!" She shook her head from side to side, her silver locks coming loose of their twist. "Get away! Help me," she called. She darted from side to side, like a bird trapped in a house, confused and desperate for escape.

If he could just get her back to her rooms, maybe the familiar surroundings would calm her.

He lunged and grabbed her arms. Vanessa twisted and pulled against his grip, still screaming like a banshee.

Ethan hooked a foot behind her ankle, pulling her off balance. When her legs buckled, he guided her to the floor and pinned her by the shoulders. "Nessa, stop!" he cried, panic rising in his throat. Even in her worst states, she'd always calmed for him before.

The sitting room door flew open. The housekeeper took one look at the scene and gasped.

"Get her laudanum," Ethan ordered. The housekeeper nodded and hurried away.

A crowd of servants gathered at the door, watching their mistress come unhinged. Ethan heard the words "lunatic" and "asylum" more than once.

"Get out!" he yelled. "All of you!" The servants stepped back, but only a few dispersed.

Vanessa managed to yank one of her arms loose. She landed a slap on his cheek; her nails raked painfully across the skin. "I hate you," she snarled. "Get away from me. Get away, get away, get awaaaay!"

Ethan redoubled his efforts at restraining her. *Where in the blazing, bloody hell was that laudanum?* Beneath his shirt, sweat poured down his sides and back. Frustration and despair gnawed at him. "I hate you, too!" he bellowed at her infirmity.

At last, the housekeeper arrived with the medicine. Ethan laid on top of Vanessa while the servant pried her mouth open and poured in some of the liquid.

Finally, she calmed in her struggles. Ethan carried her to bed.

When he left her house, he considered whether it would be bad form to stop in at the Bachmans' house. He wondered what Lily would be doing right now—something witty and refined, he imagined. Or perhaps something to do with her school. There wouldn't be any madness there, at least, or the poverty of his own empty abode. Maybe if he asked nicely, she would allow him to just sit in a quiet corner and breathe in the normalcy.

No, he thought with a weary sigh. It was growing late. She'd be preparing for the evening's entertainment by now. He would be an unwelcome intrusion in her plans. Besides, he didn't even know her direction.

He started to trudge toward home, but couldn't bear the thought of his cold, silent house. Instead, his feet carried him to one place he knew he could forget himself.

An hour later, he owed Ficken a hundred pounds.

Chapter Eight

Lily lifted a lump of…something…from a display shelf in the shop of Strombold and Jones, purveyors of exotic imports and curiosities of every description.

At first glance, the object in her hands appeared to be a polished slice of rock, but it was unlike any stone she'd ever seen. She glanced up at Naomi, who was running a gloved finger down the length of an intricately carved elephant tusk. "What do you suppose this is?"

Behind her veil of netting, Naomi furrowed her brow at Lily's mystery object. She took it and turned it in her hands, examining first the rough black-brown exterior and then the smooth, polished interior. "Petrified wood." She handed it back to Lily and exhaled a bored sigh.

"How do you know?" Lily frowned at the thing she still thought was a rock.

"See here?" Naomi pointed to faint lines in the dark surface. "Those are growth rings."

Lily arched a brow, impressed at her friend's knowledge. She glanced toward Aunt Janine, who stood at the counter talking to the shopkeeper. "Runs in the family, does it?"

Naomi pursed her lips. "If by 'it' you mean Auntie's bluestocking tendencies, they most certainly do not. When one has a botanist for a brother, one cannot help but absorb some trivial information about plants." She stuck her tongue out, then blushed and looked around quickly.

Smiling, Lily returned the piece of rock-wood to its place on the shelf. "How much longer do you suppose she'll be?" She nodded toward Aunt Janine.

"There's no telling. If Auntie's taken it into her mind to hunt down some arcane bit of bric-a-brac, we could be here all day."

Lily groaned. When she'd received an invitation this morning to join Naomi and Aunt Janine for shopping, it had seemed like a pleasant outing. Now they were trapped inside the stuffy, dim shop while the sunny day passed them by.

Nearby, two gentlemen conversed quietly while they examined the shop's wares. One of them laughed. "Well, what do you know? There's Thorburn."

A tingle shot up Lily's spine. She peeked at the men. They were looking out the window at the parade of people going up and down Bond Street.

"Didn't know he saw the sun these days," said the other. "Seems to slink in the shadows more often than not."

"If he's avoiding the shadows," mused the first, "it must be because he's indebted to them now, too." They laughed and returned to their shopping.

Lily strolled to the front window, feigning interest in a brass figurine of the Buddha. She peered into the crowd going by the shop, searching for Thorburn.

"There he is." Naomi materialized at her side. "At the jeweler's across the street."

He stood in the doorway, shaking hands with a man in a dark suit. The loupe spectacles shoved up on the man's forehead gave him away as the proprietor of that shop.

"What is he doing?" Lily mused aloud. "A man in such dire straits has no business buying jewelry!" This was it, then—proof of his irresponsible behavior.

"Maybe he's selling something," Naomi suggested.

Bollocks. That would be a reasonable thing for a man in his position to do.

Thorburn donned his hat and started down the walk.

Naomi's hand clamped around her elbow. "What are you doing?"

Lily blinked. She hadn't realized her feet were already carrying her to the door. "Following him," she admitted. "You people keep telling me he's no good. I want to see it for myself."

Naomi gaped, appalled. "You can't do that," she hissed.

Lily shrugged. "Why not?"

"It's as bad as eavesdropping!"

Lily adopted a tone of *hauteur*. "It's a public street. I can walk down it if I please."

Naomi folded her arms under her bosom, her reticule dangling from her wrist. "What about Aunt Janine? She won't approve."

Lily craned her neck. Thorburn was almost out of sight. "She doesn't have to. I'm going."

"Wait!" Naomi yelped. She hurried to their footman patiently waiting in a chair in the corner. "We're—ah—stepping out for air."

Lily was already outside by the time Naomi caught up with her. She scanned the crowd, searching for her quarry as she walked. She spotted him strolling at a sedate pace down the other side of the street, his lean form a head taller than most of the people around him. He glided through the throng, his broad shoulders creating a bit of space behind him as he passed.

She sighed miserably. "Why hasn't he come to call?"

"You don't *want* him to call," Naomi reminded her. "His outrageous debts and wild reputation make him a terrible match for any woman, title or no."

"But, look," Lily argued. Thorburn tipped his hat at a passing acquaintance. "He isn't doing anything questionable whatsoever." Her cheeks burned when she recalled the extremely questionable kiss they'd shared, but he *had* apologized for that. "I'm beginning to think he's been misjudged. You, of all people, should understand."

Naomi stopped dead in her tracks, pulling on her companion's arm to bring her to a halt. "Lily, no," she said in a flat tone. "I know how vicious gossip can be, how a rumor can become regarded as truth whether or not it is. But Thorburn truly *is* a rake. Everyone knows how badly he's in debt, because he owes money to most everyone. His reputation with women—"

Lily's temper flared. "Is he a despoiler of virgins, as well?" she fired. "Eats babies at satanic orgies, perhaps?"

Naomi rolled her eyes hugely. "Oh, really now, Lily, be reasonable."

"I *am* being reasonable!"

Lily turned on her heel and started down the walk again, skipping around slower pedestrians to catch up with Thorburn. Naomi had to half-jog to keep pace with her taller friend's stride, pressing a hand to her hat to keep it in place.

"If he's such a blackguard," Lily reasoned, "then his character should soon evidence itself." She skittered to a halt when she spotted him. He stood in front of a shop, examining a pair of Hessians in the window. "Oh, boots," she said in a sarcastic tone, "very shady."

Naomi huffed.

Thorburn continued on his way, then ducked into a building a few doors down.

"That's the lending library," Naomi said.

Lily exulted. "You see? Books are improving. He has a curious mind. Even Aunt Janine would approve. And reading is an economical entertainment for someone of modest means."

"The right kinds of books are improving," Naomi countered. "Not all are."

"Then we must discover what he's reading. Come on." Lily grabbed her friend's hand and dragged her across the street, weaving between lumbering carriages and encumbered servants carrying stacks of packages for their employers.

Lily slipped into the library and ducked behind a tall shelf. She peeked around but didn't spot Thorburn. She pulled her head back, fearful of her bonnet giving her away.

Briefly, it occurred to her that she had taken complete leave of her senses. Lily Bachman did not skulk around stalking after handsome gentlemen. *She* was the pursued party, the one who rejected at her own whim. Her cheeks burned at her utter lack of self-discipline. If she was willing to follow the man down Bond Street, what would she do if she was alone with him in another secluded garden? Damn the man!

She sank to the floor, pulling her knees against her chest.

Naomi, clearly not a raving lunatic like Lily, made an annoyed sound in her throat. She looked around the library, then flipped through a volume on the shelf next to the one Lily was hiding behind. She replaced that book, then bent her knees, as though examining a selection on a lower shelf.

"I see him," she said in a low voice.

Lily's interest flared back to life. "What is he looking at?"

"Histories."

Lily's brows drew together in vexation. History! That was altogether improving. She peevishly struggled against her estimation of the man, which was rising yet again. Beside his one lapse in propriety when he kissed her—which Lily had to admit she'd participated in as fully as he—he had done nothing to earn her disapproval. Even her poor first impression of him at his home had been caused by her mistaking him for an ill-mannered butler. Had she known his station to begin with, she never would have thought ill of him at all.

Her legs were beginning to go numb in their cramped position. She pressed her hands against the floor beside her hips to rise, but a warning hiss from Naomi stayed her.

Thorburn came into view carrying several books. Lily waited until he finished at the counter and stepped back out into the street, then clumsily extracted herself from her hiding spot. She stood and smoothed her skirts, glancing around to see if anyone had noticed her shameful behavior. Her legs tingled as they stretched out.

She gathered Naomi and approached the door. Every step shot hot arrows through her, a tormenting punishment for her hoydenish antics. She couldn't help but peer after Thorburn as she crossed the threshold. His retreating back was only a few yards away.

Lily took another awkward step and tumbled off the doorstep. Her still-tingling legs were unable to correct her misstep, and she fell headlong into a library patron carrying a stack of books.

Lily, gentleman, and books all went down in a tangled heap. She extended her arms to break her fall. A slice of pain shot through her hand and up her arm. Surprised cries from onlookers drew the attention of passers-by.

Suddenly, two strong, capable hands were under her arms, hauling her to her feet. She turned on unsteady legs to thank her rescuer.

Ah.

Of course.

"Are you all right, Miss Bachman?" Thorburn's eyes searched her face, his brows knit together in concern. His hands remained on her upper arms, holding her steady.

She nodded. "Just a little shaken, I think." She raised her hand to right her bonnet.

He snatched her wrist. "You're bleeding!"

Lily blinked at her hand. Her lace glove was torn, and a cut on the fleshy ball of her thumb oozed scarlet, staining the ruined fabric.

With a nimble quickness that suggested practice, Thorburn plucked at the fingers of the glove and then pulled it off. He tucked it into his pocket, his hand reemerging with a handkerchief, which he pressed against her wound.

The feel of his touch against her bare skin quite took her breath away. If only he weren't wearing gloves as well, she thought. She gazed at his serious face while he concentrated on her injury, barely registering the dull throb emanating from her hand.

"I do not believe it is serious, but if you'd like a surgeon to attend you, I would recommend—" His words died in his throat when he raised his eyes and their gazes met.

Lily's tongue went dry and her knees trembled. She swallowed. "Thank you."

Thorburn's eyes flicked toward the dispersing crowd. Lily pulled her hand back, acutely aware of her conspicuous mishap. She forced a laugh. "So clumsy of me. We were just returning some books." She waved at the library door and then remembered Naomi. Glancing over her shoulder, she spotted her friend standing against the wall, holding Thorburn's books.

Naomi's wide eyes were not on Lily, however. Her gaze was fixed on someone else.

Lily turned to look down the street. A sinking feeling settled into her stomach when she spotted Aunt Janine approaching at a brisk pace.

"There you two are!" the older woman declared. "James said you'd stepped out for air, but I couldn't find you anywhere. You gave me the fright of my life!" Her fists came to rest on her ample hips as she leveled her formidable glare first on Lily, and then Naomi. "What are you girls doing all the way down here? You've wandered quite a distance from Strombold and Jones."

Lily glanced guiltily at Thorburn. He turned to look back up Bond Street in the direction from which they had all come, and then his eyes narrowed on her in a piercing gaze. She wished a lightning bolt would strike her where she stood and put an end to her humiliation.

"Here's your handkerchief." She held the bloodied cloth like an offering of contrition.

He raised a hand. "Keep it." He retrieved his books from Naomi's care.

Aunt Janine bustled her and Naomi back up the street like a mother hen, scolding them both for their inconsiderate behavior.

Lily held back just long enough to chance a glance over her shoulder. Thorburn still stood in front of the library, his books held at his side. His lips were drawn in a line and his gaze shot right through her from a distance as effectively as it did at close range. She sucked her breath and whirled, glad to be swept away from his too-knowing eyes.

*

Ethan followed Lily's progress down Bond Street until she was lost to the crowd, then turned and walked in the opposite direction.

Idly, he patted his pocket. Vanessa's ring, which he'd just picked up from being repaired at the jeweler's, was nestled in its velvet bag against his chest. There was something else there, too.

Her glove. Her ruined, bloody glove. There was no reason in the world for him to hang onto such a macabre token, but even as the thought to toss it out crossed his mind, he knew he would keep it.

He shouldn't, though. This was getting dangerous. For both of them.

He'd seen her attraction to him plain as day across her features. He'd seen lust often enough to recognize its various symptoms— the parted lips, the dewy gaze, the slight flush to her cheeks.

But there was something else there, as well, the admiration he'd noted from their previous meeting. It was as though she actually believed him to be a worthy human being.

Now that she seemed to be truly ripe for the plucking—earning himself both her sizable dowry and Ghita for his mistress—he wasn't sure he wanted to.

In spite of her sometimes-brusque manner, Miss Bachman was an eminently decent woman. She would hate him forever if she found out his true designs on her. She ought to marry someone worthy of not just her fortune, but her goodness, as well.

And that certainly wasn't he.

Drat.

Chapter Nine

Ethan climbed into the carriage behind Quillan and Ghita. Quillan rapped the roof twice with his walking stick, and the carriage lurched forward to convey the trio to Vauxhall Gardens.

In the opposite seat, Ghita wore a satisfied smile as she gazed out at the passing streetscape, her hand anchored around Quillan's. She'd become demanding of late, insisting Quillan spend virtually every evening with her, even as she seemed to anticipate moving into Ethan's protection.

The only motivation Ethan could think of to account for her behavior was the imminent birth of Quillan's first child. When his friend began making noises about spending time with his expanding family, Ghita suddenly developed an overwhelming desire to go out every evening.

The three people in the carriage all had stakes in Ethan's marriage to Lily. Miss Bachman herself was responsive to his attentions. It was all coming together so nicely.

And he felt absolutely sick about it.

Ghita rapped him on the knee with her fan. "Why do you sulk so?" Her eyes cut to Quillan. "He broods like a little boy denied a sweet." Returning her gaze to Ethan, her plump lips turned up in a teasing smile. "Let's talk of something happy to cheer you up. How is your Miss Bachman? Have you seen her?"

Ethan frowned, reluctant to discuss Lily with Quillan's mistress. "I have seen her, in fact. Twice this week."

"Courting like a proper swain, then?" Quillan asked. He took a pull on a silver flask and returned it to his coat pocket. "You've been very tight-lipped about this whole thing. Tell us something about your intended. What barbs has she thrown your way? Have her other suitors challenged you to a duel yet?"

A bitter taste settled on Ethan's tongue as he recalled his two serendipitous meetings with Miss Bachman. While she had been a touch frosty with him on the first occasion, she'd quickly warmed to her subject and even sought his advice. And the second meeting, he'd caught her following him around like a silly schoolgirl. He smiled inwardly as he remembered the surprised dismay on her face when she realized she'd been found out, and the delicious response they'd both experienced when he'd tended her scraped hand. None of that was for public consumption.

"She is planning a school." That seemed the most innocuous subject to discuss.

Quillan frowned, the corners of his mouth vanishing into his great jowls. "What kind of a school?"

"A charity school for disadvantaged young women. I believe the aim is to train them for the gentler trades—governesses, ladies' companions, and the like."

For a moment, Ghita only stared at him. Then she waved her hand in that flamboyant, dismissive gesture of hers. "Every *tonnish* lady has a cause. It's fashionable these days to care."

Quillan nodded in agreement. "Even Lady Umberton sits on the ladies' committee at church, and you know the only soul she cares about is her own."

Ethan's jaw tightened in frustration. "You misunderstand, both of you. Miss Bachman is actually creating this school from scratch. She's overseeing everything—" He ticked off points on his fingers. "The purchase of the property, the hiring of the headmistress and staff, the subjects the students will be taught, everything! She's doing it all."

Quillan eyed him thoughtfully. "You'll have to put an end to that. 'Twouldn't be at all the thing for your viscountess to be seen fraternizing so much with the *dreks*."

Ghita laid a hand on her lover's arm. "No, no, Quillan, he must leave her to it." The smile she turned on Ethan had a mean-spirited edge to it. "Let her work herself to death at her fashionable charity. She won't have time for anything else." The look she gave him conveyed multiple layers of meaning. He knew she meant that if Lily was busy with her school, she wouldn't notice that her husband was otherwise occupied with his mistress.

Ethan stared frankly at the fiery Italian. She was physical perfection incarnate—large eyes, willowy limbs, and a figure that hearkened back to Botticelli's *Venus*. But there was something else there he had never noticed before—something hard and icy that soundly countered the effect of every one of her feminine attributes. For the first time since meeting the woman, Ethan looked at her and felt no physical response whatsoever.

A shout of confusion sounded from the driver's box, and the carriage suddenly lurched to a halt.

"What the devil?" Quillan began turning toward the door; the carriage rocked with his movements.

"Allow me." Ghita leaned out the window and looked up the road. From his own rear-facing position, Ethan couldn't make heads or tails of the situation.

"The carriage in front of us has stopped," Ghita reported. "A lady comes out. Now she's helping another. That one looks like there's something wrong. I think she's sick." Her voice rang with delight, entertained by the spectacle of another's discomfort.

Quillan exhaled an impatient sigh. "Well, can we get around them?"

Ethan scowled at his inconsiderate friends. "Maybe they are in need of assistance." He started to rise.

Ghita opened the door and hopped down, tossing propriety to the wind. "I'll go. Your glowering face would make them think you'd come to kill them." She shut the carriage door and vanished into the gloom.

*

Mrs. Bachman clutched Lily's right hand with both of her own in a vice grip and howled in pain. Lily ran her other hand across her mother's back. Beneath her palm, she felt the spasming muscles bunch and twitch.

She made a shushing sound. "It's all right, Mama."

Lily had nearly jumped out of her skin when her mother had stopped mid-sentence and yowled just a moment ago for the driver to stop.

When her back spasmed, sitting was an excruciating exercise, so Lily had quickly helped her down from the carriage. She needed laudanum and bed, but neither was close to hand. They were nearly a mile from home.

The footman clambered down from his seat on the back of the coach, his brow creased in concern. "What's happened, miss?"

"Mrs. Bachman's back is complaining. She needs her medicine."

Another spasm rippled across her mother's back; Mrs. Bachman twisted in agony and cried out. Tears pricked Lily's eyes. Rarely had she felt so helpless.

She glanced up and down the walk. Pedestrians passed by with barely a second glance, and those were the nicely dressed ones. Lily well knew they were prime targets for the seedy elements who came out to play when the sun went down in London. They had to get off the street before they were robbed, or worse. "I'm sorry, Mama, but we have to get back into the carriage now."

Mrs. Bachman protested weakly. "The ball…"

Hot anger flashed across Lily's cheeks. Even now, her mother was more worried about Lily's marital prospects, with no thought for their safety. "Hang the ball!"

An elegantly dressed lady stepped into the light of the street lamp in which they stood. She regarded them with large eyes and smiled kindly. "You are in distress, madam?" Her voice carried a heavy Italian accent.

Mrs. Bachman struggled to straighten, her breath coming in shallow pants. "No, everything's fi—ow!"

Lily staggered a step as her mother fell against her. "My mother's in pain. It's her back."

The Italian lady tut-tutted and laid a delicate hand on Mrs. Bachman's shoulder. "My dear woman, what can I do to be of assistance?"

Mrs. Bachman's eyes turned on Lily, her face a grimacing mask. "Perhaps a ride to the ball—"

"No!" Lily insisted. "I'm not going. I've quite decided, so do stop arguing." Their footman hovered close to hand, nearly jigging with anxiety. Lily nodded to him. "Help me get her back into the carriage."

Finally, Mrs. Bachman's shoulders slumped in resignation as the footman pried one of her hands off Lily to lend his own assistance, and the trio started back to the carriage. "Very well. I suppose you can jot a note to Lady Ainsley's once we're home so Mr. Bachman doesn't fret over us."

The Italian lady straightened, her attention trained on Lily. "Are you, perhaps, Miss Bachman?"

"I am," Lily affirmed. She continued guiding Mrs. Bachman to the awaiting vehicle, the woman a half-ignored presence behind her.

She heard a throaty laugh. "But that is too wonderful!" The lady clapped her gloved hands together. Lily glanced over her shoulder. The woman followed a step behind. Lily smelled her perfume, an exotic floral scent. "I have heard much about you," she continued. "I am so happy to meet you at the last. You should come with me." She waved her other hand toward the carriage behind theirs. "Lord Umberton will be happy to offer you a ride."

Mrs. Bachman paused with her foot on the step. "Are you Lady Umberton?" she asked breathlessly, ever awed by persons with titles attached to their names.

The woman's eyes widened, and then a slow smile spread across her lovely face. "Lady Umberton, yes."

To Lily's ears, it almost sounded as though Lady Umberton was trying the name on for size, but then she dismissed the notion as a quirk of the woman's accent. She'd never met the Countess of Umberton, only seen her from afar at huge gatherings last Season. Memory painted Umberton's wife as fuller-figured, and she didn't recall hearing she was Italian. Allowing for the fact that she ignored three-quarters of what anyone told her about the *haut ton* and scoffed at the rest, it was entirely possible she *had* heard mention of Lady Umberton's nationality and forgotten it again.

Mrs. Bachman pinned Lily beneath a fierce gaze. "You must go," she hissed. "It's a sign from Providence."

Lily snorted. "It's not at all miraculous that another carriage on our route would also be headed toward the same destination. It's logical."

Another spasm threw Mrs. Bachman off balance. The footman's support kept her from falling. When the spasm passed, she rounded on Lily, her cheeks in high color and her eyes flashing. "Now you listen to me! I am your mother and I refuse to be dismissed. For years, you have behaved as though Mr. Bachman is the only parent you have to answer to. Well, I won't stand for it another moment—not one more. I shall not be ignored!" She pointed at Lady Umberton. "This kind lady has offered to take you to the ball, and I demand you get into that carriage at once."

Lily blinked, stunned at her mother's vehemence. It crossed her mind to rejoin, but then she looked at the amused expression on Lady Umberton's face. She would not sink to arguing with her mother on a public street, in front of an aristocrat who had actually offered assistance.

"All right," she grumbled. Turning to Lady Umberton, she bent her neck. "Thank you, my lady. I accept your kind offer."

She saw her mother settled into the seat and instructed the footman to convey Lily's order for medication and rest to Mrs. Bachman's maid. Though her mother's face was still contorted in pain, her anguish seemed somewhat eased by Lily's promise to attend the ball and make the best of it. She patted Lily's hand. "Such a good girl." The footman closed the carriage door and hopped to his place on the back, giving the word for the driver to head for home.

Lady Umberton touched Lily's elbow. "Come now. Let's away." She laughed again as she started toward her own conveyance, Lily following in her wake. The sound was musical and rich, and altogether mystifying. What on earth was so funny?

*

Ghita's laughter rolled down the darkened street. A moment later, the carriage door opened, and the female herself appeared. She smiled shrewdly at Ethan as she climbed into the carriage. "I have brought you something." Resuming her place next to Quillan, she gestured to someone outside the carriage, whose identity was hidden from Ethan by the door. "Yes, yes, come in." Turning to the gentlemen, she explained, "We have a passenger."

A slippered foot and the skirts of a satin gown appeared, followed an instant later by the remainder of the newcomer.

The shock on Lily Bachman's face when she caught sight of him surely mirrored his own. Then he snapped his jaw shut and moved over to make room for her on the seat beside him. His lips compressed into a hard line as that statuesque assortment of impossible curves settled into the squabs. He shot a glare at Ghita; she caught his eye and, without a scrap of shame, winked.

As the carriage shifted and started forward, Lily straightened, pulling her arms close to her side, obviously attempting to maintain space between them in the coach's tight confines. In doing so, however, she pressed her ample breasts further together, boosting them out of the low neckline of her gown, revealing even more creamy flesh.

Ethan squeezed his eyes shut and stifled the groan rising in his throat. It was a test. Somehow, some way, this was a test of his resolve. He must not look at Lily Bachman's sumptuous breasts. He must not *think* about them. Or how they felt pressed against him when they'd kissed. Or how they would look gloriously bare. In his bed.

Damn.

He pressed himself as far into his own corner as he could without climbing the walls.

Lily nodded to Quillan. "Thank you for your assistance, Lord Umberton." She related the circumstances that led to her parting ways with her mother. When she came to Ghita's involvement, the other woman cut into the narrative.

"And so I am thinking, since we are all going to the same place, why not take Miss Bachman ourselves?" Ghita smirked, triumph blazing in her eyes. She had delivered Lily into Ethan's hands, to further his suit.

He chanced a glance at Lily, careful to keep his eyes above her décolletage. She gave him a small, nervous smile. She was amongst almost perfect strangers. Ethan was the only one with whom she had any rapport whatsoever. As dangerous as it was for him to allow his attention to focus on her, he felt duty-bound to ensure her comfort for the duration of the carriage ride.

It occurred to Ethan that Vauxhall Gardens was an eccentric choice for a family outing. The draw of such a place to an older couple such as the Bachmans eluded him. His tongue flicked over his lips. "Ah, Miss Bachman. Just to be clear, you are also going to—"

"Yes, she is." Ghita pasted a bright smile on her face, but it seemed to Ethan more a baring of her fangs.

"My father will meet me there," Lily confirmed. "But since going was Mother's idea to begin with, we likely won't stay long. Neither he nor I have patience for these things."

Ah. That sounded more like what Ethan knew of the staid Mr. Bachman and his equally redoubtable offspring.

"It might be pleasant."

She turned to regard him. Since he'd forbidden his gaze to wander south, he searched her face, taking note of every feature. Sooty lashes framed her rich brown eyes. The tip of her nose turned up ever so slightly, suggesting the pert personality within.

Color rose in her cheeks as he watched, her lips parting a fraction. His fingers twitched, tempted to touch that plum mouth.

Ethan felt the heat beginning to mount between them. *Blast it, this isn't working, either.* He couldn't look even at her face without becoming aroused. He tore his eyes away and scowled at the window. As the shade was now drawn, this exercise provided little satisfaction.

Ghita's mocking voice cut through the heavy silence. "I hear you have many admirers, Miss Bachman."

Lily's eyes went wide. "Well, I..."

Quillan snorted. "With a dowry like yours, I'm surprised there isn't a mob outside your door."

Ethan cringed. It was rude to mention Lily's dowry to her face. Ghita had no compunction about shocking people, but Quillan should know better.

She ducked her head. "There aren't really all that many—"

"Come now," Ghita cut in. "Tell us who you prefer." She waved her hands theatrically. "With so many gentlemen to choose from, there must be *someone* who captures your eye." She leaned forward, as though offering her confidence, but a subtle twist of her torso displayed her cleavage to Ethan—a pointed reminder of where his attention was supposed to lay.

Unfortunately for her, there was no comparison in that regard. With the appraising eye of a connoisseur, Ethan found Lily's pillowy bosom much more to his liking.

Laying a hand on Lily's, Ghita pressed her offensive. "You must tell me. It is all the talk, is it not?" She glanced over her shoulder at Quillan.

He grunted in affirmation. "The book at White's is brimming with entries betting on the identity of the lucky man."

Lily gasped, horror spelled out across her face. The color in her cheeks drained away. Ethan ground his teeth, his patience with his friends coming to a rapid end.

"Fortunes to be won and lost, all because of your marriage." Ghita clucked her tongue. Her eyes narrowed and her fingers tightened into a white-knuckled grip on Lily's hand. She already regarded the other woman as a rival, and poor Lily had no idea. It ran afoul of Ethan's intrinsic sense of fair play. "So do be a good girl and tell us—"

"It's a damned bloody nuisance, is what it is," Ethan snapped, surprised at his own vehemence. "Pardon my mouth, ladies."

Lily's startled eyes flew to his, full of gratitude. "Yes, it is." The smile she gave him conveyed an appreciation for his understanding.

He cursed to himself. There it was again—the way she looked at him, as though she saw someone admirable, someone worthy of respect. Were they not in a closed carriage, he might have thought she was looking at a man behind him, because he was surely not deserving of her approbation.

Maybe you could be. The intrusive thought sprang from somewhere deep inside, from the same deluded portion of his mind that wanted to restore his family's good name after the muck his father had made of it. It took up residence alongside all the other dreams that had no hope of coming to fruition. They were a pitiful lot, those dreams, mostly keeping quiet but sometimes piping up like a bunch of beggars on the church steps. And like the actual beggars who had shocked and saddened him when he'd first come to town, Ethan had learned to ignore them, refusing to listen to their weak suggestions that he could be better than he was.

Still, right now, at this moment, Lily Bachman needed someone to stand with her against Quillan and Ghita. It wouldn't hurt anything if—just for the duration of the ride, of course— he played the knight-errant coming to his lady's rescue. It wasn't much of a rescue, anyway; he just had to steer the conversation elsewhere.

He thought fast for something to say and nabbed the first coherent thought that wandered past his tongue.

"Along the lines of dowries and marriage and the like," he said, drawing the attention of his companions, "there are island tribes which use whale's teeth as a bride-price."

For a moment, everyone stared at him—Ghita with a perplexed crease in her brow, Quillan with a bored expression, and Lily, blessedly, with a look of relief.

Her gaze cut to the other pair, then skittered back to Ethan. "They use the teeth as money, you mean?"

Ethan cleared his throat, happy to declaim on the topic if it kept Ghita's venom in her fangs. "Not in the conventional sense, no. I believe the teeth are only for particular ceremonial purposes."

"Well, that's a relief," Lily stated. "Can you imagine using whale's teeth for coinage? How big they must be! I don't suppose I could carry more than one or two in my reticule."

"What difficulties that would present the fashionable lady," Ethan mused. "I can envision a stream of women heading to the shops with great sacks full of enormous teeth."

Lily laughed, her eyes dancing with amusement. She shook her head. "No, no, it wouldn't come to that. The fashionable lady would still proceed at a sedate stroll, unencumbered by her weighty currency. But her footman would have to follow behind with a dogcart full of pin money."

Ethan chuckled at the silly image. Lily's shoulders relaxed a fraction. She settled back against her seat, no longer unnerved. He was glad of it. Though his acquaintance with her was still new, he'd detected that Miss Bachman did not do well in situations beyond her ken. This was a woman who needed to feel in control of things. Helping her find her footing in present company was the least he could do.

Ghita's large eyes tightened at the corners as she looked back and forth between them. She smiled nervously. "H-how much would items cost in whale's teeth?" The uncustomary stammer caught Ethan's notice. The unflappable Queen of Her Domain was struggling against another formidable female. For the first time in his recollection, Ghita was in the company of a woman who surpassed her in both station and intellect. Both women were beautiful, as well—Ghita fair and willowy, Lily dark and curvaceous. As looks went, it came down only to the observer's preference. And Ghita knew it.

Her hands waved in an agitated gesture. "What would they be worth? It's so ridiculous, this notion."

Lily's full lips quirked. "They'd be worth their weight in pearls, of course."

"And you could rub pearls against your pocket money to tell the real from false," Ethan pointed out.

"Save your own teeth." Lily bit her bottom lip as a bubble of mirth slipped out.

Quillan cracked a smile and joined in. He grinned and nodded at Ethan. "You, for one, should be on your knees thanking God England's not on the whale tooth standard."

Ethan's shoulders jostled with another laugh. "Oh? Why's that?"

"With your debts," Quillan deadpanned, "you'd have to take up whaling full-time."

Beside him, Lily gasped and stiffened a split second before a whoop of laughter tore from his throat. He felt her eyes on him, and she joined him in laughing at his own miserable finances.

The playful banter lasted the duration of the carriage ride. Miss Bachman made her fair share of witty remarks, engaging both the gentlemen with her repartee. It seemed there was more to Lily Bachman's fabled tongue than biting insults.

For her part, Ghita sank into her seat and glowered at the others. It occurred to Ethan that the puns and word play they were engaging in exceeded her grasp of the language. The arch looks she cast in Lily's direction were especially vitriolic, but Miss Bachman appeared too caught up in the jovial conversation to notice.

When the carriage drew to a halt, Lily sniffed and dabbed the corners of her eyes. "Thank you so much for the conveyance, my lord." She nodded to Quillan. "It was most obliging of you." She cast an easy smile around to the other occupants of the carriage.

Ghita's jaw worked in a smirk, as though she held a trump in her hand. Ethan wondered at this until the footman opened the door. Ethan stepped down and offered his hand to Lily.

Her fingers were warm and firm against his. He noticed a hint of color rising in her cheeks. Then her gaze rose, and her mouth dropped open in surprise. She gasped.

Ethan turned, thinking to see some kind of disaster underway—a roaring conflagration, perhaps. Instead, he saw only the colonnaded entrance to the gardens.

"Vauxhall Gardens?" Confusion clouded Lily's features and she turned wide eyes on Ethan. "I'm supposed to be at the Ainsleys' ball."

Behind her, Ghita disembarked from the carriage and took several sauntering steps. "Is that so?" She tsked and pressed a hand to her cheek. "I must have misunderstood." She took Quillan's arm and headed for their seats.

The hard glint in her eye betrayed the pretense. Simmering anger built at the base of Ethan's spine. She had duped Lily into coming to Vauxhall, unaccompanied by a proper chaperone and without the consent of her parents.

"I'm terribly sorry." He touched Lily's elbow to guide her back to the carriage. "I'll have the driver take you to your ball."

Her lips parted as she roved his face with those chocolate-rich eyes. Ethan's thumb stroked her arm, heedless of his mind's insistence that he release her from his grasp.

Lily's eyes slid over his shoulder as she took in the entrance to the gardens. "No," she murmured. She shook her head; her eyes cut back to his and she smiled. "If it's all the same to you, I think I'd like to stay." Her gaze went sultry, though the quirk of her lips betrayed her nerves. An intriguing dichotomy.

Ethan swallowed, his throat suddenly dry. He had to strangle out an objection, marshaling every last scrap of scruples remaining to his immoral soul. "I must insist you return to your father. It would be improper—"

Her eyes—soft and inviting only a second before—narrowed. "And just who are you to insist I do anything, my lord? Do you speak to all women so masterfully? I'm not one of your milksop aristocratic females. I am not dictated to. By anyone."

Ethan felt himself knocked back by her sudden change of demeanor. "I'm not dictating to you, you silly twit. Don't you have a care for—"

"What I don't care for is the tone you are taking." Her hands planted on her hips, but Ethan noticed the hurt tone in her voice. "Really, to resort to name calling…" She whirled away from him. Her hand went to her face and her shoulders shook.

Oh, God, he'd made her cry. Ethan's eyes squeezed together. Could this night get any worse? He hadn't meant to call her a twit; she had a way of getting under his skin faster than any female he'd ever known. He reached out for her shoulder. "Please, Miss Bachman—" She jerked away and made a sniffling sound. His male instinct to stop the crying at all costs kicked into action. Before he knew he'd reached into his pocket, he was pressing a handkerchief into her hand. Glancing over his shoulder, he saw curious gazes aimed in their direction from other new arrivals. "Miss Bachman," he whispered, "I'm sure you don't wish to cause a commotion. People are starting to notice—"

"You're the one causing a commotion," she shot back. "Just take me to Lord Umberton's seats and stop harassing me!" A louder wail rose in the air.

Exasperated and nearing panic, Ethan thrust his arm out to her. "All right," he hissed. Her hand settled on his sleeve and he led her into the throng funneling toward the dinner theater. Almost immediately, her sniffling stopped, and blissful relief washed through Ethan, draining away his agitation. A moment later, he glanced at her. She turned a triumphant smirk up at him, no evidence of a crying fit anywhere on her features. Hot breath whooshed from his nostrils as he realized he'd been played for a fool. "I congratulate you," he snipped. "That was quite a performance."

Her brow arched as she nodded, accepting his comment as a compliment, much to his annoyance. "As I said, my lord, I am not dictated to. Not even by you."

Ethan stopped dead in his tracks. Lily sailed on without him, leaving Ethan to stare after her swaying hips and lush derrière and, eventually, to follow in her wake.

Chapter Ten

Lord Umberton poured Lily another glass of wine. It was her third already, and the meal was not yet over. As she sipped the rich red liquid, she glanced over the rim to where Thorburn sat across the table from her, fork and knife clenched in a white-knuckled grip. She frowned at his tense demeanor—where was the man she'd seen in the carriage, who had made her laugh until her ribs ached and she could scarcely breathe?

It was *that* man with whom she'd decided to spend her evening, not the brooding presence lurking in the supper box like he was maintaining a deathbed vigil. For once in her rigidly structured life, Lily wanted to cut loose and have *fun*, and Thorburn's change in mood was spoiling her plan. She watched him mechanically chew and swallow a bite of the thin, buttery ham as if he hadn't even tasted it.

For herself, Lily was in bliss. The first bite melted against her tongue and she'd savored every one since. The atmosphere left nothing to be desired. Entertainment provided by a band of musicians filled the air, and the twinkling lights of the thousands of lanterns hanging from the trees lining the nearby walks lent a magical ambiance to the surroundings. Lily glimpsed shadowy pavilions and pagodas in the distance. Other groups were already descending from their boxes to go explore. Her feet itched to join them.

"More wine, Miss Bachman?" Lady Umberton's distinctive voice drew her attention. The lady's brilliant eyes twinkled in amusement.

Abashed, Lily noticed that she'd yet again drained her glass while she'd been occupied observing the other revelers. Quite a few *tonnish* ladies and gentlemen had openly gawked at the Umberton box—all part of the entertainment of people-watching, she supposed. "No, thank you." She set her glass aside and glanced around for a footman. "Perhaps some lemonade?"

Lady Umberton waved a hand, her many rings catching the light and twinkling. "Lemonade is fine for children. But you're right— the wine grows boring. Quillan," she said, "champagne now, yes?"

With her husband's compliance granted, the beautiful woman turned back to Lily and pouted. "I still feel terrible about the confusion. I hope your mother will not be too put out with me for delivering you to the wrong place."

Lily pressed a hand to her chest. Since their arrival at Vauxhall Gardens, Lady Umberton had been the perfect hostess, kind and attentive to her unexpected guest. "Please don't apologize again, my lady. I'm having a marvelous time," she assured her hostess, turning to include the gentleman in her thanks. Lord Umberton was more focused on his meal than the conversation, and seemed not to heed her at all. Thorburn, however, stiffened at her words. He cast a hard look at Lady Umberton, who smiled sweetly.

Why on earth did Thorburn act so put out?

Lady Umberton disregarded his glowering expression and concentrated on Lily. "Is this your first time to the pleasure gardens?"

Lily shook her head. "I came once, four years ago. We only stayed for supper. My father hated everything about the place and vowed he'd never return. I must confess, his complaints quite colored my own ideas, and I've had no desire for another outing since." She waved a hand. "But this is all so lovely."

Lady Umberton's eyes widened. "So you have not walked through the gardens?" At Lily's negative reply, she gasped. "But you must!" The champagne arrived, and Lady Umberton pressed a glass on Lily. As Thorburn took a glass, she said, "Be a dear and escort Miss Bachman about the gardens, Ethan."

He flicked a glance in her direction. Though his features gave nothing away, Lily sensed his reluctance. She recalled the last time they'd strolled through a garden and felt heat crawl up her chest and neck. Perhaps the memory was not as pleasant for Thorburn as it was for her.

"That isn't necessary," Lily blurted, unable to sit by while Lord Thorburn weighed the evident unpleasantness of strolling with her against the rudeness of refusing. "One garden is much the same as any other. Lord Thorburn kindly escorted me on another occasion; I wouldn't wish to make a nuisance—"

A muted, strangled sound from Thorburn's direction halted her. His eyes were pinched closed. Slowly they opened—smoldering like a banked fire—and settled on her.

Lily's stomach flipped and a nervous knot formed in her chest. She pulled her eyes away from his and located her champagne, which she dispatched with undignified haste. The scrape of a chair, several heavy steps, and then he stood at her shoulder. A hint of warmth grazed over her nape, as though he'd come very near to touching her there.

A delicious, slow shiver began at the base of her skull and worked its way down her back, causing her to inhale sharply. The plunging neckline of her gown pressed against her breasts, cutting into the soft flesh. She realized that from his position, Thorburn would have a clear view of her displayed cleavage. Oddly, the thought pleased her. The shiver dissolved into a pulsating heat at the base of her spine then wrapped around her belly and pooled between her legs.

"Shall we, Miss Bachman?" His voice was soft like thick velvet. A hand appeared in front of her. Before she could rationalize herself out of it, Lily pushed back from the table. Strong fingers closed around her own as she rose. With a nod of acquiescence, she allowed him to lead her away from the Umbertons and into the gardens.

Despite the numerous lanterns lining the main walks, Lily soon discerned how dark the garden actually was. She glanced down intersecting paths, which were bathed in shadow.

A jolt of apprehension shot through her when he led her off the lit path. Would he try to kiss her again? Surely, she wouldn't allow it.

Liar, said a little voice inside. Wasn't that why she'd agreed to a walk—in the hopes that he *would* kiss her again? She already risked her parents' censure by being here instead of at the Ainsleys' ball, but at least no one could complain about her being with a married couple like the Umbertons. But to walk with Lord Thorburn through a garden notorious for its secluded alcoves was as brazen an invitation as Lily had ever issued.

A new fear sprung to mind: What if he *didn't* kiss her? Well, she'd just have to see to it that he did, she reasoned. She took control of all other situations—why should this one be any different?

As they rounded a bend, she saw a little gazebo set in a tiny clearing like a miniature grotto. *Perfect*.

With a firm nod that only sent her tipsy head reeling a little, she veered off the path toward the gazebo, half-dragging Thorburn until he realized her direction and matched his steps to hers.

As they stepped into the shelter, he turned her to face him. "What are you doing?" His voice carried a disapproving tone.

"Just stopping for a moment." She greedily inhaled his musky masculine scent—it went to her brain even quicker than the wine had, further addling her already compromised senses. "You don't mind, do you?"

A flirtatious bat of her eyelashes only resulted in Thorburn sighing and shaking his head. "Marvelous," he muttered. "You're completely fuddled."

Lily drew back in offense. "I'm what?"

"Intoxicated," he said. "You're foxed. Three sheets to the wind. Your flag is out. Lushey." He chuckled softly. "You, my dear,"— his index finger slowly approached her face, and Lily followed it, cross-eyed, until it alit on the tip of her nose—"are drunk."

Swatting his hand away, she scoffed. "'m not as bad as all that. Just a little…" Her fingers fluttered around her temples, "bubbly," she finished. "Like the champagne."

He chortled. "You're *bubbly?*"

Lily laughed, too. For the first time since their arrival at Vauxhall Gardens, he finally relaxed. *Well done, Lily,* she congratulated herself. Now that she'd slipped past his dour mood, it was time to advance her cause.

Still grinning, she caught his hand and brought it to her waist. At once, his smile faltered. Lily took a tentative step forward. Her heart pounded against her ribs so hard, she wondered if Thorburn could hear it. His smell filled her nose again. It seemed to seep from the environs of his neck. With one hand still holding his firmly against her waist, she brought the other to brush across his cravat, tied in an elegantly simple knot. The masculine austerity of it entranced her.

"Lily, what are you doing?" His throat vibrated beneath her fingers.

Her fingers darted to cover his lips. "I didn't give you permission to use my given name."

Thorburn's free hand covered hers. He nipped her fingertips in turn, sending jolts of pleasure up Lily's arm. She very nearly collapsed into a puddle of molten jelly at the sensation. "I didn't give *you* permission to manhandle me," he said.

"I thought…" she began. But her brain no longer wanted to string words together in coherent sentences. Her breath came shallower and faster as he drew her close, crushing her breasts against his chest. "We both seemed to enjoy—"

Even in the darkness, she detected the heat in his eyes as they roved her face. "Did you enjoy?"

Heat flooded her cheeks; Lily nodded woodenly. She stared at his neck cloth again, afraid to meet his gaze.

"What do you want from me?"

She swallowed. "I thought, perhaps—" she told his cravat.

"Look at me."

She did, for once in her life, not bristling at a statement that smacked of authority.

His hand splayed across her lower back and he pulled her closer still, until every inch of her was in contact with some deliciously hard part of him. "Now," he said, his voice carrying a wicked promise of pleasures she could only begin to imagine, "you look at me and tell me what you want."

The thick ridge pressing into her abdomen made her arch into him. Rallying the tattered scraps of her rational self, she managed to voice her request. "A kiss."

One side of his mouth quirked up. "A kiss? That's all you want?"

He was mocking her, she knew, trying to goad her into another argument. She nodded weakly. "Just a kiss."

His head dropped, and he chastely pressed his lips against her forehead.

When he pulled back, Lily's taut nerves cried in disappointment. She whimpered, but he paid her protest no heed.

"There now, you've had your kiss. Let's be on our way." The tension around his eyes suggested that he held himself back.

She exhaled in frustration. What did a girl have to do to get herself properly kissed? "You're not being very gentlemanly, I'll have you know."

"Indeed?" A hint of amusement played around the corners of his mouth.

Thorburn's bent arm made an appearance at her side. Lily whirled away, refusing his escort. She had come here to be kissed, and by Jove, she was going to be kissed. "You're cruel," she accused. "That wasn't at all what I meant, as you well know. If you don't feel inclined to kiss me you might have just said so instead of mocking me."

His hand clamped around her upper arm like a vise and turned her to face him; every shred of humor vanished. Thunderclouds roiled across his features. Fear clapped her in the gut. Suddenly, she was *very* sorry for her curt tone. She remembered his bellowing roar and the sound of glass smashing into the fireplace when she'd fled his house after their first meeting. For all Thorburn's urbane sophistication, something dark and powerful lurked just beneath the surface. And she should not be trifling with it.

"You're playing a foolish game, Miss Bachman."

She shook her head, desperate to clear the murkiness of the glasses of wine she'd consumed.

A bitter smile twisted his lips. "Unfortunately, I find myself losing this one, too." His fingers tangled into the hair at her nape. Lightly, he brushed his lips across hers. Lily's apprehension started to give way.

"Is this more what you had in mind?" he murmured. He teased her again with his mouth, reigniting the storm of desire within her.

"No." The word was a plea, yearning for the fulfillment of something she scarcely recognized.

A groan sounded low in his throat as he captured her lips again. His tongue caressed her bottom lip, not so much begging admittance as inviting her to come out to play. Hers slid out to meet his. She exulted at the flood of warmth, at the taste of him suffusing her senses.

The first time they'd kissed, she'd been taken off guard. She still wasn't accustomed to the overwhelming surge of desire his kiss elicited. But it didn't surprise her so much this time, and she wondered if she might be the one to steer it, as he had last time.

She wound her hands around the back of his neck and pulled herself up and in, eliminating every particle of space between them. She slanted her mouth and drove her tongue forward, demanding. Thorburn obliged her. The frenzied kiss didn't satisfy anything at all, but left her plunging onward, for surely there had to be a culmination—a merciful *end*—to the urge pulsating through her entire being.

A whimper escaped her throat, and when he cupped her bottom and drew her hard against his arousal, she felt her very soul answer, *Yes*.

"Lord Thorburn?" said an amused female voice.

Abruptly, his hands flew away from her and the kiss was broken. Lily swayed; Thorburn put a steadying hand at her elbow as they turned.

A group of several couples stood at the gazebo's entrance. Lily recognized Lady Elaine, one of the most vicious gossips in the *ton*. She stood front and center, a malicious smile on her face.

"I thought that was you," she said in a sickly sweet voice. Her cold eyes turned on Lily. "And Miss Bachman! What a surprise. I thought Vauxhall beneath your notice, but you certainly threw yourself in it tonight."

A few titters sounded from the group behind her.

Lily's lips pursed together. So she'd been caught kissing Thorburn. What of it? It was no more than any of *them* had likely done at some point. She opened her mouth to say so, but Lady Elaine pressed on.

"Even though you have no breeding whatsoever, I'm still shocked you keep company with Umberton's mistress."

Lily blinked. She shook her head. Elaine couldn't mean…?

"How is Lady Umberton?" Elaine arched a brow at Thorburn. "Has the babe arrived yet?"

Babe? Lady Umberton wasn't visibly with child. She turned her confused eyes on Thorburn, who was staring down Lady Elaine with scarcely contained loathing.

The group continued on, leaving Lily and Thorburn in the suddenly very cheap-looking gazebo.

"Lady Umberton." Panic flailed at her. Lily looked at Thorburn, searching his blank face for reassurance. "That *is* Lady Umberton in the box, is it not?"

Thorburn's brows snapped together. "No, you fool! That's Umberton's mistress. Why the devil do you think I tried to send you on to your ball?"

Shock hit her like a bucket of icy water over the head. "Why didn't you stop me?" Lily wailed.

His hands flew wide and he scoffed in exasperation. "You made such a bloody scene, I thought it would be safer to try to get through dinner unnoticed. What would you have had me do? Cosh you over the head and toss you into a hackney?"

Her hands tangled in her skirts, wrapping them around her fists like bandages on a pugilist's hands. "You might have told me, at least!"

"I thought you knew!" he bellowed. "Everyone in London knows Ghita is Quillan's mistress—everyone but *you*, it would seem."

His words stung, like he was laughing at her. "But she said she was Lady Umberton," Lily muttered. "She told my *mother* so." She buried her face in her hands, feeling like the stupidest, most gullible person ever born. *How* could this have happened?

Thorburn sighed heavily. "Well, she isn't. She's an opera singer and a mistress, and a glorious liar, too, I suppose. Come on."

He took her elbow and steered her to an exit, whereupon he *did* summon a hackney and virtually toss her into it.

Lily sat stock straight, numb with shock. "Aren't you going to escort me home?" she managed.

Thorburn gaped at her in disbelief. "Do you really care to make the scandal worse?" He shut the door and gave the word to the jarvey.

As the carriage started forward, Lily blinked. "Scandal?" she breathed. She'd been seen publicly reveling in the company of a married man, his mistress, and an unmarried gentleman. Then she'd been caught in a passionate kiss with said unmarried gentleman.

So, yes, she supposed she had ignited a scandal. "Oh!"

Chapter Eleven

Lily awoke with a pounding head, a roiling stomach, and the crystal-clear certainty that she was ruined. She'd heard too much alcohol could cause forgetfulness. Unfortunately, merciful oblivion had not found her. Every sordid detail of the previous night surged upward as she came to consciousness, along with bile burning its way up her throat. She made it to the basin just in time to retch into it.

Wiping her mouth with the back of her shaking hand, she turned to look about her bedchamber. The only blurred memories came at the end. She dimly recalled stumbling into the butler, Wallace, when he'd opened the door for her. Her parents' worried faces floated in her vision. The scolding voice of Moira, her maid, rang in her ears. Lily patted her hair. Pins from the previous night's coif were tangled in her locks, evidence of her inability to remain upright long enough to have her hair brushed.

Hot shame washed over her. Lily sat at her vanity and began pulling the pins out. The delicate tinkle each made as it dropped into the cut-glass bowl in front of the mirror grated against her sensitive ears. She slowly brushed through her matted tresses.

The reflection in the mirror told a sorry tale. Dark shadows beneath her eyes and the pallor of her cheeks attested to illness, but it was one she'd brought on herself by overindulging in wine and champagne. Her lips were swollen and flushed—another effect of the wine, she wondered, or the result of the wanton way she'd thrown herself at Thorburn?

The brush fell to the vanity with a clatter as Lily dropped her face into her hands. Her eyes felt like tiny deserts, incapable of producing drops equal to the sorrow she felt.

"You don't deserve to cry," she muttered.

Tears were for grief, not for foolish women who threw their own reputations away like the contents of last night's chamber pot. Her stomach lurched again, but Lily ruthlessly clamped down on the sensation. "No," she forced through clenched teeth. She wouldn't give in to her weak stomach—not when she'd done it to herself.

She raised her head and met her own glassy gaze in the mirror as she took several deep breaths. Last night, she'd let herself loose. There would be hell to pay today, but after that—

"Never again." The words carried the weight of a vow. Lily Bachman wasn't cut out for fast living. One ill-advised night of it had taught her that much. From now on, it would be business as usual. There would be a little rough patch waiting for the gossip to die down, and then—

A gentle knock sounded at the door. It opened a crack and Moira stuck her head in. The middle-aged woman sidled in. "I expect you've something of a headache."

Lily nodded and winced.

"Would you like some tea? Toast?"

"No," Lily grumbled. "I don't think I can ever eat again."

Moira's lined lips and chin pulled downward into a frown. "Mr. Bachman wants to see you, Miss Lily, soon as you're ready."

Lily swallowed around a lump of apprehension in her throat. She knew her father must be upset with her—it was the unknown extent of his upset that had her worried. Well, the sooner she found out, the sooner everything could go back to normal.

Moira helped her into a morning dress and wound her hair into a simple knot at her nape. Her complexion still had a waxy sheen to it, her eyes were bloodshot, and she didn't know if her mouth would ever again not feel full of cotton, but at least she was presentable. With a final calming breath, Lily steeled herself to face her father.

Wallace stood beside the door to Mr. Bachman's study; he opened the door as Lily approached. A moan from the sofa immediately caught her attention. Mrs. Bachman reclined on the furniture with a folded cloth draped across her eyes. Her father sat at his desk, head bent as he wrote. Papers stood in a neat stack at his elbow. A good sign, she decided. Her careless outing hadn't brought the world to an end—life went on.

Mr. Bachman looked up at her entrance and then glanced at his wife. "The future Lady Thorburn graces us with her presence, my dear."

She halted in her tracks, as stunned by his words as if he'd struck her. He couldn't mean that!

Mrs. Bachman pulled the cloth from her face. Her eyelids were puffy and her cheeks blotched. She took one look at Lily, covered her mouth, and let out a ragged wail.

Lily sighed. "Mother, please..."

"Have a seat, Lily," Mr. Bachman ordered.

She woodenly approached her father's desk. He laid his pen aside and gestured to the chair across the desk. Her eyes skidded to the place he usually made for her at his side, now woefully empty. She sank into the chair and folded her hands in her lap. Her innards twisted under Mr. Bachman's intense glower. *Never* had that look been aimed in her direction; it was reserved for political enemies, or business associates who refused to make good on a contract. Not for his daughter—never for her.

"Papa," she started, "I can see you're angry, but if you'll just let me explain—"

"I cannot *conceive* of the explanation that would make this mess acceptable. But please, try." His lips drew together in a thin line and his cheeks around his graying sideburns colored.

Lily quailed at his bitter tone.

Behind her, Mrs. Bachman sniffled. "It's my fault," she said in a thick voice. "If I had been a better mother…"

"Why?" Mr. Bachman demanded. "What on earth possessed you to take leave of your senses?" Lily opened her mouth, but her father drove on, his voice rising in pitch. "Have you any idea how worried your mother and I were last night? When you two didn't appear at the Ainsleys', I came home—only to learn you'd been sent on to the ball but failed to arrive. Your poor mother was quite certain you'd been absconded with, and at this point, I'm not sure that wouldn't have been preferable to the truth. So, let's hear it, Lily. Why did you go to Vauxhall Gardens instead of meeting me at the ball, as you'd been instructed to do?"

"We were lied to!" Lily protested. "Both of us." She twisted in her chair to look at her mother. "She said she was Lady Umberton, and we believed her. She told us they were going to the Ainsleys', too. We can't be faulted for that!"

"It *is* my fault." Mrs. Bachman struggled to sit up. Her head lolled to the side and she turned eyes brimming with misery upon Lily. "If I hadn't been in such a state, I never would have believed that woman was Lady Umberton. No gentleman in his right mind would ever marry an Italian." She collapsed against the arm of the sofa and wept.

Mr. Bachman cast a fretful look in his wife's direction, then rounded on Lily. "So you were duped into a carriage ride with Lord Umberton's mistress. If that had been the end of it, we would not be having this conversation." He pinched the bridge of his nose. "Help me understand, Lily, because for the life of me, I cannot make sense of this. When you arrived at Vauxhall Gardens, why did you not come straightaway to the Ainsleys'?"

Lily squirmed in her seat. Perhaps it was just a fancy, but the chair felt more uncomfortable on this side of her father's expansive desk. What was she to say? That she wanted to spend time with the handsome viscount—the one man whose attention she sought, but who had so maddeningly withheld it?

Her shoulders slumped. "I thought it would be fun." Her words sounded hollow, inadequate, even to herself.

A long silence followed, in which the only sound was Mrs. Bachman's incessant lamentation.

Mr. Bachman's chair creaked as he shifted. He cleared his throat. "Well, Lily, I hope it was the most fantastically marvelous night of your life, because it came at a dear price. You may now consider yourself engaged to Thorburn. You will not leave this house unaccompanied until the wedding, which I daresay will not be long in coming."

Lily extended a trembling hand. "Papa, please, there's no reason for such a rash—"

His fist crashed against the desk. She startled back, nearly toppling her chair. "Indeed there is! *You* are the one who decided to stay at Vauxhall Gardens, unchaperoned and in the company of persons of dubious character. *You* were caught in Thorburn's arms, behaving in the most disgraceful fashion. *You* are the one whose name is splashed all over the papers."

"What?" she shrieked. Lily leaped out of her seat. The chair fell backward, landing with a heavy thud on the rug.

"See for yourself." Mr. Bachman reached into a desk drawer and pulled out a folded paper, which he tossed across the polished desktop with a flick of his wrist.

Lily snatched it up. It was a gossip rag, the kind that reported on the minutiae of society affairs. She'd earned a column on the side of the front page, outshone only by an account of the Prince Regent's most recent public gibe about his wife, Princess Caroline.

She cringed as she read the florid description of her arrival with

Lord Umberton's party, which included his mistress, *the beautiful opera singer Ghita Bellisario, and the perennially debt-ridden Lord Thorburn.* There was even a quote from *a reliable source*—she thought blackly of Lady Elaine—offering salacious information about her and Thorburn: *I saw them in the gazebo, and I do not think it would have been very long before their encounter escalated to utter indecency, though what I saw was bad enough.*

"The matter is quite out of your hands now," Mr. Bachman said. "You have no more say."

She closed her eyes against hot tears of shame. That her parents should have to read such a lurid account of her evening was humiliating beyond whatever gossip the *ton* cared to spread. Lily had never given a snap for the opinions of the dissipated aristocracy, but to have sunk in her father's estimation was almost beyond enduring.

"How *could* you?" Mr. Bachman asked. "The papers have followed you all Season. Vauxhall Gardens is a natural draw to society reporters just looking for something sensational to write. Such an egregious misstep on your part is beyond irresponsible."

Lily turned at the sound of her mother's pained whimpering. Mrs. Bachman struggled to sit up again. She caught her daughter's gaze and mustered a tiny wavering smile. "At least you'll be a viscountess," she said. "And someday, the Countess of Kneath."

Lily's hands balled into fists. "No, I won't," she ground out between clenched teeth. "I'm not marrying Thorburn—or anyone else."

Her mother's eyes widened with dismay. "What are you saying?"

She crumpled up the gossip rag and flung it into the fireplace. "I'm saying this is garbage. It's stupid, vapid talk from people who have nothing better to do than tear each other down. They're a flock of bleating sheep and I hate them all. I don't *want* to marry one of them, and if you try to make me—"

Mrs. Bachman's face drained of color, and then she cried out as she twisted. Lily recognized the attack of muscle spasms. "My dear!" Mr. Bachman hurried to his wife as she contorted unnaturally again. He put an arm around her shoulders and made a shushing sound. Lily reached out to offer assistance, but Mr. Bachman snapped, "Haven't you done enough?"

Lily drew back, stung by his words. She yanked the bell pull. Wallace materialized, and together the two men half-carried Mrs. Bachman toward her room. Mr. Bachman looked over his shoulder. "Stay here. I'm not done with you."

She stood, staring after her parents. Her father held her mother close, with an arm around her waist, and his other hand gripping hers. The simple display of affection was startling. For years, Lily had been so busy regarding her mother as a silly, frivolous woman, she'd paid little attention to her parents' marriage. Yes, Mr. Bachman was the stalwart intellectual, a formidable master of industry and political maneuvering. Perhaps he *needed* Mrs. Bachman's lightheartedness to keep him afloat, to stop him from doing nothing with his life but work. Theirs was a quiet affection of fond smiles and easy companionship. Lily was so used to it, she'd never stopped to think about it. She had foolishly assumed her father shared her annoyance for her mother's more superficial traits.

While she waited, she righted the chair she'd toppled. Then she sat back down in it and stared at her folded hands. It never crossed her mind to put the chair on her father's side of the desk—she no longer deserved that familiar privilege.

About ten minutes later, Mr. Bachman returned. "You're going to make an invalid of her," he snapped.

"I'm sorry."

Her father did not return to his desk. Rather, he paced across the rug. Lily stood and turned to face him.

"Papa," she started, "I know I made a horrible mistake yesterday. I apologize for causing you and Mama so much trouble. Please believe that I would take it all back in an instant if I could, and dance every set at the Ainsleys' like I should have done. But this idea about...*marriage*—" She could barely scrape the word off her tongue. "Surely there's no need for that. I'll keep my head low for the rest of the Season, concentrate on getting the school up and running—"

Mr. Bachman cut her off with a bitter, humorless laugh. "You still don't understand, do you?" At her blank look, he continued, "This is your second Season out, my dear; you're a woman of three-and-twenty, and have already buried a fiancé. Foolishly, perhaps, I told you I would not pressure you in the matter of marriage after we lost Ensign Handford. I thought allowing you your choice would somehow make it up to you. Well, that decision has now come back to haunt me in the most visceral fashion. I suppose I've only myself to blame, for an incident like last night's was perhaps inevitable the longer you went unwed. Your marrying has never been up for discussion, only the who and when of it. Well, the who is Thorburn, and the time is now."

As he spoke, a lightheadedness stole over her. She remembered Thorburn's scorching eyes upon her, the way she couldn't resist his touch. Perhaps marrying him would eventually appeal to her—at least he wasn't a Leech—but this was so...so *tawdry*.

"And as for your idea to concentrate on the school," Mr. Bachman said, "I have only this to say: what school?"

Lily gasped. "Papa, you're not—"

"With your reputation in the gutter," he said ruthlessly, "what gentleman would donate money to your cause? What lady would sit on the board?" She opened her mouth, but he bowled on. "Oh, yes, Lily, you *need* them, as much as you like to foster your contempt for them. I have offered my full support for the start-up of your school, but I cannot finance it forever. You will have to develop good relations with the titled class if you've any hope of succeeding in fundraising. The only redemption for you now is to marry Thorburn at once and hope they've all forgotten this mess by the time you come calling for money."

She blanched, thunderstruck by her father's insight. This consequence of her misadventure had not even begun to occur to her. The school had not touched her thoughts once when she considered the possible outcomes of her ruin—for what did impoverished girls care for their benefactress's reputation?

But now, there would be no girls for her to help. No school providing education and training to elevate those young women beyond their circumstances.

For herself, Lily didn't care what society thought. Her parents would eventually forgive her, too. But to never realize her dream of creating a charitable school? To have her work snatched away from her before she'd even begun? No, *that* she could not tolerate. Even though they didn't know it, she had made a promise to help those as-yet-nameless young women—and help them she must. If marriage was her penance, then so be it.

She swallowed and met her father's steely gaze. "All right," she said with a nod. "I'll marry him."

Chapter Twelve

A knock pulled Ethan from the light sleep he'd been in since settling into one of Vanessa's guest rooms last night. He opened his eyes just as the door opened and the butler stepped in.

"It's gone noon, my lord," the stately servant said. "I thought you might like a bite to eat before you're on your way."

Not quite a notice of eviction, Ethan decided, but not far from it, either. "Thank you, Higgins, I'll be down soon."

When the butler had gone, Ethan slipped out of bed. The chill air raised goose bumps along his naked length. He donned a clean change of clothes—compliments of Nessa's sainted maids—and stepped into the hallway.

He started toward the stairs, then paused, turned, and went the other direction. A knock at Vanessa's door was answered by the new nurse, a Swedish woman who'd come with references speaking to her experience with similar cases.

"How is she?" He glanced over the nurse's head into the bedchamber.

"Madam is doing well today," the nurse replied in a slightly nasal voice. "She is napping just now. Her new routine is helping. There hasn't been an outburst in three days."

"Wonderful news." Ethan placed a hand on his chest. "May I come in?"

The nurse's plump cheeks fell into a frown. "Of course not!" she exclaimed. "Waking her would upset madam's routine."

"Oh. All right." He blinked and stepped back, crestfallen. He'd grown so accustomed to being the only one who could calm Nessa, it was jarring to find himself dismissed. The door began to close, but Ethan stopped it with his hand. "Would you tell her I asked after her? Tell her I send my love."

The nurse pinched her lips and then gave a perfunctory nod. The door closed, leaving Ethan alone in the hallway with his fingertips resting on the cool white painted surface.

As he made his way downstairs, he mulled over why it had seemed so imperative to see Vanessa this morning.

In case it's the last time, he reminded himself. *You might be dead this time tomorrow.*

He scoffed at his own morbid imagination. He didn't think Lily's father would call him out for last night's events, but he did feel the noose slowly closing around his neck. That was why he'd come to Nessa's rather than return to his own home—no one knew to look for him here, and he needed to get his thoughts together.

In the dining room, he found a generous spread laid out on the sideboard. He helped himself and tucked into a hearty meal. Higgins might not approve of him showing up unannounced to spend the night, but most of Vanessa's servants treated him as the *de facto* lord of the household.

After eating, he accepted his hat from the frowning butler. What to do with his day? He rubbed a hand over a cheek and grimaced at the stubble he found there. To the barber, then, for a shave.

An hour later, he emerged from the establishment with a smooth face and nagging twinges of embarrassment. He'd waited while the barber finished shaving a boot maker to have his turn at the chair. And though the barber had treated him with the utmost deference, there was still something unsettling about exposing his neck to a razor wielded by a man who was not his own valet.

From there, a hackney bore him to Brooks's. He'd not set foot in the club in some time, but today he approached the place with the nostalgic longing of a condemned man. He took a comfortable chair and accepted a drink off the proffered salver. He enjoyed a few sips of his beverage and settled back into the chair, then noticed a broadsheet on the table. Ethan flicked it open.

"Ever the charmer, Prinny." He chuckled. "Poor Caroline." His eyes drifted to the right side of the page and snagged on a familiar name—his own. Hastily—and in growing horror—he scanned the article. While Lily was the focus of the piece, he made a memorable cameo halfway down, where their kiss was portrayed as one step shy of a waltz.

With this one stupid kiss in print for all the world to see, and every sentence more sensational than the previous, Ethan had the growing realization that when Lily's father caught up to him, it would not be to challenge him to a duel. It would be worse.

"Shit," he spat. "Bloody buggering shit, shit, shit!"

"Thorburn!" called a cheerful voice. "Reading your engagement notice?"

Ethan lowered the paper and cast a stony glare at the smirking Jordan Atherton, Viscount Freese. The scar bisecting his right cheek twisted up at the end near his mouth, giving him a double smile.

Ethan glowered. "Freese."

Lord Freese ignored his black mood and continued glibly. "Not the sporting way to go about it, but you've accomplished what so many men have tried to do and failed—rope Lily Bachman into matrimony. And for that, good sir," he tapped his heels together and bowed mockingly, "I salute you."

"Go to hell, Freese."

The man chuckled. "Oh, I'm sure I'll get there one of these days. Can't dodge the mamas forever. But unless I'm very much mistaken, I do believe you'll get there first. On the bright side," he said, quirking a brow, "just think of that gorgeous dowry." He let out a low whistle. "You could fill a pond with guineas and go swimming in your fortune." With that, Freese wandered off to annoy someone else with his wretched good mood.

Tossing the paper aside with a sound of disgust, Ethan collected his hat and set out for home. No sense delaying the inevitable. Freese was right about the dowry. There was that consolation. Even though Ethan had decided pursuing Lily so he could make Ghita his mistress was uncouth, it seemed fate still thought throwing him into marriage with Miss Bachman was a grand idea.

He allowed himself the remainder of the walk home to mourn the fleet passing of his bachelorhood. There wouldn't be much to miss. His house was an empty, dried-up husk. He passed his days and nights seeking his own pleasures, be they at the gaming table, in the arms of a willing lady, or—as was the case more frequently with his recent economizing—leafing through a book.

Life could continue as he wished, Ethan reminded himself. Marriage never stopped a gentleman from doing just as he pleased. *Look at Quillan,* he thought. Even with his firstborn due to arrive any day now, his friend still stayed on in town to enjoy the social whirl.

His mind drifted to another marriage he knew well, stopping him in his tracks. Surely his parents' marriage was an anomaly, wasn't it? Though many married couples were indifferent in their unions, they didn't usually resort to his father's violence or his mother's drastic escape. That was unusual, a storied scandal because of the scale of it. Ethan wasn't destined to follow in their steps. *No.*

Was he?

He frowned and kept his eyes on the walk just in front of his feet the rest of the way home, gloomy thoughts of an unhappy home rolling through his mind. What if that *was* his destiny? The thought of Ghita's lithe figure was not the temptation it once was. Though a mistress might alleviate the boredom of a stale home life, Ethan didn't think Ghita was the right mistress for him, after all.

With a heavy sigh, he trudged up his unkempt front steps and shoved the key into the lock. The door swung into the inky interior of his gloomy house.

"Lord Thorburn?"

Ethan turned at the sound of his name. A rotund man climbed out of a carriage at the curb. His face tugged at Ethan's memory. "Ah, yes, Mister…"

"Wickenworth," the man proclaimed as he mounted the steps, leaning heavily on the hand rail. "Eugene Wickenworth, Esquire, representing Mr. Bachman."

A hard stone settled in Ethan's middle. "Of course. What can I do for you, sir?"

The man patted his considerable belly. "I've spent the morning drawing up some papers for my client," he explained. "Now they must be signed. If you'd be so good as to join me, we'll be on our way." He gestured to the carriage.

Ethan's lips drew together in a grim line. "Of course. Lead on."

He closed up the house and followed Wickenworth to the waiting carriage. They rode in silence through Mayfair until they arrived at a modest house—still completely respectable, of course, but not the obvious dwelling of one of the richest men in England.

A servant led them to the study. Mr. Bachman rose from his desk, every bit as unassuming as Ethan remembered from his first impression of the man several weeks back. His features would have looked at home on the face of a baker.

"Thank you, Wickenworth." Mr. Bachman took a folio from the solicitor and shook his hand. "If you'd be so good as to wait in the parlor while Lord Thorburn and I speak."

"Of course, sir." The rotund man shot a look at Ethan before leaving the study, the door closing behind him.

A long silence followed the solicitor's departure. Ethan stared out the window, feeling the weight of the older man's gaze upon him.

"Do you care to sit?" Mr. Bachman finally asked.

Ethan turned and nodded. "Thank you." He started toward the little sitting area, but Mr. Bachman stopped him.

"This way, if you please." He gestured to the massive desk. "This *is* a business meeting, my lord."

Ethan scowled. Did the man consider his daughter's marriage no more than a business transaction? He took the chair across the desk while Mr. Bachman returned to the large seat behind it.

"So it seems I'm to have a viscount for a son-in-law." The expression on Mr. Bachman's face did not suggest this to be a welcome prospect.

Ethan cleared his throat. "Sir, if I may, I'd just like to say that I understand the distress this situation must cause you and Mrs. Bachman, to say nothing of Miss Bachman's feelings. And while this was certainly not the way I envisioned my own betrothal coming about, I assure you I am not here to attempt to dodge my responsibility for what happened. If our marrying is inevitable, then I am happy to accept—"

"I just bet you are!" Mr. Bachman's face flushed with ire. "I'm sure you're more than happy to accept my daughter's money." At Ethan's startled expression, he laughed. "Oh, please, Thorburn, everyone knows you're drowning in debt. Very low of you, my boy. Ruining my daughter, entrapping her. You had her well and fooled. She didn't want to believe you a fortune hunter."

Ethan cringed inwardly. He'd known she'd learn the truth about him, but it smarted to know he must have fallen in her estimation.

Mr. Bachman harrumphed. He settled his chin against his fist and flipped open the folio his solicitor had given him. "This is the marriage contract."

"I thought it might be."

"Your mouth does you no favors, young man." His dark eyes appraised Ethan shrewdly. "You'll want to read it over before you sign." With a smooth economy of motion, he turned the folio and slid it across the desk.

Ethan's eyes glazed at the jumble of legal jargon. He turned a page and spotted a clause about establishing a trust fund for each of his and Lily's future children, free and clear of the Kneath entail. Not an onerous request. Of course, he thought sourly, he couldn't start trust funds from the dust gathered on his mantelpiece. His brows knit together. Speaking of money, where was the dowry?

He flipped to the third page. There, about halfway down—almost as an afterthought—he spotted the term "settlement" and quickly digested the surrounding text. His eyes widened at what he saw, rage flaring to life. "Ten thousand pounds!" He slammed the folio shut and glared at the smirking old man across the desk. "What the bloody hell is this?"

Mr. Bachman's smirk fell away to an expression of blank confusion. "Whatever do you mean, my dear Lord Thorburn?"

Ethan bit back a curse. If he demanded more money, he would sound exactly like the fortune hunter Mr. Bachman tagged him to be. The hell of it was, the money *was* what sparked Ethan's interest in Lily—to begin with, at any rate. And though his mercenary motives had given way to something less unscrupulous, the fact remained that he needed the blunt, and plenty of it.

His tongue flicked over his bottom lip. Mr. Bachman sat across from him with an exultant gleam in his eyes, damn the man.

"Forgive me for being crass, sir, but I was given to understand that Miss Bachman's dowry was of a more substantial nature."

"Indeed it was," Mr. Bachman said gravely. "A hundred thousand. You know, of course," Lily's father continued, "I am under no legal obligation to gift you that amount, considering the circumstances. Besides, for all you know, I've lost everything on the market, and haven't a farthing more to spare."

Ethan's jaw clenched. "I can walk away—I haven't signed anything, and I've made no promise to Miss Bachman. Have me tossed in gaol if you want, I don't care—but I won't be toyed with."

Mr. Bachman's heavy eyebrows shot up his forehead. "Oh, ho! And just what do you think it is you've done with Lily, if not toy with her? You're slicker than the rest, but a fortune hunter all the same. You ruined my daughter to force her into marriage, for the purpose of obtaining her dowry." His fist crashed against the desk. "And I'm supposed to *reward* you for ill-using my offspring? Think again, my lord."

Hot breath whooshed from Ethan's nose as he fumed. "Now see here, Bachman. I did *not* seek out to compromise Miss Bachman. Your opinion may be as low of me as you please, and God knows, most of what you believe is probably true." He raised his hands, palm out. "I will even go so far as to admit that I did, at one time, hope to marry your daughter and win her dowry. Yet I swear to you, I would never ensnare a woman this way."

Mr. Bachman licked his lips, a shrewd, calculating glint in his eyes. "And yet, here you are—about to engage yourself to the woman who can solve all your woes. You say you were interested in her money at one time, as though that interest has evaporated. But you sit there ranting and railing because you haven't been given enough to suit you. It appears your interest persists unabated."

Ethan scoffed. "It escapes your notice, perhaps, that I am being forced into this marriage every bit as much as Miss Bachman. I did not come here to offer for her—I was summoned, and a contract with my name already upon it was shoved under my nose. As the size of Miss Bachman's dowry is common knowledge, so, too, is your desire for a title for your daughter and descendants—which, of course, I just happen to have at my disposal. This is a situation in which we each possess something the other desires in equal measure. Just compensation is not too much to ask."

"Shut up, Thorburn," Mr. Bachman snapped. "There are scores of unwed titled gentlemen in this country, but Lily alone has the fortune you need to save your own sorry carcass. Do not delude yourself into thinking this is an even match. You need her far more than she needs you. My intention had been for my daughter to have the say of her own marriage. You took her choice away."

Ethan met Mr. Bachman's angry stare. His innards writhed, guilt for compromising Lily's reputation warring with fury at Mr. Bachman's humiliating set down. Yes, he was an impoverished nobleman—so were scads of other aristocrats. Exile was almost becoming fashionable, he mused. Calais had quite the jaunty community of Englishmen hiding from the duns. That was an option he hadn't considered, but now it sprang before him. Not ideal, perhaps, but neither would he be tied down by a swindling father-in-law and his title-hungry daughter.

His muscles bunched as he prepared to rise, sharp words forming on his tongue to tell Mr. Bachman just where he could stow that marriage contract.

"You can still have the money," Mr. Bachman stated.

Ethan froze, his lips parted and his thighs hovering a fraction of an inch off the chair. He eyed Mr. Bachman warily. "What do you mean?"

"The ten thousand stands for now." He clicked his tongue and leveled a shrewd gaze on Ethan. "But you can earn the rest."

Ethan's brows drew together in a frown. "How?"

Mr. Bachman's lips pinched. "This marriage isn't Lily's choice. *You* aren't her choice. The day she tells me she is happy in her marriage will be the day I sign over the balance of her dowry. But you must sign the contract now, and proceed straightaway to apply for a special license." He shrugged. "Or, you can walk out that door and do whatever it is penniless lords do with their lives, while someone else marries Lily—for make no mistake, while she is in a delicate situation, money is a soothing balm and soon makes men forgetful of colorful pasts. She *will* marry, and well, to someone else if not you."

Blinking, Ethan considered. His eyes settled on the contract folio and he ran a finger down the leather cover, buttery soft as the finest boots.

The money was still within reach. A flicker of hope bloomed in his chest. With a sigh, he opened the folio and re-read the last page of the contract. Ten thousand pounds now, *and* Lily Bachman. That bounteous bosom of hers would be his to explore at his leisure—now *that* was a cheering thought.

With a wry smile he extended his hand, which Mr. Bachman took in a firm grip. A few strokes of ink sealed his fate. He would have the fortune and the freedom it offered from his suffocating debts. All he had to do was make her happy. Charming the ladies had always come easily to him—how hard could this be?

Mr. Bachman poured sherry for Ethan and himself. His mood considerably brighter, he smiled at the younger man. "Now that's settled, it's time to get better acquainted. You shall join us for supper, I hope, a cozy family affair. After you apply for the special license, of course."

Ethan bowed. "I should be delighted to accept your kind invitation, sir. And I shall be off to see the archbishop—but first, I believe I must have a word with Miss Bachman."

Mr. Bachman weighed him with a heavy gaze. "It isn't necessary, you know. It's all done, signed and sealed, forever and ever, amen. Lily doesn't expect gallantry."

"Sir," Ethan said, his words sharp and clipped. "I should like a word with your daughter, my affianced bride. Signed and sealed it all may be, but I'll not meet Miss Bachman at the altar without making her an honorable offer. The very notion smacks of medieval barbarism."

With a curt nod, Mr. Bachman left the study.

A few minutes later Lily appeared in the door. Her face was ashen, her usual visage of cool disdain replaced by trembling lips and a wary gaze. Her dark eyes and hair provided striking contrast to her pale skin. Lily's distress exposed something vulnerable he'd not seen in her before and contributed a delicacy to her beauty— not even the worst hangover could render her unbeautiful in his eyes. She closed the door and stiffly advanced into the room.

His heart lurched with concern at her alarming appearance. "How are you, Lily?"

It wasn't how he'd meant to begin, but the few moments he'd had to try to scrape together some pretty words had not prepared him for the sight of a pitiable creature, frightened, angry, and afflicted with her first morning-after head. "I hope you're not suffering the effects of last night too much."

Lily's startled eyes snapped to his face. And then she laughed hysterically, wide-mouthed, with tears leaking from the corners of her eyes. At once, Ethan realized his blunder. He was thinking of the copious amounts of wine she'd consumed, somehow forgetting for a moment the wretched scrape they'd landed in.

He took her hand and drew her, still laughing, to the sofa. He sat beside her and gave her a moment to compose herself, but even as she cleared her throat and straightened, her eyes still danced with craze-tinged amusement.

"Lily," he began again, "I've just spoken to your father and he has consented—"

She burst into laughter again and shook her hands. "No," she managed between gasps of air, "don't do it, my lord, I beg you." Ethan frowned, but she forestalled him before he could speak. "I thought I could get through this mummery, but I cannot. It's too absurd."

A wry smile cracked his face. "Mr. Bachman warned me you'd not be impressed with gallantry, but I haven't even gotten to the gallant part. Perhaps you'd prefer romance—an ardent proposal by a desperate lover?"

Lily sobered. "Don't, my lord," she repeated, all the humor gone from her voice. "Don't you dare play make-believe with me. You've no desire to marry me any more than I want to marry you. But we'll wed anyway, because it's the only option left to us. You must not pretend at emotions that you do not feel—it would be more lowering than all the rest of this put together."

Ethan respected her honesty, but wondered at her claim that marriage was their only option—certainly their reputations would suffer if they did not marry, but damage had already been done.

"Pray do not put words in my mouth, my dear. I did not say I have no desire to marry you. I should think offering myself would prove my good intentions."

Her face pinched; her eyes flashed. "You've proved your intentions, beyond enough. I would thank you to leave me in peace until the wedding."

Annoyed, Ethan lifted a brow. "I fear I cannot accommodate your request. Your father has invited me to supper."

Bristling with hostility, she stood and, without another word, swept from the study. The door slammed behind her with what must have been a very satisfying crash.

And that was as close as Ethan Helling ever came to proposing marriage to Lily Bachman.

Chapter Thirteen

Lily accepted Thorburn's hand and alit from the hackney that had borne them from her parents' home to her new residence. She blinked in dismay at the facade of the house, even more run-down in appearance than it had been on her first visit. Green leaves carpeted the steps, with water pooled on the verdant foliage.

"That looks treacherous," she muttered.

"What's that, my lady?" Thorburn looked from her to the house and back again. "Not awed by the grandeur of your new station?"

A biting edge to his words gave her pause. She pursed her lips and looked away.

He smirked. "Come along, Lady Thorburn."

She followed him up the front steps, careful to keep a tight hold on the hand rail, lest she slip on the wet leaves and give him more ammunition for his mockery. Standing just behind him as he fished in his pocket for the key, she found herself again drawn to him, just as she'd been the instant he'd opened this door and she'd first clapped eyes upon him. Though he had her bested in height by only a few inches, the breadth of his shoulders and back created a solid wall of male. Those were shoulders she could rest a cheek upon. This was a man who could stand with her against the world—if he but would.

Nonsense, she chided herself. The strain of the last few days was telling on her. Lily had neither the need nor the desire for any man's protection. Even if she were so inclined, *this* was not the man who would offer it. Thorburn was only interested in looking after himself.

The door swung inward, revealing an interior as dark and dingy as ever. Thorburn stepped in and bowed with a flourish. When he righted himself, he pinned her with a jeering smile. "You once told me that living in this run-down sty would offend even a bushman. Well, it's your sty now, princess. Welcome home."

Heat flushed her cheeks as she stepped past him; humiliated tears pricked the backs of her eyes, but she refused to let them fall. "Thank you, my lord." Her footsteps echoed hollowly in the vacant entrance hall. No servants greeted them, as they would do at home. No inviting smells drifted up from the kitchen. No fires warmed the hearth.

By now, she knew all about the circumstances surrounding the mysterious, empty house. Mr. Wickenworth's inquiries had uncovered the magistrate's order to seize Thorburn's property to pay his creditors. Indeed, an auction had already transpired, his possessions scattered to the wind. It was just another tick in the column of his deficiencies.

Hot anger coagulated in a ball in her middle. She drew herself up. "Right," she ground out. Though her new husband was being a boor about it, he was correct: This was now her home. And Lily Bachman—*Helling*, she corrected herself—would be damned if she allowed the unholy state of the house to continue a moment longer. He might not care a fig for the place, but she did. She was the lady of the house now; she would not allow his negligence to humiliate her.

Without a glance at Thorburn—who could take himself to the devil, for all she cared—she strode purposefully down the hall. She found the servant stairs and descended into the belly of the house, disregarding the inky blackness that enveloped her in the stairwell. In her current mood, she just *dared* an uneven board to trip her up and give her an excuse to rip it from the floor with her bare hands.

In the basement, she rummaged in the housemaid's closet and procured a stack of rags. An empty bucket was located, filled with water, and hauled back up the stairs. Thorburn was no longer in the entrance hall. She hoped he had gone out.

Up the stairs again, she went to the front parlor. Mindful of the dust everywhere, she gingerly opened the curtains so as not to stir up a cloud. She removed her gloves and pelisse and tossed them into the corner. Then she dipped one of the rags and squeezed it out. Cold water streamed over her fingers and fell back into the bucket.

She folded the cloth into a square and commenced dusting the windowsill. When she glanced up from her work to look outside, she noted the thin film of grime on the glass. That would have to be scrubbed off, but she would save it for last. No sense getting the panes back to sparkling, only to have the dust she was stirring up settle right back on the glass.

"What are you doing?" The masculine voice was rich with shock.

Lily smirked and shook her head. She didn't turn to look at him, hoping he would go away if she ignored him.

"That's your wedding dress, Lily. It'll be ruined."

And what of it? she thought angrily. So it had miraculously materialized from the modiste's in just three days. True, it shimmered in the sunlight, or under the candlelight of the wedding ball she'd never have. Adorned it may be at the neck and sleeves with the most delicate lace she'd ever laid eyes upon. Its matching pelisse might have been the perfect finishing touch to the ensemble. But it was still just a dress, the one in which she had been sentenced to a lifetime as the wife of a man she barely knew—and none of what she did know was any good.

Fiercely, she swiped at the sides of the window frame, scrubbing away the filth *he* had brought upon the house with his irresponsible indebtedness. It was only too bad she couldn't scrub away her own stupidity and undo the events that had brought her to this.

At last, his steps retreated down the stairs. The front door opened and closed again. She peeked out the window in time to see Thorburn don his hat and stride down the walk.

"Ethan," she murmured, testing his given name. He'd not invited her to use it. She rested her fingertips on the dusty glass and watched until she couldn't see him anymore, then exhaled a deep sigh.

It *had* been a sweet little ceremony, she reflected as she resumed her work. She might never fully appreciate the lengths Mr. Bachman must have gone to in bringing the event together in such a brief period of time. Her mama had still been abed with her back pain for the five short days of her engagement, so Papa had taken it upon himself to see to the details of his daughter's wedding.

They'd married at St. George's. The morning ceremony had been attended only by Naomi and Aunt Janine, accompanied by Lord Grant, and a few of Papa's friends. Though Thorburn had been urged to invite whom he pleased, he'd provided her with no names or addresses. Other than Lord Umberton, Lily didn't know who her husband's friends might be. Just another gaping hole in her knowledge of the man, she thought with a scowl. In any event, he evidently hadn't thought his own wedding important enough to share with anyone.

"And he's already left you," she grumbled as she moved on to the mantelpiece. "What a rollicking success this shall be."

At last, she stood back in the doorway to appraise her work. She swiped a bead of perspiration from her temple and nodded. "Not bad for an empty room." The carpet and draperies still wanted cleaning, and the fireplace needed a sweep, but it was a good beginning.

Lily blew out her cheeks and wondered what to do. Next week, she would resume her work on the charity school. All of her papers were still at home—she'd have to retrieve them tomorrow or the next day.

"In a hackney, no less." It was mind boggling that she was now a viscountess—someday to become a countess—and living in far meaner circumstances than she was accustomed to. "That's because you fell for a Leech's tricks, you foolish girl."

Her life had been entirely upended since meeting Thorburn, culminating with this disaster of a marriage. She growled in frustration and stomped her foot against the bare hall floor. The sound clapped off the walls and bounced back again, a satisfying reiteration of her ire.

She wouldn't regain control of herself and her life standing around pouting, she scolded herself. Lily lifted her bucket and trudged down the hall, opening doors until she found the library.

Remarkably, the bailiff's lackeys had spared this room. The book collection seemed intact; most of the shelves were densely populated with volumes. There was plenty of furniture, too— wing chairs in front of the fireplace, a table near the back wall, and two sofas facing one another in the middle.

She opened the curtains to admit the weak remnants of the afternoon's light. The room was drafty; Lily looked longingly at the fireplace, a cold, gaping mouth in the middle of the wall.

"Get moving," she told herself. "That'll warm you up." A quick appraisal of the furniture showed it to be of good quality and in general repair; however, she grimaced at the ubiquitous layer of dust on the upholstery. "Couldn't be bothered to cover your own chairs, even?" She made a disgusted sound in her throat at the additional evidence of Thorburn's incompetence.

Her annoyance fueled her efforts. She made short work of dusting the windowsill and turned her attention to the frames of the landscapes adorning the walls.

The sound of the front door closing made her breath catch. She turned expectantly, waiting for Thorburn to appear.

He did not.

After a moment, she furrowed her brow in confusion. What was the man doing? A few more minutes passed without his making an appearance, so she resumed her work and swiped her rag over the wall.

"Still at it?"

She yelped and spun, clutching the dirty cloth to her chest. "You scared the life out of me!" she scolded. "What are you doing, creeping about?"

Thorburn leaned against the doorframe, his broad shoulders filling most of the portal. A smile flitted across his lips. "I don't creep about. You must have been engrossed in your task." He leaned over and lifted a bucket from beside his feet.

Lily's face flushed. "Fresh water? How exceedingly thoughtful." Her words dripped acid. It was one thing for her to choose to do some cleaning—it was quite another for him to expect it of her!

He brought the bucket to her work area and set it down. Then he unfastened the buttons on his coat. "If you need fresh water, you're welcome to share mine."

Lily's eyes widened in alarm as his coat parted, revealing the brocade waistcoat beneath. When he pulled the coat from his arms and draped it over a chair, she looked away and reminded herself to breathe. "What are you doing?" she asked in a bewildered rush.

"There's a bit of a chill on the room, don't you think?" Thorburn arranged some kindling on the cold hearth and produced a match from the small pocket on the front of his waistcoat. In short order, a small fire crackled in the gathering dusk.

Lily watched, mystified, as the near-stranger she'd married just that morning came to stand in front of her. Her heart pounded against her ribs. She suddenly realized they were alone in the house—utterly, completely, entirely alone. There was not so much as a maid anywhere in the place. In fact, Lily had never been so thoroughly alone with any man in the entirety of her existence— not even her own father.

Banked heat smoldered behind Thorburn's eyes. Her lips parted in surprise as he plucked the rag from her hands. Was he going to kiss her, she wondered, or demand his rights as her husband right then and there? She knew very well what would be expected of her, but already? Now? In the library? Her eyes flew around, looking for an escape.

"You look like you could use some assistance." He squatted and dipped the rag in the clean water, wrung it out, and commenced dusting the wall.

Tension drained out of Lily like sand through a sieve. "Oh," she breathed, lightheaded with relief.

She took up a clean, dry cloth and carefully wiped down the ornaments on the mantel. The fire sent shadows dancing around the library. They all seemed to point their long fingers at the silent man working nearby. Her eyes kept cutting to him, taking in the smooth, even strokes of his long arms as he slid his hands up and down the wall.

They worked together without a word passing between them for a time. Lily found it impossible to ignore his masculine presence, though he seemed not to pay her one iota of attention. What did he mean by assisting her in menial work? Her agitation only mounted as time passed.

Thorburn stepped back from the section of wall he was wiping and dropped his rag into the bucket. Lily looked away and hastily swiped at a table, hoping he hadn't caught her staring at him. His footsteps carried him out of the library and down the stairs.

Gone again, she thought, forlorn. She sighed and then caught sight of his coat still lying across the chair. Not leaving, then. "What's that man doing now?"

Lily liked order; she liked knowing what was happening around her. Thorburn continually knocked her off balance with his erratic unpredictability. She felt as though she were hurtling down a precarious mountain path in a speeding carriage, every wild curve threatening to send her over the edge. She longed for a return of her orderly life, the one that she had well in hand.

His heavy steps came back up the stairs. Lily paused in anticipation, but he continued up to the second floor. A little while later, she heard him descend again. She followed by sound as he went into his study. Then that door closed, and his steps came nearer.

Lily's rag dangled from her limp hand as he entered the library without so much as a glance in her direction. He turned his back to don his coat. A sinking feeling overcame her as she realized he was going out again.

Probably to see Lord Umberton and his vulgar mistress. Wasn't it just like an aristocrat, she mused. Married in the morning, and already forgotten it by evening.

"Wife?" He looked at the hand holding the rag, a crooked smile on his lips.

Glancing down, Lily saw that her hand was shaking, releasing dust from the rag in a dirty snowfall onto the floor. "I'm sorry," she muttered, dropping the cloth into the bucket. She spun around, looking for a fresh cloth to clean the mess.

"It's all right." Thorburn laid a hand on her shoulder. Lily froze; her stomach leaped into her throat at his touch. "You've done enough." His voice was firm, but not unkind. "Come with me."

Lily stared into his cravat, then uncertainly met his gaze. Amusement danced at the corners of his mouth. His hand slid down her sleeve to her bare forearm, trailing fire over her skin. It was the first time she'd felt his hands without gloves—they were warm and strong and stoked heat low in her belly. His fingers slipped around hers. Lily watched their twined hands, mesmerized, as Ethan brought her fingers to his lips. His eyes were scorching upon her face as he brushed his mouth against the inside of her wrist. She let out a little gasp at the intimate gesture.

He tucked her hand into the crook of his elbow. "May I have the honor of escorting you to the table, my lady?"

Lily wrinkled her nose. "There *isn't* a table, my lord."

Thorburn's head cocked to the side. "Please play along, Lily. Your maddening literalism is putting a damper on the surprise."

She drew back, abashed. He had a surprise for her? Her curiosity was well piqued. She glanced at the door, checking for the ever-present onlookers she was so accustomed to in her father's fully staffed home. Of course, there was no one to see if she played along with Thorburn's charade.

She nodded regally. "You may have the honor, my lord husband." Her lips twitched. "Just don't forget that it *is* an honor."

He chuckled as he escorted her to the stairs. "I don't think I'll soon forget."

*

Ethan smiled to himself as he led Lily downstairs, pleased with his own cleverness. Females, in his experience, *loved* to be surprised in silly little romantic ways—and this gesture was as silly and romantic as they came. If only Lily would be as impressed as he hoped she'd be. The day had not gone swimmingly so far, and he truly would like to see her smile.

But besides the comfort of knowing his new wife didn't hate him, Ethan had to make her happy if he was to stand any chance of coming into her fortune. Having her throw a colossal fit and clean house in her wedding dress did not qualify as a definition of "happy" in any language he knew.

The one thing he knew they could both find enjoyment in was the considerable attraction between them. Ethan would have to seduce his wife. And if the passion she'd shown in her temper and kisses up to now were any indication, he was going to thoroughly enjoy the exercise.

They stepped into the dining room. Ethan watched Lily while her eyes widened at the sight before them. On the floor, he'd arranged a picnic supper, complements of Nessa's cook. There was cold soup, roasted quail, vegetables wrapped in bacon, bread, cheese, two bottles of wine, and plum cake for dessert. The candles he'd lit just before collecting her from the library stood in silver candlesticks at each corner of the blanket occupying the center of the room.

Lily exhaled a sound of delight. "My lord, how did you—"

He pressed a finger to her lips. "Ethan," he corrected. "There's no other in all the world, through all of time, who shall be my wife. You must not stand on ceremony with me, Lily."

Her plump rosebud lips curved into a smile beneath his finger, and he had to resist the temptation to devour her mouth. He tamped down on his baser appetites, telling them to wait their turn. Instead, he kissed her hand before leading her to their meal.

Lily folded her legs beneath her skirt. She smiled shyly as he poured the wine and offered her a dish of soup. As the meal progressed, however, Lily ate little and grew increasingly nervous. Ethan found himself grasping for conversation. Lily answered him with the least degree of verbiage necessary to hold up her end and finally lapsed into silence, which hung thick and heavy around the room.

When they finished eating, her eyes flicked to his face. "I think I should like to retire now, my...Ethan."

His name sounded alien on her tongue, as though she had difficulty pronouncing it. Ethan frowned. *Make her happy,* he reminded himself. So he blew out three of the candles and grasped her by the hand. In his other hand, he held the remaining candle high to light their way upstairs.

At the master suite, he pushed the door open. Lily stepped in and turned. Her hands wrung together at her waist as she regarded him. "Supper was lovely, Ethan, thank you. Well, good night." She nodded and made to close the door.

Ethan stopped the door with his hand. Disregarding her startled expression, he turned sideways to move past her into the room.

"My lord, what are you doing?"

"Coming to bed, of course."

Lily went ashen, her dark eyes wide in alarm. "But surely you have your own room—"

"This *is* my room, Lily—or our room, I should say." His lips curved up in a lazy smile as he considered the pleasant task ahead of him tonight. "Look around you, my dear. There's your valise at the foot of the bed, right where I deposited it. And what is that adjacent to your valise?" He looked from the pair of Hessians on the floor to his bride, whose agitation mounted as she took in her surroundings and saw his things scattered around the room.

She shook her head emphatically. "It wouldn't be proper. The lady of the house always has her own bedchamber."

"I'm sorry, love, but this is a bachelor's home," he pointed out. "I obtained the place from another bachelor. If there was ever a lady of the house, it's been many years past. Consequently, there is no lady's chamber."

Her tongue flicked over her lips; then she drew the bottom one between her teeth and worried it while her eyes settled on the middle distance. Ethan could practically hear the gears turning in her head.

Her smile was nearly a cringe. "A guest room, then?"

"Afraid not."

He set the candlestick down on a bedside table. He shrugged out of his coat and turned his back to hide the devious smile he couldn't contain. If she'd explored the house earlier, she'd have discovered that there was, in fact, a furnished guest room just down the hall. There were no linens on the mattress, and it was as dusty as the rest of the house, but if she wanted to take herself off to sleep elsewhere, she could have. *Not that she needs to know.* No, tonight, her place was with him, in his bed.

A startled squeak drew his attention. Lily's back was to him, her shoulders hunched up around her ears. Ethan frowned. "What's amiss?"

Her chestnut coif moved side to side as she shook her head. "It's your, ah, state of undress, my—Ethan."

He glanced down at himself. Yes, he'd begun disrobing, but he'd only gotten as far as removing his waistcoat. There wasn't another inch of skin showing yet, and she was already turning maidenly.

This timidity on her part did not mesh with his vision of the passionate hellcat he'd come to expect in Lily Bachman—Helling, he amended. He was certain she would come to enjoy this aspect of their marriage, but it seemed the going would be a little slower than he'd anticipated.

He put his hands on her shoulders and gently turned her around. Her eyes remained downcast, her arms folded across her middle. Ethan squeezed her shoulders and worked his way down her upper arms, easing the tension in her muscles. His hands glided down the ivory silk of her ill-treated wedding dress.

"Lily," he murmured, "do you know what happens between a man and a woman…in bed?"

Color stained her cheeks and her eyes flashed annoyance, a glimpse of the woman he was familiar with. She cleared her throat. "Though I don't have all the particulars sorted out, I understand the gist of connubial relations. I'm not ignorant."

He gave her a lopsided smile. "I never dreamed you were." While her eyes flashed defiance, her posture suggested she would fall to the floor and curl in a ball if he released her.

Ethan considered the best tack to take. What did he know about his new bride? He knew she was fiery and vivacious when her temper flared. He remembered, too, the chance meeting they'd had in the park. She had been trying to choose a headmistress for her charity school and had page after page of neat, organized notes in which she'd tried to distill the selection down to a comparison of facts.

Ah, yes, that was it.

Trusting intuition to steer him in the right direction, he took her by the hand and led her to the large bed. Lily's arm stiffened. He sat on the edge of the mattress and drew her closer. "Don't be alarmed—we're just going to talk a bit."

She sat beside him, careful to maintain a polite distance. Her hands folded into a tight ball in her lap; her eyes remained trained on them.

"Unless I'm off my mark," Ethan began, "I believe you are an eminently capable woman, prepared to undertake any task, so long as you have all the facts at your disposal. Am I correct?"

Her startled gaze flew to his face. He didn't need any further confirmation.

"If you need information, if you have questions, just ask. Sexual intimacy will not be an unspeakable taboo in this house. There is nothing you cannot say to me, Lily—there's to be no shame or embarrassment between us. I'm an open book, at your disposal."

She scoffed. "I just bet you are." Her lips twisted as she turned hard eyes upon him. "It hurts," she stated bluntly. "Doesn't it? How can you…how can *men* enjoy doing something that hurts women?"

"It often does hurt the lady a bit, the first time. But after that, it can be just as pleasurable for women as it is for men." He smiled wryly. "There wouldn't be nearly so many babies born if women howled in pain every time men touched them. There would be no delight in that, I assure you."

Her eyes slid over his shoulder as she seemed to consider his words. She nodded slowly, accepting.

He slipped an arm around her waist. She was resistant, but he did not detect the panic that had been there earlier. Before she could bombard him with more questions, Ethan took her face in his hands and brushed his lips over her lush mouth.

She exhaled a shuddering breath, then brought a tentative hand to his shoulder. He deepened the kiss, slanting his mouth and parting his lips. She responded freely; their tongues dueled and darted.

So willing and passionate…the idea of bedding her was fast becoming irresistible. He envisioned Lily pliant in his arms, responsive to his touch. His tongue thrust deep and steadily in a rhythm mimicking the pace that would follow, once he shed them both of their layers of clothes.

He broke away from her mouth to tease at her earlobe. Lily let out a little gasp, part pleasure, part surprise. "Tell me what you want, Lily," he whispered, his voice a dark invitation.

She panted as he trailed his way down the creamy column of her neck. "I don't know," she whimpered.

Ethan lifted his head to catch her in a challenging, smoldering look. "Yes, you do." He quirked a brow. "I refuse to believe you have no imagination, princess. You've lain awake in the dark hours of night, playing something out in your mind, and you wonder what it would be like in truth."

Color flooded her cheeks.

"No embarrassment, sweetheart, not with me. Everyone has fantasies. It's only too bad females are made to feel they're wrong for having them."

His wife's brow puckered as he withdrew the combs ornamenting her coif, enameled butterflies with wings embellished by tiny gemstones. He reclined against the pillows and pulled her down to lie facing him.

Working his fingers into her thick, long hair, he unhurriedly pulled loose the remaining pins. When they had been deposited on the nightstand beside the combs, he propped up on an elbow and looked down at his bride.

Lily's eyes roved his face. She bit her bottom lip, leaving the flesh red and inviting.

"What is it you want to say?" he asked.

She drew a breath, lifting her breasts into tantalizing proximity to his mouth. *Not yet.* There would be time for that soon, but not yet.

"These fantasies you mentioned—" She spoke haltingly, still struggling against the shackles of propriety. "Maybe if you offered an example first, I would know what you mean." She lowered her eyes, her lashes sooty crescents against her cheeks.

Ethan chuckled low in his throat. "You want an example? All right. I've got a dozen fantasies about you, princess." Her eyes widened. He kissed her hand and nodded. "It's true. I imagine what you look like with no clothes on." At her shocked expression, he clicked his tongue and nodded. "I *think* you must have very long legs." His gaze roamed down her length, over her shapely hips and down to where her skirts bunched around her legs, offering a tantalizing view of her ankle. "I should like very much to run my hands up and down those legs, to feel your soft skin and explore every curve and crook."

His eyes skipped back to her face. Lily's lips were slightly parted. "Oh," she breathed.

He nuzzled against her cheek and drank in her warm scent before resting his forehead on hers. "Now you."

Lily's eyelids fluttered. He watched her eyes move beneath the delicate skin. Ethan wondered what erotic images she was concocting. She drew in a stuttering breath and spoke, her voice low and her words tumbling out in a rush. "After we danced and you took me to the garden, I was astonished by how your arms felt, and I wondered what they looked like, and what it would feel like to touch them…" Her voice trailed away as the blush deepened on her cheeks.

He smiled at the tameness of her words, but was touched that she'd had the courage to say them at all. Ethan straightened. His eyes never left her as he untied his starched cravat and tossed it aside. Pulling the shirttail free of his trousers, he grinned. "Lily."

Her eyes blinked open.

"We're going to explore your fantasies, princess." Her eyes roamed his torso as he removed his shirt and tossed it beside the discarded neck cloth. Then he leaned over, his hands sinking into the mattress on either side of her. "Go ahead."

Uncertainty shadowed her eyes. Ethan lowered his face and took her in a hot, scorching kiss. As they kissed, he felt a shy tickling on his forearms. He groaned his approval, and soon her hands swept up his arms. Her fingers clung, testing the resilience of his flesh. Her palms flattened against his biceps, traveling up to his shoulders. He felt himself rising to attention at her touch, and they'd only just begun exploring one another. It was going to be a long night.

Ethan lifted his head. "How was that?"

Lily gave him a coy smile. "Very agreeable," she demurred.

His eyebrows shot up. "Just agreeable?" he teased. "Now, then, princess, I want you to do a little more thinking for me."

Her fingers brushed back down his arms, tracing the contours of his biceps. Ethan shuddered low in his back. "Think about what?" she asked.

"Of something else you might enjoy."

She tugged her lower lip between her teeth. "May I…touch you? More?"

The thought of her hands roaming his body brought his cock to full erection. "Lily," he said solemnly, "I'm your husband. I'm your lover. Touch me as much as you'd like, whenever the fancy strikes you. Consider yourself in possession of a *carte blanche*."

She inhaled deeply.

He groaned at the irresistible pull of those magnificent mounds of flesh—once again brought into temptingly close proximity by her respiration—his self-restraint testing the tight leash he kept it on. In so many ways, this night was new for him, too. Had she been any other woman, she'd have been naked an hour ago. He would have already plumbed her depths, taking his pleasure and fulfilling hers.

There would be plenty of nights like that to come, he reminded himself. Tonight was an introductory course in sexual pleasure. Finding himself in the role of teacher was both novel and trying.

She took her time exploring his bare torso, testing with her palm the springiness of the hair on his chest. "So different," she murmured. Her gaze followed the scatter of chest hair down the path to his flat stomach, and then skidded to a halt at the trail disappearing into his breeches.

"What do you mean?"

"Your body's so different from mine." Her eyes lit with the delight of discovery mingled simmering arousal. "I don't have hair like this." Her fingers fluttered over her own chest and stomach before returning to her tactile exploration.

He raised a brow. "How can I be sure? I've not been afforded the opportunity to compare." He inhaled sharply as her nails raked across his nipples.

"I'm sorry," she cried. "Did I hurt you?"

"Quite the opposite, actually."

His stiff arousal strained against the constraint of his clothes. His hips rocked against her. Ethan tamped down on his lust. *Not yet, you randy bastard.* "That's two for you." His voice rasped, gravelly with need. "I believe my turn's come 'round."

Fear flashed across Lily's features. Then she huffed a breath and nodded. "That's fair."

Ethan smirked. This was the first time he'd brought equity into bedplay. His rational brain was presently sluggish, but he'd long since cataloged the myriad things he'd like to do with his new wife's delectable body. His baser mind had no problem taking charge.

One desire refused to be shuffled aside. And she *did* seem concerned with keeping the score even.

"Why are you grinning?" Lily asked, suspicious.

Ethan struggled to repress his smile. "I'm without covering up top. It would be fair if you joined me in that state."

She sat bolt upright. Her hands flew to her throat and she swallowed. "That's your desire?" she whispered.

"The fairness bit wasn't part of *my* imagination." He took her hands, pulling them from her chest. "But, yes, Lily, I have wanted to see and touch your breasts since the moment I met you."

Her brow furrowed and she shook her head as though she didn't believe him. At last, she swung her legs over the side of the bed and stood.

Ethan rose and squeezed her shoulders as he gazed into her face. Emotions warred there—her own fledgling desire struggling against fear.

"There's nothing to be frightened of. You enjoy my kisses, yes?" She nodded.

"You'll like this, too." He dipped his head as he pulled her into his embrace, his turgid erection twitched as it pressed into her belly. He kissed her with abandon, channeling his pent-up lust through his mouth. Lily whimpered in response, tilting her head back to give him full access to her depths.

Ethan's hands tangled in her hair, securing her face to his. Then he twisted her hair into a rope, which he pulled over her shoulder. He spun her around to unbutton her gown; tiny fasteners separated from their loops as rapidly as his nimble fingers came to them.

Offering a supporting hand, he helped her step out of the gown. Next went the corset, leaving her in her stockings and thin chemise. Dark hair fell in a tumble down her back almost to her narrow waist, drawing his eyes to the round globes of her derrière—and those legs. He was nearly overcome by the desire to fall to his knees and lick them.

Not yet. Not yet. Not yet.

He turned her to face him again, keeping his eyes on the ribbons at the neckline of her chemise as he untied them. Having pulled them loose, Ethan's fingers slid under the shoulder straps, pushing the fabric down to pool around her waist.

"Oh, my God," he whispered hoarsely. They were perfection. Abundant mounds of creamy flesh, tipped by rosy nipples rising in the chilly air. "Oh, my God," he repeated reverently. Once more, he considered dropping to his knees, this time in a prayer of thanksgiving for the twin gifts from above that were Lily Bachman's magnificent breasts.

He breathed a laugh. For so long, everything good had been taken from him, but here was this gorgeous specimen of woman— the most womanly woman he'd ever seen—his for the rest of his misspent life.

"You're disappointed?" Her voice held a note of despair. Her chin lifted at a haughty angle. "You don't have to laugh. You're the one who wanted to—"

"No!" His eyes widened and he shook his head. "You misunderstand." He took her by the waist, her milky skin warm and soft against his palms. He explored the long length of her sides until he came to the soft thickening where her breasts began. He brought his hands around the front, testing their weight and squeezing gently. She squeaked. Her hard nipples pressed against his palms. "You are incredible," he said. "More beautiful even than I imagined. I still have one more desire to be fulfilled." Her hazy eyes raised to his in questioning. "I want to worship you all night long."

He bent his knees, circled his arms around her thighs, just below her bottom, and lifted. She cried out in surprise. He dropped a kiss to one breast and then the other, savoring her delicate scent, before depositing her in the center of the bed.

Before she could protest, he claimed her mouth and covered her body with his own, brushing his chest against hers. The coarse hair on his chest teased at her nipples. Lily responded with a moan.

Ethan fluttered kisses all over her face and neck, and then settled in to properly introduce himself to his two new best friends. He covered her left breast with his hand—or tried to, anyway. Even with his fingers splayed wide, he could not contain all its glorious mass in his hand. He squeezed and pulled while his tongue flicked around the areola of the other. Lily let out a little cry as he drew her nipple into his mouth and suckled. As he feasted there, his other hand drifted to her belly, tormenting the sensitive skin with light touches.

He laved the other breast with the same attention he'd given the first. Soon, Lily's breaths came in short gasps. He felt her tensing; her nails nipped into his shoulders.

"What do you want?" he asked in a husky whisper.

She squeezed her eyes and shook her head. "I don't know. I want—" She cried out when he boldly cupped her sex in his hand.

"What you want comes from here, doesn't it?" He pressed her through the cloth of her chemise, feeling the damp warmth seeping through the material.

Lily let out a guttural groan.

"I can give you what you want, princess. Will you let me?"

"Yes."

She was giving herself to him in the most intimate way, trusting him with her body, believing him when he said he could please her. It was akin to the misplaced trust she'd put on him in the past—but in this, he would not fail her.

Wasting no more time, Ethan tugged her chemise over her hips. She wore only stockings and garters, the length of her legs finally bared for his examination. The single candle lent a shimmering luminosity to the silk encasing her legs. His throat went dry at the sight; he could scarcely wait to feel those limbs wrapped around his haunches while he—

Not yet. He swallowed. *But soon.*

He eased out of his trousers.

Lily's wide eyes focused on his engorged member. "Is that really going to…" She left the question unfinished, her trepidation hanging in the air between them.

Ethan knelt between her legs. "Not yet," he said with a smile, finally vocalizing the thought that had kept him on a tight leash all night. "But, yes, it will. And all will be well, sweetheart, I promise."

Then his fingers trailed up her legs, grazing over the whisper-fine silk. He untied the ribbons of her garters and rolled one stocking down a luscious thigh. Ethan plucked it off from the toes, and then set about removing the other. He kissed, nipped, and licked his way down her velvety skin. By the time he had her utterly, blessedly nude, they both quivered with desire.

While it was inevitable that he break her maidenhead, Ethan was loathe to *take* her virginity. He wanted very much that she give it to him freely, that the experience cause as little pain and as much pleasure as possible. "Tell me," he commanded.

Lily's gaze settled on his face. "Would you touch me again? Please," she added in a charming afterthought.

Ethan brought his hand to her woman's mound and rocked his wrist back and forth; the dark curls were already damp. Lily let out a mewling sound and wriggled against his hand. Ethan leaned over and again laved her breasts with his tongue while his fingers parted the delicate petals below. Slick warmth greeted him at her entrance. Slowly, he eased a finger inside. She tensed around him, then relaxed. He relished every involuntary gasp and twitch.

Lily's hands splayed wide, tangling into the bed sheets. Ethan pressed another finger inside, stretching and preparing her even as he drove her closer to the brink. His thumb rubbed lightly against her sensitive bud.

"Wait!" High pitched and bewildered, her voice cut through the air. "What's happening?" she asked. "My heart...Something is wrong."

"Nothing is wrong," he assured her. "You're going to climax." Ethan kissed her furrowed brow. "Trust me, princess, it's a very good thing."

"But what will it be like? How will I know?" Her wild, dark eyes searched his face as her thighs began to close. Ethan sensed her withdrawing, allowing doubt to creep in.

"Lily." It was both her name and a word of command. Her chin trembled as she met his steady gaze. "You have to let go, love—just let it happen." After a moment, he sensed her calming.

Ethan resumed his caresses, dipping in and out of her core. He kissed her, his tongue darting in the same rhythmic pace as his hand. When she tensed with the impending orgasm, he pulled back to watch.

Her back arched and her mouth fell open wide as her climax broke over her. Her sheath clenched around his fingers, grasping and releasing in waves. Lily's wordless cry was sweet music to his ears. Her features relaxed into a blissful glow, a sheen of perspiration on her forehead.

"That's my girl," he murmured.

She was the most beautiful thing he'd ever seen. He'd never been so aroused in his life, so driven to claim a woman. His raw nerves would take no further denial. He eased between her legs, his blunt tip pressing against her entrance.

"I'm going to enter you now, Lily." He was astonished he still had a scrap of rationality left in his mind to form a coherent sentence, much less take the time to explain to her what was about to happen. But some part of him needed this as much as the fulfillment—needed to take care of this woman, to prove her trust was not misplaced this time. "I'll try not to hurt you, princess, but—"

Words failed him as he slid into her slick heat. She was swollen with arousal and so, so tight. She whimpered. When she shifted beneath him, Ethan's vision went hazy and he was lost to the overpowering need thrumming between his legs.

He drove forward, scarcely slowed by her maidenhead. She cried out in pain. Ethan cursed himself and clutched her head to his chest. "I'm sorry," he rasped. "I'm so sorry, Lily. That's it, now, the worst is done."

She bit her lip, her eyes welling with tears, and nodded bravely.

"I promise this will feel as good as the other." Ethan shook his head and growled, unable to fight it any longer. "Oh, God, princess."

"It's all right," Lily said. "I'm all right."

Ethan moaned and leaned heavily over her as he worked long, slow strokes, trying to keep her first time easy. Lily brought her hands to his shoulders.

"Yes." The word tore from his throat. "Touch me."

She clung to him, her nails biting into his back as he drove on. Her hips rocked in time with the rhythm he set. Then those long legs crept up his sides and slipped around his thighs, pulling him in further and settling against him like the missing piece of a puzzle.

All at once, ecstasy tore through him. He roared to the ceiling as he emptied into her. An instant later, she joined him, this time crying out his name as she tightened around him, prolonging his orgasm.

Ethan collapsed on top of her, burying his face in the ample cushioning of her breasts. A trickle of sweat ran in the cleft between those magnificent globes; he lapped it up, savoring her salty musk.

After a moment he rolled to the side. He gathered her in his arms, a warm, loose-limbed bundle of woman. Lily smiled, a contented, lopsided grin. He'd never seen such a natural expression on her face before, absolutely free of artifice or guile. Something in his chest constricted at the sight. *He* had done this. A warm sensation of satisfaction spread through him at having done something right for a change. Maybe there was hope for him yet.

"So," Lily said in a tired, happy voice, "now I know."

His eyes crinkled as he smiled against her neck. "Yes," he agreed, "now you know." He nipped the place where her neck and shoulder met. Lily gasped. He felt himself already stirring to life again. "Would you like to know more?"

Chapter Fourteen

Sunlight crept through the spaces behind and between the heavy drapes, pulling Lily to groggy wakefulness. There was a dull ache between her legs and residual stickiness on her upper thighs. The evidence of the previous night's activities drew a grimace as she rolled to face the sleeping man beside her.

Ethan's features were slack; he lay on his side, his parted lips pushed into an irregular shape by the pillows. Dark stubble shadowed his jaw and cheeks; his sleep-tousled hair was barely more unruly than it was during his waking hours. A soft smile touched her lips as she allowed herself to do something she'd wanted to do since the moment she'd first seen him—she reached out and skimmed her fingers over and through his clipped hair. The wavy thatch on top tickled her palm, while the very short sides were like velvet.

He slept soundly, undisturbed by her touch. *And no wonder,* she thought wryly. He'd exerted himself a great deal last night.

Her eyes drifted closed as she recalled her initiation into the world of marital relations. It had been dark and pagan and wonderful. At his behest, she had relinquished the tight control she kept on herself and given her very body into his keeping.

Ethan had summoned a part of herself she hadn't known existed—a carnal creature who had no thought other than the fulfillment of desire, chasing pleasure and operating on base instinct. They'd made love two more times after the first—and each time the urgency of her need seemed greater than the previous. Each time she wantonly offered herself and welcomed his invasion.

And therein lay a problem.

Ethan snored and swiped at his nose before grumbling and burrowing deeper into the sheets. Lily sighed and looked up at the ceiling. Her eyes followed the circular, cloud-like whorls a fanciful artisan had brushed into the plaster.

The problem, as she saw it, was that she wasn't sure she liked that wild Lily. If she had learned anything during the past week, it was that she was not a woman who could simply lose control of herself—that way lay disaster, as evidenced by the marriage in which she had very suddenly found herself.

Further, the Lily who had been born last night—the lustful creature—was dependent upon Ethan. Last night, as she took him into her arms and body, she had allowed herself to imagine he harbored tender feelings toward her beyond physical attraction. In the light of day, she knew that simply wasn't true.

Lily had stood outside the study door when he'd talked with her father. She'd heard his angry roar when he discovered the dowry clause in the contract.

He didn't want to be married to her. He didn't care for anything but her money. Oh, he might have whispered endearments while he bucked against her, but that was just lust talking, not any true expression of sentiment. Last night had done irrevocable damage—she'd given up control of herself. Some part of her heart was already his, and she wasn't sure she'd ever get it back.

She couldn't afford to be foolish like that again. Her mind skipped to the future, envisioning herself as a bitter, lovelorn shadow of her former self, hoping and yearning for something that would never be.

Lily had to be smart about this. She had to regain and keep her footing. There had to be boundaries, parameters. Lily needed a *plan*. There was nothing she couldn't do if only she knew where to begin.

She jostled his shoulder. "Eth…Thorburn."

First boundary: no first names. It was a practice that only served to create an illusion of intimacy.

His hand clamped around her wrist and he rolled, pulling her arm around his side. He pinned her hand against his chest, his heart beat steady and firm beneath her palm. She felt it all the way up to her elbow, working its way into her own being.

The skin of his back was warm and smelled faintly of soap and his own potent maleness. She squeezed her eyes shut and fought the urge to kiss the place between his shoulder blades. Denying herself caused an unexpected slice of sorrow. Her breasts flattened against the plane of his back, yielding to him.

Everything about her body conspired to give way, she thought in despair, to be overwhelmed by this large, masterful man. How easy it would be to turn herself over to him completely. But if he was as reckless with her heart as he was with his money, she'd be destroyed. A shudder coursed up her spine at the thought.

"Thorburn," she said with more force, her resolve strengthening. When he still did not respond, she pursed her lips in annoyance. Vexed, she pinched his buttock, sinking her fingers into the firm muscle.

He let out a muffled groan and rolled onto his back. Lily propped up on an elbow as he awakened. His lids rose, revealing the startling slate blue of his eyes. They gradually focused on her face and then drifted down to where her bosom rested against his chest. His lips turned up in a crooked, sleepy smile as his heavy lids drifted closed again.

His hands lazily grazed up her sides, then patted her breasts. "Good morning, ladies."

Lily scoffed and rolled her eyes.

Ethan cracked one eye open. "And a good morning to you, lady wife. All rejuvenated now? Ready for a morning delight?" His hands moved to her back. One cupped her neck, while the other traced down her spine, caressing the cleft between her buttocks.

An orb of heat thrummed in her belly. Ethan's hand slipped between her legs, probing and parting. She whimpered. *No!* She reminded herself. This would not do.

Lily disengaged herself and sat up, pulling the bed sheet to cover her chest. Her tangled dark hair spilled over her hands onto the snowy white linens. "My lord, I did not wake you to do *that*."

Ethan flung an arm over his eyes. "Pity."

"I should like a word," she continued. "I would appreciate it if you'd attend."

Ethan's arm shifted; she saw one shaded eye narrowed on her face. "I'm listening."

She cleared her throat and licked her lips. This would have been easier if she'd already had her chocolate. Briefly, she wondered if there was even any chocolate in the house. "Concerning the subject of our marriage," she began, "I think it best if we establish some rules—let each other know up front what we can expect." She plucked at the sheet, her gaze sliding sideways.

Ethan lowered his arm and laid his hands atop his chest. His face was shuttered, his expression guarded. "What kind of rules?"

A nervous knot twisted in her middle. Why did she suddenly feel as though she was wronging him in some way? That was ridiculous. In truth, she was protecting them both—herself from his inevitable rejection and him from having to reject her at all. He was an aristocrat. Gentlemen did not want to be bothered with their wives' emotions.

"You should know," she blurted, "that I am only interested in a conventional society marriage. I do not plan to interfere with your life, nor do I wish you to interfere in mine."

Ethan pushed himself up to a sitting position. The sheet fell around his thighs, granting her full view of his naked torso and groin. She jerked her eyes back to his face.

"A society marriage?" His lips curled around the words as though they tasted bad. "What does that mean, Lily?"

She gestured with a hand. "That—*that*, for instance. You ought not call me by my Christian name, and I ought not use yours. I would prefer to call you Thorburn, if it's all the same to you."

Storm clouds seemed to gather around him, sucking all the light out of the room. "And what am I supposed to call you, princess? Shall I call you Thorburn, as well?"

Heat flooded her cheeks. "If you'd like," she said archly. "Lady Thorburn would do."

"You like the sound of your title, then? How fortunate that I could give you a wedding gift without spending a shilling." He punched up a pillow before leaning back, arms crossed over his chest.

She flinched, but pressed on. "And I should like to have my own room. That's what is done."

Ethan exhaled loudly through his nostrils and pressed a hand to his forehead. His little finger trembled. "And just how do you suppose that's going to happen? Now's as good a time as any to inform you I'm still entirely penniless. Your father—"

"I know what my father did," she snapped.

Lily swung her legs over the mattress and hurried to retrieve a fresh chemise from her bag. With his icy gaze on her, she felt more naked and exposed than at any time during their passionate night.

She turned her back as she struggled with the garment. Lily missed Moira, but her pauper of a husband couldn't afford to pay her maid. "I know, too, what you have to do to earn the money. I shall tell my father when I'm happy, and I'm telling *you* what will make me happy." She selected a morning dress and pulled it over her head. As she smoothed the fabric over her hips, his voice drew her attention.

"So we're to lead separate lives?" His mouth twisted in a bitter frown.

Lily faltered. "Well, yes, my lord, that's how it is done. Is this not what you want?"

His brooding demeanor puzzled her—was it possible he wanted something from this marriage besides her dowry?

For a long moment he stared at her, fury roiling through his eyes. Lily remembered the wolf-hungry look, the flashes of temper that left her trembling. Then he drew a steadying breath, his features arranging themselves into perfect aristocratic blandness.

"Of course it's what I want." His words were clipped, precise. "Thank you for sparing me from having to broach the subject."

The minuscule bit of hope she'd harbored sizzled away like a drop of water on a hot skillet. She made to leave.

"Lady Thorburn," he said in a polite tone that still somehow came out dripping with disdain, "one more thing."

Lily turned and was startled by the glacial coldness of his stare.

"You shall have your society marriage, but I shall have my heir. You may not deny me your bed. Do you understand?"

She quailed. This was the one aspect of their marriage she wished she could stop dead, the part that would erode her soul until there was nothing left of herself, if last night was any indication. "I…I…" she stammered.

The sound of a bell broke the tension. "I think someone is here. I shall see who it is." She fled before he could demand her compliance.

Lily flew down the stairs. The bell rang again, but it came from below, not the front door. She made her way to the servants' door and, curious, opened it.

"There you are, Miss Lily!" Moira's face broke into a wide grin. Behind her lady's maid were five other servants from home, all carrying carpetbags.

Lily marveled at the sight of so many friendly faces. "What are you doing here?"

"Mr. Bachman sent us, Miss Lily," said a footman. "He said we was to come take care of you."

It was like every birthday of her life had come all at once. Laughing and clapping in delight, she stepped aside to admit the servants.

"What's this?"

She glanced over her shoulder to find Ethan standing there in his breeches and shirt, filling the hallway with his imposing presence so none could pass.

"My father's sent them," Lily explained.

"Send them back," he snapped. "I can't pay them."

"Begging your pardon, my lord, but Mr. Bachman is still paying our wages," the footman interjected.

Ethan's jaw worked side to side as he cast a scrutinizing look over the servants, whose cheerful faces had begun to fall under his glowering expression. "Do as you will." He turned on a heel and strode into the gloomy depths of the basement.

Moira patted her shoulder and made a comment as the Bachman servants filed into the house, but Lily didn't hear her. Her eyes remained where her husband had disappeared, taking the joy she'd felt in her father's gift with him.

Chapter Fifteen

Ethan checked his watch again. Seven forty-five. He muttered in annoyance as he returned the timepiece to his pocket.

"Now, now," Lord Hollier said. His gray head bobbed up and down. "You mustn't be too put out, Thorburn. New brides are flighty creatures and we must grant them allowances. I daresay she's beside herself learning to manage a household for the first time."

Ethan quirked a brow and shook his head. "Many descriptors fit my wife, Hollier, but flighty is not one of them. And managing things comes as naturally to her as breathing." He cast a regretful look at his hostess. "My sincerest apologies, Lady Hollier. I can't imagine what's keeping Lady Thorburn." *Other than her desire to make a complete fool of me,* he thought blackly.

"Perhaps she's indisposed," the old lady suggested. "Young women are inclined to take ill this time of year. All the parties and balls do begin to wear on one after a while."

Ethan hadn't the heart to remind Lady Hollier that he and his new wife were not widely received. The scandal surrounding their hasty marriage had dropped them from many guest lists, although Ethan knew all would be forgiven by next Season. In the fortnight they'd been married, Lily had only been called upon by her intimate friends, Ladies Naomi and Janine Lockwood.

"Shall we go on with supper?" Lord Hollier asked. He patted his midsection. "I hate to not wait upon a lady, but my dyspepsia flares up if I go too long without eating."

A cold knot of embarrassment twisted Ethan's stomach. How could she do this to him? How could she be so rude to their hosts—especially when they'd received next to no invitations as it was?

"I'm terribly sorry," he apologized again. "I know you've gone to such trouble on our behalf, but if it's all the same, I should go home." He nodded to Lady Hollier. "Maybe Lady Thorburn is unwell. 'Twould be remiss not to look in on her."

Lord Hollier made a clicking sound. He patted his wife's knee. "You go along, my dear. I shall have a word with Thorburn and join you in a moment."

The butler was summoned and the aged retainer escorted Lady Hollier out of the parlor. Ethan couldn't be sure which of that pair offered more support to the other.

When they'd gone, he blew his cheeks out and turned his gaze back to Lord Hollier.

"Rocky start?" the older man asked.

Ethan exhaled a rueful sigh. "Still trying to find our stride, I suppose."

"Give it some time," the old man advised. He laughed, a dry, wheezing sound. "When Lady Hollier and I were newly wed, I once called her by my mistress's name in bed."

Ethan winced and made a sympathetic whistle.

"It all works itself out in the end."

"Does it?" His parents' marriage had never worked out, except to a miserable failure—which was one kind of end, he mused. *And look at you, already heading down that path.*

Lord Hollier leaned forward in his seat. "Speaking of..." He waved a hand as he spoke in a low voice. "Do you still see Mrs. Myles?"

"I do," Ethan affirmed, "as often as I can—at least two or three times each week."

The old man grunted. "You're a good lad. How is she?"

"Not well, unfortunately. But her new nurse has her on a routine that keeps the worst of her episodes at bay."

A heavy sigh escaped Lord Hollier's lips. "That's too bad. Give her my regards, if you would be so kind." He slapped his thighs and hauled himself up. "I suppose I must join Lady Hollier now. If I'm not quick enough, she'll eat all the pudding."

They parted ways in the entry hall. Lord Hollier smiled genially as they shook hands. "My compliments to your lady," he said. "You'll come again, of course—when you've got it all sorted out."

Ethan felt another stab of chagrin.

He stopped at the curb. There was a hackney stand at the corner. "Blast it," he muttered. He strode on past the tired old carriages available for hire. In his present mood, it would do him good to burn some energy off before he got home. The brass tip of his walking stick tapped an every-other-step tattoo against the walk.

The dark streets held no terrors for Ethan. He almost hoped a footpad did accost him—it would give him a marvelous excuse to beat something to a bloody pulp.

His confounded wife had, in the short span of just a few weeks, humiliated him at almost every level. She didn't give a thought for how his own reputation had suffered when the Vauxhall Gardens fiasco was made public. True, he was already considered a rake, but now he was seen as a seducer of virgins. She and her father had colluded to embarrass him in regards to his finances—first by withholding her dowry, and then by sending servants to his house to rub in the fact that he couldn't provide for his wife. And now, she furthered his social degradation by failing to put in an appearance at the Holliers'. There were few people left in the world who held Ethan in good esteem. Lord and Lady Hollier were amongst that dwindling group, and her actions threatened to take even this away from him.

He growled and swung his stick at a manicured boxwood, sending a spray of little green leaves flying into the air.

The hell of it was, of course, that he had to sit back and take it if he stood any chance of her reporting herself happily married. Once he had his hands on that money, though…

He smirked as he considered the possibilities. He could send her to the family heap to keep his father company. They could pass their days being nasty to one another. He could pack her off to Greece to live with his mother, who might find a daughter-in-law a diverting addition to her household. He could remove himself to the Continent, he mused. He'd never had a Tour, but with Bonaparte exiled, travel would soon be safe again.

Ghita would be his mistress soon, he supposed. She might like a trip home to Italy. Together, they could travel the world and leave Lily behind to stew in her proper society life.

Ethan could live very well on that dowry money until he came into his own inheritance. And eventually, Mr. Bachman would pass on, leaving everything to Lily. But since everything belonging to his wife was legally his…

A great, rich future loomed before him, wherein he could do exactly as he pleased. So why did his ideas make him feel vile and wretched? He scowled all the harder. All he had to do was wait. Until then, he would bide his time, try to make Lily happy, and get her with child, too.

A vision of Lily round with his child danced in his mind. It was an erotic thought. Sadly, they'd not had another night as unrestrained as their wedding night. Lily had shut down sexually, keeping her eyes squeezed shut while he went through the motions of intercourse. The last time, he'd been so put off by her frigidness, his erection wilted before he completed the act. He hadn't touched her in a week.

She would enjoy a babe, though. Having a child to direct her energies toward would take the sting off their eventual separation—if she even noticed him leaving. A pang of regret shot through Ethan. He wished it weren't this way, but Lily made it abundantly clear through word and deed that she was uninterested in anything beyond the most superficial of marriages. As long as it didn't disintegrate into violence and hatred as his parents' relationship had done, Ethan could say he'd done better than they. The thought did not cheer him.

He mounted the steps, the swept bricks secure beneath his boots. The Bachman servants may be symbolically emasculating, he mused, but they did make life more pleasant.

A footman opened the door. "Good evening, my lord."

Not knowing the man who opened one's door was unsettling. When that dowry materialized, hiring a staff of his own choosing was on his list of priorities. "Is her ladyship at home?"

"No, sir. I believe she had a meeting with Mr. Wickenworth."

"At this hour?" Ethan frowned. "When is she expected back?"

The footman's pleasant demeanor began to crumble under Ethan's piercing scrutiny. "She didn't say, my lord."

Ethan made a disgusted sound. He turned toward the stairs and was halted by the jarring sight of two marble pedestals flanking the banisters, each supporting a porcelain urn.

He pointed at the alien objects and pinned the servant in an accusing glare. "Where did these come from?"

The footman's weight shifted back and forth on his feet, as though preparing to make a dash for it. "They were delivered this afternoon, my lord. I believe the pillars came from a statuary merchant on Piccadilly—"

"Were they a gift?"

The servant's eyes widened and he took a tiny step back. "No, my lord."

"Have them returned," Ethan ordered.

The servant straightened. "But Miss Lily—"

"*Lady Thorburn* should know better than to make purchases she can't afford," Ethan bellowed.

He hated the way the servants were all so unflinchingly Lily's. She'd made him a guest in his own house. It occurred to him to sit them all down and make them write *Lily Helling, Viscountess Thorburn* a hundred times apiece, but it wouldn't matter. They'd all call her Miss Lily in the next breath.

The blood drained from the footman's face. His eyes lifted to the staircase.

Ethan turned, expecting to see someone, but there was no one there. "I know it is difficult to see your mistress do without the comforts to which she is accustomed," he said in a more moderate tone, "but this household is on the tightest of budgets. For God's sake, man, you're on Mr. Bachman's payroll, not mine. Please see to having those pillars and urns returned tomorrow."

The footman made a whimpering sound, then nodded.

Odd fellow, Ethan thought as he ascended the stairwell.

He blew out his cheeks, trying to wash away his annoyance. Bad enough that he must confront Lily for not showing at the Holliers'—he didn't want another argument about a silly couple of pillars.

A soft glow from the parlor spilled into the corridor as he reached for his study door. He paused and stared at his closed door. Golden lamplight cast a yellow gleam onto the white painted surface. Something was wrong. His brows drew together as he tried to put his finger on the source of his disquiet.

Lamplight.

He turned, a sinking feeling in his chest. Ethan crossed the hall slowly. He braced his palm against the partially opened parlor door and pushed.

And stared, in horror, at a room full of furnishings.

He stepped into the room to gawk at the interior. A claw-footed sofa dominated the new seating area, upholstered in brilliant canary. Bolsters trimmed with black tassels were nestled against each scrolled arm. The sofa faced the fireplace, and was flanked on one side by a chaise longue upholstered in striped damask, and on the other by two generously cushioned chairs. A two-light bronze oil lamp stood on a little stand between the sofa and the chairs, providing the light that had drawn his attention. At the far end of the room, four wooden armchairs stood around an elegant circular table. It would be a lovely setting for tea, or an after-dinner game of whist.

"What have you done?" His voice rasped with disbelief. Now he knew what the footman had been so worked up about, and with good reason, he supposed. Two little pillars in the entrance hall were nothing compared to this.

"It has to go back." He turned on a heel to see his own stupid decorative platter still residing on the mantelpiece over the fireplace, now nestled amongst an assortment of other *objects d'art*. "Everything. It has to go." He raked his hands through his hair.

How *could* she? She knew he didn't have the money to pay for any of this. Unless she was trying to tell him something. The thought niggled at his mind. He plopped into one of the chairs and grimaced at the supreme comfort of the piece. She *would* select chairs he'd fall in love with. "Damn it all," he muttered.

His fingers drummed against the padded arm, a dull sound swallowed up by the fortune of furnishings he suddenly found himself owning.

Perhaps she meant to have her father give him the dowry money, in which case he could afford a hundred parlors similarly appointed. That was a cheering idea.

Or, said a cruel voice inside, *perhaps she already hates you just as your mother hates your father, means to destroy you completely, and is having a bit of a lark as she drives you into the ground.*

At last, he heard the front door open and close. Her footsteps sounded light on the stairs. She paused on the landing. In his mind's eye, he saw her pivoting to continue up to the second floor.

"Lil-ady Thorburn," he called, wincing at his trip of the tongue. It wasn't as though he'd been calling the woman by her given name for years—why did it rankle so to not use it?

The female in question materialized in the doorway, wearing a fetching ensemble. A white dress skimmed her hips and thighs, while the light gray spencer on top clung to her breasts like the skin of a fruit, tempting him to peel it away. A smart plaid hat ornamented with a black plume sat atop her head at a becoming angle. Neatly arranged curls peeked from beneath the brim, accentuating the perfect curve of her brow and jawline.

His body hardened. Ethan ruthlessly clamped down on his lust. For her own indiscernible reasons, Lily had chosen to pretend their one night of unrestrained passion never happened. He couldn't toss her into bed as he longed to do. There were other matters to address, besides. Though stoking his ire for her failure to make their dinner appointment was difficult when she looked so delectable.

The briefest of smiles flitted across her lips, never touching her eyes. Her hands tangled in her reticule cord. "Good evening, my lord."

Waving a hand, he beckoned her in. "Come and see, my dear. The patron saint of furnishings has paid us a visit. He must have taken pity on our sorry home and granted us a parlor for entertaining."

With a guarded set to her jaw, she lifted her chin. "There's no call for sarcasm."

He raised a brow. "I am not being sarcastic, and I resent the implication. To the contrary, my lady, I feel certain to the deepest marrow of my being that we must have been granted a boon by some supernatural entity—be it sprite, saint, or demon—because the constraints of the present household budget do not allow for costly decorating. Tell me, Lily, where have you been?"

She pressed a hand to her temple. "The way you careen from one point of conversation to another quite makes my head spin."

Good. Just looking at her made his head spin, and he couldn't do anything about it. Fair enough if she was likewise discombobulated.

"Furthermore," she said, adopting the governess tone he was coming to abhor, "I must once again remind you not to take liberties with my Christian name, please."

He gave his most self-deprecating smile. "Of course, my dear Lady Thorburn. And yet, I still find myself ignorant as to your whereabouts this evening. If you'd be so good as to enlighten me?"

Lily twitched her skirts to the side as sat on the sofa. She fingered the black tassel on the bolster. "What happened to not interfering in each other's lives?"

Impossible woman! Why did she have to bristle up like a hedgehog at every turn? "I do not mean to interfere," he explained. "The Holliers, however, were disappointed that you did not come to supper as we'd committed to do." *And me,* he thought petulantly. *But you don't care about disappointing me.*

Gloved fingers covered her mouth. "The Holliers!" she exclaimed from behind her hand. "Oh, dear, it quite slipped my mind. When I heard from Mr. Wickenworth, I had to go to his office straightaway. The bill of sale and transferring the deed took longer than I expected. It was careless of me to forget—"

"A moment." He raised a hand to halt her speech, waiting to quell the surge of disbelief and shock ringing in his ears. He cleared his throat. "A...deed you say? Bill of sale?"

She nodded. "I bought the property for my school. A lovely situation in King's Cross—convenient to Mayfair, but still respectable."

"*You* bought a property?"

Lily shrugged. "With my father's money, of course. It's in his name, but I have full legal authority over it. Power of something-or-other, they call it."

He straightened. "Your father's..." His gaze darted around the parlor, taking in the furnishings in a new light. "Did he...?"

She shot him a half-smile. "No, I did. He gave me the money, yes, but I bought these things. Last week, actually." She stood up and took a turn around the room. "It's not finished yet, of course—rugs, new draperies..."

Humiliation burned his cheeks. "My dear, I must say, I don't agree with having Mr. Bachman furnish the house. For one thing, I was never consulted in the matter, and this *is* my house. You can't just begin filling it with things willy-nilly. Secondly, how do you suppose it looks from the outside for..."

From the mantelpiece, she plucked a bundle of fabric Ethan had not previously noticed. At first he took them for rags, but then he noticed the binding holding them together.

He craned his neck. "What's that?"

"Fabric samples," Lily explained. "For the draperies. It would very much *please me* to order the new ones within the week."

Ethan bit his tongue and slumped back into his chair. She was going to make an issue of this, setting it as a condition of marital happiness. *Fine.* What were a few sticks of furniture, if it ended with him having her dowry?

She brought the fabric samples back to the sofa and sat next to the lamp. Ethan watched her flip through them.

"You missed supper," he said.

Lily glanced up from the fabrics. "We've already discussed that."

"The Holliers are my friends," Ethan continued, his tone growing more terse. "You were rude not to send word; I was personally embarrassed, and still haven't eaten. Not to mention, we've scarce done anything together since the wedding."

"By all means, eat something," she said, seemingly absorbed in the selection of fabrics. "Oh, I do like this damask," she breathed. "It would make a lovely spread in my room."

Her room. Ethan glowered.

The day after the second bout of wretched sexual intercourse, she'd moved into a vacant guest room. Her blasted servants had fetched her entire bedroom ensemble from her parents' home. She had practically resumed her old life, pretending he wasn't even there.

Unfortunately, most ladies *did* have their own rooms—he could not deny his viscountess the same. Forcing her to sleep in his bed when she'd made it clear she found the practice distasteful would be counterproductive, in any event.

"I'm sure it would be lovely," he said.

"Are you?" Her voice carried a shrewd tone that set him on edge. She flipped through the fabrics. "I think this one would do for the draperies in here. What do you think?"

Ethan gave the scrap only a cursory glance, just enough to detect a revolting checkered pattern in black and pea green. Any fool could see it wouldn't suit the décor, at all. "An excellent selection, my dear."

Her cheeks flushed in high color. "Fine," she snapped. "This it shall be, then."

"I look forward to seeing the finished pieces grace the parlor. They are sure to provide many years of enjoyment." He slapped a thigh with his hand. "Well, I'm off, then. I just wanted to be sure you hadn't missed our engagement for reason of illness, injury, or untimely demise."

When Ethan rose, she inhaled, her lips parted.

He paused, expecting her to speak. *Ask me where I'm going. Ask me to stay. Tell me you miss me like I miss you.*

She didn't, of course.

"Good evening, my lord," she said with a cool incline of her head.

"My lady." He nodded once and stepped purposefully out the door, though he hadn't the foggiest idea where he was going.

*

"I 'ear congratulations are in order, milord."

Ethan looked over the rim of his glass of Scotch. Edmund Ficken stood before the corner table where Ethan had ensconced himself, wrapped in a cloud of cigar smoke like a mist-shrouded wraith in a graveyard. The skinny man clutched the brim of his hat at his chest. Ethan made a disgusted sound before tossing back the remainder of his beverage. "Save the humble butcher act for the rest of this lot." He jerked his chin to indicate the other patrons of the hell.

Ficken's gaze skipped over the tables occupied by men and women deep in game and even deeper in their cups. He smiled, a cold, calculating twitch of the lips that cut through the haze in Ethan's brain like a dunk in an icy pond. "So I shall, milord." He nodded, a signal of recognition from one swindler to another.

It was the most honest moment Ethan had ever shared with the man, and it unnerved him. In a flash, the ruthless gamester was gone, tucked away, replaced once more by the socially inferior Ficken the *ton* accepted as an entertaining novelty.

The butcher ran a hand over his thin, slick hair. "Are y'not playing? The hazard table looks to have good action tonight."

Ethan's eyes slid to the game Ficken indicated. A merry group stood around the table, men with their arms twined around the corset-slimmed waists of painted ladies. As the fellow with the dice rolled them in his hand, the group chorused an anticipatory sound. He threw, and the group let out a simultaneous, "Ah!" Then they cheered and clapped, while the caster let out an exultant whoop—he'd rolled the main.

"Lucky bastard," Ethan muttered under his breath. To Ficken, he said, "Don't care to play."

Ficken snorted. "That'll be the day, eh?" Without invitation, he pulled out the chair opposite Ethan and folded himself into it, resting his hat on his knee. Ethan's jaw clenched. He occupied himself watching the gamers, hoping Ficken would go away if he ignored him.

"You've just married the biggest stack of blunt this side of the Exchequer," the grating, reedy voice proclaimed.

Ethan staunchly ignored him.

"I've still got a pile of notes with your name scrawled all over them. Now that you've the means and then some—"

"How much?" Ethan ground out. He turned a glacial stare on Ficken, who cleared his throat and shifted.

"Sixty-five hundred." Ficken swallowed; the lump in his throat bobbed down and then up again. He shrugged and affected an air of long suffering. "I should hate to sell them notes to a lender, but a man deserves what he's due, I say."

Ethan leaned back in his chair and crossed his legs at the ankle. "Mr. Ficken," he said in a bored drawl, "I do hate to be put in the position of illuminating a deficiency on your part, but I wouldn't like your ignorance to cause you undue difficulty."

Ficken's brows drew together. "Whaddya mean?"

It was nice to see the uppity mushroom squirming for a change. Ethan's lip twitched. "What I mean, my chap, is that gentlemen settle their debts with other gentlemen first and foremost. For one so firmly latched onto the teat of the privileged class, you exhibit a shocking lack of insight."

Ficken's face darkened. "Now see 'ere, Thorburn. These days, I'm a *gentleman* every bit as much as any of yer cronies. Soon's I buy m'self some land, won't you nor anyone else be able to deny—"

In one swift motion, Ethan was across the table, his fist tangled in the limp lapel of Ficken's cheap suit. "All the money in the world won't buy you what you want," he growled. The butcher shrank back, sinking into the voluminous coat. "No matter how much wealth you fling about, you'll always be on the fringe—too jumped-up for your old world, and never good enough for mine. You're a *poseur*, and you always will be."

Ficken's mouth worked soundlessly.

Ethan blinked, then tossed the man to the floor, as though flicking an insect from his hand.

The butcher scrambled to his feet, wiping the saggy knees of his breeches and then his sleeves. He placed his hat on his head and tugged the brim, concealing his beady eyes in shadow. "Be that as it may, milord, you're gonna wish you hadn't done that." The gloomy, smoke-filled gaming pit swallowed his retreating form.

After he disappeared, Ethan poured himself another drink. He industriously set about becoming blindingly drunk, hoping that by morning he'd have forgotten that from the instant he launched himself across the table until he released the man, he hadn't been talking to Ficken at all, but to his beautiful, scheming wife.

Chapter Sixteen

Miss Cuthbert, the new headmistress of the freshly dubbed King's Cross Vocational School for Young Ladies, cast a dubious expression at Lily. She hovered on the other side of the desk in Lily's new office, a stack of papers clutched to her chest in her work-worn, capable hands.

Lily scooted her chair over a bit. "I'm quite serious, Miss Cuthbert. Please, come 'round and join me." As if to punctuate the remark, a hammer pounded home in a nearby room.

The middle-aged woman set the papers on the desk and brought a chair around while wearing a guarded expression, as though awaiting the punch line of Lily's jest. Lily wrinkled her brow and shook her head at Miss Cuthbert's suspicion. It had always felt natural for Lily to sit beside her father when going over business matters, but it seemed not everyone found the gesture as reassuring as she.

The unease in the woman's eyes put Lily in mind of how her husband had looked at her this morning when she'd joined him for breakfast. What else was she supposed to do? He was the one up unusually early—and of course, Lily had to exercise good manners. It didn't hurt that her breath had hitched in her throat at the sight of him in his dove gray morning coat. Why couldn't people just trust her good intentions?

"Now then," she began when the headmistress settled herself, determined to put Ethan out of mind for the time being, "tell me about the progress you've made on tutors."

Miss Cuthbert nodded once, a firm motion of her silver-streaked head. "Yes, my lady. As you can see," she said, pulling a paper from her pile, "I've received quite a few letters regarding our various positions. Here are the names, and those are the references to go through."

Lily watched Miss Cuthbert peruse the list. The woman seemed to contemplate each name, weighing her choices. While it remained to be seen how Miss Cuthbert would perform once the school was up and running, Lily was thus far pleased with her first hire.

Heavy footsteps in the hallway preceded a knock on the door.

"Enter," Lily called.

The door opened, admitting a man covered in plaster dust and wood shavings. He took one look at the neat office and its two very clean inhabitants, and stayed in the doorway. When he ducked his head, a shower of white particles slid from his cap to Lily's rug. "Beggin' your pardon, milady."

"What can I do for you?"

The large man shifted in his scuffed shoes, the color of which was eradicated by drifts of dust and dirt. "Things are goin' along well downstairs, milady, it's jus' we came to this part on the plan for one of the rooms, and I wasn't sure what it means, is all."

Lily tilted her head. "Which room would that be?"

"Well, milady, the architect's note says 'bath-room,' with some lines comin' out the wall, and me and the lads don't know what to do with all that."

"It's exactly what it says—a *bath-room*."

A look of consternation passed over his face. "You mean a whole room jus' for taking a bath?"

She sighed. This was the third time this week she'd had to explain the concept. Lily was disappointed that those around her did not seem as willing as she to embrace architectural innovations. "Yes, a whole room just for taking a bath. With a dozen girls living in one house, the kitchen boiler might do nothing but heat bathwater all day. It is much more sensible to have a bath-room with its own supply of heated water."

The laborer's thoughtful eyes rolled to the ceiling, his mouth slack.

"It is quite efficient," Miss Cuthbert contributed.

Lily smirked. Just a few days ago, the woman had railed against the idea, citing what she was sure were prohibitive costs and waste of space.

"Well…" the man responded. "I s'pose it's your place and you ken do as you want with 'er, but I can't make heads nor tails of them plans."

"You don't have to," Lily snapped. "The architect will be here on Thursday to oversee the bath-room himself, since pipes will have to be laid and…" She made an exasperated sound. "Don't fret over it, all right? Now, if you'll please excuse me, I have other things to—Good God, what are you doing here?"

Ethan's eyebrows shot up his forehead. "And a very good day to you, m'dear." He glanced sideways at the dusty fellow beside him, who shrank back from the impeccably dressed nobleman.

Entering the small office as if it were his own study, he turned the full force of his charming smile on Miss Cuthbert. "I don't believe I've had the pleasure, madam."

The seduction dripping from his words made Lily roll her eyes. Miss Cuthbert let out a little squeak.

"Miss Cuthbert," Lily said, "please allow me to introduce my husband, Lord Thorburn. My lord, this is Miss Cuthbert, headmistress of King's Cross Vocational."

Ethan came around the desk and took the older woman's hand, which he made a show of bowing over. "Your servant, ma'am."

The woman's arm went limp like a noodle beneath Ethan's touch.

Lily shook her head. "That'll be all for now, Miss Cuthbert."

The headmistress turned and looked at Lily over her shoulder, a blank expression on her face. She blinked. "Oh, yes." A flush crept up her cheeks. "Until later, my lady. My lord." She scurried from Lily's office.

The sound of the door slamming home still rang in her ears when Lily rounded on Ethan. "Nicely done, Thorburn. You've proved you can charm the virtue out of a spinster with next to no effort—you must be proud of yourself."

His jaw cocked to the side. "I am, actually."

Lily snorted in disgust. He'd spent the month of their marriage either blithely going along with whatever she said—his way of ignoring her, she was convinced—or dashing off sarcastic remarks. She hadn't heard a sincere statement pass his lips since their one ill-advised night of passion.

On the one hand, his boorish behavior made their uncomplicated society marriage easier to maintain. On the other, however, she missed him. There was something there, she was certain, if only he would reach out for it.

Shut it, she scolded herself. *She* might feel something there, but that didn't mean *he* did. Without the proper defenses in place, Lily knew she could be reduced to a limp bit of quivering female as easily as Miss Cuthbert had been.

"What do you want, Thorburn?"

He shrugged. "My day brought me into the vicinity, so I thought I'd pop in and see the place." Sunlight streaming through the picture window caught his irises as he inspected the office, lending them a blue translucency. The clear depths evidenced there quite took Lily's breath. Had she not already been seated, her shaky knees would have unceremoniously deposited her in the chair.

She cleared her throat and straightened the stack of reference letters to cover a sudden fit of nerves. "Does it meet your approval, my lord?" Her eyes latched onto the applicant's name in the top letter, but she felt the weight of his appraising gaze settle on her.

"Ethan. And as to my approval, I really can't say, as I've not been afforded the opportunity to inspect the property." Lily glanced up. "I should like to know how my wife passes her days." His voice was quiet, only a few notches more than a whisper. "Would you give me a tour, princess?"

Lily's chest tightened at the endearment. She'd not heard it in weeks, and it speared right through her carefully maintained walls. Damn the man! No matter how she tried to shut him out, he found a way past her locks and barricades as swiftly as a master housebreaker.

"All right," she demurred. "I'll show you about, but then I must get back to work."

A brief smile flitted across his lips. "Thank you. After you, my dear."

"We'll begin at the kitchen," she blurted. She flew down the stairs, wanting to get through the tour and send him on his way without allowing him to see what a besotted little fool she was.

This way, he might come to respect her and her work. But if he knew how she wanted to bury her face against his chest, how she longed to feel his arms wrap around her and hear words he could never possibly say…

Ethan Helling wasn't capable of love, she thought as she rounded the landing to descend to ground level. He was too damaged by his wretched childhood, too cynical as an adult. Rejection was the only possible outcome if he learned of her blasted feelings, and that would destroy her. It was far better to prevent herself from loving him—better for them both.

Smells of dirt and fresh-cut wood filled the air as she led him into the spacious kitchen. Several workmen chipped away old, broken terra cotta tiles to make way for the new floor. The sound of hammers striking chisels rang through the air. Lily covered her ears. Ethan took a cursory look around the room and nodded. The cacophony of demolition followed them down the hallway, but conversation became possible.

"There's a gaping hole where a range and boiler ought to be," Ethan said.

"We ripped out the old open range. A fully enclosed one will be installed in its place. It should be here next week."

They came upon another group of workmen gathered around a table where the renovation plans were laid out. One of them jabbed at the paper and made agitated gestures with his head. Disapproving and confused expressions marked the faces of the other men.

"They don't understand my bath-room," Lily explained.

His head cocked to the side. "Bath-room?"

Lily sighed. "You, too?" She folded her arms beneath her breasts and prepared to explain, yet again, the concept of a room set aside for hygiene.

"I know what a bath-room is, Lily," he said, forestalling her lecture. "But I've not seen one yet. When will the work be done?"

Lily blinked. "Oh! Well, the architect will be here on Thursday to oversee the beginning of the work." She turned and gestured toward the room next to the work crew. Envisioning the completed project, her words came out in an animated tumble. "It'll be quite an undertaking—pipes must be laid to tap into the water main. Fortunately, we can go on and run water to the kitchen, as well. Then the walls and floors will have to be finished, and finally the bathing equipment will be installed. The bath-room will have a dedicated boiler, of course, and the tub will feature a shower mechanism, as well. I think that would be the most efficient way to get a dozen girls in and out." When she looked up at Ethan, he was watching her with an amused turn to his lips. The corners of his eyes were soft. Lily flushed.

"It's marvelous," he said. "Ingenious, even." He stepped closer to Lily. She backed away, halting only when her shoulder blades met the cool wall. The tender gleam in Ethan's eyes turned hungry as his large frame boxed her in. Lily swallowed and then ducked to the side.

"Let's continue," she said in a breathless rush. "I really don't have all day to give you, my lord. Things to do, you understand."

Ethan chuckled as he followed her up the stairs.

In a front room, tattered wallpaper hung in strips and plaster dust covered the floorboards. Lily's voice reverberated off the bare walls and floor. "This room shall serve several purposes—pianoforte, singing, dancing, and etiquette instruction, as well as functioning as a proper drawing room."

Lily planted her hands on her hips and looked around the space. Its dilapidation reminded her of the house she shared with Ethan, but while the home she'd come into through marriage had the sad air of a structure in decline, this space was filled with the happy anticipation of renovation and renewal. Her mind swirled with desires and hopes for King's Cross Vocational. It would be a marvelous place, a sanctuary from her unhappy marriage.

Ethan's hand on her elbow brought her out of her reverie. "I'm not interrupting an angelic visitation, I hope?" Lily scowled, at which Ethan quirked a brow. "That's more like it. For a moment there, you were so ensconced in a beatific glow, I wondered if the Rapture was upon us."

"You *would* have to ask," Lily shot back.

"Just so," Ethan merrily agreed.

Lily harrumphed and swept out of the parlor, Ethan's steps hounding her from behind. The man was unflappable when he wanted to be, refusing to take offense at outlandish remarks. In Lily's experience, it didn't take much to wound a man's pride. The smallest slight against a fellow's character could have him crying for pistols at dawn. Yet Ethan took slander against the state of his eternal soul in infuriatingly good stride. What did it take to provoke this male?

Perhaps he just doesn't care about you enough to be provoked. Lily winced at the stinging thought, but she couldn't deny its plausibility.

"My dear," Ethan said behind her, "don't forget we're engaged to dine with the Holliers this evening. After the fiasco last time they invited us, we should make every effort at punctuality. We're expected at seven."

Lily frowned. He only cared about maintaining appearances for his friends. He wanted to be accompanied by his *wife*, not by her. Abruptly, she swiveled. Ethan was too close to stop in time, and walked right into her, knocking her off balance. An arm as firm as steel clamped around her waist and pulled her hard against him from shoulders to knees.

She inhaled at the unexpected contact. It was marvelous to be pressed against him, to feel him holding her, if only for a moment. A heated look passed between them, but Ethan released her and took a step back. "I beg your pardon," he said coolly.

She lifted her chin and narrowed her eyes in challenge. "I don't know whether I'll be able to attend this evening. As you can see, there is much to be done here. You will please give my regrets to the Holliers, in the event I am unable to join you?"

His eyes darkened and a muscle in his jaw twitched.

Lily quailed in the face of his temper, but saw in it the faintest glimmer of hope. If her missing their supper engagement could upset him, maybe it wasn't all lost, after all.

But as fast as his temper had flared, it cooled again. His lips flicked in that sarcastic little smile of his that she was coming to recognize as the mark of his disdain. "As you wish. Although, I must insist you commit yourself one way or another. I shall not inconvenience our friends again."

So bland, so indifferent—it was infuriating! "They aren't *our* friends, they're *your* friends."

"They would like to be your friends," he said in a reasonable tone.

Lily batted away a pang of conscience at the rudeness of reneging on the social obligation. He was merely trying to manipulate her; this was no show of affection. Her hand flew up in dismissal. "Then I shan't go."

The smallest tightening at the corner of his eyes was the only indication that he was at all affected, but even that melted away to be replaced by his bland aristocratic mask. "As you will."

Lily started back toward her office at a brisk pace. "I'm afraid I must bring our tour to an end. There isn't much else to see at this point, and I have a great many responsibilities demanding my attention."

His silence only further incensed her. Why couldn't he request a few more minutes with her, or at least express disappointment at their time together coming to a close?

He's giving you what you wanted. That little voice inside was altogether too sensible of late, doling out multiple perspectives of the situation. As much as Lily liked to consider all possible angles of most issues, in this case, every new insight only added another facet to her misery. Now her stupid conscience boldly suggested she might have brought all of this down upon her own head.

After all, the little demon continued, *he didn't demand a superficial society marriage—you did. Maybe your husband wanted more, but you'll never know now. Whatever tiny sprout of affection might have been there, you ripped up by the tender roots and strangled it with your own hands.*

Lily's feet increased their tempo, nearly running the last few steps to her office, trying to outpace both the man and the voice dogging her.

She flung open the office door and raced inside. Whirling, she threw a hurt stare at the arrogant, placid man looming in the doorway. "I'll be refurnishing the dining room," she blurted.

His brows raised in inquiry. "Oh?"

"Father is paying for it," Lily shot, digging for something to wound him as his indifference wounded her. "He said his daughter should be able to take a meal like a lady, instead of like a fishwife."

Ethan closed the door. "How generous of him."

Lily's heart fluttered wildly against her ribs. She took a step back. "It was good of you to come, my lord, but you should go now."

In two ground-eating strides, he was upon her. His hands planted on her hips and he drove her backward until the edge of the desk cut into her thighs. He was already hard against her belly before his mouth came down onto hers, forcing every coherent thought right out of her mind. Around her, the room tilted and spun. Lily clung to the front of his coat, crushing the superfine in balled fists.

Ethan's tongue plunged into her mouth, igniting the lust she'd fought so desperately to keep at bay. Like a master potter working clay, his hands moved up her back and down again, molding her body against his. Lily's treacherous nerves sparked at his touch.

His large hands cupped her bottom and he rocked against her. Her abdomen trembled and she ached between her upper thighs.

"You want it again," he rasped.

His tongue flicked her earlobe, then he drew it between his lips. A moan escaped her before she could stop it. Her breasts felt overfull, trapped in the confines of her gown. As if he knew her body as well as she, he grasped her nipples through her layers of clothing. His clever fingers rolled and tweaked them to hard pebbles. She restlessly worked her shoulders, pressing harder into his touch.

His dark words seduced her. "It could be good all the time, princess. We don't have much, Lily, but we do have this." He nipped a trail down her neck, sending a shiver coursing up her spine. "I've missed having you in my bed. I know you've missed it, too."

Desperate need swamped her. He overwhelmed her with his scent, his touch. Her womb tightened and her thighs clenched. She was about to come apart. His fingers fractured her body, her voice splintered her mind, his hunger for her pulled at her heart—

Unshed tears choked her as she pushed him with increasing force until he lifted his head. Ethan's blue eyes were opaque with desire. Lust, she thought bitterly—she was only a roll in the hay. And she was money, of course. Always the money.

"You're mistaken, my lord," she said in a quavering voice. "I do not miss you or your bed. Please leave now." She turned her head so he'd not see the tear slipping down her cheek. She didn't even dare wipe it while he gaped at her, for fear he'd see what he'd done to her—what he was doing to her.

In the space of a few heartbeats, his heavy breathing returned to normal. "I apologize for intruding upon your time, Lady Thorburn," he said in a flat tone. "Good day."

The door closed. Lily waited until she could no longer hear his footsteps, then she collapsed into her chair, put her head down on her forearms, and wept.

Chapter Seventeen

The brass tip of Ethan's walking stick rapped an angry cadence against the cobbles as he made his way from the hackney stand on the corner to Ghita's house. The carriage ride had done nothing to abate the frustration and humiliation simmering in his chest.

Lily—*Lady Thorburn*, he corrected himself with a sneer—had once again demonstrated he meant nothing to her, that their marriage only served as a vehicle for her social aspirations. He'd gone out of his way to visit King's Cross Vocational, to prove his interest in her work. Not only had he hoped to gain ground toward the ultimate prize of her dowry money, but, blast it all, he *was* interested in her work. Never in his life had Ethan Helling been even peripherally involved in a charitable undertaking of the magnitude of the institution. When Lily left home this morning after their unexpected breakfast together, he'd found himself wishing he was going with her to pass the day in a constructive fashion, rather than while the hours away writing letters to his creditors, begging time to make good on his debts. Unable to put it out of mind, he'd gone to see the school for himself.

And she'd shut him out in every possible sense, as efficient in her rejection as her new bath-room would be in issuing hot water.

Ethan rapped on Ghita's door, painted a lustrous black lacquer. The brass knocker was polished to perfection and looked like a gold bauble set against velvet in a jeweler's window display.

Late last night, he'd had a note from the Italian woman. She was growing impatient, eager for Ethan to take her into his protection. The note had brought things to a head for him. Could he really do this? He thought he owed Lily one more chance, but she made it clear she didn't want him.

If only he didn't become as randy as a goat every time he saw his wife. Hungering for her made everything exponentially worse, especially since Ethan knew how fulfilling that aspect of their marriage could be, if only she'd stop pushing him away. He cast an angry scowl at the gleaming door knocker. Sexual frustration did not agree with him, not in the least.

"Not much longer," he muttered under his breath.

This was just a preliminary call, of course, the opening parlay of contractual negotiations. In short order, though, Ghita would be Ethan's mistress. He dearly hoped she wouldn't mind receiving her first quarterly allowance after her first quarter of service, rather than in advance. Surely he'd have this whole dowry mess straightened out by then.

The butler admitted him and, when he returned from carrying his card to his mistress, led Ethan up the stairs, past the public areas of the home, past the informal sitting room, all the way to her boudoir. She was admitting him into her inner sanctum, where she entertained her lovers. A grim smile touched his lips.

The door stood ajar, and the butler showed him into a sitting room. "Signora will be with you shortly, my lord." Then the servant bowed and withdrew, closing the door as he left.

Ethan's gaze roamed the room's sumptuous arrangement of luxury. The walls were a rich amber hue and marbled to give the impression of that extravagant stone. An intricately carved chimneypiece dominated the room. There was a collection of gold and jeweled snuffboxes on a shelf near the fireplace. Overhead, a chandelier dripped with crystals. The carved rug beneath his feet was of the highest quality. Gilt arms and feet adorned the silk-upholstered settee and chairs.

He turned at the sound of a door opening.

Ghita sauntered into the room, her hips undulating from side to side in a translucent white dress. The dampened skirt clung to her figure, revealing every turn and curve of her thighs and calves. Her eyes bore down on him with the full intensity of her fiery nature, while a seductive smile teased, yet promised nothing.

She was a vision of raw female sexuality. Ethan braced himself, expecting the full onslaught of his frustrated desire to spring to life at the sight of her. Nothing just yet, but he was sure it was only a matter of seconds....

"Eeethan," she let out in a breathy voice. She held her hands out as she crossed to the center of the room where he stood. As he took her hands and dropped a kiss to her cheek, her fingers wrapped around his, tight as talons.

There was a shared moment while they looked into one another's eyes. Ethan frowned when he realized his manhood still had not stirred at her proximity.

Ghita's smile faltered. She released his hands and poured them each a glass of claret from a decanter on a little table in the corner.

"Lady Umberton has given birth," Ghita said as she handed him the glass. "Have you heard?"

He shook his head and took a sip of the wine. "When?"

"Earlier this week." Ghita lowered herself to the settee and patted the cushion next to her. "It's a girl." She threw her head back and laughed, her white teeth flashing.

Ethan winced in sympathy. He sat at the opposite end of the settee. "Poor Quill."

"He came to see me before he left to go meet his daughter." Ghita's voice was rich with mirth. "He said he had to do his duty and look the child over, and then he was going hunting for the closest male relative he can find to make his heir, even if it's a... how do you say? Cousin away?"

"Distant cousin," Ethan replied. "But who can say? Maybe he'll try again for a son."

Ghita chuckled and shook her head. Tendrils of her fair hair swung beside her jaw. "I don't think so." She bit her lip and lowered her eyes. If Ethan didn't know her better, he might think she'd been overcome by a fit of demureness. "It's over with Quillan," she said.

Ethan closed his eyes for a moment at her words—the ones he'd been waiting so long to hear. But they left him empty. There was no sense of triumph or joy. And his nether regions still seemed not to have caught on to the nubile bit of female sitting inches to his left. What was wrong with him? He'd been fantasizing about this moment for months, and now that it was here—nothing!

Ghita rose before him, her legs pressed against his knees. He looked into her seductive gaze. *If this were Lily,* the thought suddenly intruded, *I wouldn't be able to see past her breasts to get to her eyes.*

Now, that was an arousing thought. Desire finally stirred. Ghita took his hand and drew him to his feet. As close as they already were, there was nowhere for his length to go but against hers.

Slender fingers worked the buttons of his coat while her eyes remained trained on his. "This is why you've come, yes?" Her throaty whisper sent a ball of dread plunging like a rock into his stomach.

"Yes," he managed. This *was* why he'd come, by Jove. She removed his coat and tossed it onto the settee.

Her hands snaked their way to his shoulders. She stepped backward, leading him to the closed door leading to the bedchamber.

Ethan was unaccountably nervous. No, it wasn't nervousness, he decided—not quite. What was the emotion?

"There, you are frowning again," Ghita teased. "I have never seen you frown so much as since you meet your Miss Bachman."

"Lady Thorburn," he corrected by rote.

Ghita smirked. "Yes," she said in an icy tone. "She is your lady. But I shall be your woman." She stopped with her back pressed against the door. "Kiss me," she murmured against his neck.

Ethan scowled, still trying to puzzle out the emotion nagging at him.

"So fearsome," the Italian seductress said with a smile. "I can't wait to have such passion unleashed in my bed."

Standing on her toes, she came after his mouth hungrily; Ethan turned his head so the kiss landed on his jaw. She lowered her gaze, her eyes guarded. "Why, Ethan, you disappoint me."

He sighed and stepped back, running his hands down her sides. His fingers nearly met again, circling her tiny waist. Ghita was just so…small. It wasn't her fault, but he couldn't deny the fact that he no longer found her attractive. Pretty to look upon, but her body just didn't arouse his anymore. What little bit of curves she possessed felt stingy. There were other, more generous curves he'd rather feel against his palms.

God, Lily, it's all gone wrong. But it's not too late, is it? A pang shot through him, and he squeezed Ghita's waist without knowing what he was doing.

Her mouth found its target that time. Nails nipped into the nape of his neck as she pressed hard against him.

Revulsion slapped him across the cheek, and a vision of Lily's hurt face floated behind his eyes. Firmly, he grasped Ghita's arms and pushed. "No," he said, shaking his head. "I'm sorry, Ghita, but I can't."

She stared at him quizzically. For a split second, he wondered if he needed to try expressing himself again in Italian.

"What is this?" she asked. Her eyes slid low. "You...*can't?*"

Ethan snorted. He turned to retrieve his coat. "I assure you, everything is in proper working order. But this wouldn't be right."

"What do you mean?" she asked, a wounded tone in her voice. Ghita reached a tentative hand to his arm.

The gesture was so small and pleading that for a moment Ethan second-guessed himself. After all, it was Lily who wanted a detached marriage. He was well within his rights to keep a mistress.

Then her face flashed in his mind again. He saw her looking at him with eyes full of trust and adoration on the street outside the lending library. He recalled her relief when he diverted Quillan and Ghita from their cruel questioning in the carriage on the way to Vauxhall Gardens—the same night she'd discarded her reputation just to spend a few hours with him. That had not been the face—those had not been the actions—of a woman who only wanted a society marriage.

It wasn't too late, he realized, hope dawning within him. She wanted him—*him*, Ethan Helling. Not a title or status. His wife wanted him. And he wanted her, too.

He glanced at Ghita, her eyes brimming with lust, yes, but also something hard and calculating. And then he thought of Lily again, saw her trusting eyes filled with hurt, hurt that he'd come close to bringing to fruition. Bile rose in his throat at the vision.

"No," he rasped, shaking off Ghita's hand. He finished buttoning up his coat. "I'm sorry, Ghita, it's not you, it's—"

"Your new lover," she said scornfully. "You have a new female to play with."

Ethan thought of the decided lack of sexual relations in his marriage to this point and barked a laugh. If only Ghita knew. "It isn't that," he explained. "But, you see, Lily—"

"Lily!" Ghita's lip curled back over her teeth in a snarl. "Is that what you call her now?" Jealousy contorted her pretty features into an ugly mask.

Ethan started toward the door. "That is her name," he said. "And she's my wife, Ghita, thanks in no small part to the mean trick you played on her. I have to give this a proper go."

The Italian woman stood in the center of the costly rug, quivering all over with barely restrained fury. She pressed shaking hands against her face. "This is not happening," she said behind her hands.

Then Ghita lowered her hands and drew several deep breaths, her features once again serene. But Ethan knew it for the artifice it was. He had no doubt the woman was still furious.

"This is good," she said in a mocking tone. "Your devotion to your wife. I know you only turn me down because she is new. I have seen this Miss Bachman of yours. I'm sure she's fun for now." She stalked to him, her swaying hips issuing a challenge, and hooked a finger into his cravat. "But soon you will grow bored with your dull wife," she said in a low voice. "You will regret this moment, and you will come back to me." Icy hazel eyes slid over his jaw and lips, her chin lifted as she spoke. "There may be no coming back, Ethan. I will not wait for you. I may have a new lover then, one who is not acting ridiculous about another. Because listen to me, my Ethan: I do not play the second violin to any woman."

He cleared his throat and straightened, extracting his neck cloth from her hand. "I hope you do find someone who makes you happy. You know how fond I am of you, Ghita. I wish you every happiness."

She let out a disgusted sound, her face collapsing in bitter disappointment. Turning away, she flung up a dismissive hand. "Just go," she said, her voice thick. "Get out of my house. I'm tired of looking at you. You bore me to tears."

Ethan let himself out of the room. As he stepped into the street, he felt his spirits lifting. For the first time in weeks, he couldn't wait to get home.

Chapter Eighteen

Lily stared into the vanity mirror, watching Moira's placid face as the maid brushed her hair in preparation for bed. The brush strokes against her scalp were gentle but firm, a perfect reflection of the older woman's demeanor.

As if in response to her mistress's musings, Moira lifted her kind eyes; their gazes met in the mirror. "What's bothering you, Miss Lily?"

Lily sighed and shook her head. Half-servant, half-companion, and half-friend—no matter how illogical the mathematics, it was the truth—there was no use prevaricating with Moira. She'd been with her since Lily was sixteen and knew her nearly as well as Lily knew herself.

"You get paler and unhappier every day, miss," the maid continued. She set the brush down and exchanged it for a comb, which she used to divide Lily's heavy hair into thirds. "You don't have to tell me anything," Moira said in a kind tone, "but I think I can guess the problem. Why don't you just talk to his lordship?"

Lily laughed bitterly. "How can I talk to him? I don't even know where my husband is." She'd come home from the school and found Eth—Thorburn—out. He hadn't gone to the Holliers' for supper—one of the footmen said he'd carried the note of regret his lordship had written. He'd left directly thereafter, but none of the servants knew where he'd gone.

"He'll be home soon enough," Moira said.

"It's useless." A tear slipped down Lily's cheek; she swiped it away. "He likes it this way, this marriage in name only. Free to come and go and do as he pleases. I asked him for this," she whispered miserably. "I can't take it back."

"Oh, I don't know." Moira's nimble fingers brushed against Lily's back as she wove her hair into a long braid. "I've seen the way he stares at you when you're not watching, miss, especially at your backside."

Lily's startled eyes flew to the mirror in time to catch Moira's wry smile. "I wasn't always a dried-up widow, Miss Lily. My Robert and I had quite a healthy—"

"I take your meaning," Lily interjected, heat rising in her cheeks.

Moira leveled a quelling look on her in the mirror. "Well, if you don't mind my saying so, seems to me neither you nor his lordship are content with the way things are now. Your own parents, bless them, have a happy marriage. A husband and wife living two different lives might suit some of the Quality, but you weren't brought up to live this way. You're not hard enough for that, milady."

Lily frowned. Not hard enough? She most certainly was. Or would be, anyway. She'd show Moira—she'd show everyone—that she didn't need anything from her husband.

A sharp rap at the door startled her; panic constricted her throat. She shook her head, pleading with her eyes for the maid to leave the door unanswered. But Moira was already on her way.

She opened the door and bobbed a curtsy. "My lord."

Lily leaned back in her chair, but could not see her husband from her vantage. "Ah, Moira," Ethan's voice floated from the doorway, "just the woman I wanted to see. If I may have a word…" The maid cast a worried glance at Lily, then nodded her acquiescence and followed Ethan into the hall.

For a minute, Lily sat at the vanity with half-braided hair. She shifted on the little stool, wondering what on earth Ethan was up to. When the door opened again, the man himself strode into her bedchamber. Moira followed close behind and resumed her work on Lily's hair, keeping her eyes studiously on her task. A flush to the maid's cheeks piqued Lily's curiosity.

She watched in the mirror as Ethan paced behind the two women, prowling back and forth like a caged beast. Summoning her courage, Lily cleared her throat. "As you can see, my lord, I'm preparing for sleep. Whatever you'd like to discuss can wait until morning, if that is agreeable with—"

"It is not agreeable," Ethan snapped. He stood directly behind the women. The trio were framed in the oval mirror, Lily's and Ethan's gazes locked in a clash of wills and Moira pointedly avoiding looking at anyone. "That'll do, Moira. You may go now."

The maid dropped Lily's hair. "But, my lord, just a moment ago you said—"

"I've changed my mind," Ethan replied. "I'll see to her ladyship myself. Out you go."

"Don't go, Moira," Lily pleaded.

The maid's hands wrung together at her waist, and her eyes darted back and forth between Ethan and Lily. At last, she murmured, "I'm sorry, Miss Lily," curtsied, and fled the bedchamber.

"Traitor," Lily grumbled.

With a resigned sigh, she stood and turned to face Ethan, her arms crossed under her breasts. She felt at a decided disadvantage in her nightclothes and bare feet, with her unbound hair hanging in an unraveling braid, while his high and mighty lordship was impeccable in his evening clothes. He radiated an intense confidence she'd not seen in him in a long time.

He resumed pacing the room. The occasional looks he shot her were dark and predatory. Lily shivered. "What do you want?" she said to his back after he stalked past her again.

Abruptly, he spun on his heel. His jaw set in a hard line and his eyes bored into hers. "I've scarcely seen you for weeks, Lily."

"I've been so busy at the school—you know that." She turned to face the bed. Why couldn't she have already been in it and asleep when he'd come home? He wouldn't have bothered her then. "Things are coming along nicely. Miss Cuthbert is enthusiastic and hard-working. She'll have the staff assembled in a month or so, and we can start taking applications for students soon after. If construction remains on schedule all through the summer, we'll be open for Michaelmas term—"

The soft *thwump* of cloth falling to the floor caught her attention. Her throat suddenly dry, Lily turned.

Ethan stood beside her vanity. His coat lay across the back of her chair, while the material she'd heard hitting the floor belonged to his waistcoat. His untied cravat hung, limp, around the back of his neck, while his shirt had been pulled from the waist of his breeches.

"What are you doing?" she breathed in a rush.

Ethan smirked as he removed his cufflinks. "I know it's been a while, my dear, but I trust you can recall what it is I'm doing." A quick tug on his shirtsleeve had that garment off and on the floor with the waistcoat. He sat on the little feminine vanity stool to tug his boots and stockings free of his feet.

Lily's heart galloped wildly. "I have a headache, my lord, a terrible, terrible headache." She put a hand to her temple and winced.

He snorted. "You're a bad actress, princess, and a liar." He stared at her for a long moment, his eyes roaming her every feature. "You've been lying about a great many things, I believe," he murmured. "But the time for lies is over, Lily."

She drew herself up, her lips tightening. "I'm sure I don't know what you mean, my lord. And I must once again ask you to refrain from using my given name."

"I will not," he said. "You're my wife, and I'll call you whatsoever I damned well please. I've been dancing to your tune, trying to make you happy your way. All that's gotten us is a wagon full of misery. Now we're going to try my way." He unbuttoned his breeches and peeled them off to join the rest of his clothes in a pile.

The dim light played across the taut muscles of his abdomen as he approached. He was such a beautiful sight, she nearly cried with longing. Lily turned away and wrapped her arms around herself. "My lord, I beg you, please do not."

"You cannot deny me your bed." His voice was a rumble close behind her. "You promised."

His tone was not unkind, but dread coursed down her spine. She hadn't succeeded in pushing him away altogether, and now he'd come to claim his rights. The unnerving encounter at the school this afternoon had proved that she wasn't strong enough to withstand him. She still wanted him, still wanted him to want her.

Warm arms wrapped around her middle. Ethan's lips brushed against her neck. "Besides," his voice teased her ear, "this is the best time to start trying for our heir."

Lily gasped and spun. "How could you possibly—" she sputtered. Then she recalled her maid stepping into the hall to converse with the man now standing gloriously naked in front of her. "Moira," she ground out. "You might as well keep her for your valet, as her loyalty has taken a turn in your direction. Is there no female you cannot seduce into your good graces?"

Ethan chuckled and rested his forehead against hers, the tips of their noses glancing across one another. "Only you. You are the most magnificent thing I have ever beheld when you're in a snit, princess. I shall have to concoct new ways to vex you at least twice a month." He dropped a feather-light kiss on her lips. "If we had been sleeping together—" *kiss* "—every night as I wanted to do from the beginning—" *kiss* "—then I should never have had to ask your maid such a personal question."

As he kissed her again, he untied the ribbon at the neck of her robe and slid it off her shoulders. It slithered down Lily's back to land in a soft heap at her heels. He lifted his head and caught her face in his hands. The warmth radiating from his body was deliciously inviting. She leaned in a little and caught the faintest hint of roses on his skin. Her brow creased in confusion. "What is—?"

"Listen to me." The vehemence of his tone shooed away any thought of roses. "I want to know everything about you, Lily. I want you to tell me about your amazing bath-room, and Miss Cuthbert, and everything to do with your school, because it's yours. It's marvelous, and I am in awe of your goodness and generosity."

A lump formed in her throat, making it difficult to breathe. Could he really mean this? Was he actually interested in her, Lily? Her head swam with a jumble of emotions.

Ethan's hands splayed against the small of her back and over the globes of her buttocks, pulling her closer, molding her body to his. Heat suffused his words as his erection pressed into her abdomen. "I want to know everything there is to learn about your body, Lily. I want to see you and touch you and feel you. I want to know how many ways we can find to pleasure one another." His hands worked into her hair, undoing the sad remains of the braid. "Don't you want that, too?"

Even in the dim light, she was struck by the earnest pleading in his eyes. He craved her acceptance as much as he desired to take her to bed. And God help her, but she wanted him, too. Her heart leaped with hope, but fear still tugged at her. She worried at her lip while meeting his gaze. What if this was all a ploy on his part, a ruse to obtain her money?

The money. Lily was tired to the tips of her toes of thinking and worrying about money and whether or not her husband only wanted her for her fortune. How much energy had she expended in forbidding herself happiness, all in the name of keeping her heart and her money out of his hands?

Her lips curved up in a little smile and she nodded. "I do. I want that, too," she affirmed. The soft crinkle at the corners of his eyes gratified her as he returned her smile.

"Very well, then," he said matter-of-factly. "To bed." His eyes scorched a path over the thin white night rail concealing her body. Without a word, he bent and gathered the hem. Lily raised her arms so he could pull it over her head.

The tips of her breasts grazed over his chest as he straightened, teasing her nipples to hard knots. His eyes went hazy with lust, but there was something softer there, too, and it fed her fledgling hopes. Forcing her fretful thoughts to the back of her mind, Lily took his hand and led him to her bed. It was smaller than his imposing four-poster and dressed all in white sheets and coverlets.

She started to climb onto it, but Ethan nudged past her and sprawled on his back in the middle of the mattress.

"Come here," he said, reaching out.

Feeling as nervous as she had the first time they'd lain together, Lily settled into his embrace. She rested her head on his shoulder. Her hand slipped across his belly to hook around his side. For several long moments, they lay entwined, clinging together. Lily welcomed the silence and the opportunity to reacquaint herself with the sensation of his sturdy, masculine frame against her own body. She closed her eyes and breathed him in, savoring the spicy hint of cologne.

His fingers brushed her hair away from her temple; her eyelids fluttered open. The somber look on his face quite took her by surprise. "Tell me why you're afraid," he said.

Lily felt her hackles start to rise.

"No," he said in a commanding tone. "I see you starting to put walls up again, Lily, and I won't have it. I just won't. Not when you and I both know this could turn into something…" His lips turned up in a slow smile while he looked away. "Spectacular," he finished.

Her breath hitched in her throat. Exhaling a soft laugh, she shook her head. "You always say exactly what I don't expect you to say."

His grin deepened. "Good." His arms tightened around her middle and he rolled onto his back, pulling a squealing Lily on top of him.

The soft curls on his chest crushed under her breasts, tickling and teasing her aching nipples, while his hands roamed her back and thighs. Every touch was joy, each caress more arousing than the last. Lily's dark hair tumbled over her shoulder and pooled beside his face on the snowy pillow. Ethan's fingers tangled in her tresses and he guided her downward until their mouths met.

Like a spark on dry tinder, his kiss set her aflame. Her lips slid across his, parting to tease him with the tip of her tongue. A low groan escaped his throat as his mouth opened to hers. His hands swept down her sides; his fingers kneaded her bottom, then dipped into the cleft, stroking along her sensitive folds. She arched her back and whimpered. He explored more, slipping a finger inside her wetness and whispering erotic endearments as she moved on top of him.

Unable to maintain her position for all her own writhing, Lily's thighs fell open and her legs slipped down his sides to straddle his hips. His blunt tip pressed against her damp entrance. Could she—? Startled at the idea, she lifted to look at him in unspoken question.

"Yes," he whispered. "You're in charge, princess."

Lightheaded with arousal, Lily pushed herself up to sitting, with her knees sinking into the coverlet on either side of his torso. Gently, he guided her back. She rose further, poising herself above his penis. She cast him another questioning glance. He nodded in encouragement. "Go on, then," he said through tight lips.

Lily bit her lip, aroused at the realization that she had him on tenterhooks. He was as desperate to couple with her as she was to be with him—and there was not a damned thing he could do about it, pinned beneath her as he was.

Her lips curved up in an impish smile as, inch by inch, she lowered herself onto the head, rose up, and then sank down a little further. As he stretched and filled her, she inhaled deeply, tensing and easing in turn as her body melded with his. Between her thighs, she felt him shudder. When she'd taken him in to the hilt, Lily regarded her lover with a heavy-lidded gaze. "Now what?" she asked.

Ethan gave her a hazy, lopsided smile. His hands skimmed up her thighs, squeezed her waist, and continued on up to cover her breasts. "Whatever suits you, princess, anything you—Christ!" His eyes rolled back.

Lily chuckled with delight as she released her tensed inner walls. She'd wondered whether she could willfully clamp herself tighter around him, and was very gratified to know she could.

"There's my princess," he managed. "Always thinking, my clever girl." He grabbed her hips and drove upward. Lily cried out and tumbled forward, her fingers digging into his chest to steady herself.

"You said I was in charge," she scolded playfully, clenching her muscles around him again.

"Then take charge," he whispered hoarsely. "Take your pleasure from me as you wish—I want you screaming before this is over." He pulled her down for a scorching kiss. She sensed how he held himself in check, allowing her to guide their intercourse. A thrill shot through her at the realization of her own power. As their tongues tangled, she rocked her hips back and forth.

He moaned his approval, and Lily exulted in knowing she was pleasing him. She straightened and continued rocking—and was startled by the change in sensation. He was so deep—filling her more than she knew she could be filled.

Ethan's hands rested on her haunches. He watched her with lust and need and warmth. Lily's heart lurched when she saw that look in his eyes. In such a moment of raw intimacy, surely he couldn't hide his true feelings from her. And there was something there to hope for—something worth reaching for.

Coherent thought flew from her mind as the mounting pressure between her legs overshadowed everything else. There was just the two of them, and the molten bliss emanating from the place where they were joined.

Lily increased her pace, driving them both to the brink. Her breasts bounced against his chest in time with her movements; he gripped them and held tight while she rode. Even though he'd begun their mating urging her to take her own pleasure, Lily was determined to make him climax—she *needed* him to do so, to prove that she could please them both when she was in control. Despite her own orgasm building deep inside, she kept her eyes trained on Ethan—her Ethan. Hers. She didn't hear her own cries and gasps, so focused was she on ensuring his release.

Her name tore from his throat in a guttural growl. He took her hips and yanked her down, over and over while he rose up to meet her. She felt a flood of warmth and still he drove on, pushing her right over the precipice where light exploded behind her eyes. Distantly, she heard herself crying out—words tumbled over her lips, interspersed with primal screams.

Finally, panting, trembling, she returned to her senses. Ethan gave her that lopsided smile, his eyes still brimming with those good things that made Lily feel like she might float away with happiness.

Her thighs quivered in protest of being clamped around his middle for so long. She collapsed in an exhausted, happy heap into his welcoming embrace.

"Well done, my girl," he murmured as she burrowed into his arms. He kissed the top of her head. She kissed his neck, damp and salty with perspiration. Beneath her palm, his heart gradually slowed from a gallop to a more sedate trot. Lily bit her lip, grinning as she thought how *she* had brought him to this sweaty, sated state. Feeling mischievous, she pinched his bottom and was rewarded with a surprised, "Oi!"

He snatched her wrists and pulled her mischievous hands away. "Aren't you the saucy one tonight?" He pinned her wrists with one large hand and tickled her ribs with the other.

Lily squealed and squirmed until he released her. Then she turned on her side and let him pull her close, her back nestled against his chest. She still smiled as drowsiness tugged at her. As her mind relaxed, the negative thoughts she'd pushed away began creeping back in. Could she really trust him—trust this tenuous feeling between them? Her throat clenched in fear. What if—*no*, she scolded herself. *No more what ifs.*

He'd said he wanted them *both* to be happy. Ethan deserved happiness, and so did she. The way there was uncertain, but maybe if they took the journey together…

"Lily," he said against her temple, "I've something to say to you."

She shifted onto her back. Ethan propped up on an elbow. Her hand went to his cheek and stroked from his jaw to his hairline and down again. "What is it?" she murmured.

"Two somethings, actually." His brow furrowed. "No, three."

She poked his chest. "Out with it, before you've thought of thirty-seven somethings to tell me, and I'm kept up all night while you declaim them one by one."

His lips pressed together in false severity. "Very well, madam, *thing* the first: You acquitted yourself tolerably well just then."

She swatted his shoulder and laughed. "Just tolerably well?"

"More than tolerably," he said with a wink, "but I don't want to feed your conceit."

Lily snorted. Ethan's blue eyes were full of mirth. His happiness fed her own; for so long, she'd seen nothing in his eyes but hardness and bitter sarcasm.

"*Thing* the second…" He turned to look around the bedchamber before returning his attention to her. "I don't like your room," he said, shaking his head. "Everything in it is small and feminine, and I worry even now that I'm going to break the bed. It doesn't do for you, either."

She frowned. "What do you mean?"

"You're far too tall for that ridiculous little stool at your vanity. You'd do better dressing in my room, using furniture more suited to your frame. From now on, that's where we're sleeping."

Lily felt her hackles rising at being dictated to, but she pressed her lips closed again. The truth was, her father had bought her bedroom furniture when she was fourteen—lovely trappings for a fashionable young lady. However, she'd continued growing until she was eighteen, and had been uncomfortable in her things ever since. She'd never breathed a word of complaint to her dear papa. But Ethan had known right away that it wasn't right for her anymore. She relented with a nod.

"Good." He kissed her lips. "Thank you."

Lily's fingertips played in the hair at his nape. His breath quickened just a bit, and she felt her own arousal stirring low in her belly. "What was the third thing you wanted to say?" she asked.

Ethan took one of her nipples in his fingers and squeezed. Lily gasped and arched into his hand, desire flaring to life at his touch. "*Thing* the third," she heard him say as he parted her legs with his knee, "I'm in charge this time."

Chapter Nineteen

Lily awoke the next morning as she'd not done since the morning after their wedding—with her husband gloriously naked beside her and snoring softly. Joy flooded her to see him so content. Lightly, so as not to disturb his slumber, she brushed his stubbled cheek with the back of a finger.

I love him, she thought. She grinned with delight at the light, giddy feeling around her heart. *Can I make him happy?* A few of the previous night's doubts still worried her, but fresh determination rose within her with the new day's sun.

So far, Lily hadn't been a good wife to Ethan, but now she was determined to do better. If only there was something she could do, an olive branch she could extend…

Her brows shot up as an idea clapped her over the head. Slipping out of bed, she kept a wary eye on Ethan to make sure he still slept. Hastily, she donned her dressing gown and padded downstairs to his study.

She hesitated with her hand on the knob. Lily had not set foot inside Ethan's study since the first day she'd met him as a prospective house buyer. Remembering her disdain for the handsome, ill-mannered "butler" still brought heat to her cheeks.

She made her way to the window and pulled the drapes. Her heart sank when she turned and beheld a mess seemingly unchanged since her last visit to the room. The Bachman servants had dusted the floor and furniture, she observed, but the study was still overwhelmed by the desk buried in disorderly piles of paper.

"Oh, well," she grumbled. "A scavenger hunt, then." She sat down in Ethan's chair and began sifting through the papers.

237

Later today, she would go to her father and ask him to release her dowry. Ethan would inevitably have it eventually, and it would be a gesture of trust on her part that he was sincere in his desire to make theirs a happy union. It would take some time, however, for the papers to be drawn up, signed, and the money transferred.

In the meantime, Lily could immediately make Ethan's life a little easier by paying off some of his debts right now, this morning. She had a nice sum of pin money she'd been squirreling away for years, hidden in a hatbox. Now, though, that money would get some of these bills off his desk and the creditors off his back.

However, the sheer volume of letters requiring payment soon overwhelmed Lily. Numerous tradesmen demanded remittance. And the gambling debts! What had seemed to Lily like a fortune in her hatbox would evaporate entirely if she paid off just two or three of the gentlemen to whom her husband owed money. Little wonder Ethan seemed so distraught when Lily spent anything—if these were her debts, she should lock herself in her room and cry for a week. What a burden her husband carried.

Fortunately, the debts all seemed to predate their marriage. If they paid off what he owed, and if he would stop gaming for such outrageous sums—

Lily's brow puckered as she moved aside a paper and found a creamy sheet of stationery beneath it. This was not an invoice, and the script had a feminine appearance. Had Ethan been gambling with ladies as well as gentlemen? An embossed V stood in florid relief against the thick paper, and a floral aroma teased her nostrils. Lily's stomach clenched at the scent. Her fingers trembled as she began to read.

Thorburn,

Days have passed since our last meeting. I cannot say how many, for time itself loses meaning when I am not with you. Every hour is an agony, each day an eternity. Deliver me from my misery, I implore you, and come to me.

My mind torments me with visions of you in the arms of another. It cannot be avoided, I know, but the heart does not willingly receive the sound advice of reason. Memory takes me to the eve of your wedding, when we wept together for the inevitable change in our dealings. For a while, I contented myself that though you were with her, your preference still lay with me. But now, as days drag by and you do not approach, my love, I cannot still the disquietude in my breast. Are her charms more attractive to you than my own? Has she usurped my place in your heart? Oh, the wretchedness of my station! Would that I could repent of every man before you—and yes, you as well, my dearest!—if so doing made me worthy of now holding the lawful position at your side inhabited by another.

Were it not for the certainty that God long ago abandoned me for the sin of our arrangement, I would pray for deliverance from the agony of our separation. Mayhap there will be forgiveness for me in the eternities, but I confess it difficult to trust in Providence when all the world is indifferent to one such as I, but for the passing novelty of my company. No, love, my salvation lies only with you, and yet you keep yourself from me. I shall try to endure a little longer, but show mercy upon she who has loved you well these years and end my suffering.

Only yours,
Vanessa

The letter slipped from Lily's hand and fluttered to the floor. For a moment, a strange numbness pervaded her senses. She could only blink in confusion while her heart futilely attempted to keep at bay the truth her mind had grasped.

He had a mistress. Her Ethan loved another.

Pain unlike any she'd ever known tore through her middle. Leaping to her feet, she clutched the lapels of her dressing gown to her throat. Her eyes flew wildly around the room but saw nothing of the unkempt study. No, she saw Ethan again in the park, tucking away a letter topped with a V—this very same stationery. Even as he'd sat beside her on a bench while she nattered on about headmistresses, he'd been on his way to see this woman, this Vanessa.

Trembling fingers covered her face, still scented with the paper's perfume. Roses. Last night, Ethan had smelt of roses. He had answered the summons of this missive but yesterday. Lily had lain with him, given her body and heart to him—while the scent of his mistress still clung to his skin.

The pain of betrayal ripped Lily in two; nausea surged through her middle. A keening wail escaped her throat as she sank to the floor beside the love letter. She buried her face against her knees, sobbing for the long and lonely life that stretched before her as the wife of a man who had given his heart to another woman.

"No!" she strangled out. "No, no, no!" Struggling against the waves of self-loathing that beat upon her like a squall on the shore, she pushed to sit upright on her heels and swiped at her cheeks. She was a fool. Deep down, she knew he only wanted her money, but Lily had chosen to believe his seductive lies. She cast a scornful look at the horrible letter; her lip curled up in a sneer. "Of course he needs my money. A mistress is very expensive." A bitter laugh shook her belly before the tears fell once more.

*

Ethan awoke in an unfamiliar location, with an unfamiliar sensation residing in the environs of his chest and abdomen. A moment's observation allowed him to recall the location—Lily's bedchamber with its dollhouse furnishings.

The sensation took longer to puzzle out. There was something familiar about it, though it oddly reminded him of sailing with his grandfather, which was not at all the situation in which he now found himself—burrowed as he was in a nest of feminine bedding with the faint, lingering ache of last night's exercise burning his thighs.

His eyes drifted closed again and a smile flitted across his lips while he replayed some of the previous evening's more spectacular moments. Lily possessed a commanding quality that would come off as indecorous at best in another female, hoydenish or domineering more likely. But in her...he groaned with the happy recollection how she'd taken control of their lovemaking, striving to please him with every trick in her as yet sparsely stocked arsenal—and please him she had. Abundantly. And what a joy it had been to then focus on her needs, a pleasure all its own.

At that moment, Ethan was able to put a name to the still-abiding sensation: peace. There were no knots of anxiety in his gut, no dread at facing the coming day. This peace had not come about through a cessation of his financial worries; no, those were as present today as they were yesterday. It had come because of Lily.

Last night, in the throes of passion, she had cried out the three-word declaration of extreme sentiment that had, up to now, been his cue to depart from the company of the female uttering the words. But when Lily said, "I love you," Ethan had not felt the urge to run.

To the contrary, he felt even more strongly the need to make things right with her, to ensure the happiness of their marriage.

As he recalled that startling moment, a twinge of conscience reminded him he had not responded in kind. He had not acknowledged it in any way, in fact; but Lily seemed not to have noticed. Ethan rolled onto his side and punched up the pillow beneath his head. His eyes fell to the indentation in the mattress where his wife had spent the night beside him. It occurred to him that she might not remember—or even mean—the words that had passed her lips.

In his experience, women became creatures possessed at the moment of orgasm, letting loose all manner of verbiage they might otherwise never pronounce. Cries to the Almighty were common, though Ethan himself did not care to invite the notice of deity whilst engaging in acts generally frowned upon by those who claimed to speak for the higher power. Mild ladies with the most inoffensive vocabularies imaginable could turn into firebrands with mouths to make a sailor blush. And then there were the women—like Lily, he supposed—who proclaimed themselves in love at the critical moment.

The thing was, he mused, frowning at the empty place in the bed, he quite liked the idea of Lily loving him. Before they married, there had been moments when she'd seemed inclined to think well of his character, to admire him as a man. How novel it would be to truly deserve her love and approbation. Maybe she hadn't meant it last night—but maybe she had. "Wouldn't that be something?" he whispered.

He shoved up to sitting, the sheet falling down his bare torso to collect across his lap. Where the devil had his wife gotten off to, anyway? He pulled on last night's breeches before going to his own room to don fresh clothing.

For the first time in ages, Ethan looked forward to his day. Lily might love him. And he just might love her, too. The woman had enough intelligence and personality to keep him interested for a few centuries, at least. Her generosity knew no bounds; truly, Ethan had never seen its like. He knew no other female who had single-handedly taken on a task of the scope of King's Cross Vocational. And he was completely enraptured by her lush body. A surge of desire pulsed through his pelvis. Ethan abandoned the rest of his toilette, stepping into the hallway in only clean breeches and shirt.

He had to find her. *Lily, Lily, Lily...* He was a hound honing in on her, seeking out his mistress, and he didn't care. They had a foundation to build upon now. Ethan wanted the peace to remain, to grow. He wanted it to envelop the whole sad house and drive away the emptiness.

He went down the stairs to the first floor. He peeked into the newly furnished parlor—no Lily. Thinking she must be breaking her fast, he started to descend to the dining room, but the cracked door of his study caught his eye.

Curious, he approached. With his fingers splayed wide, he pushed the door inward. Lily stood at his desk, furiously flipping through the piles of papers on the much-abused surface. She paused just long enough to lick her middle finger and recommence her search.

His eyes flicked to a collection of papers on the floor beside her, scattered as though she had dropped them from where she stood. As he watched, she pulled a sheet from the mess, glanced it over, and released it to fall to the floor with the others. A strangled sob escaped her as she raked through his things.

Unease gripped his lungs, dispelling the all-too-brief peace he'd enjoyed this morning. "Lily," he ventured, stepping cautiously into the study, "what are you doing?"

Her eyes flew up to meet him, wild and bright with tears. Her cheeks were mottled with red blotches and her mouth twisted into a tight sneer at his appearance. Sleep-tangled tresses spilled over her shoulders. She leaned forward and braced herself on the edge of the desk, allowing the top of her robe to fall open. In other circumstances, the sight might have allured him; now, it terrified Ethan, as it bespoke a complete leave of Lily's sensibilities.

"What am I doing?" she seethed. "What am I doing?" Her voice rose in pitch, and a white-knuckled fist struck her chest. "No, Ethan! The question is not what am *I* doing, but what are *you* doing?" Her index finger pointed in accusation.

Bewildered, he held placating hands out toward his distraught wife and took a few steps toward her. "You must calm down, Lily, so we can discuss…whatever it is we need to discuss."

"Stay back!" She pushed a pile of papers onto the floor and fled to the far end of the desk, keeping the oak structure between them. "I don't want you to touch me ever again. It'll be the death of me, if you haven't given me a pox already!"

Ethan's jaw dropped open, aghast. "What the devil are you talking about, madam?" he demanded. Anger suffused his confusion, lapping at his temples. He rounded the end of the desk where Lily had stood, his bare foot crunched against paper. Glancing down, he noticed the pile his wife had made. At the opposite end of the desk, her breath came in rapid pants, near to hyperventilation.

He stooped to pick up the papers. His hands froze when he caught sight of the first *V*. A quick appraisal confirmed that every sheet was a letter from Nessa. He was accustomed to receiving letters dictated by the woman's infirmity, but instantly grasped how they must look to his wife.

"Oh, Lily," he murmured. With a heavy sigh, he glanced at his fuming spouse. Once she understood—

Years ago, when Nessa's dementia first began to make itself apparent, he'd sworn never to reveal her ailment to anyone. A woman in her condition was too easy to take advantage of. With the exception of a very few others who knew her situation, she had been his alone, his closely guarded secret to protect. She was now forgotten by most of the world, and he preferred to keep it that way.

Lily isn't like everyone else, he reasoned. She could be trusted with Vanessa's secret. Last night had meant more to Ethan than he would have thought possible. He'd asked Lily to trust him, and she had. Perhaps it was time to return the favor.

"This is not what you think," he assured her. "I realize these letters must shock you, but if you'd only—"

She cut him off with a crazed whoop. "Oh no, my lord," she said, wiping away tears that slipped down her cheeks even as she laughed. "There is nothing you can say or do to shock me. Indeed, I've only shocked myself by hoping you might have been something other than what everyone warned me you are." Her bottom lip quivered. Lily clamped one hand over her mouth and the other arm across her middle.

Ethan let out an exasperated sound. "Lily, please." A few strides brought him to her side. He made to put an arm around her shoulders, but she twisted away from his grasp.

"Do not touch me!" she screeched. "I told you not to touch me. I told you not to use my name. I reassert those demands right now! I'll not be sullied by a tongue that lavishes endearments upon two women in one night, or by hands that would rather touch a whore."

Ethan's mood plummeted dangerously. His instinct to protect Vanessa roared at the slander. "Don't speak of her that way, Lily. You don't know what you're talking about."

Scorn emanated from every fiber of her being as she cast a look of disdain upon him. "And so you have done it again. Not a second after I tell you not to, you have once again abused my Christian name." Drawing herself up, she lifted her chin at a haughty angle. "As you refuse to capitulate with my desires regarding a detached marriage, I shall have to press the issue. I'm leaving, my lord. Once I'm gone, you may 'Lily' me all you like, for I shan't be around to hear it. Bring your wretched mistress here, for all I care." Her shoulders stooped a fraction as sadness swept over her eyes. "I wish you'd married her instead of me, my lord. How much happier we'd all have been."

"I wish I could have," he snapped, "as Vanessa has never once cast aspersions upon my character the way you do."

Lily's eyes narrowed.

"And yet that would be altogether impossible, as you would understand if you would only listen, Lily."

"Do not speak her name and mine in the same breath! How *dare* you, sir?"

She started toward the door and Ethan cursed. Grabbing her from behind, he clamped his arms around her in a punishing embrace and pulled her back against his chest. Bending his neck, he spoke into her ear in a low voice. "Stop this, Lily, just stop. You don't know what you're doing. I need you to believe me—"

"I shall never believe another word that passes between your lips, my lord." He had to strain to hear the near-whisper. As he leaned closer, his lips and cheek brushed against her hair—a silken, sweet-smelling torment tempting him even as frustration and anger continued to mount between them. "You are a cad of the highest degree, a libertine, degenerate, lying, amoral—"

"Your point is made." He released her, stepped back, and crossed his arms, grasping his elbows. "So this is your opinion of me, Lily? You won't give me the benefit of the doubt, even after last night?"

She turned, but did not raise her eyes to meet his. "Yes, my lord, this is my true opinion, as it has been since I was forced into this marriage. Last night was a mistake."

Despair unlike any he'd ever known snared him around the middle and pulled him down until he felt his heart crashing through the floorboards.

With arms stiff at her sides, Lily departed and went upstairs. A moment later, he heard the soft click of the lock on her bedchamber door sliding home.

Ethan turned back to his desk, his eyes sweeping disconsolately over the madness piled before him. His life was a disaster, he thought as he stooped to retrieve Vanessa's crumpled letter from the floor. His finances were ruined with no hope of ever recovering. He was caretaker to an elderly woman with an infirm mind, and his marriage—

Guilt swamped him as he slumped into his chair. The only good thing in his life had been demolished by half-truths and omissions. Ethan had managed to follow in his parents' footsteps and create a colossal ruin of his marriage. Staring at Nessa's letter, he cursed himself. If there was anyone in the world he could trust with Vanessa's secret, it was Lily. Maybe, when she'd had time to calm down, she would let him explain.

He heard a knock at the front door downstairs and frowned. "Too early for callers," he mused. The Bachman servants were competent, though, and would send whomever had shown up at this unseemly hour on their way.

Putting the caller out of mind, Ethan resumed his glum perusal of the letters Lily had collected. Each one read like heartfelt words from a mistress to her lover. Ethan knew them to be the recollections of a mind lost in itself, able to detail and relive events of years past, but no longer capable of retaining information pertaining to the present. Nessa's infirmity was the most tragic thing he'd ever beheld; losing her through the gradual degradation of her mind was horrid.

And now I've lost Lily, too, he thought.

In a way, he reflected, he was as lost in the past as Nessa—held hostage by debts that forbade him any kind of freedom until he could put them to rest. If only there was someone he could talk to who could give him some sound advice...

"Oh, you blind beggar!" He shot to his feet. Did he not have a financial genius for a father-in-law? Ethan hadn't been able to look past the man's monumental fortune to consider how he—a man of humble beginnings—had built his wealth. Perhaps Mr. Bachman could offer some guidance in the matter.

Once he had a plan in place for repaying his debts, Lily might look on him with a little more kindness. Even if she didn't, he would do this for himself, to prove he was a man who could take charge of his responsibilities.

He opened the study door and nearly collided with the footman who had raised a hand to knock.

"I beg your pardon, my lord," the servant said, hopping back.

"Not at all." Ethan aimed for his bedchamber to finish dressing. "Who called, by the way?"

"I called," said a voice.

Ethan skidded to a halt and noticed a small man hovering a few steps down the stairwell, his lips turned up in a far-too-satisfied smile. "Mr. Laramie, is it?"

The bailiff rose to the landing and bent in a slight bow. "Indeed it is, my lord."

Ethan huffed. "What is your business, sir? Are your brutes with you? I've nothing left for you to haul away—"

"I'm sorry, my lord, but it's much more serious this time." The bailiff reached into his coat and withdrew a document. Unease gripped Ethan when he noticed a wax seal affixed at the bottom. This was very official, and very bad.

Mr. Laramie cleared his throat and read: "On behalf of Dunraven Bank, Complainant, and by order of the Court, Ethan Faraman Helling, Viscount Thorburn, is hereby placed under arrest for failure to satisfy repayment of funds as contractually obligated to the afore-named Complainant. Ethan Faraman Helling, Viscount Thorburn, is hereby summoned to Fleet Prison, there to remain incarcerated until such a time as the Court determines resolution satisfactory to the Complainant. Issued and sealed this day, *et cetera*, signed by. . . Well, you get the gist."

A muffled sound from above caught Ethan's attention. He glanced up to see a wide-eyed Lily leaning over the second floor railing, all the color drained from her face. Their gazes locked, and he felt misery compounding misery that he was causing her this new grief.

Mr. Laramie cleared his throat. Ethan swallowed hard and watched the bailiff refold the arrest warrant and return it to his coat pocket. "Come along, my lord," he said with that mean little smile of his, "it's debtor's prison for you."

Chapter Twenty

Lily straightened, unable to tear her eyes from her husband. He spoke to the bailiff in a low voice. With her heart hammering against her ribs, Lily drew a deep breath and then another.

So now he's to add debtor's prison to his list of deficiencies, right behind keeping a mistress with a penchant for the epistolary, she thought, forcing herself to think dispassionately on the matter. *I am to watch my husband led away to gaol—just what every bride hopes for.* She squeezed her lips tight as a cry threatened to escape.

Now was not the time for tears. Now was the time to distance herself from this man, to leave him to the fate he'd made for himself through his debauches and excesses.

Below, the bailiff nodded once. "Very well," she heard him say, "but if you've not presented yourself at Fleet by noon, it will be much worse for you. Evading arrest shall be added to the charges."

"I understand." Ethan reached out to grasp Mr. Laramie's hand. "I shall be there. Thank you."

Mr. Laramie started at the handshake, then turned to depart. He glanced up and caught sight of Lily. "My lady." He bowed.

She clutched her dressing gown and drew back, listening as the bailiff descended the stairs and the door closed behind him. A moment later, Ethan appeared at the top of the stairs. He paused when he saw her, his eyes brimming with anguish.

Good. She lifted her chin, determined not to show that her heart lay in pieces inside her chest, that his having a mistress had hurt her more than she could ever begin to express.

His lips twisted. "It would appear you're getting that separation you wanted."

She could not find humor in the dark joke as the enormity of the situation began to settle on her shoulders. "Arrested," she hissed. "You're going to prison, Ethan! All because you didn't pay your bloody debts! What is the matter with you? How could you be so reckless?"

His mouth worked for a moment before he shrugged and looked dispassionately over the banister.

"Was it worth it?" she persisted. "The boots, or hats, or wines, or whatever it was you didn't pay for?"

"It was the mortgage, actually." His eyes—which had taken on a flat appearance—slid to her face and then away once more.

Lily sputtered, aghast. "Mortgage? You mortgaged the house? What happened to the ten thousand pounds my father gave you?"

"I gave it to Quillan," Ethan explained, his tone as flat as his eyes.

Her throat constricted and she felt herself quivering with anger all over. "Quillan!" she strangled out, her hands balling at her sides. "You gave that boorish lout ten thousand pounds but left the bank waiting?"

"A gentleman repays his debts to gentlemen first," he said in an even tone. "That's how it's done." He brushed past her to go into his own room.

She cursed under her breath before following him. Why was he so calm all of a sudden? It would be so much easier to maintain righteous indignation if he would yell back. Instead, he accepted the arrest with grim dignity—an arrest which had come about, she hated to admit, because of his adherence to a gentleman's code of honor, misguided though it was.

For all his many faults, Ethan seemed to be striving to do the right thing. Her heart constricted, reminding her of the bruised love she held for this man.

He emerged from his dressing room with a dark waistcoat and coat. He buttoned the coat as he crossed to a trunk against the wall, from which he retrieved a bag. Ethan cast a few glimpses in her direction as he packed some clean shirts and toiletries into the case.

Panic clawed at her gut as she watched him. This was really happening. Her husband was going to gaol. Lily's breaths came faster as an overwhelming sense of loss crashed over her. She sank onto a chair—one much better suited to her frame, she noted with despair—and dropped her head into her hand.

Then she was in his arms, scooped up and crushed against his chest. "It's all right," he murmured against her temple.

Lily wrapped her arms around his neck and buried her face in his shoulder. "How can you say that?" she wailed. "You're going to prison, leaving me…"

He rubbed her back with soothing motions. "I never wanted to leave you."

The gentleness of his words broke her heart all over again. She had to stop this! "I don't want you to go," she whispered. "Please don't go."

Ethan's hands clutched her hair, pulling her closer. "I have to. But it won't be for long. The bank is just trying to scare me into paying—as if I wouldn't have already, if I had the money. If I don't pay soon, they'll seize the house and that'll be that. One way or another, I won't be there long."

Lily pushed back in his arms and looked into his face. His expression was somber as he brushed her cheek, wiping away hot tears as though it were the most important task in the world.

At that instant, Lily put aside her hurt at his having a mistress. That wasn't the most pressing matter now. With a firm nod of resolve, she cleared her throat. "I'm going to my father right away. I'll tell him to sign over the dowry, and he will give me enough to pay the bank so you don't have to go to that dreadful—"

His fingers against her lips silenced her. "Don't do that, Lily."

Confusion tangled her thoughts. She could fix this! "But—" she started.

"No." His eyes hardened in resolve. "I've not been good enough for you." She started to protest, but he forestalled her once again. "I'm sorry, Lily. Truly sorry for not being the husband you needed me to be. I promised your father I would make you a happy woman before I took your dowry, and I intend to do just that. I *will* make you happy, princess."

"It would make me happy if you didn't go to gaol!" she insisted.

He smiled ruefully and rested his forehead against hers. "I'll figure it out, Lily. Before I go, I only want to swear to you that Vanessa is not my mistress. You must believe that." Lily flushed at the mention of the other woman. Her lips parted; Ethan shushed her with a quick kiss. "There's not time now to explain, but I will do so when I return. And return I shall, princess, and soon."

He took her face in his hands and kissed her properly, then broke away. Lifting the valise from the bed, he gave her hand a final squeeze before slipping out the door and down the stairs.

Lily stood in stunned silence as she heard the steady beat of his boots against the stairs and crossing the entry hall.

"Wait!" she cried just as the front door slammed home behind him. She ran to the window and ripped the drapes aside in time to see him step into a hackney.

As the hired coach pulled away from the curb, Lily slapped her hand on the glass to catch his attention. He was already out of sight, shut inside the shabby carriage. "Wait," she whispered hoarsely. "Don't leave me. I love you." She rested her head on the glass, watching until the hackney disappeared around a corner.

Lily's mind whirred. No matter what he said, she had to do something. Lily Bachman—Helling, she corrected herself—would not stand idly by while her husband was held in debtor's prison. Not when she could save him.

Chapter Twenty-one

She flew to her chamber as if the devil were on her heels, yelling for Moira to attend her and for a footman to summon a hack. Lily dressed in haste, forgoing any attention to her hair in favor of getting out the door as quickly as possible. Snatching up her reticule, she bounded down the stairs, her loose hair streaming behind her, only to discover that the carriage had not yet arrived.

A frustrated cry caught in her throat, and Lily swung her reticule as though slashing with a saber. If she hurried, she could prevent Ethan from spending more than a few moments in that dreadful place, but here she was being delayed by some anonymous jarvey who hadn't the slightest concern for her need.

She prowled around the entrance hall, stopping every few seconds to make the servant open the door and see whether the coach had arrived. When at last it did, she burst from the house and issued the address while clambering inside.

The whole of the maddeningly slow ride to her parents' house, Lily was tormented with visions of Ethan being subjected to every horrible degradation. He would be deprived of his own bed to sleep in. He would be housed alongside likewise deprived and degraded men, who may be capable of doing him harm. She had to get him out of there!

His instructions rang in her mind. She swatted aside a twinge of guilt at defying his wishes. "Flexing that awkward honor of his," she murmured—the same honor that held him responsible to his ridiculous gambling debts before the mortgage. If she lived a hundred years, Lily would never quite grasp this gentleman's code that men spoke of, not when aspects of it flew in the face of all reason. Surely, he'd not hold her interference against her once she'd secured his release from prison. The alternative was for him to remain in gaol—unthinkable.

After an eternity of clogged streets and lumbering progress, the carriage finally drew to a stop in front of the Bachman house. Lily paid the jarvey and accepted the hand of the footman who appeared at the carriage door. She stalked past the butler without a glance, aiming straight for her father's study.

The door was closed, but Lily pushed her way in, paying no heed to the startled man sitting across the desk from Mr. Bachman.

"Father, I must speak with you." Her fingers twitched in the material of her skirt.

Mr. Bachman's heavy brows drew together. "Lily, I'm in the middle of a meeting! What is the meaning of—"

"I'm sorry, Papa, sir," she added, nodding toward the other man. "Were the matter not of grave importance I wouldn't have—" She pressed a fist to her mouth as her throat constricted and tears welled. "I wouldn't ha-have in-terrupted." Lily stood stock-still, her eyes squeezed shut, while her father made a hasty apology to his associate and closed the door behind him. She opened them again only when they were alone and she felt his warm hands on her shoulders.

"What has happened?" His words rang with alarm.

She met his concerned gaze and wrung her hands at her waist. "Oh, Papa, Ethan's been taken to gaol!"

Mr. Bachman's face darkened and his jaw tightened. "Has he now?" He turned from Lily and shoved his hands into his pockets while he stalked to the window. A hard knot formed in Lily's belly while she looked at his back. She gleaned no insight from the square set of his shoulders, nothing to suggest empathy for her plight. "His debts have caught up with him, I assume?" he asked in a clear voice.

Swallowing down the lump in her throat, she summoned her courage to proceed. "It was the mortgage, Papa; the bank took out the warrant. If you would only sign over the dowry—"

Mr. Bachman's fist slammed against the window frame. "The blasted dowry again!" He whirled to face her, thunderclouds marring his usually placid features. "I wish to God I never promised anything like it. I should have sent you off with ten thousand like every other chit on the mart. But no, I felt remorse for you still being unmarried at your age. I felt guilty for your having had to endure a year of mourning, further delaying your debut. I wanted the world to know what a treasure you are, that there was no blemish upon you, how I—" he touched his fingertips to his chest, his voice growing thick. "How *I* treasure you," he said in a more even tone. A deep breath lifted his ribs. Love and sadness mingled in his eyes. Lily hated having to come to him like this. What a disappointment he must think her now.

"But it's never brought us anything but grief," he continued. With a heavy sigh, Mr. Bachman looked toward his desk, still littered with the papers from his unfinished meeting. "So Thorburn sent you after the money."

Lily shook her head and reached a trembling hand to her father's arm. "No, I came on my own, Papa. Ethan doesn't know I'm here. In fact, he told me not to ask you for it." She breathed a humorless laugh and shrugged. "But here I am, anyway. I fear I'm hopeless at the 'honor and obey' part."

Mr. Bachman gave her a half-smile before running a hand along his jaw. "I must confess, I'm pleasantly surprised to learn of Thorburn's instructions. You'll not like this, Lily, but I stand with him."

Lily's stomach plunged. "What can you mean, Papa?"

Mr. Bachman groaned as he settled himself into his chair at the desk. "I spoke plain, my dear. Your husband is quite right. I shall not turn the dowry over at this time."

Desperation sent icy claws reaching around her. How could he not come to her aid? She quivered as she looked at the impassive man before her, anger stiffening her spine, putting words on her tongue before she'd even thought them through. "I don't think you ever mean for us to have it!" Her hand cut an arc in front of her. "Your prejudice against Lord Thorburn has tainted your view of me, as well. Papa, I have done *everything* you've ever asked of me! I honored a betrothal to a man I scarcely knew, who was ten years my senior, fully prepared to marry him only because you wished it of me. I mourned that same man, though I did not grieve him. I married Lord Thorburn because you told me I must! And now that I find I do love him—" At his astonished expression, she nodded. "Yes, Papa, it's true. I love my husband, and though he's not said the words, I think he loves me, as well. But now that we've a chance at happiness, you would keep us apart with meanness and spite and—"

"That will do, Lily."

"And—and *hate*, is what it is. You are being hateful—"

"Madam, that will do!" he roared.

Lily flinched back at his fury, startled into silence.

Mr. Bachman's nostrils flared while he pinned her in a ferocious stare. "Never before have you spoken to me with such impertinence, Lily. I will not begin to countenance it now; indeed, I will not. If you mean to continue in this fashion, you may leave this instant, for I'll not hear another word of it."

Lily's head bowed under the shame washing over her. Where was the self-control she used to pride herself in owning? Ethan had dispossessed her of it. Rationality fled before her when she so much as thought of him. "Forgive me, Papa," she murmured. "I'm only worried about Ethan. I never should have spoken so. It was unseemly and ill done and I apologize with my whole heart."

Mr. Bachman rose and took her hands, cold against his warm palms. "There now, it's done," he said. "Let's not quarrel, my dear."

He led her to the sofa in the study's seating area and Lily sank into the welcome support of the cushions. She felt tired and sick, weak with concern. The tinny chime of the clock on the mantelpiece caught her attention. Noon. Even now, Ethan would be at Fleet Prison. What was happening to him there? Was he being treated respectfully, or was he being abused by jailers, happy to see a nobleman brought low?

Her eyes slid to her father, whose lips turned up in a sympathetic smile. "Please, Papa," she whispered.

Mr. Bachman patted her hands. "I'm sorry, my dear, no. In the first place, I feel obliged to honor your husband's wishes. If he does not want your dowry put to this use, I'll not do it. Secondly, I see that I have engendered in you a dependency on my generosity. When you were my unmarried daughter, it was both my duty and my delight to provide for you to the best of my ability. Now you are Thorburn's responsibility, and I should not have given you so many monetary gifts after your wedding. It was a disservice to you, my dear, and I do apologize for it."

Lily stared at him, bewildered. "You apologize...for *spoiling* me? Is that it, Papa, are you calling me spoiled?"

Her father's jaw worked from side to side. "Well, no, my dear. But you must admit you are *accustomed* to having my resources at your disposal."

"That's not my doing," Lily said weakly. She felt hope slipping from her grasp. If her own father would not help her, what could she do for Ethan?

"I know it's not," Mr. Bachman said, "which is why I apologized."

"But surely you must see that this is an extraordinary circumstance, Papa. I'm not asking you for pin money to buy a new bonnet!"

He shook his head, his jaw set in resolve. "No, Lily, I'm quite decided. It's time for you and Thorburn to do for yourselves. You never saw the first home Mrs. Bachman and I shared in Brighton. What a mean little apartment it was, my dear. Just one small room, but I paid the rent myself." He patted her knee. "Struggling together can bring a couple closer. If you truly have formed an attachment to Lord Thorburn, then you will find a way to muddle through and be better for it in the long run. Though I daresay that if he returns your regard, then it shan't be long before the conditions Thorburn agreed to for the relinquishment of your dowry are met."

Lily felt depleted, empty but for the aching need to bring Ethan home. "I'm happy," she ventured, a final attempt to sway her sire.

He snorted at her words. "Far from it, m'dear. You're miserable. You children get through this, and then we'll see where things stand."

Where things stood, Lily thought as she pressed a dutiful kiss to her father's cheek before slipping from the house, was this: she had failed in procuring from her father any material support for her cause. She was a woman alone. There was no one else she could turn to. If only Isabelle were home, she might know what to do. *Perhaps Naomi,* Lily thought, before discarding the idea a second later. No, she could not draw her friends into her woes.

She pressed her fingers to her forehead as she walked toward the hackney stand on the corner. Mortgages and properties and money…all men's affairs. Hazy images swirled through her mind as a driver handed her up into a carriage. The little bit of money she'd saved was laughable in the face of the sum needed to satisfy Ethan's debt to the bank. If only she had property of her own to mortgage—

Lily's eyes flew wide open.

"What direction, my lady?" the driver inquired.

Her lips trembled in hesitation for a moment before she firmly instructed the man to take her to the office of Mr. Eugene Wickenworth, Esquire.

Chapter Twenty-two

Ethan scraped his tongue against his teeth and spit out the barred window, casting the wretched taste-smell of Fleet Prison onto the street just on the other side of his cell. He took a swig from the mug of sour ale standing on the little wooden table in the corner, swished it around his mouth to obliterate the remnants of the previous offensive taste, and then cast that out the window, as well. "Gah! That may be worse," he muttered.

With a heavy sigh, he grasped hold of the bars and gazed out. A spectral fog lay over the city, reducing buildings to mere shadows of themselves and all of the inhabitants to shades. Little eddies of the fog fell through the bars into his cell. The dampness permeated his clothes; his shirt clung in places and hung limply in others. *There's not enough starch in the world to make a cravat stand against this mess,* he reflected. And so, he wore neither cravat nor waistcoat—the latter having conspired with the dampness to make him sweat like a sausage in its casing, despite the cool temperature—only a dark blue coat over his shirt, trousers, and boots. Water droplets gathered on the shoulders and sleeves of his outer garment; he swiped them away before resuming his glum inspection of the outside world.

Nearby stood the sponging houses, their roofs jutting up into the mist like drowning men struggling to regain the surface. Upon his arrival, the Keeper had smugly informed Ethan the sponging houses were all full, thus necessitating his being held in the prison proper for the time being. The best he could offer Ethan was a private cell.

At least the fog obscured the faces of passers-by. He couldn't stand the combination of pity and scorn he saw when he met the eyes of those who walked free. Humiliation had clapped him over the head time after time in the last week. Had Ethan's father—the detestable Earl of Kneath—done his offspring the favor of passing to his eternal reward, all of this could have been avoided. Not only would he already possess the funds needed to repay his obligations, but he'd be a peer in his own right, immune from arrest for debt.

"No," he ground out, his hands tightening around the bars. Such thoughts were worthy of the Ethan Helling of several months ago, the man looking for quick money and easy answers, but not of the man he was striving to become.

For a long time he stood at the window, almost hypnotized by the undulating fog, its tentacles embracing and releasing pedestrians like some denizen of the deep.

A finely dressed woman passed nearby his window. He startled, thinking for a moment it was Lily. Excitement flooded his veins, but quickly turned to icy shame that she should see him in such squalor. The shame gave way to weary relief when he realized the woman was not Lily at all.

Turning his back to the window, lest he go mad attributing his wife's persona to every passing female, Ethan collapsed onto the mean cot in his cell. Straw poked through the worn, stained ticking and dug into his thighs and back, a torment not nearly as great as that which he inflicted upon himself.

Resting the back of his wrist across his brow, his eyes closed and visions of his wife sprang before him. There was Lily in his bed on their wedding night, nervous and brave and passionate. There were her chocolate eyes and dark hair spilled across white sheets. Milky skin and eternally long legs and those breasts— Lord, those breasts! Desire, with no hope of fulfillment, thudded heavily through his veins.

He stifled a groan and squeezed his eyelids even tighter, forcing the erotic images away. The innocent vixen was now dissipated and replaced by Lily, sitting beside him on a park bench, looking to him for advice and guidance; Lily, standing in his vacant parlor, pertly dismissing him as an uppity butler. He chuckled at the memory. He'd been drawn to her from the first, entranced by her spirit and beauty even as he'd wanted to put the arrogant girl in her place.

But then, there was Lily in that same parlor, scrubbing walls in the wedding gown she valued no more than the dirty rag in her hands. And finally, there she was, barely glimpsed from inside the hackney that drew him away to gaol—at his bedroom window with her hand pressed to the glass and tears staining her cheeks, hurt beyond all recall by the penniless blighter she'd been forced to wed.

Prior to meeting Ethan, Lily had been *the* talk of London. For good or ill, everyone took note of her goings and comings. She commanded a legion of hopeful beaus and struck terror in the hearts of every matchmaking mama. Since their first twirl around the ballroom, he'd managed to topple her off that pedestal and drag her down to the barely respectable depths he inhabited.

Unexpectedly, Ethan thought of Ensign Handford, Lily's deceased fiancé. He never knew the man—knew nothing of him, even, except for the little he'd gleaned from Quillan and Lily's vague comments. But Ethan pictured him now, a brave, upright man sacrificing his life in defense of an occupied nation and his own country's security.

"I wish you hadn't died, sir," he whispered. Charles Handford would have been a good husband to Lily. He never would have humiliated her as Ethan had done.

Further, had Handford survived and married Lily, Ethan wouldn't be suffering this torment. He never would have known this despair, or the maddening need he had for her, the unrelenting desire to be in her company, in her good graces, in her bed. If she'd been Lily Handford, rather than Lily Helling, she never would have come to town seeking a husband. Her dowry would have passed to the eminently deserving Ensign Handford. That good man would have had her fortune, as well as her respect, companionship, and—

"Damnation, he would have had her in bed, too." A frustrated, possessive growl ripped from his throat at the vision of his luscious Lily in the arms of the suddenly despicable Charles Handford. He sat upright, his chest heaving. No, she was his—Ethan's. He had claimed her body with his own as surely as she had claimed his. There was no other woman for him. They were bound together, and he had to get home to her. This separation was driving him mad. "Does it drive her mad?" he mused. "Or does she welcome the respite?"

A sharp rap on the wooden door interrupted this new volley of self-inflicted mental flagellation. "Thorburn," called the guard in the hall, "visitor." Ethan stood as the door opened. Mr. Wickenworth entered at a trot, as though to escape the cell-lined corridor with all haste. The solicitor removed his spectacles to mop his forehead and eyes with a large handkerchief and startled when the door slammed home behind him.

Replacing his spectacles, the solicitor blinked once, twice. As Ethan watched, Wickenworth toured the confined space with a slow rolling of his eyes and head, even tilting his chin upward to observe the dank, dripping ceiling.

"Oughf." The man's appalled sound vibrated from the back of his throat, filling the air with his disgust.

Ethan smirked. "My sentiments exactly. Please," he said, gesturing to the rough little chair beside the rickety table. "I take it you received my letter?"

Wickenworth set a leather binder on the table and gingerly lowered himself onto the chair. It groaned in complaint, but held firm as the man settled into it. "I did, my lord. It was printed last night." He picked up his binder and unwrapped the thong holding it closed. Opening it, he removed a sheet of newspaper and handed it to Ethan. "Worded just as you instructed." Ethan found the notice toward the bottom of the page:

OFFERED FOR SALE:
The sailing vessel *Star Rover*, 48 feet in length.
Mahogany decks with teak appointments.
Hull, masts, and rigging in excellent condition.
Ideal yacht for pleasure-cruising, river or coastal travel.
Asking £1000.
Please inquire to E. Wickenworth, Esq., No. 82, Cheapside

Ethan gave a sad half-smile when he read the advertisement. His grandfather's sailboat was the last bit of valuable property he had to his name. It had been an instrument of solace and joy to him as a child and young man. The days he'd spent on the water in the care of his grandparent had been bright spots of happiness and reprieve from the darkness of his father's house.

More than anything, though, Ethan needed to get home to Lily, which meant he had to raise money to satisfy his debt with the bank. *Money*, he thought with bleak exhaustion. *It always comes back to money.* He hated to part with the boat, but he couldn't see any other way.

He must have voiced the thought aloud, for Wickenworth cleared his throat, intruding on Ethan's thoughts. "I beg your pardon, my lord, but if you don't mind a bit of advice, it might be a better idea to sell the Bird Street house. After all, a thousand pounds might not meet your obligation with the bank—"

Ethan jabbed him with a piercing stare. "No. That's Lady Thorburn's home. I will sell the clothes off my back before I make a homeless woman of my wife."

The solicitor's fingertips rubbed together on his thigh as he gazed thoughtfully at Ethan. He bent his neck in an approving gesture. "Very well, my lord. You'll be glad to know I received an offer for *Star Rover* this very morning."

Ethan's brows raised. "Already?"

Wickenworth opened the folio again. "A man came to my office at ten o'clock, bank draft in hand. Here it is."

Scarcely able to believe the speed of his good fortune, Ethan took the bank draft and looked it over. The numbers had the painstaking appearance of someone recently introduced to their formation by a primer. The signature was likewise scrawled with deliberate accuracy, rendering it utterly, awfully legible. Ethan felt the blood drain from his face. "Oh, no."

There, at the bottom of the cheque, was the name Edmund Ficken.

"No, no, no!" Ethan growled out a curse and spun, driving the side of his fist against the stone wall of his cage.

"My-my lord." The chair scraped as Wickenworth clambered to his feet. "Are you displeased? Do you not wish to sell to Mr. Ficken? I brought a bill of sale for you to sign, but if you do not desire—"

"Does he know?" Ethan interrupted.

The solicitor's brows furrowed, burying themselves behind the rims of his spectacles. "I beg your pardon?"

"Does Ficken know it's my boat?"

The solicitor's mouth worked soundlessly for a moment, his jowls bouncing up and down. "We-e-ll," he said at last, elongating the word and glancing nervously about the room, "he did say to me—and these were his exact words, 'Ain't that Thorburn's boat?' and I affirmed it was your lordship's. He seemed pleased, and handed over the bank draft straightaway."

Ethan scoffed. "I just bet he did."

"My lord?" Wickenworth's brows once again retreated to await enlightenment.

What to say? Should Ethan tell the man of law that he was offended by Ficken's very existence? That the man's social climbing exploits left a bad taste in Ethan's mouth? That he hated the bloke for having the devil's own luck, while Ethan had lost everything at the tables? When he thought of it that way, his distaste for Edmund Ficken was not worth speaking aloud. He shook his head. "Nothing. I'll sell. Where's the bill?"

Business concluded, Wickenworth replaced the signed document in his folio, along with the other papers. He glanced at Ethan, his countenance conveying that something else tickled his tongue.

"What is it?" Ethan asked.

"My lord, I took the liberty of looking into your mortgage obligation to Dunraven Bank."

Ethan straightened, flabbergasted at the man's audacity. "You did what? I requested your assistance in the sale of my boat—that was the extent of your involvement."

"Forgive me, my lord, for prying into your personal affairs, but Lady Thorburn came to me, seeking advice in the matter."

He flinched. If he could magic away Lily's knowledge and recollection of this whole sorry affair, he'd do so. Was it possible to sink any lower in his wife's estimation? Clearly, she did not believe him capable of ensuring his own release. Planting his feet in a wide stance, Ethan fixed Wickenworth in a dark glare. "When?"

The other man dabbed at his forehead with his much-abused handkerchief; the gold ring on his little finger winked at Ethan.

"The very day of your departure from Bird Street, my lord."

Ethan cringed. "I don't want her involved in this," he said, casting his eyes out at the fog-shrouded city.

"My lord," Wickenworth ventured, "Dunraven Bank demands a security of five thousand pounds." The man's unease became palpable as he paused. Ethan's stony gaze flicked to his face. The solicitor squirmed where he stood. "You do not have five thousand pounds, my lord."

Sneering, Ethan turned on a heel and paced the confines of his little cell, his legs aching from lack of exercise. "And here I thought you were to tell me something I didn't know. Go away, Wickenworth."

"My lord," pressed the solicitor, "even with the sale of *Star Rover*, you are a long way from release. Lady Thorburn is working to raise the funds. I believe you should allow—"

"No!" Ethan roared. He rounded on Wickenworth; the rotund man stumbled back and fell into the chair. Ethan leaned forward, bracing one arm on the little table, boxing the solicitor in. "I—told—her," he seethed, every word forcing its way past his clenched teeth, "not to go after her dowry." He pounded his chest with his free hand. "I can do this!"

Wickenworth regarded the raging viscount with pity. "She did request the dowry from her father, my lord."

Ethan's eyes slid closed and he exhaled slowly, his sense of degradation mounting with every word from Wickenworth's mouth.

"Hear me out, my lord! Mr. Bachman refused her request."

His shoulders slumped with relief. "Well, that's good news," he said, turning away and pressing his hands to his eyes.

A pounding at the door announced the presence of the guard again. "Thorburn, guest!" barked the voice. Ethan frowned and for a split second wondered whether Lily had come. But he'd jotted her a note the day he arrived, telling her in no uncertain terms she was not to set foot in Fleet Prison. The thought of his lovely wife in such a hellhole made him sick to his stomach.

The visitor was, however, female, if not a lady. She stepped into the dank cage with the skirt of her turquoise blue pelisse sweeping behind like the plumage of a peacock. A frivolous matching hat, adorned with fluffy plumage, rested atop her golden hair. Her lovely lips curled and her doe eyes were wide and full of mirth.

Ghita's unexpected presence put him on guard. They had last parted on less-than-friendly terms, which made her guileless smile all the more suspicious. Her motivations in coming were likely questionable, yet he couldn't deny that seeing her was a welcome reprieve from the drab gray sameness of his prison existence. Her unrepentant superficiality reminded him that life outside these heavy walls went on as it always did.

"Ethan, the air of this place makes my body feel as though there were a hundred thousand creepy things all over—spiders and bugs and a snake going down my back."

He gave her a tired smile. "The English expression is 'it makes my skin crawl.' But your turn of phrase is much more evocative."

Ghita preened at his compliment, ducking her head and glancing up in a coquettish fashion. The chair creaked as Wickenworth shifted in his seat. Ghita's eyes narrowed upon him, as though just noticing his presence, despite the fact that he took up a third of the available space. "What is this person?"

"Forgive me." Ethan turned to include Wickenworth, who rose for the introduction. "Ghita, this is Mr. Wickenworth, my wife's family's solicitor. Mr. Wickenworth, Signora Bellisario."

Wickenworth's eyes lit up. "Not Ghita Bellisario!" he gasped rapturously. He grasped her hand and pumped it up and down.

Ghita's startled face turned to an amused Ethan. "Madam," Wickenworth continued, "I saw you last year in *Figaro*—three times, in fact. You were divine, *signora*, just divine."

Ghita's head fell back and a musical laugh escaped her creamy throat. "Thank you, sir, you are too kind." For an instant, her face was free of guile, and her teasing smile reminded Ethan why he had once been so ensnared by her charms. "I did not think to find a patron of the arts here."

"But tell me," Wickenworth continued, "why have you not performed this year? I am disappointed with every production that does not feature your talents."

A brow arched over Ghita's eye, and she flicked a sidelong glance at Ethan. He wondered what answer she'd concoct, for surely she'd not give the man the truth—that she'd grown too comfortable in her position as Quillan's mistress to continue with the stage.

"A singer," Ghita started, laying a delicate hand upon Wickenworth's arm, "such as myself must sometimes give the voice—" here she touched her throat, drawing the poor, defenseless Wickenworth's eyes there "—an extended holiday, to rest and stay strong."

Ethan turned and covered the snort he couldn't contain. When he looked back, Ghita was throwing daggers at him with her eyes, while her ardent admirer stared, slack-jawed, at the graceful lines of her neck, reverent in the presence of the soprano's instrument.

Like a hypnotized bumpkin at a country fair, Wickenworth nodded and mumbled his assent. "Yes, that makes perfect sense. Well," he said more loudly, "take care of yourself, *signora*, and I hope to see you perform again."

"Be assured of my coming forth triumphant return to the stage."

"Oh, good, good." Wickenworth vigorously nodded his head, setting his jowls to bouncing again.

The conversation having wound down, Wickenworth looked from Ethan to Ghita and back again, as though waiting for someone to initiate the next round of discourse. Ethan looked at Ghita, who cleared her throat and cast a meaningful glance at the solicitor.

Taking her meaning, Ethan extended his hand to the other man. "Thank you for coming, Mr. Wickenworth. Your assistance is appreciated."

The solicitor's mouth tightened as he looked disapprovingly between the two other parties. *He wonders why I wish to be alone with her,* Ethan realized. At length, Wickenworth took Ethan's hand. "My lord," he said curtly. "*Signora.*"

With a harrumph, he gathered his folio and knocked on the cell door, which was opened in short order by the guard.

"Mr. Wickenworth," Ethan called. The man turned in the doorway, filling it up with his girth. "My warmest regards to Lady Thorburn, if you please."

The solicitor's face softened, and he nodded. "Good day, my lord."

When he'd gone, Ghita took a turn around the little room, with Ethan standing in the center of it—a one-man audience to her display of each turn of her figure. "What a funny little man," she said with a wave. "Falling over me one second and ready to scold me the next. You English are a nation of passionate prudes. Did you know? I wonder you do not all drive yourselves mad with the pushing and the pulling against your natures." She emphasized her words with theatrical gestures, as though she were ripping her own self in two.

Her performance wore thin. Time to end the game. "Why have you come, Ghita?"

She stopped in front of his cot and blinked in surprise. "Is it not natural for a woman of tender sensibilities to visit a dear friend who has fallen upon hard times?" She tilted her pretty head in a close approximation of innocence.

He eyed her warily. "Dear friends, are we?" He shook his head once, uncomfortable with the close confines of the cell, despite there being more open space in the room now with Wickenworth gone. Leaning against the wall, he crossed his arms in front of his chest, hands braced on opposite elbows.

Ghita rested a hand on his. "Not as dear as I should like." She stepped closer still, her expensive skirts brushing over his scuffed boots. "We are so alike, you and I. We're both of us too wicked for good society, but we don't care."

His brows snapped together. "You're mistaken, Ghita. I do care. My wife's reputation has already suffered through her connection to me. Would that I already got on better in polite society, but from now on, that's just what I shall strive to do."

Ghita's lips pursed. "And where is your Miss Bachman?" She tossed her head flamboyantly. "Is she here to comfort you in your hour of need? Did she bribe the Keeper, the warden, and the guard to be allowed in to see you? No! I did. Here I am, Ethan. Where is she?" Her eyes burned with feverish intensity. "And I want to do more for you, too, my love. Let me get you out of this awful place. I hate seeing you like this, a man so great and fine as you, caged like a toothless bear. You are more than this place! I can have you released today, right now, if only you'll tell me we will be together."

Ethan pushed her away, appalled at the proposition. "I told you I won't keep a mistress."

Ghita laughed. She reached a hand toward him again, which he avoided by turning to the window. Damn this cell! If he could, he would crawl through the cracks in the mortar to get away from her.

"No, don't you see?" she continued, her face beatific. "I don't want to be your mistress, Ethan. No, no, I see now that would never do—not for you."

He pinched the bridge of his nose. This visit had taken a turn for the nightmarish. "You should go."

"Listen to me!" she cried. "I want only to be your friend, your lover, your companion—a true affair of the heart. I gave up Quillan to be with you. It was all understood between us, Ethan. We'll be able to support ourselves with that dowry, and soon, I will return to the stage—I spoke true to that silly man. The conductor has already contacted me to come back for a winter production of—"

A fierce growl tore from his throat as he rounded on her. "I want you to leave." He wiped the back of his hand down a stubbled cheek as though flicking crumbs to the floor. "I tried to let you down easily before, but let me put it to you plain." She stepped back toward the door. He stalked onward, driving her. "It's never going to happen, Ghita. I. Don't. Want. You."

Her back hit the door and she swallowed, color rising in her cheeks. Then she straightened and met his glower with a challenging look. "You will regret this, Ethan. More than anything in the world—except maybe marrying your stupid Miss Bachman."

Ethan's vision went red at her catty insult. He shook with the force of holding himself in check. His fist crashed into the door two inches to the left of her ear. She jumped with a shriek. "Guard!" he bellowed. He lowered his face to look Ghita in the eye, on the level of kissing her if he'd been so inclined. At present, he'd much rather slam his forehead against hers and see whether she'd bounce off the door or just collapse in a heap. "That's *Lady Thorburn*," he seethed. "And don't you ever, *ever* forget it."

Ghita trembled all over, and then she grew still. A little too still. Uneasiness seeped up Ethan's spine as he straightened. The

Italian's eyes glittered dangerously. Behind her, the door opened. She smirked. "Don't worry, my lord. I won't forget."

With one of her dismissive waves, she turned and swept from the room in a swirl of silk and feathers.

Something about her final words haunted Ethan. He paced the room, turning them over and over in his mind. Such a very few words, but they carried an ominous tone. And then it struck him. He stopped and stared blankly at the gray stone wall. Ghita had never once called Ethan "my lord." In so doing, she had acknowledged the end of their association. She had turned on him, which meant—

"Oh, God, Lily." His wife was the target of a scorned woman— and she didn't even know it.

Chapter Twenty-three

E. Ficken, Lily read. It was a name with which she was unfamiliar, but she felt gratitude toward the mysterious gentleman, along with a twinge of sadness. Sighing, she pushed her bit of melancholy aside. Ethan would be home soon—in time for supper, she hoped—thanks to the papers bearing Mr. Ficken's name.

Lily tucked the papers into a drawer, then glanced around the room and smiled. It was a small thing, to be sure, but she hoped her husband would be pleased to discover some of her things in his room—just a few, enough to show she intended to share the room with him at night. Her own decanter of water stood on a bedside table. She'd purchased a new brush set to nestle alongside Ethan's combs and pots of hair pomade. These last items she smiled at fondly; no pomade succeeded in taming his short, unruly hair. Judging by the variety of containers on the stand, he must have tried nearly every formulation.

The bulk of her things she'd left in her own room. Despite Ethan's protest, Lily did need a place to keep her clothes and to dress. "But that will be all," she pronounced with a toss of her head. She and Ethan could begin anew. Peace and light filled her at the joyous thought; her heart bathed in the golden glow of her growing love for her husband.

Repairing to her own room, she summoned Moira to help her dress for supper. For the occasion of her reunion with Ethan, Lily selected a dress of creamy India muslin with a floral print around the hem and gilt spangles worked into the skirt and bodice. The neckline plunged daringly low to skim across the swell of her breasts, while short sleeves clung to her shoulders, including the expanse of her collarbones in the display. Combined with the tasteful arrangement of her hair—swept back and adorned with a simple bandeau—Lily was quite pleased with the general effect. It suggested, not demanded; it offered, but demurely. It was a sartorial lifting of the brow, a subtle cut of the eye toward a secluded nook. After a separation of nearly two weeks, Lily longed to hide with Ethan in a secluded nook or three.

Just as Moira stepped back from fastening the last hairpin in place, a knock at the front door reverberated through the house. "Ethan!" Lily shot up, a tangle of delight and nerves buffeting her middle. She cast a glance over her shoulder at Moira.

"Go on, Miss Lily," the maid urged. "Don't keep his lordship waiting."

Lily breathed a laugh, and decorum flew out the window. Biting her lip, she raced down the stairs to the foyer. As she rounded the landing, a grin spread over her face. A footman held the door ajar. Lily ran toward it, ready to throw herself in her husband's arms. "Eth—"

His name died on her tongue as she skidded to a halt. The smile fell from her face as she stared in disbelief at the person darkening her door. The…liar, the actress, the Italian mistress inclined her head in greeting.

"What are you doing here?" Lily fumed, offended that the very woman who had engineered her social disgrace would have the compunction to approach her at all, much less intrude into Lily's home.

"My dear Lady Thorburn," Ghita said, "I apologize for calling at this awkward hour."

Lily pinched her lips together. Her hands clasped at her waist. "It is, I'm afraid, a most inconvenient time. You see, I expect my husband any moment." Behind Ghita, at a nod from his mistress, the servant opened the door again. "You will please understand I cannot receive you—"

Ghita raised a gloved hand. "I beg just a moment of your time, my lady. How happy I was to read in the paper today the news that Lord Thorburn's release from that dreadful prison had been secured. But it was this which prompted my hasty call. Please, my lady, a single moment."

Lily's eyes narrowed. The shorter, fairer woman's countenance held no artifice, and her large hazel eyes shone with pleading. "Very well," she relented at last.

Lily led her unexpected visitor to the newly furnished parlor. Gesturing with a hand, she waited until Ghita had settled herself onto the chaise longue, and then she took one of the chairs opposite. There would be no hint of intimacy with this woman, no innuendo of pleasure at her visit.

Ghita looked at Lily, who fixed her caller with a glacial stare. "Your moment is passing," she snapped.

"I—I'm sorry," Ghita stammered. "You have every reason in the world to dislike me."

"Then you cannot take it ill if I do," Lily rejoined.

Ghita shook her head. "No, my lady, I cannot. Indeed, when I saw that Eth—Lord Thorburn would be happily returned to you this very day, I felt moved to come and offer my apology." Here she paused and glanced down at her hands knotted together in her lap.

Lily frowned. Could it be this creature had a conscience, after all?

"You see," Ghita continued, "I wish to apologize for misleading you and your worthy mother both. It was a bit of sport on my part, answering to Lady Umberton's name when dear Mrs. Bachman called me so. All was intended in fun, and I never meant for you to suffer. Please believe me, my dear Miss—Lady Thorburn," she corrected herself with a pretty blush, "we Continentals do not have the same rules of decorum as you English. It is no great thing for a woman such as myself to be received everywhere—even into her lover's wife's parlor—and no sin to make friends with an unmarried lady. I apologize most sincerely for not remembering the English rules and for causing you such trouble." Contrition marked every line of her posture.

Her explanation lacked nothing, and her accented words felt sincere. Grudgingly, Lily's spine softened a fraction. "That is very generous of you," she acknowledged. "While your mischief did do me harm, I must allow that my own sense of propriety was sadly lacking that evening." Recalling the brazen way she'd demanded Ethan's kiss, she colored and cleared her throat. "And it seems I'm the only person in London not aware of your arrangement with Lord Umberton."

Ghita relaxed visibly at Lily's words. Merriment lit her face as she waved a hand. "You must not take any of the blame, my lady. I have missed the stage, and could not resist playing a part. As for Lord Umberton," she shrugged, "I no longer have any arrangement with him—not since the agreement with Eth—" Her eyes flew wide and a hand clapped across her mouth.

Lily blinked. Her head tilted in question. What in the world had Ethan to do with Lord Umberton's mistress? "I beg your pardon?"

Ghita shook her head emphatically, sending golden curls swaying beside her cheeks. "Ah, no, my lady, I spoke wrong. Nothing, nothing at all." The slight woman started to rise.

"Sit down!" Lily snapped.

Ghita sat.

Cold iron bands tightened around Lily's chest. "You did not misspeak. Explain yourself, madam."

Ghita's hands twisted and she offered a simpering smile. "I would not dream of speaking to you of it."

Quivering, Lily forced herself to draw a deep breath before continuing. "You came to my home for this purpose, did you not? To tell me what it is you pretend to withhold."

The other woman's eyes tightened a fraction, triumph glittering in the irises.

"Say it," Lily hissed. She pounded the arm of her chair with a fist, her lips curled in a snarl.

Ghita's mask of false humility crumbled as she smirked and straightened. "Very well; it is a simple little thing," she said with a breezy wave of her hand. "I encouraged Ethan to marry you. In fact, I quite championed the cause." She inclined her head again, but there was nothing of the supplicant in the gesture this time; rather, the sharp movement mocked Lily. "That, of course, would allow Ethan and I to come to an agreement of our own, something we have both wished since we met. That is all," she shrugged, "no more, no less."

Lily's eyes moved from Ghita to the fireplace, where the evening's fire had been laid out but not yet lit. A whooshing sound flooded her ears, threatening a swoon. "I don't faint," she whispered, squeezing her eyes shut and pinching the inside of her arm. "I don't faint!"

The full meaning of Ghita's words washed over her and through her, filling her mouth with the taste of bile. So Ethan had only married her so he could take Ghita as his mistress! Oh, this was beyond marrying her for her money to pay his debts. What Lily wouldn't give to have been roped into matrimony with nothing worse than a Leech, rather than this, this…

"Rake," she muttered.

Hadn't Naomi warned her so? Hadn't her friend done everything she could to steer Lily away from Ethan? But like an imbecile, Lily hadn't listened until it was too late. Bad enough about the money, worse the mistress—*or mistresses,* she thought in disgust, recalling the love letters from the mysterious Vanessa. Had her husband two paramours? But the very worst was the pain tearing through her heart, as deep an agony as her love for him had been a joy. *To love such a man. How could you let this happen?*

Opening her eyes, she pressed a hand to her temple to still her swimming vision. Across the room, Ghita wore an amused expression, clearly enjoying the effects of her performance.

Suddenly, the sound of feet pounded up the stairs. Lily looked up just in time to see Ethan burst into the room, a heartbreaking grin on his face. "There you are, you magnificent girl! However did you do it?"

With lips pinched tight together, Lily held silent. Why did she still yearn to throw herself into his arms? Even now, she wanted him to hold her while she cried, though it was he who caused her distress. Taking in her stricken appearance, Ethan's face fell.

Ghita rose and turned to face him. "My lord." Ethan's expression turned to outrage. "I've just had a delightful visit with your lady wife. I shall leave you two to your happy reunion—"

"Stay," Lily snapped.

Ghita tittered, her eyes darting between Lily and Ethan. For his own part, Lily noticed, Ethan looked on the verge of pitching Ghita out the window.

"Signora Bellisario has just apprised me of some startling intelligence," Lily stated. Ethan took a step backward, his features shuttered and wary. "Is it true, Ethan?" she asked in a low voice. "That you wanted to marry me so you could make her your mistress?"

Ethan's shoulders slumped a fraction, pain scribed across his handsome face. "Yes, Lily, it's true. But listen, listen to me, princess." He crossed the room and took her hands, pulling her to her feet. Lily whimpered and attempted to withdraw from his grasp, but he held tight to her fingers. Kissing the back of each hand, he then pressed them against his chest. Behind him, Lily caught a glimpse of motion as Ghita slipped out of the room, away from Ethan's wrath.

"Yes, I said that before I knew you, darling, but once I had the opportunity to talk with you, to learn about you, I wanted nothing to do with it."

Lily shook her head and looked away.

"It's true," he insisted. "The night of Vauxhall Gardens, I was disgusted with myself for contemplating such a course. But then, you were in the carriage with us, and everything happened so fast." He pressed kisses to her hands again and started to draw her closer.

Wrenching violently, Lily succeeded in excising herself from his arms. She could not trust herself there—even now, her flesh betrayed her, awakened by his presence.

She fled from the parlor and ran up the stairs, tears staining her cheeks. Instinct carried her to the bedchamber, where she flung herself face-down onto the coverlet. Ethan's measured steps followed her. "Go away!" The soft bedding muffled her indignant demand.

"Have you taken up residence in my room?" he asked, bemused.

Lily raised her head and groaned. She hadn't realized she'd gone to her new bedchamber—his. Ethan's weight sank into the covers beside her. Scooting back until she touched the mound of pillows against the headboard, Lily drew her knees against her chest. Ethan's hand came toward her.

"No!" Lily slapped his hand away, lashing out with all the hurt and anger in her broken heart.

Ethan rubbed his hand with the other. "That was uncalled for, Lily." His lips pressed together, and the corners of his eyes tightened. "I have never struck you, despite the many times you've tempted me. I should appreciate reciprocal restraint."

Lily gasped. "You're wrong, dead wrong! You *have* struck me, again and again." Her voice rose in pitch and cracked with emotion. Her belly was in knots as she quelled the rising urge to vomit. "You struck me by duping me into this marriage for my money. You struck me with your lies."

He shook his head in emphatic denial. "It's not like that—"

She pressed a fist to her chest and left her arm there, suddenly ashamed she'd put her bosom so much on display for her cad of a husband. "You only married me to get the woman you really want, that horrible little opera singer. Have you any idea how humiliated I am?"

"Listen to me," he snapped. In a flash, Ethan knelt before her and leaned in close, his nose mere inches from hers. "I don't want Ghita," he said. "*You* are the woman I want. Only you." Rocking forward, his mouth crushed her lips.

In vain, Lily fought against the raw need snaking its way down her back to twine in her abdomen. His smell surrounded her, clean, warm and spicy—somehow he'd managed a bath between Fleet and home. Where had he bathed? The question distracted her from the kiss.

Mistress. He would have the run of her house; he had probably been soaking in the tub even while Ghita came here to mock Lily with their affair.

With a mighty effort, she shoved him away from her while a sob wracked her body. "Go away!" she cried.

Ethan blinked, his eyes desire-hazed but quickly cooling. "Where would you have me go?" He stood and prowled the room, his long strides eating up the floor. In reply, Lily only shook her head and swiped tears from her cheeks. Raking a hand through his hair, he pinned her in a fierce glare. "Answer me, Lily. What is it you want?"

"Time," she said, her voice threadbare in her tight throat. "I need some time to sort this all out. Settle on where I can go, or where you can go—"

"What?" he roared. Wrenching his arms down and back, he looked like a prizefighter ready to round on her. "You would throw our marriage away?"

"Yes," she shot back. "It's been rubbish all along—we might as well toss it in the midden heap."

He stepped forward, rage blazing behind his eyes. Grabbing the vase from the bedside table, he howled as he flung it into the fireplace, where it exploded in a spray of porcelain shards, water, and shredded flowers.

Lily cowered against the headboard, pulling her legs against her all the harder. "Stop!" she cried in terror, "You're frightening me." She buried her face into her knees. Her heart galloped against her ribs; the hair on the back of her neck stood on end.

A moment passed, and nothing else happened. She chanced a glance up and saw him standing in profile, a trembling hand covering his eyes. A few seconds more, and his shoulders rose and fell as he took a deep breath. Long fingers wiped down his face, and he regarded her, frowning.

Their anguished gazes met for an instant before he looked away again. "My profoundest apologies, my lady." His fingers flexed and released at his sides. "That outburst was unpardonable, and I don't blame you if..." Shaking his head, he laughed bitterly and swiped his lips with the back of his hand. "It seems I can't escape my birthright, after all."

Lily's brows drew together in confusion. What did he mean about his birthright? Fear still held her tongue, so the question remained behind her teeth.

"Just as well my bag's not been unpacked." He strode past her and out the room.

Lily shuddered as she followed his progress down the stairs. When the front door closed, she relaxed for a moment, heaving a great sigh of relief. Another moment later, though, the tears came again, great wracking sobs that sprawled her out on the bed, screaming and pounding the soft bedding.

Not even two months after it had begun, her marriage was over.

Chapter Twenty-four

"Ow!" Lily pulled her pricked finger from behind the handkerchief she was embroidering. She sucked the wound, grimaced at the stain on the white linen, and tossed the scrap of material to the floor with a sigh of vexation.

A week had passed since Ethan's departure, and Lily had not yet adjusted to life as a woman estranged from her husband. A note from Wickenworth the day before informed her that Lord Thorburn had taken up residence at the home of one Mrs. Vanessa Myles. Now there was no question that the mysterious Vanessa was, in fact, Ethan's mistress. By moving into her home, he had announced his intention to leave Lily for good.

She stared around the room, her shoulders slumping. "Too many hours in the day," she muttered, her voice cracking with disuse. Lily had not ventured outside since Ethan had left. She had not touched a newspaper, for fear of the sensational gossip her marriage must have given rise to. She'd been a ghost rattling around in her own home, shying away from windows and cringing at the sound of a knock at the front door. Rather than tell her parents what a muck she'd made of matrimony, Lily had avoided their missives and had staunchly been "not at home" for a week. She had even avoided Naomi's letters and calls, too ashamed to admit she'd been wrong about Ethan.

Flopping onto the chaise longue with a heavy sigh, she picked up a novel and flipped through the pages before tossing it to the rug and sighing again. A soft tap sounded at the door. "Come in," she called.

A maid entered, carrying a salver. "This just came for you, Miss Lily."

She smiled wanly. Whatever strides the servants had made toward recognizing her as Lady Thorburn had evaporated with what they viewed as Ethan's desertion. She was once more their Miss Lily.

She plucked the creamy package from the tray and noted the familiar hand that formed her name. Frowning, she broke the seal.

> *My dearest Lily,*
> *Forgive my forwardness, but I must beg you to make all haste to Monthwaite House. It is a matter of utmost urgency. Please come this very morning—now.*
> *Your friend,*
> *Naomi Lockwood*

At her friend's alarming words, Lily sat bolt upright and stared in anguish at the maid. "What's happened?"

"A carriage awaits you," the servant said.

She stood and shook her head, clearing away the cobwebs of idleness. Had Aunt Janine taken ill? Was Naomi herself in distress? "Why could you not have given me a clue, silly goose?"

Lily made ready her departure. A cream lacquered carriage adorned with the Monthwaite crest stood at the curb. She took no pleasure in the vehicle's plush interior, distracted as she was with worry.

Though her mind was plagued with numerous questions and dark prognostications, she realized after some moments that she had ceased moping for her own misfortune. Nervous energy had her feet tapping for the first time in days. Whatever the crisis, at least she could think about something besides Ethan.

When the carriage pulled into Grosvenor Square, Lily craned her neck for a glimpse of the great house, searching the exterior for any clue of the emergency within. A footman sprang to the curb to lower the stairs and hand her down. The front door swung inwards as Lily ascended the steps.

"You came!" Naomi grabbed Lily into a hug the instant she set her foot in the door. Lily pulled away and searched the young woman's face. Naomi's cheeks were in high color, but otherwise she did not look particularly discombobulated. Her plaited hair was wound around the crown of her golden head, and her dress was the very crack of fashion. "It's good to see you, Lily," Naomi said with obvious pleasure. "It's been too long."

"My dear, what's happened?" Lily questioned. "Your note frightened me nigh to death."

By way of reply, Naomi took her hand and tugged her toward the stairs. "Come. You'll see."

Apprehension caused Lily to hold her breath as they made their way past generations of imposing-looking Lockwoods glowering out of their frames on the walls. There was a wedding portrait of Naomi's mother and father. Caro Lockwood had possessed a cold beauty even as a bride, Lily noted. A shiver of dread coursed her spine.

Naomi stopped at last at the door to the morning room at the back of the house. She hesitated with her hand on the knob. "Ready?" she whispered.

"What for?" Lily's eyes were wide in alarm.

Naomi's face split into a wide grin and she threw open the door.

Lily shrieked with glee as Isabelle, Duchess of Monthwaite, glanced over her shoulder from the sofa on which she sat, a delighted smile on her lips. His Grace, the Duke of Monthwaite, regarded the scene with fond warmth in his eyes from where he stood with his bent arm braced on the mantel. Naomi slipped out and closed the door.

"Isa!" Lily hurried around the back of the sofa as Isabelle rose, revealing a rounded middle.

Isabelle took Lily's hands, and the taller woman held the other at arm's length, delight bubbling up in her throat and spilling out in happy laughter. "Oh, a baby!" She embraced her closest friend— careful not to press against Isabelle's blossoming abdomen. "How I've missed you," she whispered.

"I've missed you, too," Isabelle replied, her green eyes dancing with joy.

Lily couldn't help glancing down at Isabelle's middle again. "From the looks of you, Isa, you must be—" Remembering she was in mixed company, she clamped her lips together, color rising in her cheeks.

"A little more than five months," Isabelle supplied.

Lily turned, still holding fast to Isabelle's hand, and clucked her tongue. "And you did not bring her home straightaway, Your Grace? I am all astonishment."

Marshall glanced from Lily to his wife, the hard planes of his handsome face softened with a glow reflected in Isabelle's countenance. "To the contrary, Miss Bachman, I was eager to abandon the expedition at once, but Isabelle wouldn't hear of it. She insisted we see the whole thing through." He looked back to Lily with a teasing smirk. "I'm delighted to find you in such excellent health, Miss Bachman. Your forthright nature has come to no harm in our absence."

Lily blushed at his jibe. She'd never been able to restrain herself when it came to speaking up for Isabelle. But looking from Marshall to Isabelle and back again, Lily realized the time for defending her friend had passed. These two obviously adored one another. Even as her shoulders relaxed a fraction, a pang of sadness shot through Lily that she would not know the same happiness in her own marriage.

"Oh, but Lily," Isabelle said, drawing her friend to sit beside her on the sofa. "I was in a very bad way with the sickness early on. Thankfully, we stayed in a village of Yanomani Indians, and the women gave me tea steeped from the root of a jungle plant, which quite settled my stomach. I've never had another worry from it, so long as I remember to drink that tea each morning."

"Astonishing!" Lily proclaimed. "I do hope you thought to import this plant for the benefit of all Englishwomen," she directed to Marshall.

The botanist-duke's lips twitched. "Unfortunately, no. I brought but two specimens back with me for the purpose of establishing its proper Linnean classification and registering it with the herbarium at Kew." He heaved a happy sigh. "If you had seen our cargo hold, you'd understand my predicament."

"Filled to the brim! Such sights, Lily, you wouldn't believe," Isabelle said. "The very air was *thick*. My hair fluffed out and refused to behave nine days out of ten." She waggled her fingers beside her neat coif, miming the wayward actions of her locks.

"Until the Yanomani helped you with that, as well," Marshall reminded her.

"Indeed," Isabelle replied. "With a nut oil rubbed into the scalp, and then combed through the hair."

Lily leaned back and tapped her chin. "Gad, it sounds as though the Yanomani have the answer to every problem an English lady could encounter."

"True enough," Isa agreed. Her green eyes looked toward the window, a distant, thoughtful expression on her face, as though she were once again seeing the marvels of the South American jungle. "They live in paradise," she said softly. "The scent of flowers hangs in the air and clings to your clothes—and such flowers! In vibrant colors you wouldn't believe, Lily. They look like a child's fanciful painting, I declare."

"Don't forget the animals," Marshall added, taking a seat in an armchair and crossing his long legs at the ankle.

"Oh, gracious, no, I never could! Remember the first time we heard those howler monkeys?" She laughed at a memory Lily wished she could experience, too. "It was the middle of the night, and I woke from a dead sleep with this dreadful noise in the trees just outside our hut. I thought a jungle monster had come to devour us. Make the sound for her, Marshall—you do a credible imitation."

Marshall frowned and shook his head.

"Oh, please!" Isabelle begged, clasping her hands together at her chest.

Marshall's countenance was stone, and Lily was certain her friend's pleas were in vain. Astonishingly, though, after another moment of Isabelle's fervent imploring, the man relented. "Very well, my love, if you insist."

"I do." Isabelle gave an imperious nod, then winked at Lily.

Marshall sat forward in his chair and braced his elbows on his knees. He cleared his throat and dropped his head from side to side, as though loosening up for a round in the boxing ring.

"Quite a build-up," she whispered to Isabelle.

Isabelle waved her hand. "Shh, shh, listen."

The duke formed his mouth into a wide oval, drew a breath, and bellowed. The cry was something like the roar of a great cat, punctuated with a wheeze at the end. The eerie sound sent a shudder through Lily.

His performance concluded, Marshall straightened. Isabelle clapped her appreciation, and Lily joined her applause. With a mocking incline of his head, Marshall accepted their accolades.

"Gracious me! What on earth is that racket?" Lily glanced back to see Aunt Janine and Naomi entering the morning room, followed by a house maid bearing a tea tray.

The ladies settled in while Isabelle poured. "Marshall was imitating a howler monkey for us," she explained.

Aunt Janine eyed Isabelle over the rim of her spectacles as she stirred her beverage. "I trust you've sufficiently reacquainted yourselves, then, since you're making animal calls for entertainment."

"I'm afraid we've monopolized the conversation with tales of our expedition," Marshall said. "Miss Bachman has graciously humored us."

Aunt Janine's spoon clattered to her saucer. "Miss—" She shot Lily a disapproving stare. "You haven't told them yet, girl?"

Isabelle's brow furrowed as she looked from Aunt Janine to Lily. "Haven't told us what?"

Lily cast an inquisitive glance of her own to Naomi. "I'm gossip for half of London, but you didn't see fit to tell them?"

"It's your news to share, not mine," Naomi rejoined.

"What news?" Isabelle interjected.

"I've always been glad to share happy news," Lily continued peevishly, "even if it is not my own. But it seems Lady Naomi does not view my news as anything worth rejoicing, and really—" she scoffed "—I can't fault her. Not now."

"Come now." Aunt Janine leaned over to pat Lily's knee. "It will all work out, m'dear, you'll see."

Isabelle huffed in frustration. "Will someone *please* tell me what is going on?" Her voice rose over the other women's, drawing all eyes to her. "Lily? I think you'd best illuminate us."

Fortifying herself with a sip of tea, Lily met Isabelle's worried expression. "I have been married these past two months."

The worry evaporated from Isabelle's eyes as a smile replaced it. "Why that's wonderful news!" she exclaimed.

"My congratulations," Marshall added. "This is, indeed, joyous news." His gaze drifted from Lily to Isabelle and back again. "I find the institution agrees with me most excellently."

Lily couldn't help but share her friends' joy. She was truly happy that they had found their way back to one another after the disastrous divorce that should have alienated them forever.

Isabelle's hand covered Lily's. "But tell us the name of your groom, my dear! I am in such suspense."

Lily set aside her tea before answering, "My husband is Ethan Helling, Viscount Thorburn."

Isabelle stared at her blankly for a second, while Marshall sputtered on his tea. "Thorburn?" he croaked.

"So…" Isabelle started, rallying from her shock. "So, you are the Viscountess Thorburn. That's…that's wonderful, Lily, truly…" Her voice trailed away as she apparently couldn't bring herself to utter any more empty compliments.

Lily's cheeks burned, and hot tears stung the backs of her eyes. Her friends were shocked at her marriage, appalled even. *And what would Isa say if she knew I loved the man? She must think me the most foolish female who ever lived.*

"Thorburn?" Marshall repeated, his vocal cords recovered from their clash with his beverage. "But he's not at all…that is, what they say…he's so very much…"

"Marshall, stop," Isabelle gently ordered. She scooped up Lily's hands and kissed them. "Can't you see we're distressing her? Lily, if you're happy, then I'm happy, too."

Her friend's kindness was her undoing. Lily's chin quivered. "But I'm not happy," she whispered. Isabelle made a sympathetic moue, and all of Lily's hurt came out in a great tumble. "I've made a horrible hash of things. But so did he. He was going to treat himself to a mistress if he married me."

Isabelle's mouth fell open in a gape of horror; the other ladies likewise gasped at this new, salacious intelligence. Marshall's brows shot up his forehead. "Naomi," he began in a low voice, "you'd best go. This isn't appropriate for a young lady's ears."

Naomi scowled but dutifully started to rise until Aunt Janine waved her back into her chair. "She won't break, Marshall. I've been looking after her for half a year; I feel qualified to issue that guarantee. We've both been with Lily since the beginning of her dealings with Lord Thorburn. If the viscountess doesn't mind including us, I see no objection."

Marshall grunted.

His sister took it as permission to stay and leaned toward Lily.

Discombobulated by the interruption, Lily hesitated in continuing. "He…didn't take up with this mistress."

"Well, that's good news." Isabelle encouraged. "How could he, with beautiful, wonderful Lily for his wife?"

"I wasn't a wonderful wife." Lily's hands tangled in her skirt. "He came to our marriage very much in debt."

"That is my understanding of the man," Marshall contributed with a tone of disapproval.

Isabelle shot her husband a look and pursed her lips. "Go on," she said to Lily.

"I was determined he shouldn't have my dowry. I insisted upon a detached society marriage. I thought he ruined me on purpose, you see—"

"Ruined!" Isabelle's hand flew to her throat as she shared a look of pained camaraderie with Lily. She knew all too well the sting of social exile. "My dear, what happened?"

Lily glanced at Marshall, whose penetrating gaze bore into her. She did not care to divulge the details of her misconduct in his company. "It was in the papers," she said in a rush. "Everyone knows."

"Never mind." Isabelle patted her hand. "It sounds like a rocky beginning. Marriage can be difficult." Her lips quirked up at the corners. It was good to see her friend distanced enough from her own scandalous woes to find the humor in them, Lily mused. She hoped she would likewise arrive at a similar place someday.

"But all is well now, I trust?" Marshall asked. For all the casual air exuded by his lounging posture, Lily did not miss the hard lines around the duke's eyes and mouth. He hadn't jumped to any conclusion of domestic tranquility, despite his inquiry.

"No," she admitted, "all is most unwell, in fact."

Heavy silence hung over the room. There was not so much as the sound of a teacup tinking against a saucer as the four other occupants of the parlor awaited Lily's explanation.

Her head bowed and her shoulders slumped, weighed down by the unhappiness of the past week and the knowledge that she'd driven her husband into the arms of another woman. "He's left me," she confessed.

Isabelle cooed. "But he'll be back soon. It's just a quarrel."

"No." Lily, dejected, shook her head and stared at the toes of her kid slippers. "He's living with his mistress."

"But you just said—" Naomi protested.

"Another one." Lily lifted her head and looked out the window, too humiliated to meet the pitying eyes of her friends. "He did not take up with the one mistress, but now he lives with another—one he previously assured me was not his mistress at all, when I found her love letters." She scoffed at her own stupidity. "What a dolt I've been." A humorless laugh fell from her lips as she cast a sidelong glance at Isabelle. The petite, fair woman frowned. "Mrs. Vanessa

Myles," Lily said, drawing out the name of her husband's lover. "It just drips sin, doesn't it?"

Aunt Janine startled. Lily saw the older woman's face had gone quite pale, and her eyes as wide as if she'd seen a ghost. "Vanessa Myles?" she said in a rush. "Are you sure?"

"Of course I'm sure!" Tears clung to Lily's lashes. She swiped them away, determined she would not cry for her faithless husband. "I should think I know the name of the woman for whom I've been cast aside."

"But no one's heard from Mrs. Myles in years." Aunt Janine spoke to herself more than to the others; she seemed not to have heard Lily. She tapped a bent finger against her thin lips in thought, then her sharp eyes trained on Lily. "You are absolutely certain Lord Thorburn is at the home of Vanessa Myles?"

"Yes!" Lily's cheeks burned, her hands clenching the edge of the sofa in a white-knuckled grip. "Yes, I'm sure."

"And the letters you found, they were written recently?"

Marshall rose. "Aunt, that's enough. You're upsetting Lady Thorburn."

With an irritated wave of dismissal, Aunt Janine forged ahead. "Are the letters recently written?"

Lily's lips went cold as the blood drained from her face. "Why does it signify? Please stop!"

"Aunt Janine, leave her be!" Isabelle pleaded.

"Were they recent?" Aunt Janine pressed. She was trained on Lily like a hound on a fox, and no amount of protesting from the others would cause her to relent.

"I think so," Lily answered. "I don't remember the dates on them, but the ink was unfaded, the paper fresh." Her chin trembled and she turned her anguished face to Isabelle. "They smelled of roses," she whispered. "The paper bore her perfume."

Isabelle pulled her close in a tight hug. "Aunt, stop this at once," she insisted. "Why are you doing this?"

Staring at the rug, Aunt Janine continued on with a conversation no one else was privy to. "No, the question is: why should Vanessa Myles send amorous letters to Thorburn? That doesn't make sense, unless—"

"Auntie, enough!" Naomi tugged on Aunt Janine's sleeve, pulling the old woman's attention away from her own train of thought.

Aunt Janine blinked and finally looked—really *looked*—at Lily, who was huddled against Isabelle. "I'm sorry, my dear," she tutted, "I do not mean to cause you grief. It's only that I've not heard the name Vanessa Myles in years—more years than I can recall. If it's the same—but it must be," she muttered to herself again.

Setting aside her tea, Aunt Janine rose and smoothed the front of her plain gray frock. She stood before Lily with her lined hands crossed at her soft waist. "My girl, stand up."

Her heart sick with trepidation, Lily did so and looked down into Aunt Janine's kind face.

"You know I am terribly fond of you, don't you, dear?"

Lily nodded slowly.

"I think of you as a niece of my own, every bit as much as Naomi or Isabelle. Your sharp mind reminds me much of myself at your age." Aunt Janine pressed a cool hand to Lily's hot cheek. Her eyes were magnified in the lenses of her spectacles, enlarging the tender expression Lily saw there. "I do hope you know how it has pained me to see you unhappy these last months. I wish you only the very best in all things, Lily. Do you believe that?"

"Yes," Lily answered.

Aunt Janine nodded once. "Good." She held Lily's hands firmly in hers. "Now, I need you to trust me."

Lily frowned. "What do you mean?"

"I believe Lord Thorburn. Vanessa Myles is not his mistress—the very idea is preposterous." Behind her, Naomi gasped.

"Auntie…" Isabelle said in a warning tone.

Lily's brows knit together. "How can you know that?"

"Because I do," Aunt Janine answered. "You must be a very brave girl, Lily. I don't know why your husband has gone to Mrs. Myles's house, but you must go there and find out."

Lily gaped at her in disbelief. "You would have me set foot in the house of a…" Words failed her as her tongue refused to articulate the station of her husband's lover.

"Yes," Aunt Janine said hotly, "I would." At Lily's sputtered protest, she raised a hand. "Lily, I don't know what the truth is, but I do know it is not *that*. I cannot promise you happiness in your marriage—that's up to you and Thorburn—but I can promise you relief from your fears. Go to your husband, Lily."

Confusion and fear gripped her soul; Lily looked to Isabelle for guidance, but her friend only shook her head. She had no better insight than what Aunt Janine had offered. More than anything, Lily wanted to cling to Aunt Janine's words. How marvelous it would be if they were true! The bluestocking spinster spoke confidently about this Vanessa Myles woman, as though she knew something about her Lily did not. There was only one way to find out.

"Very well," she blurted before she could think better of it, "I'll go."

Chapter Twenty-five

Not thirty minutes later, Lily stared out the window of the carriage Isabelle loaned her at a terrifyingly normal-looking house. Nothing about its stuccoed exterior hinted at the secrets within. It was situated on an alarmingly respectable street. Lily would have felt better had the address provided by Wickenworth led her to an obvious house of ill repute. She longed for some clue as to what she was stepping into. "Shouldn't there be a shingle, at least?" she mused. "'Here There Be A Mistress' would suffice."

She climbed the front steps like a convict approaching the gallows and was given further pause by the fact that the knocker had been removed. The house was closed—or not receiving visitors, at the very least. Lily drew a deep breath. "Trust Aunt Janine," she murmured, then felt an instant of panic at the idea of entrusting the matter of her husband and his mistress to a dear old woman who had never been involved in any relationship as complicated as marriage. "Oh, Lord," she said, pressing her hand against her stomach. Reminding herself that while Aunt Janine might be a spinster, she was sharp as a tack. Lily could trust Janine's intellect. She took a moment to steel her resolve. "What's the worst that can happen?" she reasoned.

She pounded on the door with her fist, to no effect. A few minutes passed, and no one answered her summons. After another unanswered knock, Lily stepped back and regarded the silent portal. "Just like the first time."

The door jerked inward and for a split second, Lily half-expected to see her husband there, tousled and ornery, just as he'd been when they first met on his doorstep.

Rather than a handsome young man, a cantankerous butler greeted her. "What do you want?" he hissed. "Madam is not at home."

Knowing "not at home" did not necessarily mean not in the house, Lily lifted her chin, disregarding the servant's demeanor. "I'm here to see Lord Thorburn."

"His lordship is not receiving anyone," the butler snapped.

The bold frankness of the servant's statement punched the air from Lily's lungs. So Ethan was here—the butler freely admitted as much. And neither he nor Mrs. Myles was "at home"? What could that mean, but a romantic assignation? *Oh, Aunt Janine, what have you done to me?* Lily had been sent on a fool's errand, straight to the door of Ethan's mistress. Could she truly pry him away and bring him home? Would she want to, if he preferred this other woman to her?

If that's the case, so be it, she thought. *Let me find them in the very worst situation imaginable—let me! Then I shall know for sure what I am up against.*

"I am Viscountess Thorburn," she declared, "and I have come to see my husband."

The butler's eyes went wide. "My-my lady," he stammered, "forgive me, but his lordship has ordered that no one is to be admitted."

Her nostrils flared. "So he gives orders here, does he?" Her voice brimmed with hauteur. "I'll see about that." Gritting her teeth, Lily pushed past the old man with minimal resistance and headed for the stairs. They would be in a bedchamber, doing the good Lord knew what.

The butler hurried to the bottom of the stairs. "My lady, please!" he called in a loud whisper. "I don't think you should—"

Lily ignored the man. He could issue no warning more dire than the vivid scenarios her imagination concocted. She knew she might find her husband in the arms of another woman. It would destroy her to know that her husband's love was not hers, but this had to stop.

Lily stepped down a hallway, opening doors, looking for her husband. Here was a parlor with fanciful mythological scenes painted on the ceiling. And a light, airy library.

This kept woman's house was as fine an establishment as any in Mayfair. It easily rivaled the homes of any but the greatest lords and ladies. Ethan and Lily's house on Bird Street was a mean little hovel by comparison. "No wonder he's desperate for the money," she lamented. It would take nothing less than a fortune to maintain this luxurious household.

She climbed the stairs again to the third floor. The rustle of her skirts, the slide of her hand along the rail, each tiny sound of her movement seemed overly loud. It was then she discerned the heavy silence pervading the house. No maids whispered gossip as they worked; no ajar windows admitted the noise of the neighborhood. Besides the butler, Lily had met no other living soul. Her brow furrowed in a frown. "Where is everyone?" she muttered into the silence.

On the third floor, Lily tried a few doors again. The first was a guest room, closed; white sheets covered all the furnishings. Across the hall from that room was another closed bedchamber. Farther down the hall, she tried one more.

As she opened it, the air from the chamber rushed out to tease her, to mock her with his scent. The door swung inward to reveal Ethan's belongings scattered around the room. Lily stepped inside and was enveloped by the lingering spice of his cologne. She ran a hand down the brocade cover of his bed—freshly made, she noted; not all the servants had vanished, after all. With a light touch, she examined his things on the vanity—comb, shaving implements, soap, and his hopeless collection of pomades. Lily lifted one of the tins and cradled it in her hands as though it were a priceless treasure. She bent her head over this tiny piece of Ethan's existence—this ridiculous tin evidence of the domestic normalcy from which Lily was now excluded.

Reverently returning the tin to its place, she opened the armoire and pulled one of his shirts from a shelf. Though it was freshly laundered, a hint of his smell still clung to the collar. Lily stroked the white broadcloth. Tears choked her as she lifted the shirt to her face and pressed her cheek against it where she had grown to love resting against his chest. "I've missed you," she breathed.

Clutching the shirt to her chest, she wiped her face and calmed herself. Her bottom lip quivered; she bit it to keep herself from crying again. *This isn't right,* she decided. Ethan, her husband, must not continue to live with another woman. No matter what, Lily had to win him back. It was inconceivable to her that he might actually love this Vanessa woman. What was it Ethan had said to her on their wedding night? *"There's no other in all the world, through all of time, who shall be my wife."*

Lily Helling, Viscountess Thorburn, was Ethan's wife. Not Vanessa, or Ghita, or anyone else. No other woman on earth held her position; no other ever would. Just Lily. They would have to reunite eventually—heirs to produce, after all. But, oh, how she longed to bring children into a loving family, instead of these broken shambles.

With a resolute nod, Lily laid Ethan's shirt at the foot of the bed and went to find her husband. "No matter what, you must remain calm," she ordered herself. She walked out of the room and down the hall to the last door—the one she was certain had to be Vanessa's. "No matter what, you can't fly off the handle. You can talk it out. You can work it out. Be brave, just like Aunt Janine said."

With her heart pounding and her palms cold with sweat, Lily reached for the bronze knob set in the white door. She turned the knob and pushed, bracing herself to behold a visceral betrayal of her marriage.

She sucked her breath at the scene before her, for which she was utterly unprepared.

Ethan glanced up at the sound of her intake of breath, his face somber and wary. He sat on a chair beside the bed, clutching the hand of its occupant, a slight old woman.

"Oh!" Lily approached her husband, her gaze riveted on the slip of a figure beside him. The woman's white hair was pulled back from her face; a neat braid rested on her shoulder. Beneath parchment-thin lids, her eyes darted back and forth, dreaming. Lily sank to her knees beside Ethan. When he did not say anything, she finally looked away from the ailing woman and turned to him.

Her heart lurched at the sight of red-rimmed eyes and several days' worth of stubble on his jaw. He looked to her with such anguish, she wanted to throw her arms around him and take away his pain.

Still, she proceeded cautiously. "Who is she?"

"This is Vanessa, Lily—Vanessa Myles."

She glanced back to the bed. Ethan still held Vanessa's hand, and did not look as though he would relinquish it in the near future. "Yes, but who *is* she?" Lily pressed. "The letters—"

"Vanessa was a celebrated courtesan in her youth—beautiful, enchanting, received everywhere. King Louis himself pursued her when she spent a year at the French court. She was my grandfather's mistress," Ethan concluded, "the love of his life."

His eyes drifted to the bedside table, where a framed miniature portrait faced the bed. Lily turned it and startled. "You look just like him," she murmured. But for the longer hair on the man in the portrait, the outmoded style of dress, and a subtle difference around the chin, it could have been Ethan's framed visage.

"Vanessa's been unwell for years, Lily." Ethan's voice was hollow as he spoke. "An aggressive dementia has taken away her mind, bit by bit." She pulled the chair from the vanity to sit beside him. She laid her hand on his knee. Ethan exhaled and relaxed a fraction. He turned to her, sorrow etched in every line of his posture. "She always treated me like her own grandson. When Grandfather died, Nessa was the only family left to me, though we share no blood."

Lily recalled Aunt Janine's story about Ethan's troubled childhood and the grandfather who cared for him when no one else did. And there was a woman, too—this woman—who loved him. Lily felt a sudden wellspring of gratitude for Mrs. Myles. Lily knew what it was to be out of place, alone in the midst of a crowded ballroom. At least she had good friends like the Lockwoods, as well as her own parents, to stand beside her. Who did Ethan have? His grandfather's mistress.

Before she realized it, she was huddled beside him with a hand at his neck, rubbing her fingers into the taut muscles. Ethan showed no response to her touch, but neither did he reject it. "May I ask you something?" she said, all the while reveling in the feel of him under her hands. "Mrs. Myles's dementia. Did this cause her to…the letters."

Vanessa whimpered and Ethan sprang to his feet, ripping himself out of Lily's grasp. "I'm here, Nessa," he said. "It's all right, darling, I'm here." With the gentlest touch imaginable, he smoothed a wayward strand of hair away from her face, endowing the gesture with such tender devotion, Lily's heart constricted.

Ethan tugged the bell pull beside the bed, and when a maid answered the summons, he ordered a basin of clean water and some broth. The requested items came, carried by a stout nurse. Ethan led Lily from the room so the nurse could try to get Vanessa to take a little sustenance.

Ethan tucked Lily's hand into his arm as they descended the stairs. Her husband was restless from inactivity, she could see, but loath to stray far from Vanessa. "Perhaps we could stroll the halls a bit?" she suggested. "I feel in need of some exercise."

Together they walked from room to room. They entered the airy library Lily had already discovered and Ethan crossed to the window, his hands clasped behind his back. "I didn't answer you before, about her dementia and the letters."

Lily joined him at the window. Side by side they stood, together but not touching, looking down on the quiet street but not seeing it.

"I've been Vanessa's guardian for the last five years," he said. "When the gravity of her condition evidenced itself, she entrusted her financial affairs to her solicitor, and the running of her household and her own care to me."

Lily cast a sideways glance at his exquisite, strong profile. His throat moved down and up as he swallowed. "I've been the guard at the gate," he continued, "shielding her from gossip and those who would take advantage of a helpless old woman. She's been forgotten, and I've allowed that—encouraged it, even. I spoke of her to no one, and after a while, people stopped asking." He drew a deep breath and caught Lily in a pained expression. "Three years ago, her mind began to slip in earnest. Little by little, day by day, she forgot me. Have you ever been forgotten by someone you've known and loved all your life, someone you see almost daily?"

Lily's face scrunched up as a bolt of sympathy shot through her. She couldn't imagine such pain. "No," she whispered, shaking her head.

"After a while, she'd forgotten nearly everyone and everything, except for the early years of her affair with my grandfather, Jophery Helling. She remembered him as he was in his youth, when *he* was Viscount Thorburn. She became trapped in that time." He shrugged.

"Oh," Lily said, understanding dawning. "So the letters weren't written to you, at all, but to your grandfather."

Ethan nodded. "Just so. And my resemblance to him has been a double-edged sword these past years. On the one hand, she's trusted me and allowed me to care for her even in her worst states, when she was too confused and frightened to allow anyone else to come close. On the other hand—" he sighed "—I think it hastened her forgetting me for myself. She only saw Jophery when she looked at me."

"I'm so sorry," Lily whispered. It was a grief she couldn't quite understand, but grief nonetheless.

"And now the end has come," Ethan said flatly. "It hurts to watch her go, but I'm relieved her suffering will soon be over. The truth is, I lost Vanessa to her illness years ago. It's a ghost that's passing now."

Lily looked out the window again, down to where the Monthwaite carriage stood at the curb, the driver awaiting her directions. "I'll leave," she said. "Now that I know, I beg your forgiveness for intruding. You rightly covet your remaining time with her; I shan't take any more from you. I'll . . ." She looked up and met his intent gaze. Her mouth went dry and her stomach flipped. "I'll be waiting at home," she finished in a harsh whisper.

Ethan's hands settled on her waist and he drew her close. "Please stay," he said, resting his forehead against hers. Lily couldn't stop herself from touching his face, from snaking her hands around his shoulders as he pulled her into an embrace. "Please stay, Lily," he said again, burying his face against her neck. "I need you."

Her heart lurched at the raw truth in his words. Lily nuzzled against his temple as her bruised love came roaring back. "Of course," she answered. "Of course I'll stay."

*

It was past midnight when they left Vanessa's bedside again. The physician had come, and Ethan received his grim words after he'd examined her. "Her heart and lungs are lapsing, beating and breathing irregularly," the physician explained. "In cases of severe dementia such as hers, it's almost as though the body forgets how to live. It won't be long now."

Ethan extracted a promise from the man to remain through the night, then he led Lily down the hall to his room.

Weary, she leaned into the support of his arm, having spent all the afternoon and night attending to Vanessa's needs and his own. She had refreshed his glass of water, reminding him to drink. She'd brought a little supper on a tray and insisted he eat to maintain his strength. It hadn't occurred to Ethan until later that she had not eaten with him, and he didn't know whether she'd ever taken any supper of her own.

Lily's generous heart had evidenced itself a dozen times today. She had walked into the chamber of a dying woman she did not know and had turned herself into Vanessa's nurse. She'd rubbed her arms with a cool cloth, adjusted her blankets, and shushed her sweetly when she cried out. Ethan's chest tightened as he recalled that moment. As Lily smoothed her brow with a soft hand, Vanessa's eyes fluttered open.

Lily had gasped at the sight of those violet irises. "You have beautiful eyes, ma'am."

Nessa gave the faintest ghost of a smile. "Thorburn loves my eyes."

"As well he should," his wife said, seamlessly stepping into the appeasing role Ethan had been playing for years. Vanessa murmured and slipped again into sleep and had not roused again.

In their room, Ethan closed the door and leaned his head against it. He hadn't meant for Lily to find him here. He'd come to allow both their tempers to cool after the Ghita fiasco, but then Vanessa had declined so rapidly, he couldn't leave. He'd intended to return home to his wife when it was all over, but now that she was here, he couldn't bear to let her go.

Though he'd hoped to spare Lily all his anguish over Nessa's passing, he couldn't deny what a relief it was to have her beside him. Just her presence made his soul feel a little lighter. Now that she'd come, he had to make things right with her.

He turned from the door and approached Lily, who struggled with the buttons at her back, swaying with exhaustion. Ethan stilled her hands with his and wrapped his arms around her from behind. "Allow me," he murmured. Lily reached to release her hair, but Ethan shooed her hands away again to do it himself. She'd dressed in haste this morning, he saw—only a few pins held her locks in a simple knot at her nape.

Her chestnut waves fell over his hands, rich and warm. It had not been so long ago that he'd first seen her this way on their wedding night. She was beautiful—breathtakingly so—but he was too distracted and sad to give her body the attention he ought.

Having come unprepared for an overnight stay, Lily had no nightdress to wear. She slipped between the sheets in her chemise. Despite the tired bruises beneath her dark eyes, they shone with alertness as she watched him undress. *She's probably scared you'll take her,* he thought dourly. After all the unrest they'd known in their brief marriage, after all the untruths, Ethan couldn't hold it against Lily if she never wanted him to touch her again. But he needed her tonight—if not quite *that* way.

She scooted over to make room as he joined her in bed. For a moment, Ethan lay on his back with his hands on his bare chest, staring up at the ceiling. He felt her eyes on him, waiting.

"I apologize again," he said, turning to meet her gaze, "for those terrible things you heard. It was cruel to you."

"Yes, it was," she answered.

"I haven't touched another woman, though, Lily—not since the day I met you."

"Which time?" she asked, a smile spreading across her face. "The time you were a mannerless butler, or the time you swept me into a scandalous waltz?"

He returned a tired smile, relieved to see her easiness. "The first. However, I was not a mannerless butler; indeed, you were a mannerless buyer."

She pinched her lips in mock severity and swatted at his shoulder. Ethan caught her hand and brought it to his mouth. Still holding her gaze, he kissed each fingertip in turn. Lily's smile faltered.

He couldn't bear not to touch her more; need overpowered his senses. "I know you must find the thought loathsome," he said in a husky tone, "but if I could hold you—just hold you—for a little while…"

Lily was against his chest in an instant, nestling into the crook of his shoulder and sweeping her hand over his torso. Ethan exhaled comfortably for the first time in weeks, finally rejoined by the other part of himself. He brought his arms around her, holding her close and letting her warmth and scent seep into him. A knot of anxiety released in his chest. She was a soothing balm, able to cheer and comfort him even on this darkest of nights.

"I love you." The words slipped from his lips as naturally as breathing, though he hadn't known the instant before that he would say them. A flash of apprehension worried him, but he couldn't deny the truth any longer. Lily had his love; what she chose to do with it was her decision.

She lifted her head, her eyes soft. "I love you, too, Ethan." He raised his head and met her lips, drawing her into a tender kiss.

Inevitably, heat flared between them; the kiss grew urgent. Lily's arms clamped around his neck, while Ethan squeezed her waist and pulled her close, relishing the molding of her soft flesh against him. Sitting upright, he pulled her chemise over her head and then lowered her onto her back while he covered her.

Their hands roamed, exploring and enjoying. He collected her breasts in his palms and squeezed while she arched against him. When her hand closed around his shaft, Ethan hissed. He throbbed in her fingers; desperate need coiled tight at the base of his spine.

"Are you sure?" he rasped. "With everything that's been wrong—"

"But this is right," she interrupted. Love poured from her gaze and put to rest all his anxieties.

He moaned as he entered her slick core; each thrust both satisfied and stoked desire. Ethan went slowly, relishing the sensation of being inside her, the feel of her nails nipping at his shoulders, the sound of his name on her panted breaths. When his climax broke over him, he felt more than his seed pour into her. Ethan's heart left him irrevocably to enter into her keeping. There was no going back for him—not now, not ever.

They clung together, shutting out the sadness of the night to enjoy the bliss of their joining for just a few more moments. Whispered declarations of love fell between kisses, an entire conversation of the same three words over and over. And for Ethan's part, each "I love you" still felt hopelessly inadequate.

"There aren't words," he said at last, frustrated. "Those don't say quite what I mean."

"You'll have to show me." She pressed a kiss to his damp chest.

"It'll take years," he warned.

"We have years."

He smiled at the thought of years—*years*—with Lily. His own Lily. He turned onto his side and pulled her against his chest. Her hair tickled his nose. He brushed it out of the way and kissed the back of her neck. A delightful shiver coursed up her spine, and she burrowed against him.

"I was thinking," he said.

"Hmm?" came her sleepy reply.

"I'm going to have more time on my hands soon, and—" His voice hitched in his throat. *She's not gone yet*, he reminded himself. "Could I help with your school, Lily? I should very much like to do something useful with my life."

She stiffened in his arms. When she turned, tears clung to her sooty lashes. "I'm sorry, my love, but there isn't a school anymore."

Ethan frowned. "What do you mean?"

"I sold it," she whispered.

Dismay rolled through him. "You what?"

"I tried to mortgage the property." Tears leaked from the corners of her eyes to run down her temples. "Mr. Wickenworth must have taken me to every bank in London, but none of them would give me a mortgage."

"So you sold it. And that's how you raised the money to free me from Fleet."

She nodded.

Ethan grimaced. Holding her tight, he pressed kisses to her forehead and nose. "You magnificent woman. My brave princess. I'm not worthy of such a sacrifice. I wouldn't have asked it of you. I'd rather still be in gaol now, than—"

She pressed her fingers to his lips. "Don't say that. I was dying, knowing you were there. I love you so much, Ethan—I was crazed, not being able to do anything. I had to. You'd have done it for me."

"Yes, I would have," he acknowledged.

"Then don't reproach me," she said, shaking her head. "I gave it up willingly."

He extinguished the candle on the nightstand, plunging the bedchamber into darkness. There were no more words between them. He held her close, his own eyes wide in the night while she sank into sleep. When he finally felt her relax, her breathing even and shallow, Ethan let his own eyes drift shut.

It was still dark when a jostle at his shoulder awakened him. "My lord, please wake up. Quickly, now." Ethan let go of Lily and rolled onto his back. The butler stood beside the bed, holding a candle high, his stately features ashen.

"Nessa." He shot up and took the time only to pull on a shirt and trousers before he darted to her room. The physician stood at her bedside, his fingers perched on her frail wrist. Ethan quailed. "Is she...?"

"Not yet, but soon."

The physician stepped aside to make room. Ethan scooped up Vanessa's hand. He pressed a kiss against it. "I'm here, Nessa." Her chest barely rose and fell under the coverlet. Fear gripped him as he looked down on her beloved face, worn with age, but still possessed of a beauty neither time nor infirmity could take from her. Hers was the only face that had looked on him with kindness all his life. Vanessa was the sole person, besides his grandfather, who had loved him unconditionally from childhood. And when Grandfather died, he and Vanessa had grieved together for the man they'd both loved and lost. And now she was leaving him, too, leaving him alone, without—

A hand touched his shoulder, gentle but firm. No, he wasn't alone. Ethan would never be without love again. "Go to him, darling," he said, emotion tightening his throat. "I'm all right now, Nessa. Thank you for staying, but I'm all right now."

He kissed her hand again and clung to it, his eyes riveted on her face. She exhaled a soft sigh and sank against her pillow. The physician went around the other side of the bed to check for her pulse, but Ethan already knew she was gone.

The hand on his shoulder tightened as Ethan's chest constricted beyond enduring. He turned on his knees and buried his face against her belly. Lily wrapped her arms around him while his tears dampened her dress. He heard the door shut as the physician and maid left them alone.

He swiped at his eyes. When he looked into Lily's face, he was stunned to see tears tracking her own cheeks. "You loved her," his wife said simply, "and I hurt for you."

It did hurt—God knew it hurt to lose Nessa—but he wasn't alone. He had Lily. She would see him through.

Chapter Twenty-six

Lily felt a hand creeping up the sheet, gliding over her hip toward her breasts. She swatted it.

"Oi!" came the laughing protest behind her as the hand retreated.

"You've no heart for your poor wife," she said, rolling onto her back. "You can't stand to let me sleep more than three hours at a time. I shall perish of exhaustion."

Ethan kissed her on the nose. "You should have thought of that before you usurped half my bed, madam. Keep to your own room, and this wouldn't happen."

Lily sputtered in pretend outrage. "My lord! How dare you…?" She couldn't get through her statement of scorn without laughing.

"What shall we do with the day, princess?" Ethan leaned back against his pillows, his hands clasped behind his head. "The sun's up, we might as well be, too."

Beaming at her husband, Lily marveled that it had only been a few months ago that Ethan preferred gaming half the night and lying abed until noon. The change in his schedule was just one difference she'd seen of late. His demeanor had changed, too. No longer did he wear a mask of bland indifference or biting sarcasm. Love had brought those walls tumbling down. Finally, fully open to one another, they could still stand strong as they faced the world together. Lily might not have needed a man at *her* side, but she found she quite liked being at his.

"The lending library?" she suggested. "You've read all there is to read about the rising and falling of the Roman Empire, and I've gone through all my novels."

Ethan seemed to weigh the idea with a tilt of his head. "We could," he mused, cutting his eyes to her. "Or we could stay in bed all day."

Lily groaned. "If we hadn't done that very thing two days past, I might be more inclined to consider it."

"Do you mean to say you vote against my proposal?" Ethan quirked a brow.

"I do." Lily inclined her head.

"Then I move that the motion be carried to the floor for a vote." Lily giggled. "What kind of nonsense—?"

With one smooth motion, Ethan rolled onto his side and pulled the sheet down to her waist. His slate blue eyes simmered with banked heat, and Lily felt an answering need stir between her thighs. "All in favor," he murmured, "please rise."

Before she knew what he was about, he drew her right nipple into his mouth. Lily gasped; her fingers tangled in his hair, clutching him close. After driving her mad with wanting, he moved to suckle the other side. His teeth grazed the sensitive flesh, dragging a whimper out of her throat. He lifted his head and gave her a satisfied smile, a wicked glint in his eyes. He glanced at her erect nipples. "The ayes have it. Motion passed."

Lily shrieked at his outrageous jest. Her cheeks burned even as she laughed. "My poor mother would fall to the ground and *die* if she knew what a shocking reprobate I'd married."

Ethan fell back as though stricken. "Reprobate? I?" He pressed a hand to his chest, his face the very picture of wounded innocence. "Need I remind you, Lady Thorburn, that it was not *my* unbridled lust that ruined the both of us." When Lily started to protest, he raised a hand. "Nevertheless, despite my ill use at your hands, I have heard your complainants and been moved to mercy. You said yourself just moments ago that you've not had enough rest— you should get some now." His eyes softened and he kissed her lips. "I've seen how tenderly Monthwaite treats your friend, the duchess. I've determined to follow his example."

Fierce love blazed through her. Even in his serious moments, he continued to surprise and delight her. How touching that he should try to learn from Isabelle and Marshall's marriage and emulate the duke's husbandly behaviors, since Ethan had been deprived of such an example in his boyhood home. "But, love," she reminded him, "Isabelle is with child. She warrants such treatment, while I am not, and do not."

He favored her with a boyish grin. "Then we shall have to remedy that." As he scooped her into his arms, his face grew more serious. "I love you, Lily, and I cannot wait to have a child with you."

Happy tears pricked the backs of her eyes. "Oh, Ethan—"

"You are so good and generous and kind, princess. You will be a wonderful mother."

Lily raised her head to kiss him.

A soft tap at the door broke them apart. "My lady? My lord?" Moira called.

Ethan covered himself with the sheet, while Lily scrambled to don her dressing gown. "Come in."

Moira bobbed a hasty curtsy. She glanced at Ethan and then quickly down at her toes, color rising in her cheeks. "There's a gentleman waiting in your study, m'lord." She handed a card to Lily. She read the name before passing it to Ethan. *Mr. James Logan, Esq.*

"A solicitor?"

Ethan nodded. "Nessa's. It must be something to do with her affairs." He swung his legs over the side of the mattress, and Moira scrambled to exit the room before his lordship rose from the bed, gloriously bare in the morning sun.

Lily attempted to help him dress. She made a muck of his cravat before cursing the scrap of material and allowing Ethan to tie it for himself. She held his coat for him, then affixed the black mourning band around his upper arm. "There now," she said admiringly, smoothing his lapels, "handsome as can be—though I do wish you'd hire your valet back. Maybe he could do something with your hair."

Ethan looked at her askance. "I can't, darling. We're still economizing."

She huffed. "If you would just use my dowry—"

He tapped her on the nose. "No," he said, his tone brooking no argument. "I told you I want no part of it. We'll have what's left of the Kneath fortune one of these years. Until then, we'll muddle through. The Bachman money belongs to our children."

He kissed her before exiting the room and going downstairs to meet the solicitor. Lily sighed and shook her head. No matter how she raised the issue, Ethan adamantly refused to touch her dowry, except for a small portion he had asked Mr. Bachman to help him invest—the profit from which he intended to use to repay his debts. The rest, he'd left alone to collect interest. She supposed it had become something of a proving ground for him. After all the trouble that money had caused, he swore he didn't want it at all—that he already had the greatest treasure Mr. Bachman could have given him in Lily.

They were poor as church mice, and the dunning letters hadn't stopped, but Lily had something more precious to her than all the money in the world: a man who loved her for herself, and one whom she, in turn, loved and respected with all her heart.

*

Ethan strode into the study and greeted Mr. Logan, a middle-aged gentleman of average stature with graying hair, ordinary features, and ink stains around his fingernails. Ethan invited him to sit in the new chair on the far side of his desk, while he took his seat behind it. He clasped his hands together on the oak top, now cleared of the drifts of papers. He and Lily had worked together to create an orderly system of folios so that each letter demanding money now had a cheery home inside a cover marked CREDITORS—UNPAID.

"My apologies for calling so early, Lord Thorburn," Mr. Logan began. "I've just come from the bank, and hoped to catch you at home. It's good to see you again, my lord. I regret we did not have the opportunity to speak at Mrs. Myles's funeral service—which was lovely, by the by. She was blessed to have you, if I may say so."

Ethan gave a slight nod. He never would have made it through the trial of arranging Vanessa's funeral and burial without Lily. She'd lent him quiet strength when he'd depleted his own, granting him courage with a smile or a squeeze of her hand. She had seen to the notice in the paper and even thought to wrap his walking stick in bombazine to complete his funeral ensemble. In the two weeks since, he had taken great comfort in being with Lily as much as possible. She distracted him from his grief, which receded a little each day.

"I take it her affairs bring you here?" Ethan asked, setting aside the somber memory of the funeral.

Mr. Logan nodded. "I have spent these last weeks distributing Mrs. Myles's estate as her will directed. A great and generous woman, my lord—I have crisscrossed England issuing her bequests to orphanages and hospitals. She also left the amount of two years' salary to each of her servants, quite above and beyond the normal way of things."

Ethan smiled to himself. How good it was to hear of Vanessa's final requests. It reminded him of how she was, before the dementia robbed him of her.

"This very morning," Mr. Logan continued, "I established an account that will see to her pensioned servants for at least the next five years, which brings me to the final item of business in regards to Mrs. Myles's will." The solicitor lay a folio on the desk and opened it. "You are aware, my lord, of the arrangement between Mrs. Myles and your grandfather, the late Jophery Helling, Earl of Kneath?" He drew a steel pen out of his inside breast pocket.

"Of course," Ethan replied. "She was his mistress for some thirty-five years—until the day he died."

"Just so, my lord." He made a check mark beside an item on his papers.

Ethan frowned. "What are you marking off?"

"Mrs. Myles instructed that I make certain there were no surprises, my lord. She wanted you to be clear on all points."

"Vanessa knew I knew all of that! For God's sake, when I stayed with Grandfather, I saw her almost daily, why should—" Understanding lifted a veil. "Oh," he said sadly. "The dementia. Even then. She wasn't sure anymore that I knew." He clasped a hand to his mouth.

"It could have been different the next day, my lord—the next hour," Mr. Logan said. "But at the moment when she dictated my instructions, I believe your assumption to be correct, my lord. I'm sorry for any pain this arouses, but you understand I must follow Mrs. Myles's directions."

Ethan nodded. "Go on."

Mr. Logan cleared his throat and consulted his notes. "Mrs. Myles would like to know whether you, Ethan Helling, continue to play at games of chance in a fast, irresponsible fashion?" *Check.*

He sputtered a laugh. "She would like to know?"

"It's what she said, my lord." Mr. Logan pinched his lips.

"No, I do not. I've not regularly engaged in games of chance since the time of my marriage."

"Hmm." Mr. Logan nodded his approval. "Mrs. Myles would like you to know she is proud of you for ridding yourself of that vice, which she saw as the one flaw in an otherwise remarkable young man." *Check.*

Ethan smiled, imagining a younger, healthier Vanessa chiding him for his rakehell lifestyle. "Thank you, Nessa," he murmured.

"In light of your reform, Mrs. Myles wishes you appraised of the following: Your grandsire, the second Earl of Kneath, never liked the man his son, the third and present Earl of Kneath, became. Mrs. Myles shared his opinion." *Check.*

Ethan couldn't help but sputter a laugh. "No, Grandfather never had much good to say about my sire."

"Indeed, my lord. Might I trouble you for a glass of water?" With the requested beverage procured and his parched throat refreshed, Mr. Logan once again referred to Vanessa's unusual final words for Ethan. "Mrs. Myles would like you to know that your grandfather feared your sire's heir, Lord Walter Helling, followed your father down a likewise brutish path." The solicitor's face reddened, and he hastily added, "'Brutish' is her word, my lord. You see? Here. Please understand I intend no disrespect to the deceased."

Ethan waved away his apology. "Walter was still alive when she dictated to you." He didn't broach the claim, although Vanessa was right. Walter had been a bully and a brute; he learned well from their father that he who shouts loudest or hits hardest gets his own way.

Mr. Logan dabbed his forehead with a handkerchief. "Thank you, my lord. Mrs. Myles goes on to say that in you, however, Jophery Helling saw a good man in the making. He took an especial interest in you not out of obligation, but out of preference. In light of your father expressing little concern for your welfare, and as you stand to inherit nothing from your sire—"

"But I will inherit," Ethan cut in. "She didn't know Walter would die and make me heir."

Mr. Logan shot him a withering gaze. "My lord, if I may?"

"Please." Ethan waved, biting his tongue to keep himself from interrupting again.

"Your grandsire, the second Earl of Kneath, was bound by law to leave the entirety of his entailed fortune and property to your father, the present and third Earl of Kneath. Yet he desired to see your future provided for, and therefore established, along with Mrs. Myles, an inheritance for you, Ethan Helling, free of the Kneath entail." *Check.*

Ethan stared at the solicitor, dumbstruck. "My…You mean Grandfather? When I heard you'd come, I thought perhaps Vanessa had left me a little portion, but you're saying *Grandfather* is behind this?"

"Indeed I am, my lord," Mr. Logan affirmed. "Additional monies were contributed to Mrs. Myles's quarterly allowance, which she set aside for the purpose she and Lord Kneath devised." *Check.* "She would also like to advise you," Mr. Logan said, glancing up, "that the earl was overly generous with her allowance, and she also put aside a portion of her own money."

Disbelief allowed Ethan to do nothing but gape at the solicitor. Never in his wildest dreams would Ethan have believed that fifteen years after his grandfather's passing would he learn of a legacy.

"All monies being held in Mrs. Myles's name," Mr. Logan continued, "prevented the present earl from making any claim on them. Upon the occasion of Mrs. Myles's passing, this inheritance now passes to you, Ethan Helling, a joint gift of seventy-five thousand pounds from Jophery Helling, the Earl of Kneath, and Mrs. Vanessa Myles."

The number struck Ethan in the gut. "Seventy-five…*thousand?*"

"Oh, she left you her house as well." Mr. Logan blew his cheeks out and drank the remainder of his water.

Ethan went numb all over. He stared at the man, all agog. "Seventy-five thousand and her house."

"Yes, sir."

"Seventy-five *thooooooouusand*," he experimented with the articulation, hoping to no avail it would make the situation more believable, "and her house."

"That's correct, my lord."

His fingers drummed against the desk. Lily would be astonished to learn of this inheritance. He could discharge every penny of his debt in short order. She would be so relieved. "If you'll excuse me," he said, rising, "I have to tell—" He halted as a thought sprang up. "Oh, you idiot!" he proclaimed, clapping himself on the forehead. "Why didn't you think of that first thing, you ridiculous lout?"

"My lord?" Mr. Logan frowned at him.

Ethan commenced an energetic pacing of the room, eager to be done with the meeting. "Mr. Logan, my good man," he said boisterously, "is this fund already in my name?"

"Yes, my lord."

"And I can draw on it right away?"

"As soon as you'd like, sir."

"Excellent!" Ethan clicked his heels and cut a slight bow. "Forgive my hasty departure, Mr. Logan, but I must attend to some business."

*

When he returned home, he found Lily in the parlor, stitching a thistle into the collar of one of his shirts. She rose to greet him, concern etching lines between her brows. "You went to meet Mr. Logan and then disappeared for two hours. Is everything all right?"

Ethan smiled as his arms slid around her waist. "Everything is more than all right." He pressed a kiss to her lips, delighting in the effusive warmth that spread through him at her touch. His beautiful wife rested her cheek against his shoulder, a gesture so simple, but so replete with love. Ethan stroked her hair and back. "I have something for you, princess."

As he reached into his pocket, Lily quipped, "Is it a table for the dining room?"

"Not yet," Ethan answered, "but soon." He handed her the paper he'd purchased from Edmund Ficken. Lily unfolded it and scanned the lines. Happiness filled him as he watched her face light up.

"The school!" she exclaimed with glee. "You bought it back! But how...?"

"Vanessa," he said simply.

Lily clasped her hands to her heart, then the next instant flung them around Ethan's neck, nearly toppling him backward. "Thank you so much." She kissed his cheek, his lips, his other cheek, his neck, his jaw, his lips again—

Laughing, he captured her face in his hands. "It was my pleasure, princess. This is a marriage of equals, is it not?" At Lily's happy nod, his heart leaped with joy. "You bought me a house." He jerked his chin, indicating the very home in which they stood, for which Lily had sacrificed her dream of King's Cross Vocational. "I thought it was my turn to do the same for you."

He scarcely had the words out of his mouth before Lily stood on her toes and kissed him with such erotic sweetness, he was sorely tempted to dash her upstairs to bed. "I love you, Ethan Helling," she said, her eyes brimming with love and desire.

"And I love you, Lily Bachman. Helling," he amended.

Epilogue

"My lady!" Miss Cuthbert exclaimed.

Lily glanced up from her notes, where she was painstakingly laying out the schedule for Michaelmas term. She'd lost a month when the property had been out of her possession—and several instructors, as well. There were only four months standing between her and the opening of King's Cross Vocational School for Young Ladies. Four short, busy months. There wouldn't be a chance to catch her breath if the school was to be ready in time. Every day between now and the first of October would be filled with meetings, planning, arranging...Lily loved it.

"Yes, Miss Cuthbert?" she said.

The headmistress held a letter over her pile of correspondence, a happy grin splitting her face. "Lord and Lady Hollier have—"

A loud crash in the room above Lily's office—followed by shouted curses between the workmen—ran over the older woman's words.

"I beg your pardon?" Lily squinted.

"Lord and Lady Hollier have donated a pianoforte," Mrs. Cuthbert repeated. "Brand new!" She held the letter out for Lily's perusal. "They invite you to select an instrument and have the invoice sent to his lordship."

A rush of gratitude touched Lily's heart. Once she made the acquaintance of the Holliers, she'd quickly grown to adore them. It was easy to see why they'd always been particular favorites of Ethan's, and she regretted having ever turned their dinner invitations into opportunities to wage battle against her husband. Lily put the letter into her own tray of correspondence; she would write a note of thanks this very evening.

"How lovely of them!" Naomi said. "The Holliers are such dears."

Lily glanced to the other end of her desk where Naomi waded through the student applications that had poured in the last few weeks. Her friend let out a frustrated sigh and dropped her arms to the stack of applications. "So many deserving candidates," she lamented. "However shall we choose?"

"Miss Cuthbert," Lily said a short time later, "that will be all for today. Thank you."

When the older woman had gone, Lily sighed and leaned back in her chair. Naomi read an application as studiously as a Latin primer.

"How has the Season passed?" Lily inquired. "I've not set foot in a soiree these last few months." Being too scandalous to receive invitations had been a blessed relief, as it spared Lily the *tonnish* galas she so despised. Gossip faded, however, and invitations to modest affairs were trickling in.

"Tedious," Naomi said. "Aunt Janine is a lax chaperone, and Grant is overly cautious. Between the two of them, I've wanted to tear out my hair on more than one occasion."

Lily gave her friend a sympathetic smile. She started to say something, but Naomi continued pouring her heart out. "Last year, Marshall forbade me from forming an attachment to any gentleman. He wanted me to have fun, he said. Well, let me tell you, there was no fun to be had with the entire *ton* gossiping about my brother and former—and now again—sister-in-law. No gentleman wanted to come within a mile of that spectacle." With a dejected sigh, Naomi propped her elbows on the desk and her chin in her hands.

"This year," she went on, "Grant forbade me to form any attachment, for fear of my making a choice Marshall would disapprove. So, I've yet again had to dance and smile but discourage any gentleman's attentions. Six of my friends are either married or betrothed now, and I'm being left behind."

"You're only twenty," Lily pointed out, "hardly on the shelf. And now that His Grace is home, you can be swept off your feet."

Naomi wrinkled her nose. "I think I've given up this year. Most of the eligible gentlemen not sitting in Parliament have left town."

Lily thought of her own unlikely husband. Her blood quickened as she recalled their first disastrous meeting and the love that had come from that wretched beginning. "You never know what's around the bend, dear. Don't despair just yet."

As though she knew her friend's mind, Naomi smiled wryly. "We can't all have our future husbands greet us at the door."

"No, but yours is out there, Naomi." Lily's eyes narrowed as she cast a thoughtful glance toward the ceiling. "Just think—right now, the man you will marry is going about his day, never knowing that his future bride is longing for him at this very moment."

"You've turned romantic, Lily," Naomi said in disbelief. "Lord Thorburn has wrought a change in your perspective."

Lily blushed but could not disagree.

Naomi smiled. "I'm happy for you. I truly am." Standing, she crossed to the window. "There's Grant. I shall go down to meet him. Good evening, Lily."

Lily rose to press cheeks with her friend and stood in the hall as she started toward the doorway. Naomi stopped at the top of the stairs to give a dust-covered man a wide berth.

"Good evening, Lord Thorburn," she said. "You'll excuse me if I don't give you my hand."

He bowed gallantly instead. When Naomi had gone, Ethan came to Lily, a happy smile in his eyes. He leaned down to kiss her, careful to keep his dusty person away from her dress.

"How have you kept yourself busy?" Lily asked. "I've not seen you since noon." Her husband's appearance would shock those who believed a proper gentleman did not engage in manual labor. Sawdust sprinkled his hair like snowflakes, and plaster dust clung to his face and clothes. Only his hands were clean, thanks to his thick leather gloves.

Since reacquiring King's Cross Vocational, Ethan had thrown himself into the work of preparing the school for students as whole-heartedly as Lily, but from a different angle. He met with the architect and foreman of the work crew, then lent his own hands to speed the progress. Lily couldn't believe she had the good fortune of a husband whose enthusiasm for her venture equaled her own.

"I have a surprise for you," he said, tugging her hand. "Come and see."

Their footsteps bounced off freshly plastered walls. Lily noticed the silence filling the house. "Have the workmen gone?"

"I sent them home," he answered. "It's nearly sundown." He led her downstairs to the kitchen level. He stopped at the door of the room that had caused the workmen such consternation and turned to smile down at her. "The bath-room is finished."

Lily clapped her hands in delight. "Everything?"

He nodded, his grin widening. "Everything. Would you like to see?"

"Of course."

She bit her lip in anticipation as he opened the door and stepped aside. Lily gasped at the beautiful room. The center of the space was dominated by the massive tub and shower. The dark wooden tub was lined with gleaming copper. Four posts near the scrolled top—two on either side—supported the exotic shower mechanism. A round head rested atop the posts, covered with short spouts aiming back into the tub. It was a marvelous device, and Lily was proud to have it.

She pulled her eyes away from the domineering bathing station to examine the rest of the room. A coal-fired boiler stood in the corner, and a pipe ran from it along the baseboard, then below the tiled floor to carry hot water to the tub. When she came close, she noticed the boiler emitted heat. She turned and cast a curious look at Ethan.

He redirected her attention to the vanity table with a framed mirror mounted on the sunny, yellow wall. A little padded bench stood against the adjacent wall beneath the high window, and next to it, a shelf was already stocked with piles of folded towels and cloths. A basket on another small table held fragrant soaps. Lily picked up a little cake of soap and inhaled its lavender scent. "It's beautiful," she murmured. Turning, she gaped at Ethan, who stood bare to the waist and was unfastening his trousers. "What are you doing?"

"I want to try it!" he exclaimed.

"It's for the students," Lily protested.

"Not yet, it's not." A devilish gleam twinkled in his slate blue eyes. "That tub is large enough for two."

Lily's mouth fell open as she looked from Ethan to the tub and back again. He had finished stripping off his clothes, and the evidence suggested he had more than just washing on his mind. He grasped her arms and turned her around, making quick work of her buttons.

A thrill coursed down her spine as he stripped her. Ethan selected a soap from the basket while Lily unbound her hair. He took her hand and she giggled impishly, feeling like a girl sneaking another tart from the tray.

He caught her mood and swept her around. Lily shrieked as he dipped her backward and lavished her with a ravishing kiss until she was lightheaded with desire. "Now, princess," he said, righting her, "are you ready?"

Lily nodded and Ethan turned a valve on the boiler. The pipes made a gurgling sound as water coursed around the room and across the floor to the tub. Turning another valve on the tub produced a sputtering sound, followed by the astonishing sight of indoor rain cascading from the shower. Thrilled with the new sight, Lily held a hand into the water. The drops fell faster and harder than rain, and the warmth raised gooseflesh on her arm. She cut her eyes to Ethan and smiled. "It's perfect."

He stepped into the tub and gasped as the water poured over him. Rivulets streamed down his face and onto his chest, washing the grime of his day's labor down the drain. He reached out and took her hand. Lily stepped over the side of the tub and into the water. Ethan gripped her hips and pulled her close; his skin was warmed by the shower water. Lily lifted her face for a kiss, which he obligingly provided. Hot water rained down on their bodies as they explored one another—delighted with the new sensations offered by this modern innovation.

Ethan took the bar of soap and worked up a lather. He made quick work of washing the remaining sawdust from his hair and face. Then he soaped his hands again and turned his attention to Lily. He worked his hands over her breasts and belly. Hugging her close, he moved side to side. Lily gasped as her skin glided over his, hot and slippery. "I like that," Ethan growled in her ear. "What say you?" He kneaded the globes of her derrière as he pulled her hard against his arousal.

Lily's arms twined around his neck, clinging as he shifted to move his hand between her legs. "What I say is, may you never stop surprising me, my dearest love." A pleasured moan escaped her as he dipped into her core. "I also say," she added, laughter rising in her throat, "that we build our own bath-room."

"I knew I married an intelligent woman," Ethan said in a hot, wicked voice, "but that idea, princess, is sheer genius."

More from the Author
From *Once an Innocent* by Elizabeth Boyce

CRIMSON ROMANCE

HISTORICAL

Once an
Innocent

Elizabeth Boyce

Author of *Once a Duchess* and *Once an Heiress*

Chapter One

London, 1814

When the liveried footman in front of Jordan stumbled over a lump in the rug, a bottle of claret and two wine glasses toppled from his laden tray. Jordan sprang forward and caught the bottle 'round the neck in one hand and a glass by the stem in the other. He intercepted the second wine glass with his leg; it rolled down his shin to settle, unharmed, on the treacherous floor covering.

As he stooped to retrieve it, an audience of one applauded off to his side. "Lord Freese, my hero! You saved my rug, wine, and stemware all from unfortunate demise."

He turned to the speaker and bowed with a flourish. "Your servant, madam."

Isabelle, Duchess of Monthwaite, smiled warmly as she stepped off the bottom stair and crossed the entrance hall to where he stood. "We didn't know if you'd come tonight, Jordan. Charity events are not nearly so tempting to single gentlemen as other amusements."

Jordan affected an affronted demeanor. "And where should I rather be, if not at An Auction for the Benefit of King's Cross Vocational School for Young Ladies, as the invitation so enticingly described?" He poured wine into the two rescued glasses, then returned the bottle to the red-faced footman before turning to offer Isabelle a drink.

She took both it and his proffered arm as they strolled toward the salon, following the faint sounds of pianoforte music and laughter. "Still, it was good of you to come," Isabelle continued. "I know Lily will be grateful for whatever material support you offer, and I'm just glad to have another body in the room. This far into summer, it was difficult to fill out the guest list." Her sigh was thick with fatigue, and she leaned heavily upon his arm.

Jordan looked down at his friend's wife. Though the arm hooked through his own was still willowy and her face as slender and lovely as ever, Isabelle's lithe figure had given way to the heavy fullness of late pregnancy. Her breasts were larger than they'd ever been—scarcely contained by the bodice of her light green dress. Even so, they were overshadowed by the great roundness of her belly.

Though politeness prevented him from directly alluding to her delicate condition, he was concerned she might overexert herself. "Are you sure this is not too much?" he asked. "Would you like to take a rest?"

A frown line creased her brows. "I've just come down from taking a rest," she answered testily. "Pray do not stare at me like that, Jordan. I'm perfectly aware of my limitations."

"Forgive me, Isabelle," he said with a quick smile. "If I seemed to stare, it is only because I am dazzled by the becoming new cut of your hair." He nodded toward the blond curls framing her face. "That short style suits you—very modish."

"You're forgiven, since you not only noticed my new hairstyle, but complimented it. Poor Marshall is mourning the length I cut off."

They rounded a corner; the salon was directly in front of them, its doors thrown open wide, spilling light and music into the corridor. Inside, a respectable crowd of several dozen mingled over drinks. Jordan smiled mischievously and bent to speak in a low voice near her ear. "Since you'll not go rest, at least say you'll leave Marshall and elope with me, Isabelle. I'll take you to Paris and buy a hundred hats to adorn your new hair."

Isabelle threw back her head and laughed as they entered the room, drawing admiring gazes from the assembled guests. "You grow more outrageous by the day," she scolded, her blue eyes swimming with mirth. "If you don't hurry up and marry, you'll soon be so scandalous, no decent woman will have you."

"You've uncovered my scheme," he replied in jest, raising his voice slightly to be heard over the hired musician seated at the pianoforte in the far corner. "If no decent woman will have me, then my dear step-mama must stop badgering me to shackle myself to one."

Their private conversation ended as Marshall broke away from a group of gentlemen to meet them. His arm slipped protectively around Isabelle's expanded waist, concern etching his features. "Are you feeling better?" he asked. "You don't have to do this, darling. I'm sure among Lady Thorburn and Naomi and myself, we have everything well in hand."

Isabelle laid a reassuring hand against her husband's cheek. Their sweet, open affection moved Jordan. He was happy for the joy his friends found in one another but very much doubted he was meant for any such relationship. The permanence of marriage scared the daylights out of him. Jordan couldn't bear to stay in one geographic location longer than a month or two at a time—how could he be expected to remain at one woman's side for the rest of his life?

The duchess moved on to speak with her guests. Marshall turned nonchalantly to face Jordan, lifted his wine, and swirled it beneath his nose. "There's someone in my study to see you," he murmured, his lips concealed by the glass.

Jordan frowned. "Who?"

Go, Marshall mouthed silently. His dark eyes cut to the door.

Feeling foolish for leaving almost as soon as he'd arrived, Jordan retreated from the social gathering. Curiosity put a spring in his step as he found his way upstairs to the study. He knocked once on the door and entered. The smell of leather and ink greeted him as his eyes sought out his summoner.

A head of close-clipped, graying hair looked up from where it had been bent over papers. Jordan shook his head ruefully as he shut and locked the door behind him. Was there nowhere the man could not engross himself in work?

"Freese." Lord Castlereagh nodded once and gestured to a chair across the desk.

"Fine," Jordan said as he took a seat. "Thank you so much for asking. And how does the night find you, Robert?"

The Foreign Secretary's lips turned up in a small smile. He tossed his quill onto a sheet of paper, his hard eyes glinting in the light cast by the candelabra on the end of the desk. "I don't waste time on idle chitchat, Jordan Atherton—and if you knew what was good for you, neither would you."

"I find it singular," Jordan rejoined, "that I've been turned away from your office every time I've attempted to see you this year. But here you are," he said, spreading his hands wide, "running me to ground at a charity auction, pulling my strings as deftly as a puppet master. I should like to have a word with you."

"And I with you," Castlereagh said, leaning back in the borrowed chair. "That's why I've come."

"I'd hoped to accompany you to Paris." Jordan hadn't meant to blurt it out. He only hoped he hadn't sounded like a petulant child.

Castlereagh pursed his lips. "You'd have been no good to me there, Freese. You're no diplomat."

Jordan's teeth ground together. "There was intelligence to gather before the treaty was signed. I could have done that."

"You have your assignment."

"I'm *sick* of my assignment," Jordan seethed. "Four years is long enough. Send me somewhere, Robert—anywhere. Let me be useful again!"

Lord Castlereagh's brows shot up. "I *am* sending you somewhere." Amusement tinged his words. "Home, in fact. What in the name of God Almighty are you still doing in Town this late in the summer? You're lucky I haven't strung you up for dereliction of duty, Freese."

Jordan swiped a hand down his right cheek; his fingers automatically traced the scar he had obtained carrying out Castlereagh's orders. It ran from his ear almost to the corner of his mouth.

How could he make the impassive Foreign Secretary see that this assignment was killing him? He was hobbled, tied to England like a dog staked on a short rope, when all he wanted to do was stretch his legs on foreign soil and engross himself in meaningful work once more.

"I've always done my duty, Robert," he protested. "You cannot question my loyalty."

Castlereagh spread his hands flat on the desk, long ink-stained fingers splayed wide, and leaned forward, pinning Jordan in his fierce gaze. "Then why are you still here?"

Because Lintern Abbey is the dullest place on Earth, he wanted to say. Because estate ledgers, crop rotations, and rent tallies bored him to tears. Instead of anything approaching the truth, which Robert would only interpret as sniveling, he opted for sarcasm. "I've taken a keen interest in charity schools, you see. I had to stay to lend my support to Her Grace's benefit."

His superior leveled an incredulous look at him, his jaw working side to side. Finally, Lord Castlereagh rummaged through the papers before withdrawing one and handing it across the desk to Jordan. "Home may have just become more exciting for you."

Jordan read the intelligence report with mounting alarm. When he reached the end, he turned disbelieving eyes on Castlereagh. "French agents? Are you sure?"

The Foreign Secretary shrugged. "*I'm* not sure, but our man in York is, and that's good enough for me. Frenchmen have been sighted in villages and towns in the North, asking questions."

"But it doesn't make sense," Jordan said in a rush. He swiped his fingers through the mop of black curls atop his head. "The monarchy is restored." His eyes lit as an idea took shape. "Perhaps King Louis has sent them?"

"No." Castlereagh shook his head. "Louis would approach the government directly. They're Bonapartists."

"But Napoleon is on Elba," Jordan pointed out.

"Where he is already expanding his army and navy," Castlereagh snapped. "His exile is not secure, damn it all. And now we have nine, ten, perhaps more of his men nosing around Yorkshire, getting closer to Lintern Abbey."

With fingers and thumb pressing into his eyes, Jordan growled in frustration. "To what purpose? Do we suspect assassins?"

When he opened his eyes again, he saw the Secretary's lips drawn into a grim line. "Of course they're assassins. When have you last laid eyes on Enrique?" The pang of guilt aroused by the mention of his ward's name must have shown on his face. Castlereagh scoffed. "Go home, Freese. Do your goddamn job." He shoved another paper at Jordan. "I want you to take these men with you. Set a patrol; do whatever it takes."

Jordan glanced down at the list. He recognized the ten names as well-placed gentlemen: some sons of *tonnish* families, some men attached to high-ranking government officials—and all agents of the Foreign Office, as well, it would seem.

He scowled at the paper as a problem presented itself. "If I run home with ten men, that will draw attention. If those same ten men start patrolling, asking after these Frenchmen, that will certainly draw attention. As it is, Bonaparte's agents can't know anything for certain. They're looking, yes? Otherwise, they'd be on my doorstep in an instant. Setting out a guard like this is as good as lighting a beacon for them. It would be better to allay their suspicions. 'Nothing to see here; move along,' as it were."

Castlereagh pressed his hands together in prayer fashion and rested his chin on his fingertips. "How do you propose to do that?"

"I don't know," Jordan admitted. "But I'll think of something."

"Do whatever you'd like, Freese, but you have to take those men. You're good, but I'll not pit you alone against ten Bonapartists."

Jordan squeezed his eyes shut and pinched the bridge of his nose. Despite an overwhelming desire to be released from his assignment, he found himself even more tightly bound to it. He'd wanted Robert to relieve him of his burden and give him something more exciting, more compelling to do. Instead, he not only had to hurry home to Lintern Abbey, but he had to concoct a front, something perfectly ordinary and domestic to cover the sudden influx of almost a dozen armed men. Something boring. But, blast it all, this was his job—his duty. And no matter how it rankled, Jordan Atherton, Viscount Freese, did his duty.

"At the end of September, I'm leaving for Vienna," Castlereagh announced. "There's to be a meeting in November, a congress of the Allies. I want this settled before my departure. Anything untoward that suggests Bonaparte is still wielding power could upset negotiations."

"It's already the eighth of August," Jordan protested. "You want me to carry out a covert manhunt and eliminate all these French agents by the end of next month?"

"Yes, I do," Castlereagh stated.

"If I do this, if I succeed, will you take me with you to Vienna?" Jordan asked. "I would be useful to you there, Robert, I swear. If you only needed me to act as your page, I would do it."

"No." Lord Castlereagh's mouth held the tight O shape of his refusal for a moment as though making sure his edict was understood. "I know it's not as thrilling as your old days on the Continent or in Spain, Jordan. But it's vitally important. You must understand that your work is crucial to the very survival of Europe. If Bonaparte's agents succeed… If he escapes and returns, and we can't fight him off again…" Castlereagh's mouth pressed in a grim line. "I don't have to tell you it would be devastating. Political stability *must* be maintained while Europe rebuilds. That's what you're guarding at Lintern Abbey. Stability. Peace."

Well.

When he put it that way, Jordan couldn't formulate any further argument against his assignment. While stability and peace weren't his cup of tea personally, he certainly valued them for the world at large.

"You're in this for the long haul," Castlereagh concluded. "You might as well resign yourself to it and find some pleasure in living a more domestic lifestyle. Get married, my boy. My Amelia has been a good and constant companion these last twenty years."

Jordan rose and bowed. "Thank you for your advice, sir. I shall consider it." He tucked the intelligence report and list of Foreign Office agents into his coat pocket before taking his leave.

As he made his way back downstairs to the auction, Jordan scoffed to himself at Lord Castlereagh's final words. The last thing he needed—or wanted—was a good and constant companion. A good companion was marvelous for a night or two, but the constant part was right out.

*

When he rejoined the party in the salon, Jordan attempted to regain his typical jovial manner, but the tight pull of his scar told him he still frowned. In Town, he found it very easy to forget about his responsibilities at Lintern Abbey and throw himself into entertainments and the company of his friends. This collision of his worlds was most unwelcome.

What the devil was he going to do? He could not carry out Castlereagh's orders without amending them. If his home was being watched, an action such as the Secretary desired would bring the Bonapartists down upon his head and ruin four years of careful intrigue. Lintern Abbey itself held little draw for him, but he didn't want harm befalling those who lived there. Uncle Randell and Enrique would be as helpless as lambs before wolves without Jordan's protection. Leaving them to face the threat alone was out of the question. But how to go about it?

"I didn't think anyone could scowl as fiercely as my husband, but you may have bested him."

Lily Helling, Viscountess Thorburn, regarded Jordan with a bemused expression on her face, full lips twisted in a wry smile. The statuesque female was sheathed in chocolate satin, touched here and there with gold lace and beading—a smashing complement to her own dark hair and eyes.

"If I am scowling fiercely," he said, his charming smile once more in place, "it is only because you look—"

"You used that one on me already." Isabelle joined them and playfully swatted Jordan's forearm with her fan. "Pen some new material."

"Save your flirtation for the other ladies, in any event," Lily said. "Handsome you may be, but I am utterly immune to your charms, my lord."

The two ladies' husbands joined the group. Ethan Helling handed a cup of punch to his wife. "Freese, I warn you. If you attempt to flirt with Lily, she will almost certainly skewer you for it. I still must couch remarks in innuendo and entendre."

Jordan grinned. "I'm well aware of the lady's formidable parlance. Indeed, I admire Lady Thorburn's forthright manner." He nodded to Lily, who blushed and shared a smile with Ethan. Despite his claims of walking softly around her, Jordan knew a woman as strong as Lily could only be matched by an equal force—and any fool could see the Thorburns were as deeply in love as Marshall and Isabelle.

Good God, I'm surrounded by willing prisoners, he realized with a start. Jordan was the odd man out in the group, the fifth wheel in the midst of couples wallowing in marital felicity. He scanned the other guests for someone else to talk to. How had it happened that everything tonight kept pointing to the subject of marriage, even as he was dunked into a crisis of international security? When he should be thinking of nothing but how he would outsmart Napoleon's dogs, he found himself forced to reflect upon the distasteful institution of matrimony and all the choking restrictions it entailed.

His restless gaze landed upon Lord and Lady Hollier—married since the beginning of time—who socialized with Lady Thorburn's parents, Mr. and Mrs. Bachman—likewise possessed of a long, seemingly happy union.

A gorgeous vision stepped into the group of older guests and made Jordan suck in his breath. Naomi Lockwood made a polite curtsy to Lord Hollier. She bent her neck, and the light from the chandeliers skimmed across her strawberry-gold hair, which was knotted on top of her head and adorned with a charmingly frivolous blossom. The rose color of her dress brought out the healthy glow of her creamy skin.

Lord Hollier took her hand and patted it fondly. Mr. Bachman bowed when she greeted him. Jordan noted how the faces of all four guests lit with pleasure as Naomi moved gracefully amongst them, sharing a few words with each. She leaned over to put an arm around the seated Mrs. Bachman's shoulders, giving Jordan a view of the gentle swell of her breasts, filling out the low square neckline of her gown.

An unexpected tightening in his groin startled him. This was Naomi—Marshall's little sister, for God's sake! He'd known her since she was a schoolroom miss in braids. And while he'd always been aware—academically speaking—that she was a lovely female, it had been the awareness of an older sibling-esque personage toward a younger quasi-sisterly individual, a reason to help look over her since she'd made her debut last year.

And yet he couldn't take his eyes off of her.

She flagged down a footman to bring punch for Mrs. Bachman. Then Naomi took her leave of the older group and made her way to other guests, a welcoming smile at the ready for each.

That warm, open way of hers contradicted the rumors Jordan had heard of late. She'd been branded an ice queen, an untouchable. Two Seasons out, and the beautiful, generously dowered younger sister of an obnoxiously wealthy duke was still unattached. Naomi was *the* catch last year, a diamond of the first water. She should have been snatched up within minutes of making her bow. But for two years she had deftly, delicately rebuffed the advances of every gentleman who had attempted to court her.

The grumbling in the clubs among her thwarted suitors was that she was cold, heartless—made in the same mold as her imperious mother, Caro Lockwood.

Jordan knew that wasn't a true or fair characterization. Naomi had one of the kindest natures he'd ever encountered. His eyes followed her as she continued to move through the assembly with the ease of a natural-born hostess, helping everyone feel noticed and included, seeing to the comfort of her brother and sister-in-law's guests.

No, Naomi Lockwood was anything but heartless, Jordan reflected. The conclusion he drew was that she was content with her single status. Marshall would never force his sister to marry against her will, and she would always be amply provided for. Perhaps, he thought with rising admiration, Naomi shared his unfavorable view of matrimony. It would be an unconventional opinion for a female—especially for one as well-bred and raised to convention as Naomi—but that only made it all the more fascinating.

"Do you mind," rumbled a dangerously low voice against his ear, "extricating your eyes from my sister, Freese?"

Marshall stood beside him, matching every one of Jordan's six feet and four inches, glowering and tight-lipped. A quick glance around the group confirmed the others all had fallen silent and had been engaged, for some indeterminate length of time, watching Jordan watch Naomi.

Bollocks.

Jordan flashed his annoyed friend a smile. "If you don't want her admired, Marsh, you'd best put a sack over her head. Otherwise, I fear it's hopeless. Besides," he said, glancing back to where Naomi stood, quickly appraising the people around her and snagging on the first likely suspect his eyes found, "Augustus Gladstone has been dogging her heels all night. I'm surprised you didn't notice," he added with a hint of rebuke. Marshall's head snapped to where Naomi was, in fact, exchanging words with the pup Gladstone, who was known to be trying to prove his manhood by making his way through all the bawdy houses in London.

Marshall frowned. "I'm sorry, Jordan. I didn't realize—"

Jordan clapped his friend on the arm. "It's all right, I know your mind is elsewhere." He nodded toward Isabelle. "I just thought someone should keep an eye on things."

The duke's jaw tightened, and Jordan still wasn't certain his friend wouldn't call him to account for so publicly ogling his sister. Isabelle intervened with a hand on her husband's arm.

"We're blessed to have a good friend who shares our concern for Naomi's welfare, aren't we, my love?" She steered Marshall away to go converse with the Bachmans.

Jordan impulsively glanced back to where he'd last seen Naomi, but she was no longer there. Frowning, he scanned the salon but couldn't locate her anywhere among the guests.

A few minutes later, the musician on the pianoforte stopped playing, and Marshall's voice rang out over the crowd. "Ladies and gentlemen, if you'll please take your seats, the auction will begin."

As Jordan filed along with the others to the several rows of padded chairs standing at one end of the room, he saw Naomi slip in. She stopped just inside the salon with her back to the wall, and even from this distance, Jordan noticed the high color staining her cheeks.

Another group, several young bucks and a lady, wandered in. They passed Naomi, and she reached a hand out to stay one of the gentlemen, Wayland Hayward. The flaxen-haired young man turned and leaned while Naomi spoke to him, her fingers twisted together at her waist. Hayward straightened, a light smile touching his lips. Then he glanced around and—apparently supposing them unnoticed—grasped Naomi's hand and pulled her out into the corridor.

Jordan frowned. "What's that about?" he muttered to himself. A sharp prod in his back pulled his attention away from Naomi's peculiar behavior.

"Lord Freese, sit down!"

He glanced at the seat behind his. The Lockwood siblings' spinster aunt, Lady Janine, cast a look of sharp disapproval at him. Jordan saw that everyone else had settled into their chairs. He pressed a hand to his chest and bowed briefly by way of apology and took his seat at the end of the row.

Lady Thorburn stood at the front of the room. "Ladies and gentlemen, thank you for coming," she began. "And a special thanks to Their Graces, the Duke and Duchess of Monthwaite for hosting this benefit. I would like to take just a moment before we start the auction to tell you all about the purpose and vision behind King's Cross Vocational School for Young Ladies—"

Jordan maintained a look of polite interest while his mind wandered back to his conversation with Lord Castlereagh. How was he ever to solve this problem? What could he do, quickly, to cover an armed patrol of his property?

Lily nodded and everyone clapped. Jordan joined in, having not heard another word of her speech. Then Marshall stood and presented the first item up for auction, a sitting with the portraitist, Lawrence. The bidding opened at a hundred pounds and quickly rose. Lord Cunnington won with a bid of seven hundred fifty pounds.

While the guests applauded Cunnington's generosity, Jordan glanced at the door. Naomi was still gone. And he still had a mess of international security to sort through, by Jove! Why the devil was he even thinking about Naomi's whereabouts, much less obsessing over them?

Two more items came and went. Jordan's feet tapped restlessly against the immaculately polished floor. Another poke to his back had him turning in his seat.

"You haven't bid on anything," Lady Janine said in a stage whisper.

"Nothing's caught my eye, my lady," he replied.

"You'd better dig into those deep pockets of yours," Lady Janine insisted. "This is for my niece's school."

Jordan raised a quizzical brow. "Lady Thorburn is not your niece, ma'am."

"Don't contradict me, boy!" Her blue eyes sparked behind the lenses of her gold-rimmed spectacles. "Mind your own damned business and do as I say."

He chuckled. Jordan had always appreciated Lady Janine's spunk, even if she was a hopeless bluestocking. He turned around to see Marshall standing at the front of the room again, balancing a pie on each hand.

"The winner of this lot is in for a special treat," he announced. "These fruit pies were baked by the Duchess of Monthwaite herself, especially for tonight's auction."

Another round of applause. Isabelle nodded from her seat, acknowledging the attention.

"What are the fillings, Duchess?" someone called.

"One cherry, one blueberry," Isabelle answered.

Jordan glanced once more at the door. Still no Naomi. He huffed. *Get out of my head*, he thought in frustration. He had far more important matters to think about.

"Very well," Marshall announced, "for one cherry and one blueberry pie baked by the Duchess of Monthwaite, who will open the bidding at fifty pounds?"

French agents at his home. They would be former military, he reasoned—as well trained themselves as anyone he could bring to counteract them.

David Hornsby raised his hand.

"We have fifty pounds!" Marshall called. "Who will offer seventy-five?"

These would not be brutes, no, Jordan thought, tapping a finger against his upper lip. Their actions so far had demonstrated an organized elegance, working in small groups to cover more ground. That meant they had established a communication network. They wouldn't rely upon the English post to carry their reports to one another. Couriers of their own, then. A French intelligence network—in Yorkshire! His mind reeled.

"One hundred pounds," Mr. Bachman called.

The door still stood vacant. No Naomi. Jordan's toes tapped out a rapid tattoo.

"Thank you for your generous bid, Mr. Bachman," Marshall said. "Can one of you best it?"

Lady Janine's finger dug into the back of his shoulder. Jordan ignored it. "Where the devil is she?" he muttered. He looked at the door again and sighed.

"One hundred fifty!" Hornsby called.

Jordan shook his head. One hundred fifty pounds for two pies? Ludicrous! Lintern Abbey had twenty thousand acres. Jordan had to patrol it with ten men—eleven, including himself. And make it look innocuous. It was preposterous.

Poke.

Scowling, he turned fully to face the door. "Get back in this room," he whispered. Why was he growing agitated at Naomi? She hadn't done anything to earn his ire. Except look utterly delectable this evening and arouse an awareness in him that had never been there before.

"Two hundred," said Lord Hollier.

"Two hundred pounds from Lord Hollier," Marshall called. "Are there any more bids?" No one spoke. "Two hundred once."

Poke.

Where is she? Jordan scanned the room to make sure he hadn't missed seeing her come back in. No, she was not in the salon, he was certain. What if something had happened to her? An uneasiness tightened his chest.

"Two hundred twice!"

Poke.

"Fifteen hundred pounds!"

A collective, startled gasp filled the room, and every face turned to see who had bid such an outrageous sum for two fruit pies. It took Jordan a moment to realize they were all looking at him.

"Sold," Marshall called, grinning broadly at Jordan, "for fifteen hundred pounds to the gentleman with the sweet tooth."

The audience laughed and clapped appreciatively. Jordan stood, feeling like the biggest fool imaginable. Lady Janine wore a satisfied expression.

He realized what he'd really purchased was the right to leave. With a sharp nod to no one in particular, Jordan turned on a heel and stalked out of the salon to find Naomi.

Find out more about *Once an Innocent* when you visit:

www.crimsonromance.com/crimson-romance-ebooks/
crimson-romance-book-genres/historical-romance-novels/once-an-innocent/.

About the Author

Like all good Southern girls, Elizabeth Boyce fell in love with the past early on, convinced the bygone days of genteel manners and fancy dresses were only an air conditioning unit shy of perfection. Her passion for the British Regency began when she was first exposed to that most potent Regency gateway drug, *Pride and Prejudice*. She's remained steadfast in her love of the period ever since. Those rumors of a fling with ancient Greece are totally false—honest.

Elizabeth lives in South Carolina with her husband and three young children. She loves to connect with her readers, so keep in touch!

E-mail: *bluestockingball@gmail.com*
Blog: *http://bluestockingball.blogspot.com/*
Facebook: *https://www.facebook.com/AuthorElizabethBoyce*
Twitter: *https://twitter.com/EBoyceRomance*